One

"You're a bastard, Joe Ballen."

It might have been true in a biological sense as I never knew my parents. It was probably true in a euphemistic sense too, but I listened rather than responding. I'd like to say that was down to me being a patient guy, but the truth was Helios Station was over one A.U. from Earth, and the transmission delay at this distance was over eight minutes, so a direct two-way conversation was impossible.

I also had to admit Dollie had a point. She'd not wanted me to take the Mercury job and we'd fought—ending with me walking out and stepping on the elevator to the High-Rig. I'd been "on the job" for almost ten months and wasn't planning on going back Earthside before it was finished.

"Do you know how long it's been? You're turning me into a frustrated old maid. I swear there are cobwebs forming." Dollie looked at me with lowered eyes. "A girl deserves to be treated well. You can't expect me to keep it all wrapped up warm for you for so long."

Despite the fact that we'd gone through the legal marriage process, I thought it highly unlikely Dollie was "keeping it warm" for me. It wasn't in her nature. She had at least twice the sexual drive of a regular person, and I often got the feeling she'd have been happy if we stayed in bed 24/7.

"It's great to see you, Dollie. You look as good as ever." Even though I knew she wouldn't hear me for several minutes, the cost of the call was so high I couldn't say nothing. "I miss you too. A whole lot. The work here is important though—you know that."

I slipped into my chair, the phone pickup automatically tracking my face. The artificial gravity in the rotating habitation section felt good. As much as I liked free fall, it was surprisingly tiring, especially with the heat inside the station. "Everything is going well here. We finished installing the first four rocket launcher systems last week, and the upgrades to the Mass Driver are underway. The new crew members are doing well for the most part—though a couple need to learn more about personal hygiene in close quarters. Inestria is working on that."

Isabell Inestria was my second. She knew almost as much about Zero-G construction as I did and also had similar experience in handling construction teams. But as soon as I mentioned her name, I cursed myself silently, anticipating the response I'd get in seventeen minutes. Ever since Dollie discovered Helios was a mixed-sex operation, she'd convinced herself I'd be bedding every single female on board. The fact that Isabell was friendly, outgoing, and robustly attractive, did nothing to assuage Dollie's mistaken accusations.

"When are you coming home, Joe? Dollie isn't happy. And when Dollie isn't happy she gets restless and naughty. You wouldn't want me to be naughty, now would you? I swear I'm making all the drivers nuts, I'm so wound up. Perhaps I should organize a big orgy to settle my nerves and theirs."

My throat was dry, and not only from the ever-present traces of bitter dust from the ore processing sections. Working at Dollie's Cabs had taught me how rough Dollie could be with people at times. Her mixed-up hermaphroditic DNA gave her a sizzling personality that sometimes showed the worst of both worlds: a male-oriented harshness combined with a female spite that could peel your skin if you were unfortunate enough to be on the receiving end.

"Ballen?"

I looked up and grimaced when I spotted Delacort outside my door. He was the leader of the small MilSec unit stationed with us, and the official monkey on my back. He always dressed perfectly in uniform, completing the look with cropped regulation hair giving his narrow-domed skull a passing resemblance to a kiwifruit. He insisted he was a "regular guy" despite his military rank, but somehow he still managed to make every job we had at least three times harder than necessary.

"Personal call." I took a sip of my dark coffee. It was hot and bitter, quite appropriate since we were currently in orbit two thousand kilometers above Mercury. Whatever he wanted to bitch about I didn't want to know. "After that, I have another six solar arrays to bring online. Look me up after I'm done."

"Well, zip your pants. I've received a priority one notification from Central. The Atolls have launched a cruiser and, as near as they can tell, it's headed our way." Sweat prickled his face. Even with almost unlimited solar power the cooling systems struggled to fight off the sun's heat. The units worked well enough, the problem was getting rid of the excess heat—even the best exchangers work only marginally in a vacuum. Not only that, we were almost at closest approach to the sun, and that, combined with radiation from Mercury, made it a losing battle.

"You better keep your hands off that—" I killed the comm channel, cutting Dollie off in a way that would cause me a mountain of grief later. Assuming there'd be a "later." Even if the defenses worked, we weren't equipped to fight off a determined attack from an Atoll ship.

"How long?"

"The simulations show arrival probabilities of the enemy from eight hours to seventeen days depending on flight parameters." Delacort shrugged. "You know how it is."

Tactical sims have a habit of showing you every possible piece of information, but not the one you need to know. What you get are probabilities and estimates, but it's basically a shopping list of what-might-be's—choose your own level of optimism or pessimism. We had relatively poor monitoring capabilities, limiting our knowledge of Atoll force movements, so it was hard to see any benefit from such vague numbers. From what Delacort said, if they came straight for us they'd be here in half a day—any change from the most direct approach would place the time of arrival at any point in the future.

"They're sure they're coming for us?" It was wishful thinking, but I had to ask.

"Ninety-three percent confidence rating based on the figures they have."

"You'd think they'd give us a break. It's not like we're treading on their toes."

Three years ago the Atolls had taken out Deimos Base, a mining relay station in Mars orbit feeding raw materials to both the Atolls and Earth. It was the only operation Earth was involved in outside of planetary orbit and tolerated only because it provided resources to both sides.

But the starship Ananta changed everything, including that miserably slim piece of collaboration. It was a prototype, built by Earth, which the Atolls had scoffed at. When the possibility arose that it might work, the Atolls were ready for blood. They'd clamped down on every deep space endeavor we had. And those restrictions hadn't been lifted even though the Ananta had been lost for the past three years.

Earth had looked inward. Mercury wasn't a good bet for ore extraction. Although its orbit made it easy to deliver materials to the inner solar system, the heat and difficulty in achieving a stable orbit made the project much more expensive than the Deimos operation. But the Atolls controlled everything farther out, leaving us little choice.

"Everyone into the Rabbit Hole in seven hours. I'll pass the word."

The Rabbit Hole was a bunker deep in the heart of the station. Theoretically, it could hold the crew and protect them for nine days—long enough for a rescue vessel to get here from Earth—but we'd never tried it. It was surrounded by as much mass as possible to "armor" it: packed rock from the extraction process, water tanks, and finally several layers of matted ballistic material. It *might* survive a sustained attack, but it was probably a fifty-fifty proposition at best. I grabbed my comm-set to contact Isabell; she could handle most of the arrangements.

"How about infrastructure?" Delacort waved his hand in an all-inclusive gesture.

"What about it?"

"The solar arrays, heat sinks, cooling systems. Should we shut them down to protect them?"

I thought of telling him where he could stick his "infrastructure" but didn't. He was only doing his job the way I tried to do mine, and we'd need all those things if we survived. "Heat sinks are maxed out. We can't take them offline, not this close to perihelion. We'd fry in a matter of hours. Same with cooling."

"Right. The bastards timed it to hit us when we'd be most vulnerable."

"We could furl the arrays. That would make them less prone to damage but would only leave battery power."

I waited while Delacort thought about it. Running on batteries would mean the railguns and lasers would be useless after a few shots and, unless we got impossibly lucky, there'd be nothing left of us except for a cloud of trace elements drifting slowly inward to fry in the Sun. I knew he'd want to make a stand, his tightly muscled jawline delivered that message clearly.

"We have to be able to fight. Forty-eight rockets aren't going to save us on their own," he finally said.

"Forty-eight rockets, four railguns and two lasers doesn't sound much more effective."

Delacort lifted his chin. "Do you have an alternative?"

"Sure. Surrender. The Atolls don't want to kill us, they want to confine us. If we turn ourselves in they'll either hold us or send us back to Earth. Knowing how much they hate us, I imagine they'll send us home with our collective tails between our legs."

Delacort stiffened. "You're a coward."

Why is self-preservation always dismissed as cowardice? After surviving what I'd been through a few years earlier, was it any surprise I didn't feel like offering myself on the altar of destruction once again? "You're the one with the military background. What chance do we have? We're on a space station. We can't avoid their attacks or do any fancy escape orbits. We have limited weapons and a small crew. But they can maneuver freely and outgun us *at least* ten to one. If we had a fighting chance I'd raise a flag on the ramparts myself, but this is suicide."

"We might get lucky."

I nodded slowly. "Has Central dispatched a rescue ship yet?"

9

"What? No. Why would they? Nothing's happened. SecOps doesn't have ships waiting in line to nanny a bunch of nervous engineers."

The truth was we didn't have any ships to speak of, but that wasn't relevant to the point I was making. "They know our situation—we have virtually no chance of winning this fight. Some might survive in the Rabbit Hole, but you know how limited the time frame is. Earth could send a ship now to pick up the pieces, but they haven't. Why?"

I let him ponder the question and come to his own conclusions. Picking up my comm-set, I signaled Isabell.

"Prepare everyone to head for the Rabbit Hole. There's an Atoll ship on the way and they're not looking to get a tan."

Isabell sounded calm. "How long?"

"Eight hours, maybe."

"Will do."

Isabell disconnected, and I looked back at Delacort. He pulled a cloth from his pocket and mopped his forehead. "Central doesn't expect anyone to be left here. You're right."

"I'm glad you saw sense." I moved towards the hatch. "Let's get to the radio room and broadcast our surrender."

"That's not what I mean. Charge all the batteries and capacitors to full. We'll need everything we've got."

I groaned. Why couldn't things go the easy way? Just once.

Delacort hurried off, and I checked the personnel trackers. There were eleven people outside the station performing mainte-nance tasks, and I saw all but one start to move towards the airlocks. I picked up the comm-set again.

"Isabell. What's Abdela's assignment?"

"He's checking the guide rails on the ore launcher. Why?"

"Tracker shows he's not heading for an airlock."

Isabell cursed, then switched to the open frequency. "Abdela? What the hell are you doing? Report back immediately. This isn't the time to screw around."

I flipped through the external screens, searching for any signs of him in the glare of the station's mirrored surface. At our current distance from the Sun, the external surface of the hull was painful to look at without filters. I threw in an enhancement filter to mask some of the brightness, but that made the image grainy, making it difficult to pick out details.

"Ballen?"

I heard a voice from over my shoulder and turned back to the phone, thinking Dollie had called back, but there was no incoming connection.

"You're losing it, Ballen. You'll be talking to yourself next."

I finally spotted Abdela floating off the primary port-side stanchion. He was doubled up as if in pain, then he waved his arms several times before curling up once more.

"Isabell. Check the number seven external feed."

There was a pause. "He's praying."

"What?"

"Not sure how, but he decided that point on the station had the clearest view of Mecca. He goes there to pray."

Abdela had been born in the MusCat Alliance in Egypt but escaped when he was about fourteen. How he managed that, he never said. I'd heard rumors he was homosexual and his family had helped him escape. Other scuttlebutt said he was an atheist SecOps informer, and they'd pulled him out when his cover was blown. I didn't care one way or another, as long as he completed his work on schedule.

"How long has this been going on?"

"Since forever. I didn't want to report him, he's a good worker."

Isabell's good nature was liable to get Abdela very dead if he didn't come inside. The estimated arrival time for the Atoll ship was still hours away, but I had little confidence in the number and it didn't take into account the earliest the enemy could launch an attack. For all we knew, there could be shots incoming any minute.

Isabell tried again, but there was no response. "He shuts off his radio when he prays," she said, sounding sheepish at admitting she'd allowed such a basic safety breach.

The majority of the USP were atheists or agnostics. Religion wasn't banned as such, but viewed with suspicion after the religious uprisings over a century back. The Catholics and Muslims had decided unbelievers were more dangerous to them collectively than they were to each other. So they united, provoking a series of skirmishes and wars as they pushed their combined ideology as widely as possible. The result was predictable with most of the Middle East and Northern Africa forming a loose coalition with much of South America and the southern states of the former U.S.A. Meanwhile, the northern states and Canada had come together for mutual protection, as did many formerly independent eastern countries. It shouldn't have required as much blood as it took in the end, but that's humanity for you—they'd rather fight to the death over a pile of crap than work together to escape the heap.

I jammed a comm-set over my ear and set out for the nearest airlock. "Get everyone inside the Rabbit Hole. I'll get him."

"I should go."

I understood how Isabell felt. It was her mistake, so she should be the one responsible for correcting that. I had a more important task for her, though. "We don't have time to argue. I want you guarding the airlock at the Hole. I don't want any of those smart guys thinking it would be better to zip it up before we get back."

"Over my dead body." She hesitated momentarily. "Make sure you *get* back."

"We're going to come through this with no dead bodies, okay?" I scrabbled down the access tunnel to the ZeeGee hub and squirmed down the corridor to the right. My suit was at the main 'lock, which was unfortunately a long way from Abdela's position, but there wasn't much I could do about that—luckily I move pretty well in low gravity.

Several crew were in the staging room as I entered. The frost on their suits made them look like frozen samurai warriors before they started to shed their armor. The room reeked with a mixture of sweat and oil, and the moisture in the air condensed onto the walls, forming a greasy patina.

"Everyone stay in your P-Suits," I called out, getting a few muffled grunts in response.

My suit was in its rack and I squirmed around to slide legs-first into it. Once I felt the ankle locks tighten I crunched up, sliding my head and arms inside the tight glove of the upper suit. The "bug" crawled up my back zipping me up, then unhooked me from the tubular cage framework, and I stepped towards the inner 'lock. One of the men followed me and I looked around.

"You're going to need an EMU." The name stenciled on his helmet said "BENZING." "Can't do that on your own."

Giving him a thumbs up, I closed the inner hatch, then thumbed the cycle button, almost immediately feeling my suit stiffen as the pressure dropped. The Extended Maneuvering Unit looked like a pair of robot legs carrying a huge backpack. I stepped backward into it and Benzing strapped my legs to the augmented ones of the unit. As he worked on my legs, I hooked up the waist straps and finally locked my arms into it.

The power-up sequence was short. I flipped the switches to bring the systems online and patched the station's navigation telemetry through to my suit. Benzing leaned over and touched his helmet to mine.

"Don't let that crazy Arab die out there, boss. He owes me fifty bucks." His voice was muffled and distorted through the laminated helmet layers. "And he's the only real friend I've got out here."

I didn't imagine Abdela would appreciate being called an Arab, and Benzing had never struck me as a sentimental guy. He was one of the "toughs" who swaggered around the station as if they had a God-given right to be anywhere in space they chose, regardless of what the Atolls had to say about it. I'd have laid money on him not having a friend anywhere in the universe outside the nearest barman. Space does funny things to people, though.

I waited for the outer hatch to open, then unhooked from the station and pushed off outside. Despite my best intentions, the shove was slightly off-center and I started tumbling slowly. The automatic stability dampener kicked in almost immediately, minimizing the chance of motion sickness.

Mercury looked like a ball about the size of my fist, sitting to the left or "port" of the main axis of Helios. It wasn't the best view I'd ever seen. The planet itself was brown and looked like a Zero-G turd floating in space. Its mineral wealth made it a valuable resource but didn't improve its appearance one iota. Our orbit was taking us deeper into the planet's shadow to help ward off the heat as we approached the closest distance to the Sun. That made it difficult to see anything other than the rim of the planet, but I didn't have time for sightseeing.

I kept the thrust on constant rather than using the more usual "squirt and drift" technique. Speed was more important than saving the power unit, and the propellant was easily replenished filtered wastewater, so it didn't need conserving. All I wanted was to get there and back as quickly as possible.

A soft warble sounded to warn me the EMU was about to start deceleration, and five seconds later the small forward-facing thrusters triggered, each blast trimming my speed as I approached the solar arrays.

"Ballen. I have a signal. It's them," Delacort's voice crackled over my comm-set.

I swore silently, unable to move any faster unless I wanted to risk becoming an independent solar satellite. "ETA?"

"Less than two hours. Range approximately one million kilometers. They're set up for a pass rather than a rendezvous."

Damn those tactical reports. "I'm ten minutes from my guy. Back inside in thirty."

"No time." Delacort's words were muffled briefly. "Kill your pickups."

The missile carrier at the far end of the station swiveled, the launch doors opening as it turned. In a full spacesuit like mine you "see" using external sensors, with the information broadcast on the inner surface of the visor, suitably enhanced and augmented. This makes the suit stronger and less prone to damage from knocks or small debris, though it takes a little getting used to.

I shut down the pickups not a moment too soon as a flare erupted from the launcher. Even without the external sensors the brightness was so intense it leaked around the edges of the flip-up virtual screen. More flashes followed, and I clenched my eyes against the glare.

"You haven't a comet in hell's chance of hitting them," I called into the comm-set. It was stupid to waste what little weaponry we had at such an extreme range. No doubt the Atoll ship would be dancing around in a "drunken walk," making intercept trajectory prediction almost impossible, especially with the limits of Helios' detection equipment.

"I'm not as stupid as you think." Delacort sounded unconcerned with my criticism. "If we can make them move around more, we can push them closer to their thermal limit. It might make them decide we're not worth the risk."

Thermal buildup is the biggest limiting factor in space combat. Every maneuver requires a burn from the engines and produces heat directly from the exhaust, but also within the reactor core powering the drive. It's the same every time you fire a weapon. And even though the Atolls have the benefit of more advanced fusion reactors than we do, they still produce heat, which is difficult to get rid of in the vacuum of space.

The rockets we had were "frangible"—a fancy way of saying they break apart. This isn't through accident or shoddy workmanship. At a configurable range, they explode, forming an expanding cloud of debris and kinetic impactors traveling at several kilometers per second. This velocity means every piece has three times the energy of an equal amount of TNT. That would give you a bad day in short order. It's also a difficult mess to predict, so the people on the receiving end are forced to use their own defensive weapons, maneuver, or both. And that brings us back to thermal buildup. As a bonus, the rockets didn't contribute to *our* buildup because their energy was locked in their propellant.

I reactivated my external pickups and the helmet screen flickered back to life. "Good choice. Let's hope it works."

"I'm so glad you approve of my tactical decisions," Delacort said. "Now get your man and make it quick. They have rockets too, and we can't duck."

I saw a flash of orange from the high-viz bands on Abdela's suit and tried the open frequency again. There was still no reply, and I wondered how the hell he could have missed the rocket launch. From a distance I could see him slowly pinwheeling in space, and closer in, I saw his helmet screen was up.

"He's in trouble. Think the launcher flare got him." I tried to relay the message calmly, but this was going to make my job a lot harder.

"Acknowledged."

I aimed for Abdela's center of mass, slowing to a crawl as I closed, otherwise the combined mass of me and the EMU would break him in half. Spreading the "arms" wide, I gathered him up and gripped tightly as I spun back towards the main airlock. I told the EMU to take us back as quickly as possible, overriding the safeties as much as I could to minimize the travel time. The unit would compensate for the unbalanced load, but it reduced the speed at which we could move.

"Incoming!" Delacort yelled.

I wasn't even halfway back when the laser turrets came to life, wheeling around as they acquired targets I couldn't even see. The beams were invisible, but I caught flickers out of the corner of my eye almost too faint to see as the incoming shrapnel was vaporized. For a brief moment, it was almost as if the stars were twinkling, the way they appear to us from Earth.

The reverse thrust warning sounded and I prepared for deceleration. Abdela twisted in my arms and I struggled to hang on to him, locking my arms about his waist.

"Eyes. Can't see." His voice was hoarse.

"We'll be inside soon."

That appeared to satisfy him, and he stayed quiet, even when the thrusters started to kill our forward motion. The airlock was dead ahead and closing fast. Too fast. The overrides had been too ambitious—impact was inevitable, and there was nothing I could do to change it.

I pushed Abdela slightly to one side. It would be crazy to have gone to all that trouble only to crush him with my momentum. The EMU was still braking our progress and he slid away on the short tether I'd hooked to his P-Suit straps. We didn't look to be going very fast, but appearances were deceptive.

"It looks like we're in the clear. For now."

Delacort sounded almost as relieved as I was, but he wasn't the one approaching the airlock wall too fast. At the last second before impact, I twisted so the EMU hit first. I didn't need its thirty-five kilograms of mass slamming into my spine.

Bang! My head snapped back and my vision blurred. Abdela gasped over the comm-set. Instinctively, I grabbed the nearest handhold to stop myself from bouncing back out of the 'lock. Then I punched the "cycle" button and the outer hatch started to close.

"Second round."

I barely realized the significance of Delacort's announcement as I focused on the painfully slow movement of the outer-hatch. Finally, the indicator light turned yellow to show the seal was complete; only then did the pressure start to build. My external pickups frosted over immediately, but that didn't stop me from tearing open the straps tying me to the EMU. Luckily, it was easier getting out than in.

The light turned green. I grabbed Abdela, launched him past the inner hatch, and followed him a second later. Even through my helmet, I could hear the repeated whine as the capacitors charged after each blast from the point defense lasers. I was sweating inside my suit. The station's cooling system was struggling to combat the heat buildup. How long until thermal shutdown, I wondered.

"On board," I called over the comm-set.

I wanted to get us both into emergency P-Suits, but it would have been way too difficult and time consuming. We needed to get to the bunker before the next attack—one that might overwhelm our defenses. I stripped out of my bulky suit—at least in my shorts I'd be able to move more easily.

Abdela yelled as I slid his suit down, then gritted his teeth. It looked like his arm was broken, either as a result of me holding him too tightly or from the impact with the airlock bulkhead.

"Can you move?" I asked, pulling the suit over his legs.

I saw his jaw tighten as he tested himself. "My arm...yes, I'll make it."

He was a fighter, I had to give him credit for that. Bracing myself against the floor, I pushed him within reach of a handhold.

"Head for the Rabbit Hole. I'll be right behind you."

In gravity his injury wouldn't have been too debilitating, he could have shuffled down the corridors without much difficulty, but in ZeeGee you have to squirm around like a monkey chasing its tail, dragging yourself from handhold to handhold. More than once we had to stop while Abdela caught his breath.

Then I heard the thing that scared me the most: the deadly clatter of debris impacting against the hull.

"Dammit! You there, Delacort?"

No reply.

I cursed again more violently, nudging Abdela forward as we turned into the corridor leading to the Rabbit Hole. "Isabell? We're ten meters away and closing."

The hairs prickled on the back of my neck when again there was no reply. As we approached the bunker, I saw the hatch was sealed and locked.

"Isabell? We're outside. Open the goddamn door."

Nothing happened. I hammered against the smooth surface of the hatch in a futile gesture. Abdela groaned weakly but held tight to a handhold. I heard several pops, then the high-pitched whistle of escaping atmosphere. Something had breached the hull. The noise came from all around, telling me there were multiple breaches. Not big enough to be immediately fatal, but they needed attention or we'd soon be just so many slabs of meat.

I grabbed a bottle of VacSeal from the wall and floated down the corridor, finding three holes and quickly squirting the self-sealing foam into them. There was still a whistle, but I couldn't work out where it was coming from. Then the indicator turned green, and the hatch opened.

"I sealed the hatch as a precaution. Sorry, it took a while to cycle." Isabell grabbed Abdela and guided him through the hatch to join those inside.

"I could kiss you."

She looked me up and down. "No objections, but your timing is terrible."

Several people inside grabbed Abdela and pulled him the rest of the way into the Rabbit Hole. They didn't look happy, and I couldn't really blame them.

"There's a breach." I waved the VacSeal at Isabell. "We need to find it, or the automatic doors will cut us off from the rest of the station."

She nodded and worked her way inward while I floated the other way. I thought the whistle was getting louder, but then it faded again. I glanced back at Isabell and she waved me towards her, pointing into the mass of wiring and ducts behind the mesh screens.

"Here."

I reversed direction, pushing back against a bulkhead as the comm-set buzzed loudly in my ear.

"You there, Ballen? Things got a little busy." It was Delacort.

"What's the situation?"

"I'm seeing a pressure drop in your area. Something got through the last round." His speech became muffled, then, "Hard to tell how bad from here."

Delacort was still in the main control center, monitoring the station as well as the defenses. His men didn't have the luxury of being able to hold out in the Rabbit Hole like my crew. Their job was to fight, and if necessary, die.

"Already on it. We have several small punctures in the B-Six crosswalk. Almost finished sealing them. Any others?"

"There are similar drops in D-Three and Four. Bigger judging by the rate of pressure drop. There's also something in C-Twenty-one."

D-Three was on the way to the cooling plant—de-pressurization in that area could put the whole station at risk. On the other hand, C-Twenty-one was near the reactor, hardly a safer bet, although pressure loss shouldn't directly affect the reactor.

I filled the hole Isabell had found and shrugged. "Rock or a hard place?"

"I'll take C-Twenty-one, I know the reactor better." Her chestnut eyes locked with mine. "Stevens knows the cooling systems."

That was true, but I couldn't order a man out on a job like that. "I'll go."

"You're not suited up."

"I better work fast, then."

I pushed the VacSeal into her hand, squeezed past her and dived down the corridor. Her P-Suit helmet had been open and her perfume lingered in my nostrils despite the sweat. I tried to put it out of my mind, but it had been a lonely ten months.

"Delacort? Isabell's dealing with the reactor area. I'm taking care of D-Three. Update in ten."

I wasn't entirely suicidal. The route to the cooling section took me back past the main airlock. I grabbed an emergency P-Suit, wriggled inside, and was back on the move inside of two minutes.

19

I also grabbed a couple of large cans of VacSeal along with some aluminum patches in case there were any bigger holes.

The lights in D-Three were flickering when I turned down the corridor. The white thermal-plastic walls were constantly dirty from the ore processing dust but now looked scorched and blackened too. Whatever had penetrated must have hit some of the wiring. I switched on the headlights on the side of my visor. There were several small holes I filled easily with the sealing foam and two larger ones that needed a patch.

I emptied half a can of VacSeal onto the back of a patch and slapped it over the hole, holding it in place while the foam set.

"One down. One to go."

The second was harder to get to, and I had to reach awkwardly around some conduit. "Thirty seconds. How are you doing, Isabell?"

"Fine. Nothing but small stuff down here. Once I—"

The whole station lurched, then the roof slammed into my head like an asteroid impacting a planet. The emergency lights flickered to life, filling the corridor with a sickening pale green light. Then I blacked out.

Two

I woke strapped to a medical bed. My head was thumping like mining charges were going off inside my skull despite the fact that everything else felt numb. I guessed someone had administered painkillers, but they didn't seem to be working above the neck.

A young guy floated into the room wearing the powder-blue uniform of a MedTech, took one look at me and left without a word. I wasn't on Helios, that was certain—we had no military medical officers. Several minutes later Delacort appeared in the doorway. His oval face was strained, and he was wearing medical pajamas like me, the blue diagnostic light on his lapel blinking regularly to show he was alive.

His right arm was missing from just below the elbow.

"Welcome to the brotherhood of the stump." I held up my own arm, the scar halfway down the bicep still visible from where the regen'd limb had been joined to me.

"Glad to see you're awake finally." He looped his leg around a chair and pulled himself into it, scraping his palm through his cropped hair. "The docs were worried about you, but I told them not to be. I was sure it would take more than a space station falling on you to put a dent in your skull."

"Thanks, I think."

There was something about Delacort's manner that made me suspicious. Like he was holding something back. "How badly did we get our asses kicked?"

"The station is still intact. Thanks to you and..."

He dropped his head to stare at the gray bulkhead between his feet. I guess the drugs were affecting my brain after all because it took several minutes before the obvious occurred to me. "Isabell?"

He shook his head briefly.

Bile rose in the back of my throat, burning upwards until I thought it would explode. I fought to hold it back. "What happened?"

"As far as I can tell, we got lucky. The Atoll ship plowed through one of our impactor clouds. Not enough to kill it, but enough to give them a bloody nose. They swept around Mercury and headed back." He swallowed hard. "One of their shots got through the point defenses. I'm guessing, but it was probably an explosive sub-munition. Blew out half of D corridor. Left the reactor intact. We found her in the debris, P-Suit torn open." He gestured from his neck down to his stomach. Together you saved the rest of the crew."

"And now?"

"On the Ares. Heading back home. We couldn't wake you, so the MedTechs decided we should take you back."

That didn't feel quite right somehow. I was in charge of the operation. I shouldn't be on the way home while others didn't make it. I rolled over to face the wall.

"Go away," I said.

He did.

Being a civilian on the Ares was like being a hooker at a MusCat convention—everybody notices you, but they sure as hell don't want to talk to you. I was interested in the ship's engineering. Originally it had been commissioned as an Atoll support ship, but then the newly formed United Space Navy managed to persuade Surahman Industries it was in their interests to sell it to Earth. The Atolls had squealed loudly about it, but Surahman had obviously been paid enough to ignore it.

I wandered around the ship freely for the most part, apart from the main control room and engine areas, both bizarrely guarded by two wooden-faced soldiers at all times. Why they couldn't simply lock the bulkhead doors was beyond me. I guess they had to find something for the grunts to do.

The ship was very different from the creaking transports that had taken us out to Mercury and was spacious in comparison. The odd thing was where you came across holes—gaps where something should have been, but wasn't there anymore. Like buying a jigsaw puzzle and finding several of the key pieces were missing.

And that's exactly what it was. All the Atoll technology had been stripped out before delivery. That Earth had the confidence to take the ship over showed how much progress we'd made since the Atoll attack on Deimos Base; it also highlighted how far we were still behind the Atolls. Things would have been very different if the Ananta had come back as it was supposed to, but it was likely the ship had been destroyed by the unproven Jump drive.

I spent most of my time in the small centrifugal gym, building strength for my return. Despite my regimen of exercise while working on Helios, I still needed to improve my strength to be able to deal with Earth's gravity. Not to mention Dollie.

I was strapped into a resistance training exo-skeleton and sweating hard when Delacort came in. He was still in his pajamas but had a towel with him and floated over to the second training unit.

"You're lucky, Ballen."

He fastened his legs into the unit, locked the belt around his waist, then held on to it as he worked on his lower body. Presumably, he was still restricted from doing much with his arm.

"How's that?" I took a moment for recovery.

"You're a contractor. You get to go home whenever you choose. You're well paid for what you do and don't face any of the risks we do." He grunted a little as the skeleton forced him to push harder. "Space is something you play at."

I thought about the battle I'd gone through. The loss of Isabell. The long call I'd had with her family the previous night. The painful rehab I'd gone through after losing both my legs and arm and the excruciating regen process. I wondered if I should tell him about the joys of phantom pain, the brutal burning sensation and stabs of agony I *still* felt despite the regenerated limbs. Instead, I shrugged, he'd find out soon enough.

I started my next round of exercises, trying to get comfortable with the way the skeleton was making me move. "I guess so."

"You don't believe in fighting the Atolls, do you?"

"There's nothing worth fighting for out here." The program adapted to my movements, turning it up another notch, and my breath hissed through clenched teeth. "No one can live in a vacuum."

"So we should knuckle under to those Toller bastards?" Delacort's legs folded as he pulled against the training unit, and he breathed sharply.

"I'm saying we need to find new places to live if we're going to leave Earth. That goes for the Atolls as well. And the real estate out here isn't attractive."

I sighed as the program ended and the training unit relaxed, glad to have an excuse to leave Delacort's accusatory stare.

Six days later I watched the approach on the screen in my room. We slid in over Asia and the screens picked up the bright reflection of the Fukumuro orbital solar power plant floating over the continent like a metallic dandelion seed. The appearance was apt—I'd heard dandelion hooch was a survival commodity to the engineering crew. Those damn weeds could grow anywhere apparently, even in LoGee. I dropped back down on my bunk.

Two hours later we were approaching a docking port at the High-Rig. It looked bigger than I remembered, which was probably the result of being confined for so long on Helios. When I passed through the airlock, the main promenade was busy, the wide area filled with a high percentage of SecOps uniforms. The news had said they were reinforcing the defenses again, a project started before the attack on Helios, but no doubt taking even greater priority now. On the way in, I'd noticed the outlying hubs were being expanded and it all looked competent enough, though as with Helios, protecting a fixed point from an attack was problematic.

The one person I wanted to see wasn't there. I'd not heard from Dollie since the last call before we were attacked, even though I'd sent several messages. I wasn't sure whether it meant she was still mad or she didn't want me back, and if I was honest, I wasn't sure I wanted to find out.

I had several hours until I could board the elevator so I headed for the infamous "Heisenberg Principle"; I'd spent several nights in there with Logan while working on the High-Rig. He'd introduced me to "Old Freiskein"—a whiskey so cheap and rough they reputedly used it to clean the injectors on rocket engines. Logan called it "Old Foreskin" and claimed it was brewed and distilled from said ancillary body parts. I almost believed him. After the "dry" months on Helios though, it was a rare treat.

"You're that guy." A slurred voice drifted across from someone sitting farther down the fake Bavarian-style bar. "The Ananta hero."

That wasn't how I described myself and cringed every time I heard the nickname the media had given me. I wasn't a hero and never would be. If the ship had come back like it was supposed to, perhaps I'd have felt differently, but disintegrating on its first test flight wasn't good for anyone, especially Earth.

"Sorry, bud. Wrong person. I get that a lot, I guess I must look like him."

The guy wandered over, a little unsteady on his legs. He was wearing a SecOps uniform and had several days of stubble on his square jaw. I was surprised to see him in the bar—Sec-Ops upper ranks are usually pretty strict about such things—then I noticed the "Flaming Comet" patch on his shoulder that designated an Interceptor pilot. Those guys always took liberties. And always got away with them.

"Sure you are. I got briefed on it. Mallen? Bannen? Something like that." He emptied the rest of his glass and slid his heavyset frame into the seat next to me. "Just back from Helios?"

"Ballen." There didn't seem any point denying it further. "Came in on the Ares, heading to the surface."

"That was a shitbake around Mercury, huh?" He gestured at the barman for another. "Thombs. Lieutenant in the ever-glorious service of SecOps."

"Pleased to meet you." I raised my own drink. "Good health."

"Right...I'm a space pilot. Interceptors. No one gives a poo-pile about us."

"Maybe it seems that way, but a lot of people, me included, think you guys are the real heroes."

"You ever seen an Interceptor, Ballen?" He downed half his glass in a single swallow. "They're a shitbake, I tell you. Supposed to be the most advanced ship we have, but they're still a shitbake. Would as soon blow *you* up as the enemy."

Six Interceptors were permanently stationed at the High-Rig now. Part of SecOps *Overreach* plans to defend the station and elevator—I'd seen them docked to one side as we arrived. The PanAsians had done the same with the Tiānkōng Zuànshí station and Bengkulu elevator from what I'd heard. They were even working with USP on joint defenses as part of the USN—something unbelievable a couple of years back.

"Best we can do, I guess." I figured Thombs had got an early start and I didn't want to get into a debate with him, so I dropped into my "cab driver" persona as if he were just another drunken passenger. "I'm sure there's a tech team working overtime right now to improve them."

He didn't seem to hear me, but drained his glass and gestured for another. The barman stepped up but didn't have a drink with him. "Sorry, sir. I'm afraid I can't serve you another. You've had too much."

"What the hell? Gimme a drink, you little shiz. No one calls time on *Fireball* Thombs." He turned to me and grinned. "That's what they call me—Fireball—cos I'm hot. You tell this prick."

I should have walked away. Thombs was nothing to me, but I couldn't simply abandon him. His comrades-in-arms had literally defended my life on Helios. Instead I flashed my credit chip at the barman and gave him my biggest smile. "Another drink for my friend, please. My round. After that we'll be heading out."

The barman hesitated, even though Thombs murmured his agreement.

"And, of course, a large one for yourself..." I tossed my chip on the bar and the barman picked it up. He was getting paid a bonus for me to take trouble off his hands—why would he refuse?

"You're a real pal, Ballum...Palum?" He laughed at his own joke. "You're a bal, Palum."

He spent the next ten minutes explaining what was wrong with the Interceptors in fine detail. From what I'd seen, they weren't

26

going to win any design awards, for sure—even if they were the first newly constructed Earth ships in more than thirty years, apart from the Ananta. The front end was a standard conical command unit which connected to a central gantry spine; behind were the giant fuel and water cooling tanks. At the back the fat reactor and drive units attached to the spine along with the radiator "wings," making them look like a crucifix in space.

"Remote piloting would be better," Thombs explained. "Lower mass, fashter acceleration, and more *hic* range. And less chance of co-counter attacks."

"So how come they use pilots?" I finished my drink and was ready to leave. "Remotes would be more vulnerable to countermeasures and hacking, I guess."

His response was a bitter laugh. "Sure. That's what the brass says. Truth is ..."

He leaned in close, and I almost got high from the alcohol on his breath before I settled back a little on my stool.

"Truth is...you're not meant to come back...unlesh you win, that is."

The ultimate sacrifice. No wonder the Interceptor jockeys didn't care about following the rules.

"Let's get out of here. Go somewhere we can talk in private. We don't want these civilians listening in on this."

He noticed his empty glass. "Want another...where the barman."

"Sure. The night is young, but why pay through the nose in a dump like this? We can pick up a bottle on the way..."

"Hey! Thas a good idea, buddy." He upended his glass and slapped it down on the bar. "Lead on!"

I helped him up and we wobbled towards the exit. The barman reappeared looking relieved and nodded to me as I guided my new friend through the door.

"Let's find some slitches too. I got the dough..."

"I'm married."

"Thas funny. So am I!"

Thombs laughed so hard I thought he was going to make himself sick. I guided him to the nearest hotel via a liquor machine. No way would I be able to get him back to his barracks without handing him over to the MPs, and there was no way I was going to do that—he was already putting enough on the line.

I checked him in and dumped him in the sparse room. He'd already started on the bottle I'd bought and was busy getting more thoroughly saturated.

I threw a drink down my throat, grimacing at the unaccustomed harshness. "We need some snacks. Back in a few."

"Snacks? Good thinkin..." His head rolled loosely as he answered. "Get some SnikSnax..."

I estimated he'd be unconscious before he realized I wasn't coming back. That was the best I could do, and I weaved my way through the crowds to the elevator.

Three

Twelve hours later I hobbled into the traveler lounge at the base station on Earth, breathing heavily from the exertion. Even with the artificial gravity areas on Helios plus the intense workouts in the fitness centrifuge on the Ares, ZeeGee takes its toll on the muscles. I'd been getting the new AminoARM shots to help fight muscle-atrophy, but the change in gravity still left me feeling like someone was sitting on my shoulders.

"Here, Ballen."

The voice was a deep growl, and for a second I didn't recognize it. I started to turn, then a mass of lithe, two-legged hellcat hit me from the side, riding me as I fell backward and straddling me on the floor.

"You complete bastard! I hate you. I hate you. Hate you."

Dollie kissed me all over as she cursed me. Her lips were warm against my face and neck, and she ground her crotch against mine. I couldn't help the natural biological response, and she grinned.

"MMMmmm...So you still remember poor old Dollie, then? At least that's something." She kissed me several more times. "Did I tell you I hate you? You and that trollop female space engineer. Did you bring her home for me?"

"Could you hate me a little less and let me up?" The hoots and whistles around us were getting embarrassing. "And Isabell...well, she didn't make it..."

Dollie pulled back, her beautiful cobalt eyes almost black as she looked at me. "Sorry, Joe. They didn't say much about what happened."

She clambered off me. "Was she nice?"

What do you say in such circumstances? "Very. A good engineer, and a good friend."

"Was she better than me?"

"Nothing happened between us."

"You sure?" Dollie tried to look me in the eye and failed. "I mean, she was...normal. A real woman..."

"Dollie." I took her hands in mine, pulled her close, and looked into her eyes. "You *are* a real woman. And the only one I want."

I had no luggage beyond a small shoulder bag, so we didn't need to wait. Outside, the air was fresh in a way it never is in a recycled space habitat, and it held a tang of salt from the ocean around us. I took a deep breath and stretched. It felt good.

Dollie dragged me to the car and in less than ten minutes we were skimming over the rolling ocean waves on our way back to Baltimore. The car was spacious and luxurious and had the "new car" smell that only comes out of a can.

"No more of this long-distance stuff, Joe." Dollie looked at me, and for a moment I thought she might cry. "The bed gets far too cold."

"I thought you had a long line-up of bed warmers."

She glowered at me, and I thought she was going to lay into me again, but she held back. "Things change."

There was a look on her face I couldn't identify. I hadn't known quite what to expect when I got back—Dollie is never predictable—but her mood was unusual even for her. She slid closer and pressed herself against me; her eyes held a mischievous twinkle as she reached down and squeezed. Despite the one gee gravity, I couldn't stop the inevitable reaction. This was the Dollie I knew.

"You don't seem tired, Joe." Her eyes were wide and innocent.

"Unfortunately, I am."

Her hand tightened as she writhed against me like a cat. "That's okay. You relax. Dollie will do all the work."

It's a good thing we had the autopilot, as neither of us was watching the controls for the next couple of hours. Burial at sea isn't my style, though Dollie did go down three times. Or was it four...

Neither of us saw daylight for the next three days. Dollie

insisted that I "rest" and build my strength. Her strategy for this was deceptively simple and consisted of equal parts high protein diet alternating with intense bouts of "aerobic exercise."

On the third night, I woke unexpectedly.

I couldn't figure out what had disturbed me, and I opened my eyes, sighing. The indicator light on my Scroll was blinking regularly indicating an incoming call, otherwise the room was black. With the privacy set, the Scroll wouldn't ring, only flash. I reached over and grabbed it, thumbing the *answer* button.

"Hello?" My throat was dry and rough.

"Joe Ballen?"

The voice was a whisper. Almost too quiet to hear and curiously distorted, as if there was bad reception. I swung my legs out of the bed and walked around, hoping to catch a better signal. "Hello?" I repeated, and the line went dead. I checked the call log; there was no record of a call and I wondered if I was truly awake.

"Joe...?" Dollie's voice was gravelly as she rolled over. "If you're awake, you better come back to bed."

I slid inside the covers and she moved over me. Her mouth melted against mine and thoughts of anything else slipped away.

I sipped my coffee and swallowed a piece of toast, then sighed contentedly. "A man could very easily die between your thighs."

We were sitting at the breakfast table. Dollie had redecorated the apartment in shades of gold and bronze while I'd been away. Now it looked like the dining area for an Amazonian warrior, which in some ways perhaps it was. I had a steaming mug of fresh Jamaican Blue coffee in hand, the rich flavor playing with my taste buds and leaving them begging for more. I whistled, wondering where Dollie had managed to find it. Even for a special occasion, it was indecently expensive.

"You say the most romantic things." Dollie smiled, reaching across the table to pat my arm. "Unfortunately, I better check in at the office today. You know how antsy the drivers get when I'm not around."

It was a twenty minute hop to the taxi hub, so I checked my

Scroll as we traveled. The news was the usual depressing crap. PanAsia still had human rights issues and had imprisoned several journalists on charges of reporting the truth. Several major crop failures meant thousands were fighting starvation in Old Europe, while much of the aid being flown in from the United African Democracies was getting "lost in distribution." The Atolls had announced that the attack on Helios was a "measured and proportionate" warning and, best of all, the Tigers continued the same abysmal form they'd shown all season.

I tapped the Scroll. "Same old s—"

"Did you expect the world to suddenly discover sanity while you were gone?" Dollie barely glanced up from the driver logs she was checking.

"I keep hoping..."

"You're a born optimist, Joe." She squeezed my thigh. "That's why I love you so much."

"Me and how many others?"

She frowned and put the logs down, squeezing my hand. "I'm not a saint. You knew that when we started all this. We're married, but I'm not a corpse."

"I know," I lied. "I was joking."

Dollie looked serious. "I see who I want to. We agreed we were still free to do that, didn't we?"

It was what we'd agreed, and I even believed I'd meant it at the time. The truth was, although I might have *looked* at other people since, that was as far as it had gone. I'm an old-fashioned kind of guy, and it didn't seem right to intentionally look for another partner after making such a commitment.

"Yes, we did."

"We can discuss it, if you're not happy."

I wanted to say *something;* but couldn't think how to put it without it coming out wrong. We had a good thing going, why spoil it? We'd agreed to be adults and not crowd each other, so why did it bother me all of a sudden?

I was about to say I *did* want to discuss it, when the car settled into the cradle at Dollie's Cabs with a clunk, and the doors hissed open.

Dollie strode into the offices with me trailing behind. I was still lost in thought over our discussion or rather the lack of it. We'd gotten married because I thought it would be romantic and fun, but it didn't mean I expected Dollie to change. We were partners, not owner and owned.

I heard some heated voices in the drivers' lounge.

"You guys need to pick it up." It was Dollie, but she'd slipped into her harsher male vocal range. "The turn-around is slipping, we're not getting through as many calls as we should, and I don't like losing traffic to other companies."

"We're doing what we can. It's a tough market out there, you should try it sometime."

"I did *try it*, for years. That's how I built the business in the first place." She paused. "You need to take fewer breaks and get in your cab more, Bloch."

She'd mentioned him a couple of times while I was on Helios. He was a newer driver and sometimes belligerent. He wouldn't still have been there except licensed drivers were getting hard to find. I slipped into the room and stayed quiet. I wasn't about to interfere; Dollie was the boss here.

"I'll do what I can." Bloch spoke slowly, clearly not too distressed by Dollie's criticism.

"See that you do." Dollie moved through to the central lounge. "Sarah! Fetch me a coffee, and transfer some calls over to me."

Bloch shook his head at the other drivers. He had his back to me and shrugged his shoulders. "Stupid bitch needs a damn good..."

The other two looked at each other, then back to me, as if they didn't know whether to leave him to his fate or stay to protect him. One of them leaned in and whispered something to Bloch that I couldn't hear. He turned, and I slowly unclenched my fists, resisting the urge to put a punch where he most deserved.

"You like your job, don't you?" I kept my voice even.

His face turned a dark amber. "Sure. I mean, it's okay. Had worse."

"So show the lady some respect. She's the one feeding your family."

"Ain't a she, it's an *it*. Goddamn maffer creeps me the hell out."

33

His embarrassment quickly turned to anger, and he screwed up his face. "How'd you even manage to touch that *thing*."

"He or she, it's her choice, not yours or mine. Don't ever let me hear you bad-mouthing her again or it *will* be your job."

"You ain't the boss."

"I'm close enough." I breathed slowly. "I suggest you get out and start cruising the BWI. There's always traffic at the airport."

I left him cold and crossed into the lounge. Dollie was in conversation with Sarah, her part-time assistant controller. She'd hired Sarah temporarily when we got married and kept her on afterward. Although competent enough, Sarah didn't have the same authority over the drivers that Dollie had and tended to let things slip a little.

"Bloch by name, block-head by nature." I nodded in greeting at Sarah, then looked at Dollie. "Get rid of him before he becomes a real liability."

"I don't need you—"

I held up my hands to forestall the storm. "Not telling you how to run your business, just helpful advice."

"Who do I replace him with? The military is buying anyone who can fly a kite, in case things blow up." Dollie's eyes hardened. "And you left. Remember?"

That one was a bit close to the knuckle. I could hardly blame Dollie for still being angry at me leaving, and the last thing I wanted was to start a domestic interaction in public. "Sarah. Put me back on the roster for the duration. That might help bring the numbers back."

"Nice to see you again, Mr. Ballen." Sarah nodded, her blond hair as untidy as the clothes she wore. She was nothing if not casual.

"Thanks, Sarah. It's *Joe*, remember?"

"We were so worried when we heard about the attack. Dollie even tried to hir—" Sarah yelped, looking at Dollie.

"Sorry, my foot slipped."

I made a mental note to quiz Sarah about what Dollie had tried to do. Then I wasn't sure I wanted to know—maybe she'd had an orgy to celebrate. Perhaps Sarah had helped comfort Dollie; she was a little heavyset and not Dollie's usual type, but that didn't mean they couldn't have fun together.

I pulled out my license and passed it to Sarah. "Register me."

Dollie spoke up as Sarah reactivated me in the system. "Make it part-time. I've not finished with him yet."

The reception area suddenly seemed a little claustrophobic, and I tried to avoid looking at either of the women. I couldn't help noticing Sarah's blush, her cornflower-blue eyes widening as Dollie giggled.

Four

I slipped back into the role of cab driver with ease, despite the time I'd been away. Dollie didn't work me too hard outside the bedroom, and everything slipped into a pleasant routine. I suppose some people might have found it dull, but I'd had enough excitement to make "dull" feel good.

I'd been working for a couple of months and we were slowly pulling the stats closer to where Dollie wanted them, partly by me pitching in, partly by leading through example, and partly by pulling long shifts. My screen beeped as an assignment came in for a downtown pickup. With it was a note from Dollie telling me it was my last for the night—she had designs on my body that sounded exhaustingly pleasant.

Downtown on a Friday meant one thing, and I hoped the fare was sober enough not to fill the backseat with puke. Brayshaw's Bar was designed to look like it dated back to the days before rising seas and the big shift knocked the hell out of the world. Warm orange lights, green shamrocks and patented *olde worlde* signs that were stylish at the cost of legibility. The landing platforms were additions, not part of the original structure, making the building look as though it was festooned with strange growths.

I floated the cab down on L3 per directions and switched the turbines to idle. Almost immediately a man dressed in a dingy yellow business suit emerged from the bar, walked over to the cab, and clambered in. He was stocky with black buzz-cut hair, and the car's interior lights flashed on his high forehead. He looked like he'd be mean in a fight, and again I hoped he wasn't loaded, though now for other reasons.

"Brin?" That was the name I'd been given for him. He nodded as he strapped in and I lifted the cab into the air. "Where to?"

"Set the autopilot to fly around in circles," he said, then pulled out a small box, pressing a red button on its side. The cab filled with a barely audible high-pitched whine, like an electronic mosquito singing an insane mating song. "There. We should be safe from eavesdroppers now."

"If you're looking to make a confession, you're in the wrong place." I could smell SecOps all over him and wanted nothing to do with whatever he was pitching. "How about I drop you at Fairy Fun World? I hear they've got openings for clowns."

"No reason for hostility, Mr. Ballen." I watched in the RearView as he pulled a Scroll out and flipped through several files, the light from the display illuminating his dark skin. "You're out of work right now, I understand. I'm here simply to offer you a job."

"Your information is wrong. I have a job driving this cab. That should be obvious even to someone with your...intelligence?"

"Very droll, I'm sure." His face showed no sign of emotion. "I'm Dexter Brin, Senior Field Agent with the SIA."

The Special Investigation Agency was the branch of SecOps responsible for investigation and intelligence both inside the USP and externally. They had a wide remit and were completely separate from the branch my old friend, Logan, worked for. Not that it would have helped if they were on the same team. I dislike and don't trust secret security organizations on principle—or rather perhaps the lack of theirs. "ID?"

"You're a careful man. That's good." Brin reached into his pocket and pulled out a midnight-blue electronic card.

He held up his ID long enough for it to scan his eye and verify his identity. I made an exaggerated sigh; I was hoping he'd turn out to be fake.

"Okay, that says you're who you claim to be." I programmed a holding pattern into the car, then turned to face him. "What's it got to do with me?"

"You know what happened with the Ananta plans?"

The plans should have been made available on the worldwide

academic system, GARNET, but when the files were checked, they were incomplete. Several vital assemblies and specifications were missing, and no one could explain what had happened. "I don't have any better answers for you now than I did three years ago. Ganz and Tana said they'd make everything available. That didn't happen."

"And you still claim to have no idea what happened to the missing information?"

"I don't *claim* anything." My hands tightened on the controls. I'd been through this several times after the Ananta left. Brin must know that. "I've told you people what was supposed to happen. I've no idea why it didn't."

"I read the summary. Digital consciousness. Stored brains. An evil, dead scientist." The skepticism was clear in his voice. "They stole the world's first prototype starship and flew off, never to return."

"That's what happened."

"And you believe that this dead scientist, the evil one...Harmon...blocked the information transfer?"

"I don't know that he did. That was all I could think might have happened. From what he said at the time, he didn't think we were worthy of interstellar flight. But that's all a guess. As I said when I first suggested it."

"Yes, I see you made that claim." Brin flipped through some more notes on his Scroll. "I don't believe it. I think someone deliberately stole the information for the purpose of extortion."

I turned to unlock the controls. "That's stupid. But I'll call my lawyer and we can play legal *hoopla* again."

"I've spent two years tracking this down." Brin tapped on the PlaSteel screen between us. "You think a lawyer will stop me nailing your hide?"

It seemed unlikely, given the powers SecOps *could* use if they deemed something to be in the "interest of the state." He continued, not waiting for me to answer.

"Two days after Ananta left Earth's orbit, one of the engineers, Denny Wirkkala, disappeared. The company he worked for was involved in constructing the starship. They filed him as a no-show with the Board of Employment, and that was the end of it, seemingly."

"No law against a man walking off a job."

Brin's Scroll beeped. "One second." He reached inside his suit and pulled out a pill box, then swallowed a yellow capsule from it. "NanoBiotics. Have to take them every two hours."

NanoBiotics were the latest in high-tech healing—medical nano-scale robots that literally rebuild your tissues from the inside out. They create scaffolding from fibrous cartilage and then layer over that differentiated tissue derived from stem cells to recreate organs, muscle, bone, or any other type of tissue necessary. If Brin was taking them, then he was dealing with some serious health problems or injuries. He was also very valuable to someone—one of those pills would cost me a day's salary.

"Wirkkala resurfaced in Luna Free State. He'd taken early retirement and relocated there with his wife, who was seriously ill with aggressive osteoporosis and possibly dementia. Apparently he relocated his wife to take advantage of the lower gravity."

"That's not illegal either." SIA or not, his recap of yesterday's events was annoying. "Why the hell bring this up after all this time? Look, I need to get back to work. If I don't make pick ups, I don't get paid."

"It took me two years to piece this together. You think someone who was retiring would cover his tracks so thoroughly?"

"Perhaps he doesn't like people poking around his business. There's this thing, you might have heard of it, called privacy."

"Possibly. And I guess it's a coincidence that Wirkkala was chief technician on the Ananta's space-drive? Or that he worked every day with the very files and information that vanished?"

While it was a big coincidence, it didn't make the guy guilty of anything. "What do you want from me? I don't know anything about him."

"I want you to go to LFS and talk to him. *Maybe* he took the records, *maybe* he didn't. He might remember some of what he worked on. It might all be innocent, but *maybe*...he has the information needed to build a new Ananta."

"Great. I hope he does. And when you see him, I'll be happy for both of you."

"You think they'd let me go? It's not called Luna Free State for nothing. If it was that simple I'd have gone six months ago when I first tracked him down."

LFS was one hundred percent free. Politically independent from any Earth coalition and not allied with the Corporates or Atolls. Though not free as in beer. It was an expensive luxury resort inhabited by three classes: wealthy privileged seniors, temporary vacationing party goers, and the massed contracted minions of obsequiousness. All visitors were heavily screened. I couldn't see how a retired engineer could afford it.

"What makes you think they'll let me in?"

Brin gave a slight smile, the skin around his lips becoming paler almost as if protesting such an unfamiliar action. "Like everyone, the LFS is worried about the ongoing conflict between ourselves and the Atolls. They're looking for contractors to help strengthen their defenses, in case one side or the other decides a lunar base might be what they need. I'd say you're eminently qualified."

"Okay, I'm qualified. I still don't want it. In case you didn't know, I'm a happily married man. I enjoy going home every night."

"Logan told me you might be reluctant. He said to ask you to do it as a special favor to him."

My friendship with Logan didn't require me to go along with this game, though it did add more pressure. We'd worked on the High-Rig together, and Logan had saved my life at least twice. He'd also smoothed things over with the authorities after the Ananta had vanished. That brought a certain sense of obligation with it, but I still didn't want to touch it.

Brin looked at something else on his Scroll. "After the Ananta went missing you were still wanted for murder, I understand."

I shrugged. My alibi had effectively vanished along with the starship. "There were some loose ends..." Logan had interceded with the authorities, something else I owed him for.

"None of the murder cases have ever been closed. Ganz, Rohloff, Francis, and Sterle are marked as unresolved. It would be messy to reopen them, don't you think?"

For a moment I wondered what the penalty would be if I dropped Brin from my cab. He was annoying me enough to make me consider it, but I said nothing.

He nodded as if it was all agreed. "Here's a QuBee. When you find Wirkkala, activate it to let us know. We'll arrange to pick him up. We've taken the liberty of submitting your work profile to the recruiters, and they've already invited you to go through the pre-contract assessment. You have a double berth booked on the elevator a week Thursday."

"Double?" That seemed pointlessly extravagant or remarkably generous for a government department.

"We assumed you'd want to take your...errr...wife." Brin grimaced as he said the word. "That's your decision though."

Damn that Logan. Dollie wasn't going to be happy.

Five

Luna Free State was what I imagine pre-shake Florida must have been like—most of the permanent residents were old, retired, and well heeled. This was balanced by a near constant swarm of tourists who reveled in the combination of low gravity and tax-free hedonism. Unlike Earth-based resorts, there was no seasonal price differential other than slight travel cost differences brought about by the fluctuations of the lunar orbit. Despite their early popularity, interest in orbital resorts had declined due to the lack of gravity, although they still had their fans. If you were heading off-planet, it was far more likely Luna was your destination, especially since the Atolls threw up their borders and were no longer an option.

For the most part, the tourists were kept away from the residential zones, except around the fashionable and expensive Armstrong Park area. A wide-domed arboretum was the only place "open" to the sky and provided a view of Earth through a high-vaulted transparent dome. Many people made the mistake of thinking the park was where the historic first landing occurred. The replica of the lunar module in the center doesn't help the misunderstanding, but the actual site is the Lunar Memorial, a few hundred kilometers away and only accessible with special high-ranking permission.

We hadn't caught the elevator that had been booked, as we'd had to wait for extra clearance for Dollie. She hadn't been to Luna before and was as happy as a kitten with a ball of yarn. As soon as we'd unpacked in the shoe box optimistically called a "double" hotel room, she wanted to get out sightseeing. For budgetary reasons, I'd chosen a hotel at a distance from the park, but the Transit Tubes make any journey fast and pleasurable, so we were soon wandering through the trees.

"I thought you said everybody here was old." Dollie linked her arm around mine and pulled me closer.

Luna City was currently in its two-week "day" period, so the walkways were brimming with skimpily dressed youngsters making their way to and from the large solariums. I should have feigned disinterest, but there was far too much jiggling in the low gravity to make that entirely possible, and Dollie knew it.

"They're too young to take seriously," I said as we approached the replica lunar lander. "Can you believe the first astronauts came here in something like that?"

"I suppose I'm old and serious?"

There was an edge to Dollie's voice that instantly put me on guard. "That's not what I meant, and you know it. Stop fishing for compliments. I don't want to be with anyone else."

"Well, maybe *I* want to be with someone else..." Dollie made a show of checking out a couple nearby. "You're not exactly buff."

I couldn't argue. I was still rebuilding muscle after the weeks on Helios, and even though I was pushing myself in the gym each day, it was hard work—an unwelcome sign of getting older I didn't want to admit. "I love you, but I don't own you. If you want to play around and have some fun, then that's your choice."

Dollie looked a little uncomfortable for some reason. "Perhaps they are too young."

We worked our way through the crowds, stopping for several minutes to pay homage to "Old Queenie," the longest-living—and largest—tree on Luna. Old Queenie had been planted by one of the first residents on the moon, starting out as a pot plant and then replanted periodically as it grew. Now it's a beautiful Royal Empress which blooms several times a year in the low gravity and at that moment, was fully dressed, with each branch and twig topped with blooms like blobs of pink icing.

I wanted to check out the new GlydeTank, but Dollie decided she'd like to have lunch by the tree. We grabbed some overpriced

BLT wraps from a vendor and found an empty table near the base of the tree. There was a soft movement of air and a warm sense of comfort. Other than the faded directionless shadows from the artificial lighting and black sky above, we could have been sitting in a park Earthside. Of course, the illusion was spoiled by the low gravity if you moved too much, but was still pleasant.

"It would be nice to retire here someday," Dollie murmured, her fingers interweaving with mine. "I'm sure I could get used to starlit skies and low grav."

"Sounds good, but how would you afford it?"

The days of pensions and state handouts were long gone. If you wanted something now you had to work for it. I bit into my wrap and was disappointed by the fake bacosoy; at the price we'd paid it should have been cultured pork, at least.

"I have some savings. And the cab company can bring in money without me."

Dollie had left Sarah in charge while we were away, but I had doubts as to how effective she'd be. "You think Sarah could handle things long term?"

"Not right now, perhaps," she mused. "In time. People need to build up to things. You're always too impatient."

Perhaps it was true. But in my experience, there were two types of people: those who could and did, and those who couldn't. There didn't seem to be a way of turning one into the other, regardless of how many years they had behind them. It was like trying to make a remote manipulator into a prosthetic leg— they might have the same basic functions, but it's never going to work in the end.

"I heard what you did, Joe. With Bloch." Dollie brushed my face. "It's nice. Makes me feel all gooey inside, but I can look after myself."

"I know you can. I like looking after you, though." I thumped my chest lightly. "Joe protect!"

Dollie giggled. "It feels good when I look after you too."

She leaned over the small table and our lips met. Someone whistled nearby, and I wasn't sure if it was at us or not. I didn't think we were *that* interesting. I glanced around Dollie and saw the real reason for the whistles. A woman with a lean body similar to Dollie's was striding through the crowds. She was dressed in a tight black SkinSuit and had an angelic face surrounded by a bouncing halo of green-tipped dark hair. As she passed, I got a closer view and my leg ached with sympathy pains. I recognized her but couldn't believe what I was seeing.

I squeezed Dollie's hand, then stood a little too quickly, almost unbalancing the table. "Stay here."

"Joe? What is it?"

I didn't stop to answer and took off after the woman. Last time I'd seen her she had a shaved head and was in charge of an assassination team. I thought she'd died when the ore transport was destroyed three years ago, but somehow she'd managed to get away. Whatever Gabriella was up to, I'd bet it was no good for someone, and I had a sneaking suspicion I knew what she was doing on Luna at that moment.

I trailed after her down the long stretch of the main corridor. She didn't seem to be in a rush and even stopped a couple of times at various stores, occasionally crossing from one side to the other. The casual observer wouldn't have thought twice about it, but I knew her better. She was using her path to check for people following her, and I stayed well back, far enough that I'd be part of the melee. Luckily her black clothing made her stand out from the pastel shades popular with most of the crowd.

She turned down a smaller side passage towards one of the residential areas, and I hurried to catch her before she had a chance to disappear. But even with my haste I was careful to saunter past the entrance when I got there as though I was simply another pedestrian.

A quick side glance as I passed was enough to tell me she'd vanished, and I swore under my breath. After I'd gone another five meters I did a one eighty to return to the corridor and leaned slightly left so I could peek around the corner. She was nowhere in sight, but there didn't seem to be anywhere she could have gone. The nearest entrance was thirty meters down, and I didn't think she could have covered that distance before I'd gotten there.

The corridor widened before the first entrance, leaving a small blind spot halfway, where I couldn't see. It was possible she was hiding there, but it seemed unlikely unless she'd spotted me. I edged forward, close enough to the wall that my hand brushed the slightly grainy lunarcrete. As I approached the hidden area I slowed.

Even though I couldn't see into the blind spot of the corner I could see the edge of a door frame. I risked a quick glance and sure enough, it was clear apart from the door. I had no idea where it led but I could hardly wait around to see if she came out again. She'd see me the moment she emerged and there was no place close where I could hide. I slid backward, away from the door and then stopped as a sharp plastic blade slid lightly across my throat.

"Joe..." Gabriella cinched her arm around me and pulled back, effectively locking me into her grip unless I wanted an involuntary tracheotomy. "How delightful to see you again after all this time. Following me is a dangerous game, you should know that."

"When did you see me?"

"Oh, darling. I spotted you by that silly tree with your charming...friend. I would have stopped by to say hello, but I'm not here for a social visit."

I reached up slowly and lightly gripped her knife hand, hoping she'd relieve the pressure, but instead it bit deeper.

"What's this? A wedding band?" Her voice was as warm as a comet in deep space. "Joe, how could you?"

Gabriella pressed her lithe body tighter against me, the knife blade slicing through several layers of skin at my throat. "I always liked you, Joe. We should be friends, don't you think?"

I'd rather have wrestled a rabid tiger but didn't think it was the right moment to mention it. "I'm always in favor of having more friends."

"But you had to go and introduce this *wife* motif. Why, Joe? We had such a special relationship."

The only relationship we had was hunter and prey, with me cast as the latter, but it didn't seem a good time to remind her. "She likes girls too."

"So I've heard." She scowled. "I don't."

She reached down, squeezing between my legs firmly. "It would be a pity to lose this, Joe. Don't follow me. My business isn't yours."

I winced as she tightened her grip, blinking heavily as my eyes watered. Then the pressure was gone, and so was Gabriella.

Dollie looked ready to blow a stack when I got back, then she reached into her bag and handed me a tissue. "What the hell happened?"

My throat felt like it *had* been cut, even if the damage was minor. Still, there were spots of blood on the paper when I wiped. "Gabriella."

Dollie stiffened, her hands gripping the strap of her bag as I related the encounter. We'd both suffered at the hands of Gabriella, having shared the dubious experience of having her shoot both of us during the messed-up Ananta mischief. We'd obviously lived to fight another day, but I was sure neither of us wanted to repeat the experience.

"I thought...hoped...she was dead. What's she doing here?"

"I didn't think it was a good time to ask. Whatever it is you can guarantee it will involve someone getting hurt." I wiped my neck again, but the blood had already clotted. "I can't help wondering if she's connected with why they sent me here."

"Wirkkala?" I'd told Dollie about my meeting with Brin. "I thought only the SIA knew about him."

"Let's move." I helped Dollie up and started to amble down the promenade towards the sports stadium. "I still want to see the GlydeTank. There's a game this afternoon."

Dollie held back. "How can you think about sports with that psychotic bitch in the vicinity?"

I turned back to her. "I've never seen GlydeBall live. It looks interesting. Besides, we should try to act as normal as possible. What would you do?"

"Report her. She's a killer, Joe."

"To who? And for what?" Dollie was right, but I couldn't see how it would do anything other than bring attention to us. "She's done nothing wrong as far as we know, and even if she has, we have no idea what. Not to mention the fact we're also missing a few basics, like proof."

Dollie shook her head but caught up with me, and we continued walking.

The arena was larger than I imagined with seating climbing fifteen meters high around the tank itself. We paid the entrance fee and settled into the stands as the warm-up started.

If you've never seen a GlydeBall game, it's worth checking out. The tank is a clear box twenty meters high, twenty wide and fifty meters long. At either end there's a funnel-shaped "goal," and each half of the tank has a set of vertical and upright spars—poles used by the players to maneuver. While hidden behind grating at floor level, multiple fans pump air upwards to counteract the low lunar gravity.

Today's game was an exhibition between the local Lunar Mystics and the Jade Dragons, from the PAC community in the Mare Frigoris region. Both teams were leading contenders for the championship, so the rivalry was expected to be intense—we were getting to see the likely championship finalists for bargain prices.

Several of the players, called "Glyders" were swinging around and between the horizontal and vertical spars in complicated warm-up exercises, occasionally making long elegant glides up and down the length of the 'Tank. They wore tight body suits with webbed wings running from the arms to the legs that spread when they stretched out, making them look a little like hairless, winged squirrels.

"They look good," Dollie murmured, closely examining two muscular players from the Mystics. We should get some autographs."

I could imagine what "signature" Dollie was interested in, but I had to admit they all looked extremely fit. Each side had seven players, though only five were active at any time. The two beefy-looking players were matched by a similar pair from the Dragons. They were the enforcers. The other players were lighter in build and more athletic, apart from the goalkeepers who looked bulky in their thick air-padded outfits and had one hand attached to a large mesh net.

"From what I hear the Dragons will slaughter them." The PAC team moved with military precision compared to the wilder Mystics. It was a battle of ideologies as much as sporting ability.

Dollie laughed. "They don't look big enough. Fifty bucks on the Mystics."

I don't think I'd ever won a bet with Dollie, but there's always a first time. "You're on."

The object of GlydeBall is simple. Put the ball into your opponent's goal for a point. Imagine a cross between skydiving, basketball and gymnastic asymmetric bars, and you're somewhere close.

The warning sounded, and the teams took positions at their respective ends of the 'Tank. The Mystics were in blue and gold while the Dragons were understandably in dark green. A minute later the launcher above the Dragons lit and the ball launched into Mystics' defensive zone.

One of the Mystics caught the ball in a soaring cross dive. Holding the ball in one hand and looping around a spar, she flicked the ball to one of the enforcers. He moved close to the halfway mark before making his one touch and having to pass the ball to another player. This guy was fast and zipped close into the Dragons' goal as two of them closed in on him. Suddenly he flipped the ball high, and the first player swooped in to catch it, closely followed by the second enforcer. The Dragons' defense opened, and the ball soared into the goal accompanied by the bellow of a horn.

"Want to change your bet, darling?" Dollie looked smug as she batted her eyelids in mock innocence. "You should check out the form more."

I've worked in LoGee and ZeeGee most of my adult life but I couldn't come close to what the Glyders were doing. Seeing them swooping around like ball-playing eagles was impressive, and how they used the spars to alter trajectory and change speed was simply breathtaking.

Although I was watching the game my mind was only half on it. My thoughts kept wandering back to Gabriella. "How do you think she escaped?"

Dollie appeared to be intent on the game, but she knew what I was talking about. "I've no idea. I thought we'd left her for dead on that hulk."

When the Ananta launched, the Atolls had tried to stop it by force. Even though it was only a prototype, they didn't want to run the risk that we might have developed a practical starship. We'd taken control of an ore carrier and run "block" to give the starship time to launch. With Dollie's help, we'd kept the Ananta safe and left the carrier as it fell apart. There'd only been one escape pod and we'd used it.

A cheer thundered around the arena. The local team had scored again.

"Nice moves," Dollie commented, then waved a VendaDrone over. After buying beer and hot dogs she continued. "You're not taking in the match, are you?"

"Gabriella must be working for the Atolls. It's the only thing that makes sense." I bit into the hot dog and several hundred taste buds died. The Lunar variety was about as palatable as their Earthside equivalents and even worse than the bacosoy from earlier. I swilled it down with the beer, which was frosty cold and had a deliciously nutty flavor that made up considerably for the dog. "She works for the highest bidder and the Atolls would certainly want to get their hands on Wirkkala if they knew about him. They want the space-drive as much as we do. And she's the type of person they'd hire to do their dirty work."

"She's a dirty *piece of work*, I'll grant you that." Dollie guzzled some beer. "Call the spook, see what he says."

"There's no way to call from here that wouldn't be monitored." There was a slightly smaller cheer. The Dragons had scored, their players flying in formation to celebrate. I might not lose my bet after all.

"You sure know how to get yourself deep in the shit, Joe." Dollie cheered as one of the Mystics shot and almost scored. "You're too dangerous to be let out on your own."

The thought had occurred to me more than once. I had the QuBee, but Brin had told me not to use it until I'd found Wirkkala. I swallowed the last bite of hot dog and swilled it down with the beer, silently cursing Logan for getting me involved. Friends are good, but sometimes they get you deep in it too.

One of the Dragons got the ball and soared along the 'Tank, deep into the Mystics' territory. Two of them swooped in to block him but at the last moment, he passed the ball back to one of the enforcers in the upper middle. He was big enough to crunch past the lighter player in front of him and held the ball in the air. Seconds later the final Dragons player dived down crosswise, snatching the ball and shooting it like a missile past the goalkeeper into the Mystics' goal. It was a perfectly coordinated attack, and brilliantly executed. Maybe my luck was improving.

I cheered along with the smattering of other Dragons fans as Dollie glared at me. "How about it, *darling*? Want to up the ante?"

"One hundred bucks." Dollie smiled sweetly. "I'm going to enjoy taking your money."

We were both intent on the game which was now tied, with Gabriella mostly forgotten. There were several more plays, some of them close but nothing decisive. Then one of the Dragons made a break and launched up the field. The Mystics closed in, but it was a ruse—the Dragons player had slipped the ball to one of her team members. The goalie had been drawn away also, leaving a clear shot.

I leaned forward. There were only minutes left on the clock. This was surely the winning goal.

The Dragons player launched the ball. Unbelievably it missed, and the ricochet was caught by a stray Mystic. The player launched diagonally, looped around an upright spar to reverse, then used a horizontal bar to reverse again. The Dragons goalie was completely fooled, and the ball shot into the goal as the final horn sounded. Three to two to the Mystics.

I reached into my pocket and pulled my credit-chip out, offering it to Dollie, who had an evil grin on her face.

"Awww...I wouldn't take your money, Joe." She patted my knee. "You can pay me back in our room."

She stood, pulling me to my feet and dragging me towards the exit.

Six

"Joe?"

I woke slowly. It had been an exhausting night. The cheap beer and hot dogs had a strange aphrodisiac effect on Dollie that didn't diminish until the early hours.

"Huh?" was my witty rejoinder.

"Joe...It's me..."

The voice was muffled and appeared to be coming from the small living room area. I slid out of bed, shuffled into the other room, and looked over at the hotel phone. The light was flashing green indicating an incoming call, though how it could have connected without someone picking up I had no idea. The hotel was cheap enough that it could well just be faulty. My mind was still foggy from sleep and I looked around, half expecting to see someone in there, but there was no place to hide in the tiny three-by-five meter area.

I grabbed the phone handset and heard several clicks before the buzz of a call signal sounded, followed by the automatic phone system cutting in to offer me a selection of unhelpful choices.

"Joe?"

This time the voice came from behind me and was recognizably Dollie. After checking the door, I slipped back into bed beside her.

"Everything okay?" she asked, her voice drowsy.

"I think the phones are screwed up." I kissed her. "Go back to sleep."

"Who were you dreaming about?" Dollie roughed her fingers through her thick mop of hair, which was dark red since we'd come to Luna.

"Huh?" I was dressing, getting ready to head out for the preliminary site assessments. Regardless of the SIA, I still had a job to carry out. "Oh...I don't remember, to be honest."

"It better not have been that psycho bitch." There was an edge to her voice.

"You know me better than that."

"Exactly. I know how your sneaky, womanizing brain works." She sniffed.

"Sure you do, because you think the same." I kissed her forehead. "I'll be back in a few hours."

The Department of Critical Infrastructure Protection responsible for civil defense in LFS is a large set of offices set in a central reinforced lunarcrete bunker fifty kilometers away from the main city. Despite that, the Transit Tube got me to my meeting in plenty of time. Uninvited guests aren't exactly welcomed, as evidenced by the fact that there's only one platform at the DCIP station, and I had to show both my ticket and ID before the transit doors would allow me to leave. The platform led directly to the heavily buttressed meter-thick walls that surrounded low-carbon steel blast doors—Loonies take defense seriously.

I was guided to a cramped shoebox of a meeting room, the lunarcrete walls painted an indistinct shade that seemed to hover somewhere between pale blue and cloudy beige. After an initial introductory session, recapping the essential contract requirements, I was taken on a virtual tour of the existing defense systems via remote-piloted drone. The hardware was impressive—they had missile launchers, gigawatt level lasers, and numerous batteries of QuenchGuns in reinforced sites spread around the surface. It looked more than adequate to me, but they were looking to increase the capacity in all areas. Paranoia often sells more than the best engineering.

Marjorie Hayter was the defense coordinator in charge of the project from the LFS side. She was a thick-limbed woman with fiery red hair almost as loud as her booming voice. She hated the

Atolls, and I got the impression engineers weren't far behind in her estimation.

"Your defenses look good. The price tag on these upgrades will be substantial." I tapped the list on my DataPad. "And the changes won't increase your capabilities much."

"Spare me the arguments. I've already had them with the board. They want the upgrades and are willing to pay for them." She looked at me like I was a day-old donut with a bite out of it. "What would the schedule look like?"

I could have given her a pretty good idea of what the schedule was on the spot, but experience has told me people don't accept quick assessments no matter how accurate they are. Also, I wanted to make sure I had an excuse for staying on Luna while I was looking for Wirkkala—otherwise I'd have to eat the expenses.

"I need to do an assessment on the power lines and infrastructure support. Extra missile launchers are no problem, that's mostly physical construction, the lasers and QuenchGuns need power to support them as well as heat-sink capacity to meet the required operation levels. It will take a few days at least. I also need to do a physical inspection of the existing sites—the remote is useful but doesn't tell me enough."

"At least you're thorough. Ballpark?"

She wasn't going to let me off easily—the problem with rough estimates is they get mistaken for firm numbers all too often. "Crew recruitment, at least four weeks, site prep and construction four to nine months depending on further investigations and how big a crew you're willing to pay for."

Hayter sniffed. "The last contractor said ten weeks in all."

"Do they have LoGee experience?" She was playing games, and I wasn't going along with it. "If they do, I'd recommend going with them. But be sure to let me know when they miss their first milestone."

"You don't like me, do you, Ballen?"

I wasn't going to fall into that trap. "I don't know you well enough to dislike you."

"Would you like to?" Her voice had dropped, and she leaned forward in her chair. "Kiefer's Ritz is just down the tunnel."

I held up my hand so she could see my wedding ring.

She grinned. "Call your wife and invite her over. I'm broad-minded."

I slipped out before she could push her proposition. Although Dollie would probably be flattered and her interest piqued by the idea, I was selfish and didn't want to share her. That was what made it hard for me knowing she had her own ideas of what the word *fidelity* meant. Not that I was jealous and possessive in any way. Well, maybe a little...

Brin had given me an address for Wirkkala over in the East-side Loop. He'd been living there two years ago, but I had no information on whether it was his current address. To get there, I had to Tube back to the Transit hub in the main city and then out again, as there wasn't a cross-tube to go more directly.

G7-R133 was in the lower rent area for sure. The corridors weren't the pristine plastic-coated 'crete you usually imagine when you think of the lunar colony. The walls were discolored in places and there were even odd pieces of litter "decorating" the floor, something you almost never see with the recycle-conscious Loonies.

I waved my hand past the door signal several times with no response and wondered if I should try leaving a note or give up and come back later. Then I heard a mumbled voice from inside, followed by a dull thump. A couple of minutes later the door slid open part way and a silver-haired witch poked her head into the gap, screwing up her sunken eyes at the light in the corridor.

Okay, so not an *actual* witch, but a near-perfect facsimile. She was missing the pointy hat and hooked nose but otherwise, spot on.

"Who the hell are you?" Her voice seemed to grind over her tonsils like chains dragging along a metal floor. "Not necking awake yet."

She moved back inside, leaving the door open, and I stepped in behind her. She was scrabbling through debris piled high on the furniture and a small table marked with so many drink stains it looked like the cratered lunar surface. The walls were cloaked in pictures of a young woman dancing in a variety of glittering SkinSuits, and it took me a minute before I realized it was the same woman, but around thirty years younger.

"I'm looking for Wirkkala—he around?"

"Denny?" She lifted a square plastic container full of a foul-looking orange liquid and guzzled it, a grateful smile coming to her trembling lips after she swallowed. "I kicked that bum out years ago. He in trouble?"

"Nope. I'm an old friend. Owe him some money." The alcohol from the drink added a disgusting fetor to her breath, which didn't need the help. "Lost contact a few years ago. This was the last address I had for him."

"You a cop?"

"Engineer. Joe Ballen."

"Don't matter to me none." She gulped from the container again and appeared to wake a little more. "Yeah. Denny was some kind of engineer too. Before he retired. I'm Sinnamon. Sinnamon Bunz, cuz I'm spicy."

She'd been spicy once—the pictures attested to that. But now she was shriveled and prematurely aged from bog-knew what abuses. "You were friends?"

"Nahhh...I was his *mistress*. That's what he used to call me. His sexy little mistress. We met at Bottom's Up." She pointed to the pictures on the wall, then creaked into what was probably meant to be a seductive pose, but only made her look like a diseased corpse. "That was before, of course."

I didn't think she could tell me anything, but there was always a slight chance she might know where Wirkkala was. "Before?"

"Before his wife...you know..." She made a throat-cutting gesture with her finger. "Did herself."

Nothing in the information from Brin said anything about Wirkkala's wife being dead, and I felt sorry for him even though I'd never met him. He'd tried to do the best for his wife, even if he'd been screwing around on her. "Do you have an address for him? I'd like to get this money to him. I hate owing people, you know?"

"Oh yeah, I hate owing people too." She finished off the container and sprawled down on the sofa in the mess of old food wrappers, opening her shriveled legs wide. "I get lonely sometimes, how 'bout you?"

I couldn't help the shudder that ran up the back of my neck. "You sure you don't know where I can find him?"

"I don't remember. He wasn't the same after that bitch died. Couldn't touch me anymore. What kind of *man* is that, huh?" She flicked her stringy hair back. "I'm still as good as I always was, don't you think?"

I wanted to leave in the worst possible way. The smell of the rancid food and stale alcohol had me close to retching. "An address combo? Number?"

"You're kinda cute. Maybe I *could* remember...after a few drinks...my memory ain't what it used to be..." She hesitated. "How much you owe him?"

"Thousand bucks," I lied. "What's his address?"

"That much, huh?" She ran her wrinkled fingers along the inside of her veiny thighs. "I could pass it on to him if you wanna leave it with me."

"I have to do it myself. It's a debt of honor." I turned to leave, needing to escape the putrid atmosphere.

"Come on, soldier. Gimme something. You *gotta* give me something, for gossakes..."

Dollie sometimes calls me "soldier" and I turned back, seeing tears in Sinnamon's eyes. Suddenly, instead of something vile and repulsive, I saw her as an old woman the world had abused and broken. I pulled out a fifty-credit bill and placed it on the table in front of her, along with a contact chip. "If anything comes to you, let me know."

I stepped out and took a deep breath. Even though the corridor wasn't especially clean, it was like walking into a sweet-smelling meadow in comparison to the inside of the apartment. Life has its own way of playing the cards, and it sure doesn't always deal out winning hands.

I retraced my steps and hopped on a Tube back to the hub. It was crowded and got more so as I approached the center. The buzz of people jostling around managed to distract me from thinking about the encounter too much, lifting the dark thoughts flitting around inside my skull. I'd hit a dead end and would have to report back to Brin that I'd failed. I wasn't too unhappy at the prospect and still had the defense project to make the trip potentially worthwhile.

I opened my DataPad and sent out several information requests while I traveled. Using the delegated authority of my contractor status, I requested information on power grid loadings and transmission capacities for the potential defense sites. I already had the hardware specs, so it should be straightforward to work out the necessary modifications. From what I'd already seen, there'd need to be upgrades to load levels and definitely increases in heat-sink capacity to allow functioning to the required performance specifications.

The interior of the Tube was well lit and clean, but I still felt like I needed a shower and would be happy to get in the stall as soon as I got back. I was earlier than I'd estimated, so Dollie would be still out shopping—I hoped she hadn't bankrupted us already.

I reached out to swipe my access card when I heard voices from inside our room. Everything in Luna is packed so tight, complete privacy is almost impossible, even with the best materials. Something about the tone of the voices made me stop and listen, rather than simply walking in.

"...are you sure?" I recognized Dollie's voice clearly. "No mistake?"

The answer was muffled and I couldn't make out the words, then Dollie spoke again.

"No. I can't tell him. It wouldn't be right."

Again the muffled speech.

"I understand. That's a hard decision. How long do I have?"

It was maddening hearing only one side of the conversation, but something in Dollie's voice told me I wasn't supposed to hear *any* of this. I couldn't imagine what she'd want to keep secret from me. Unless...I pushed the thought from my head, or tried to. Dollie was a lot of things, but if she wanted to end things between us she'd say so openly. At least I thought so.

The voices went quiet. I waited a couple of minutes, then swiped my card against the lock and blustered in, making as much noise as I could. Dollie was hunched in a chair by the phone and brushed her hand over the screen to clear it, as if casually wiping dust away.

"You're early." Her voice was a little harsh as if she'd been crying. Something *very* un-Dollie-like.

"It was a bust. That address was no good, some old dancer was living there who used to know Wirkkala. The defense tour was useful, though."

"That's good, Joe." Dollie sniffed. "I'm glad it's not been a wasted trip."

I pulled Dollie up from the chair and slid my arms around her. "Everything okay?"

"Yes, sure. Why wouldn't it be?"

"You seem upset."

"Tired from shopping. I think the LoGee is getting to me a little."

"You can tell me." I cupped her chin in my hand.

"It's fine. *I'm* fine."

Her eyes told me otherwise as they darted away from mine.

Seven

Things were awkward the next morning. At least *I* felt awkward. Dollie was her usual collected self. I thought there was a slight edge in her voice, but it could have been me projecting onto her. Her appetite certainly wasn't affected, and she wolfed down several pastries covered with cinnamon and syrup, along with a large coffee.

"What's the plan today?" she mumbled in between mouthfuls. "More site work?"

"Visiting the Solar Farm. I need to confirm capacity and assess expansion costs." I hesitated, not sure how to continue. "You okay?"

Dollie nodded, swallowing the last of her pastry. "Uh-huh. There's a LoGee health spa I want to try, and then I'm going to hit the stores again."

"Why do women think the mathematical definition of a budget is an imaginary number?"

"It's important for a man to have an incentive. It keeps him from straying too far from home." She smacked my ass as I turned to leave. "Go hunting, mighty warrior. Bring back the spoils of victory in bundles of cash—small, untraceable notes preferred."

I touched my finger to the side of my head. *"Nos morituri te salutamus."*

"Poor baby. It's not that bad."

"You get to relax and have fun, while I chase Mister Green. That's a tragedy if ever there was one."

I made my way to the lobby. A bright, spacious area that contrasted starkly with the cramped reality of the rooms themselves. I don't know what it is with hotels and vegetation, but this one was planted with as much foliage as its Earth-side equivalent would have been—large shrubs and palms scattered in a way seemingly designed to make the path as convoluted as possible. As I passed a mid-sized fluffy cedar, I sensed something behind me. A fraction of a second later something hard and blunt pressed into my side as a graceful arm looped around mine.

"That's a *Malcheck Ten*, Joe. It would be a shame to make a mess on this rather elegant floor."

Gabriella guided me out through the door. To anyone who saw us we'd appear to be a regular couple walking arm in arm. I didn't try to resist. She was crazy enough to start shooting people for kicks and didn't need any provocation.

"Very good." She spoke quietly so no one else would hear. "I believe you're maturing, Joe. It must be the comforts of married life."

"What do you want?"

"The same things all girls want. Wealth, position, absolute obedience, bloodshed. And you between my legs."

The first half of the list rang true, at least. "What do you want from me specifically?"

"You're visiting the wrong people, asking the wrong questions, and generally making a nuisance of yourself, Joe. It has to stop."

"You're looking for Wirkkala as well?"

She guided me around a corner and backed me into a doorway, out of sight of any passers-by. Lifting the gun, she forced the barrel hard under my chin. "My assignment is none of your business, but my employers are getting nervous. They pay me to take away that tension."

"It's obvious you're working for the Atolls. Why try to hide it?"

"You have no idea." She pressed the gun harder against me. "You're not my assignment this time, but that can change. Stick to engineering, Joe. You'll find it far safer."

With that, she turned and walked away, moving down the corridor and into the Tube. I made no attempt to follow her this time—I'm not *that* stupid.

"Joe?"

I snapped round to see Dollie approaching. She was dressed in an almost sheer swimsuit and had an orange sarong wrapped around her hips, which rolled deliciously as she approached. "What's wrong? You left ten minutes ago."

"I stopped to check directions at the desk." I couldn't see any point in worrying her further. Besides, honesty works both ways. "We can take the Tube together."

I linked arms with her, unconsciously mirroring Gabriella's action minutes before and felt guilty for some ridiculous reason. Gabriella had threatened me with a gun; I hadn't been a willing participant.

The train hummed as we moved, and Dollie said something I didn't quite catch. "What was that?"

She pointed past me to the large viewscreen on the wall. It was showing the local news and as I watched, the picture changed to a woman's, her death-agony obvious in the contorted facial expression on her lined face and the blood in her over-whitened blond hair.

"Was that...?"

I nodded. The police report listed her name as *Sinnamon Bunz*, and from the information displayed on the screen, she'd been killed not long after I'd seen her. "That means the cops will be visiting me. I didn't cover my tracks."

"Why would you? You had nothing to do with it." Dollie hesitated briefly. "Gabriella?"

"I saw her as I left the hotel. She threatened me and told me to stop looking for Wirkkala."

Dollie clenched her jaw, squinting slightly. "Why didn't you tell me?"

"I didn't want to worry you." I sighed. "Besides, I couldn't carry on even if I wanted to—Sinnamon was the only lead I had."

"We need to be honest with each other, Joe. It's important."

My fingernails cut into my palms at her hypocrisy and I struggled to keep the harshness out of my voice. "Is there anything *you* want to tell *me*?"

She bit her lip and played with the strap on her purse, not looking at me. "This is my stop."

The capsule slowed and Dollie slipped through the opening

doors before I could say anything else. I knew something was bothering her, but why couldn't she tell me?

Luna City transport is arranged like a spoked wheel, with lines out from the center every thirty degrees and cross-tubes every five kilometers. I changed Tubes at the hub, taking the R60 in the other direction. An elevator took me to the Power Station just below the surface, where Marjorie Hayter was waiting with two of the power crew. They were already suited up and I wasted no time pulling on the loaner P-Suit they had waiting for me.

"I've authorized you for surface ops with Seattle and Koropat here." Hayter pointed to the two suited men. "They'll show you the collectors and substations. I assume you're surface licensed."

"Fully. Want to check my card?"

"Later, perhaps?" Hayter lifted her eyebrows. "If you've changed your mind..."

I appeared to have developed a fatal attraction for women since arriving on the moon. Maybe there was a shortage of local talent, though Seattle and Koropat looked satisfactorily rugged to belie that. For me the problem was that with Dollie the "fatal" aspect was more than likely, and something I'd like to avoid if at all possible, for me or anyone else.

We clambered inside the tightly packed surface crawler and rolled into the mid-sized airlock. A Hopper would have been quicker, but efficient use of my time was obviously not high enough in the project priorities to justify the expense.

The lunar surface looked the way it always does when the sun's up: dry, gray, and incredibly bright. Even with the shading on the forward windows, the glare was considerable. Koropat had his visor down, its enhanced display providing information essential to driving safely as the sharp contrast turned the shadows into black holes.

The wheels kicked up a lazy arc of regolith as we moved, floating behind us as though the crawler was steam powered rather than the mix of fuel-cell and solar technology it was.

"You from Earth-side?" Seattle had a deep voice that croaked like his larynx had been sun-baked from being on the lunar surface for too long.

"Originally." I offered my hand, but he ignored it. "Been working ZeeGee and LoGee so long I almost don't remember it."

There's a sort of snobbery that exists with people who've left the surface of the planet for any length of time. Partly because there are relatively few who do—over ninety-nine percent of humanity has never left Earth—and partly because until you've worked in space for an extended period, you don't appreciate its beauty...or its risks. Seattle was basically assessing whether I was worth talking to or a worthless "ground-grubber" with a piece of paper that said he was a spaceman.

"You the Ballen who saved the starship?"

I wasn't sure where this was leading, so I decided I might as well be honest. "Yeah, I guess that was me."

"Sheeeeit!" Seattle slapped the bulkhead next to him.

"Twenty bucks, dumbass." Koropat spoke for the first time. "Told ya it was him."

With my bona fides apparently established to everyone's satisfaction, the atmosphere in the crawler took on an almost festive mood. The guys were full of questions, both about Ananta but also the more recent skirmish with the Atolls.

"Those *split-pins* need to get their heads outta their asses and realize we all got a right to space." Seattle sucked a mouthful of juice from a flask. "Not just them and their buddies."

"Too right," Koropat agreed.

"Seems to me the LFS and USP and the other Earth States should be working together to put the boost under those stuck-up Toller bastards and striking out on our own."

"Too right."

That seemed to be Koropat's standard response to any comment about the Atolls. I couldn't argue with them, except I thought we should work *with* the Atolls, rather than wasting resources competing or fighting with them. Of course, *they'd* have to agree to work with us—about as likely as Vlad the Impaler's ghost setting up a knitting group.

The collectors were an impressive sight. The solar arrays provided both power and heat. They generated almost three gigawatts of energy and covered over four-square kilometers, making them large enough to see from Earth if you had good eyes. The power was stored in high-capacity Ganus Cells for use during the long lunar night, the hydrogen storage cells located deep underground to minimize danger from impact events. From the point of the proposed defensive systems, this also had the added benefit of protecting them from attack. Though the collectors themselves were highly vulnerable and were one of the areas that needed their defenses upgrading the most.

After finishing the tour, we rolled back to the airlock and re-entered the city. I was more than happy to squirm out of the P-Suit which fit as badly as all "loaners" and chafed my shoulders.

"Wanna make a night of it? We're gonna hit R30." Seattle pulled on a pair of embroidered cowboy boots that must have cost a month's salary on Luna. "There are some hot mamas out there waiting for our company."

"Too right," Koropat agreed.

"Sorry, boys. I'm here with my wife. Another time."

"Sure. Glad to have met you, Joe." We shook hands. "Need anything else, drop by. Check out the nightlife though, before you leave. This place has some real hot spots."

"Too right."

Marjorie Hayter was waiting inside the 'lock and waved me over. "Come with me, Mr. Ballen."

Her earlier game of playing the seductive administrator had vanished, and I wondered why, even though I was happy to not have to deal with it. She led me to an office by the elevator and knocked sharply before opening the door. "Someone wants to talk to you."

I stepped through the door knowing exactly who I'd find inside.

The room was well lit, with an impressively large, polished lunarcrete desk dominating one end. The walls were covered in various plans and a picture of Marjorie Hayter sat on the desk, complete with young child and a person I guessed was her partner. The man sitting behind the desk was not one of the people pictured.

"Officer Tare." His voice was measured and low but contained an unmistakable edge of authority. "Have a seat, Ballen."

He looked young, perhaps mid-twenties, though that didn't seem to fit his rank, and a shock of white regulation-cut hair contrasted harshly with his rich brown skin. Despite the lunar gravity, he was muscled and toned, a clear sign of someone who invested significant amounts of time in centrifugal gym sessions.

I offered my hand, but he sat unmoving, not even acknowledging my gesture with a refusal. I sat in the chair opposite and made myself comfortable. I'd been in this position before. "How can I help?"

"People tend to underestimate me. They see my face, my hair," he gestured briefly towards himself, "and think they know who I am, where I come from, and how inexperienced I must be. They're always wrong."

"I know what you mean. People are always mistaking me for Elvis VIII."

"Don't *you* make that mistake, Ballen." He sounded as if he were lecturing an under-performing student. "I had five years in USP MilSec and seven in the LFS PD before taking up my current position."

"Score one for the good guys."

He completely failed to respond to my attempted humor. "I'm not a stupid Solido cop. I'm not going to threaten you, beat you, or torture you. If you treat me with respect and answer my questions honestly, we'll get along. If you don't, you'll suffer the consequences, and if you're guilty of criminal acts, you *will* pay the price for them."

"Isn't that a threat?"

"No." His voice didn't change in the slightest. "It's a promise."

"Do I need a lawyer?"

"You tell me." He held up a Solido, the thin film projecting a 3D picture of a young, innocent-looking girl. "What is your relationship with Jessica Shappy?"

I almost didn't recognize the picture. Jessica Shappy looked very different from the *Sinnamon* I'd met, even in the pictures of her when she was dancing. "She didn't use that name. There's no relationship—I met her last night for the first time."

"She used several names in her professional work, I understand."

Tare checked his DataPad. "What were the circumstances of your meeting? Were you a *client* of hers?"

"I arrived here a few days ago with my wife, as I'm sure you know. I was looking for an old friend and the address I had was hers. I spoke to her and left."

Tare clenched and unclenched his hands. He stood and leaned over the desk. "Who was this 'friend' you were looking for?"

I hesitated, unsure of what to say. Technically I had no reason to hide the name, but my reason for tracking Wirkkala down was supposed to be a secret. If the LFS government got wind of the papers Wirkkala had stolen, they might want them too, complicating an already messed up situation.

"Don't play games." Tare mistook my hesitation for evasion. "This is a murder investigation."

"Denny Wirkkala. I met him while working on the High-Rig." That was stretching it, but there was no way he could easily disprove it. "An old friend, like I said."

Tare picked up his DataPad and made a note. "You're lying, Ballen. I can tell. It's like a sixth sense I have, and it never fails. Nothing that would hold up in court, but I know nevertheless.

"I could have you deported," he continued. "Even if you haven't done anything criminal. All I have to do is say the word, and you're on the next transport back to Earth. How does that sound?"

I was tired of the interrogation and my pulse hammered inside my ears. "Go ahead. You can also explain to your board of directors why the lunar defenses aren't getting updated."

Tare slid back in his seat and pointed to the door. "You can leave—for now. But I'll be watching you."

Eight

At the hotel, a message was waiting on the phone. It was Dr. Kinsella from the Geneium on Earth. As Dollie's Geneering consultant it was no surprise he was in contact with her—her mixed up genes meant she needed regular monitoring. The message was coded for her alone, per routine doctor-patient privacy, but nevertheless it irked me in light of her recent secretive manner. I wondered if it might have been him trying to call the other night; Earth-Luna communication is sometimes unreliable.

The shower was welcome and swilled away the sweat from being in the pressure suit. When I came out, Dollie was lying on the bed wearing nothing more substantial than a large grin.

"Shopping makes me horny." She batted her eyes at me.

"What doesn't?"

"Look what I've got." Dollie held up a shimmering plastic tab. "Tickets for *Orpheus and Eurydice* at the Moon Globe."

It was the hottest show on Luna, sold out for months ahead. I'm not a huge fan of Oprallé, but I knew Dollie wanted to see it and I hadn't been able to get tickets even through scalpers. How she'd managed it was beyond me. Perhaps it was better if I didn't know.

"As long as I don't have to wear a tie."

Dollie laughed. "No, but you do have to take me to dinner. Later..." She pulled me down on the bed.

Dinner was at the Matsutake. It was good, but I was glad we didn't stay for dessert—I don't think my credit chip could have taken it. Despite that, it was a pleasant distraction and set a good mood for the evening.

The Oprallé was impressive; they used a similar system to the GlydeBall to let the performers dance and perform in three dimensions rather than the holoprojectors and mocap booths used on Earth. That made it feel more "real," though I'm sure the singing took years out of my eardrums.

Dollie loved it, of course. At the intermission, she was positively bubbling. "You never told me how graceful low gravity is. Everything looks so beautiful."

"It's not the same in a P-Suit, with air tanks on your back weighing as much as you do."

"Don't spoil my illusions. Isn't Mimi beautiful?"

Mimi Capstyne was the female lead, and I had to admit she was good-looking, even if I was less than impressed with her warbling. "She's got a nice ass."

"Joe!" Dollie punched my arm hard enough to make me wince, then giggled. "Her ass is rather nice, though."

"Dollie?" I was going to ask her about the message.

"Is it better than mine?" She twisted around, trying to see her own posterior.

That was one of those dangerous questions usually best avoided, but luckily for me, I didn't need to. "Dollie, you're the finest piece of ass I've ever seen."

"Really, Joe? You're not just saying that?"

"Of course. You're perfect the way you are."

I expected her to be pleased, but I guess I haven't figured out the depths of the female mind yet. She looked upset, and her jaw clenched a little.

"What's wrong?" I asked.

Dollie shook her head and took a gulp of her drink. "Nothing."

Again, I knew she wasn't being honest but couldn't understand why. "I guess the search is over. No idea what we do now."

Dollie furrowed her brow. "You said Wirkkala met the dead woman in some bar?"

"Not exactly. It was a strip club, from what I understand."

"Right." Her eyes were bright. "When a guy finds a stomping ground he likes, he rarely changes it."

"You think I might find him there?"

It was a possibility I hadn't considered. What had Sinnamon called it? The Bottom's Up? I ran through the listings on my Scroll. "Over on R150. It's worth a shot. You're a genius."

"Did you ever doubt it?"

"Of course. I'm only interested in your body."

"Like all men."

I stood. "I'll see you back at the hotel."

"Sit down, soldier. There's more Oprallé and the fat lady ain't warbled yet." She finished her Strawberry Luna and crunched an ice cube. "Besides, I'm not letting you go anywhere on your own."

I thought about arguing, but the look on Dollie's face told me it was pointless. I shrugged, hoping the second half would be more interesting.

From outside, the Bottom's Up was simply a bunch of rooms off a corridor like every other place in Luna City, marked only by a discreet sign next to the door. To enter we had to join the "exclusive" club—and pay the extortionate *no-wait* membership fees. This trip was rapidly turning into a financial disaster.

Inside, the room was decorated in early twenty-first century sleaze. Lots of garish neon, mirrors, and what looked like vintage laser lighting. An oval bar dominated the center of the room, while darkened booths circled the walls. Some had drawn curtains, which made me feel unclean, not only because of what might be happening behind them, but because they looked matted from years of greasy hands opening and closing them. Several women gyrated lifelessly on plinths dotted around the room, while similar women mingled with the onlookers lining the perimeter of the bar.

Even the atmosphere had a vintage air—like breathing inside a P-Suit after a heavy day. Every breath was sticky and had a used, fetid taste I didn't want to identify. Dollie took it in her stride, not showing any visible signs of distaste. "I wouldn't bother asking at the bar." Her voice was hard to hear over the blaring rock track. "This looks like the type of place where the staff has a well-practiced sense of forgettery."

"Maybe we could help them remember." The clientele semi-hidden in the shadows didn't exactly fill me with optimism.

"We don't have enough to buy them all, and if you try any gung-ho maneuvers, I'll be taking you home in a coffee jar."

I decided she was right. "Any suggestions?"

"Substitute patience for machismo. We wait."

We slid into one of the booths and soon enough a blond came up, dressed in three microscopic triangles of silvered plastic that left no doubt as to the state of her imagination. She offered us a list of extremely overpriced drinks and I ordered a beer while Dollie ordered a Moonshot Madness—the most flamboyant cocktail they had. A few minutes later it was delivered, complete with signature comet-tail pyrotechnic and screeching sound effects that drew the startled attention of several of the other customers.

"Blending in," was her only comment.

She was taking the blending in part seriously and surprised me by gesturing one of the girls over for a table dance.

I guessed the girl was fairly new at the game. At least she looked a little younger and not quite as weathered as the others. She climbed on the table and gyrated mindlessly. She had a look of empty boredom on her face—that or she was dealing with a long-term Neopenth habit. Neither alternative suggested anything to me other than trouble.

Dollie whistled and cheered loudly as the girl wiggled her ass in front of us, then reached out to slap it playfully.

I felt a little uncomfortable. I'm not prudish, but public displays have always made me awkward. I was even more surprised when Dollie pulled the girl down from the table and onto her lap. The girl nodded at me briefly, then started grinding her ass against Dollie's crotch. Her eyes widened when she felt what must have been an unexpected reaction.

"Let's get a room." Dollie pulled the girl hard against her, leaving no doubt what her intentions were.

The girl glanced at me again. "One or two?"

Before I could answer, Dollie said, "Both."

"Dollie?" This had gotten out of hand rapidly. Honestly, I couldn't see the appeal myself, though if she wanted to get it on with the girl, I'd happily leave them to it.

"Hotel nearby?" Dollie continued, her voice husking.

"Nahh, rooms upstairs."

"Clean?"

"Enough." The girl stood and pulled Dollie by the hand, taking mine too as she passed. "I'm Misty."

Misty led us through a side door and up some dimly lit steps. The corridor at the top of them was lined with identical doors complete with timer locks. She pulled us inside the nearest unoccupied room and leaned over to take her shoes off, very deliberately giving us a long look.

"Two-fifty an hour." Misty unclipped the front of her studded leather-style bra and tossed it on the side table. "For both. Now show me." She gestured at Dollie's crotch.

"We'll give you four hundred." Dollie made no attempt to remove any clothes. "But we want something else."

Misty backed away, grabbing her discarded top and pulling it back on quicker than it came off. "Ain't done nothing. I'm registered clean. Licensed and all."

"We only want some information." Dollie nodded to me. "Show her, Joe."

Dollie was making sense finally. I pulled out the Solido of Wirkkala and held it out. "Know him?"

"No." She didn't even look at the picture.

"Five hundred," Dollie said. "Take a look. We know he comes here."

Misty leaned back against the table. "What d'ya want him for?"

"We're hoping he can help us. It will be worth it to him."

The door chirped as the lock was overridden and two large men stomped into the room. Misty ran out almost before they were inside. I hadn't noticed her trigger anything, but there must have been a silent alarm somewhere.

"We're not looking for trouble," I said, moving between the heavies and Dollie. "We'll leave now. Okay?"

"Well, you found it anyway." The bigger of the two shuffled forward, his thick jaw jutting forward like an off-balance counter-weight. "We don't like cops. Private or otherwise."

He swung at me and I ducked his punch, crouching and pushing with all my strength to pile into both men. A few years ago I wouldn't have managed it. I'd convinced myself I was disabled and weak, but now I had almost full control of my limbs, and my momentum, combined with the low gravity, was enough to send them sprawling.

"Get out." I glanced at Dollie. "Don't wait for me."

The smaller of the two guys was quicker to his feet, and as I turned back, his fist slammed into my jaw. I tried to roll with it to reduce the impact, but it was still enough to make my head spin and I crashed across the bed. He followed me over, a barrage of fists thudding against my torso, and I felt a rib crack.

I half-twisted, putting him off balance, and used the change in momentum to flip him over the bed, then turned back to his friend. The Shock-Wand caught me hard in my ribcage, and I dropped to my knees like we'd boosted unexpectedly at ten-g. The big guy grinned and lifted the Wand, aiming to whip it against my head. I flinched, throwing up my arms to protect myself—a Wand can cause brain damage if applied to the back of the neck.

His arm locked backward, his face changing from a sadistic grin to one of abject pain. Dollie forced him down to the floor, then delivered a double chop to the sides of his skull. He collapsed, groaning in agony. She pulled me up, and we stepped towards the door. Which was now blocked by a rat-faced man, much smaller than the other two, but far more deadly as he held an ancient-looking short-barreled shotgun.

"Enough!" he commanded. "Doug? Ben? You okay?"

There were muffled groans behind us, but neither of the men seemed eager to move.

"You two are gonna leave by the back exit. Don't want none of the regulars spooked. Either of yas gives me the slightest trouble, I'll let old Betsy take care of ya." He twitched the barrel of the gun to emphasize his point.

"Okay. Take it easy..." I held my hands up.

Dollie's hand shot out and the Wand slapped across the man's arm. He yelped and dropped the shotgun. It tumbled down but luckily didn't go off when it hit the floor. She held the Wand in a ready position as we left the room and scampered down the steps. The door to the main bar was closed and another one led the opposite way. Presumably, it was the back exit our rat-faced friend had mentioned.

We hurried through it and into the corridor beyond. Moving forward, I checked behind us every few seconds. At the Tube station, Dollie threw the Wand in one of the trash cans, and we relaxed only once we were headed back to the hotel.

Dollie checked my ribs as soon as we were safely locked away. She couldn't detect a crack and thought perhaps I'd only bruised them. I was going to disagree and suggest heading to the nearest MedCenter to get them checked when she pushed me back on the bed and clambered on top of me.

"God, I'm horny."

We woke with the phone screeching at us like it was the End of Days, and for a second I thought it was a depressurization warning. Before I could answer there were several loud thumps on the door.

"LFS PD," a voice shouted. "Open up in there."

"One minute, dammit."

I waited until Dollie had thrown on a gown, then triggered the door lock. I thought I recognized the voice and proved myself right when Tare pushed his way in. "Joseph Ballen. By authority of the Luna Free State Board of Governors, I arrest you for murder and terrorism. You do not have to say anything, but anything you do say, will be used against you.

"You have a right to legal representation, but such representation is not provided. Representation can be made available at your request and cost. Do you understand these rights?" He held out the flexible mesh strap of a MagCuff.

"You won't need those." I turned to Dollie. "Don't worry. Whatever this is, it will soon be cleared up."

Tare wrapped the MagCuff around my wrists anyway and triggered the magnetic lock so it wrapped tightly around my arms. Thirty minutes later I was secured to a bolted down table in an interview room facing him across a small desk. His features looked even darker than when I'd seen him the day before, and his tight-cropped hair looked like a pure white helmet.

"Where were you last night at three AM?"

"In my hotel room. And before you ask, the only witness was my wife."

Tare nodded. "Did you visit the Bottom's Up club?"

"I was there a little earlier. I didn't find it very friendly and left."

"And your wife was with you?"

"Yes."

He pulled a seat over and perched opposite me. "Do you often take your wife to sex clubs?"

"Whenever she wants me to." I leaned closer and winked. "Want to join us next time?"

"This is serious, Ballen."

"I guessed that when you arrested me." I lifted my cuffed wrists. "And these are a bit of a giveaway."

"You know something? I usually don't have much to do here on Luna." Tare sipped from a cup of coffee. "Most of our crime is small stuff. People partying too hard, occasional assaults, and similar incidents. Nothing too taxing from a policing perspective and I like it that way."

"I'm happy for you."

"But it doesn't mean I'm inexperienced or untrained. I can handle big cases as well as the smaller ones. Criminals are like cockroaches, they're all pretty much the same size, and they all squish the same way when you step on them."

"Oooh, I'm going to have a coronary from fear. What happened?"

He ignored my question. "Do you know the penalty for murder in Luna Free State?"

"I know this one." Sometimes my mouth has an unfortunate mind of its own. "A hot date with your sister and flowers in the morning?"

He grinned. The first expression I'd seen on his face. "Airlocking. Why should the taxpayer be burdened with the cost of housing a criminal? We throw you into an airlock and let the pressure out. You die. Slowly, agonizingly, as your lungs hemorrhage and the last thing you see is your own eyes bleeding. It's quite an event. Haven't had to do one in several years. It's an effective deterrent."

That was hardly surprising. "What am I supposed to have done?"

He held up a Solido that flipped through pictures of several blackened corpses—I think Dante saw something similar in the lower levels of hell. "At three this morning the Bottom's Up had a fire, the suppression systems failed mysteriously, and several people were killed including the manager, several of his staff, and some of the girls. Several witnesses said there was an altercation between the manager and a customer. You were identified."

"They're mistaken."

"We have your DNA on-scene. We have witnesses." Tare threw down the Solido and tapped his DataPad. "I don't need a confession."

"So throw me out the nearest 'lock."

He tapped a finger against his DataPad. "I've been checking on you. You were a suspect in several killings a few years ago back on Earth."

I took a deep breath. Sometimes my past was like an annoying old friend who'd outstayed their welcome but didn't want to leave. "I think you'll find the charges were dropped."

"I saw that." His taupe eyes narrowed. "Charges get dropped for a lot of reasons. It doesn't mean the person is innocent.

"You're a dangerous man to associate with, Mr. Ballen. People die around you for all sorts of reasons. Yet somehow, it's never your fault. You're a jinx. A *Jonah.*" Tare leaned back. "The question is—does death follow you, or are you the cause?"

"You should hang around for a while and see what happens."

His face darkened and for a second I thought he was going to lose it and punch me, but he blinked hard and contained the reaction, breathing slowly in and out.

The door opened and a mousy-looking man came in. He moved alongside Tare and whispered something. Tare nodded, then turned back to me. "Your wife is here." He shook his head. "And she's brought your lawyer."

I didn't have a lawyer, especially one operating in LFS jurisdiction. Even if I felt I needed one, I couldn't afford it. I hid my surprise, though, and lifted my shackled arm. "About time."

Tare made a few more notes. "Bail is posted, you're free to leave." He reached over and removed the cuffs. "Nothing is more suspicious than someone who can lawyer-up quickly."

"I'll remember that."

"By the way, Ballen. Your *friend*, Wirkkala? Records show he left LFS over six months ago."

He watched me closely. This time I couldn't control my reaction and gave away my disappointment. "Thanks for the update."

Dollie was in the waiting area with a short Asian man who looked like he was a few centuries older than God. Despite his generally wizened appearance, the lines on his face told me his smile must be an almost permanent fixture.

"Mr. Ballen?" He bowed. He had a hint of a British accent—very refined, but warm and clear. "A pleasure to meet you. I'm afraid your bail is very high. Not much I can do about that, with you not being a resident. I don't anticipate any difficulties over the charges, though, since the evidence is entirely circumstantial."

"Mr. Kiyomizu is highly recommended." Dollie kissed me passionately. "Everything is fixed."

I didn't ask who'd recommended him or how Dollie could afford him. That she'd gotten him on the spot so quickly was slightly less of a surprise; Dollie is as unstoppable as a tsunami when she sets her mind to something.

"Thank you for your help. I appreciate it." I held out my hand, but he bowed again.

"Please forgive me, I don't like to touch people." He smiled again. "It was no trouble at all. We Geneered have to stick together, after all."

That explained how Dollie had gotten him on the case but didn't explain how we were going to pay for his services.

"Dollie has told me much about you. You're very brave and obviously have exquisitely refined taste."

He turned to Dollie and bowed. For the first time since I'd known her, she blushed heavily, and her cheeks dimpled like a young girl.

"You're too kind, Kiyomizu-san. Thank you for your assistance.

It will not be forgotten." She bowed back.

"If you'll excuse me. I have a full day ahead of me and you two would no doubt like some time together." The lines around his eyes deepened. "If you are not too busy later, perhaps we could meet for dinner? I'd enjoy getting to know you both better. Around eight? I'll call you."

We agreed and Kiyomizu shuffled off, leaving us at the precinct doors. I wondered briefly about the basis of his Geneering. As with Dollie it wasn't obvious, and stood as a reminder that you can't tell the Geneered from "ordinary" people. We're all one race, despite the bigots who still try to claim otherwise.

"How much is he costing?" I asked, not really wanting to know the answer.

Dollie slipped into my arms and kissed me. "I was worried."

"You're avoiding." I almost tacked the word "again" onto the end but thought better of it.

"Kiyomizu-san graciously donates his time to help out his Geneium sib." She looked in my eyes. "Don't get paranoid on me, Joe. It's not uncommon with Geneered. You know that."

I sighed. "I don't like owing people. Not even favors."

"You don't. I do."

We could have argued back and forth for several hours, but it wasn't the place or time. "Let's get some lunch. What they served in there doesn't merit the word *food*."

We found a quiet-looking cafe a few transit stops inward, and I happily sank into one of the comfortable chairs in the patio area outside. The meal was deceptively simple but hearty, and I have to admit that for the next thirty minutes or so I did nothing but concentrate on feeding my stomach and watching people go by. After the confines of the jail, even the relatively limited freedom found in the streets of Luna City was a literal breath of fresh air.

"The news carried the story about the club." Dollie finally interrupted my gorging. "What the hell's going on?"

"It must be Gabriella." I spoke quietly, in case anyone was listening. I wouldn't be surprised if Tare had put us under covert surveillance. "My guess is she's looking for Wirkkala too and getting rough with her questions. It would suit her sadistic way of operating."

Dollie chewed her lip slightly. "But what does it get her? All she's doing is leaving a trail of corpses."

I thought about it for a while. Dollie was right, it didn't make a lot of sense, but I couldn't come up with a better explanation. For all her predilection for manufacturing dead bodies, Gabriella was also eminently practical. I didn't think she'd kill someone for the hell of it—at least not before they'd given her any information she wanted. "If she doesn't know where Wirkkala is, she could be torturing them for answers then covering her tracks."

"Or perhaps it's someone else."

That didn't make sense either. If Gabriella was in LFS she was undoubtedly there for something big, and I couldn't see what else would bring her. "Tare said Wirkkala left six months ago."

"Did he say where?"

"Nope. But I can only think of one place he could go without the SIA knowing."

"The Atolls?" Dollie looked confused and I understood why.

"Exactly," I said. "If he's with the Atolls, who the hell is Gabriella working for? The Corporates?"

The question hung around us like a PlaSteel-reinforced wall—I had no answer either.

Nine

"I'm touring the heat-sinks today." I finished my coffee and pressed my credit-chip against the receipt to pay the bill. "I better get on with it or I'll never land this contract."

"You think you've still got a chance?"

Dollie had a point. With all the interest from the police, it was likely that Hayter would scratch my name from the list. The only thing going against that was the fact I knew I could do a good job for them, and I don't give up a fight easily. "I have to assume I'm still in the running, otherwise I lose by default. Besides, we still need money."

"And you're good at your job." She smiled. "Same old stubborn professional pride. Even when it's hopeless."

"Nothing's hopeless until you give up." I detected an undercurrent of concern in Dollie's voice. "Something wrong?"

"No. But I'm not letting you out of my sight after what's happened."

I was going to object, but Dollie's expression told me it was pointless. I wasn't the only stubborn one in this relationship.

"Don't blame me if you get bored."

"Will there be some hunky lunar miners around?"

The heat-sinks were deep in the lunar rock, so it was entirely possible. "Could be."

"Then I'm sure I'll keep myself entertained."

The heat-sinks were an integral part of the LFS defenses and a key part of what would make the colony so hard to defeat. Almost all weapons generate heat, and that's a big problem. On Earth, the heat is carried away by the atmosphere, but in space or on the moon it builds up. Although you can build radiators to take the heat away, they're inefficient and highly vulnerable in a conflict. It's this heat buildup that typically limits military encounters in space more than anything else.

The situation on the moon is somewhat different. Although there's no atmosphere to speak of, they can effectively use the moon as a giant heat-sink if necessary, and that was a big part of their current strategy. The only problem is that rock isn't very good at conducting heat away rapidly. So to provide better on-demand heat management, they create vast frozen reservoirs inside the lunar crust that can be melted quickly if needed. This allows them to keep the lasers and railguns within operating parameters for extended periods before having to switch to the rock "backup." No warship—Earth or Atoll—could compete against that cooling capacity.

The tunnels around the heat-sinks were cold, despite the insulating meters between the ice flows and the passages. Several of the miners were leering at Dollie and the visible effect the temperature was having on her.

"You should have brought a jacket." My breath condensed as I spoke, coating my face with an unpleasant dampness.

"I agree." She shivered visibly. "So should you."

"I don't think these guys are interested in my nipples."

"But I am."

The lechery ended when one of the older workers produced a spare parka for Dollie. I was left to endure the chill but kept my grumblings to myself.

There was ample capacity in the 'sinks for their current needs, but if they wanted to maintain the operational lifespan they'd need to increase the capacity by around twenty percent. That meant cutting deeper, but Loonie engineers were more than used to working rock, so I didn't worry too much about it.

I was happy to leave the caves behind after finishing the tour. Looking at how Dollie's skin had whitened with the cold, I knew she was too. We made our way back to the main hubs and grabbed a quick coffee.

"That's damn cold down there." Dollie grasped her cup as if its heat was the source of all life. "Please tell me we don't have to go back."

"I'm done. I only need to do the actual analysis now. And I can finish that at the hotel."

"In that case, you can *work from home* in a Solarium, so I can defrost my frozen ass."

In other circumstances, I might have accused Dollie of wanting to check out the scantily clothed youngsters, but right then it sounded like the perfect antidote to the frozen chill of the heat-sink tunnels. Stopping only to pick up a set of shorts for me and an outrageously flamboyant electric-purple outfit for Dollie, we joined the throng and made our way to the sunbathing areas.

Lunar Solaria are essentially small craters capped by a synthetic ceramic and aluminum oxynitride composite "glass" roof surrounded by reflectors that channel as much sunlight as possible into the room inside. Most of the harmful UV is filtered out, but the light levels are brighter than the midday desert sun, and UV goggles are issued at the entrances. They're worn by everyone along with twenty-four-hour responsive tattoos indicating how long you've been exposed. Once your patch goes black, you're done—you have to leave for the remainder of the day for your own health. Though looking at some of the extremely tanned bodies, I guessed some people managed to circumvent the system.

In the middle of this man-made Eden was a large pool, complete with wave generators, creating an oasis of light and warmth that is possibly the best and safest "waterfront" vacation anywhere, although the slow-motion waves looked slightly odd.

I worked on the figures for about forty minutes, but it was a losing battle. The constant ebb and flow of nubiles would have been enough to make Rehab blush, and the spectacle wasn't lost on Dollie either. She rolled over, the artificially-weathered regolith "sand" sticking to her blemish-free skin like a coating of confectioner's sugar, and pressed herself against me in a way that did nothing to help my concentration.

I was about to suggest we make our way back to the hotel or some other convenient area of privacy when a woman spread her towel close to our heads, much closer than necessary and definitely encroaching on our personal space. Before I could say anything to Dollie the woman spoke, her voice low and hard to hear over the constant party-like screams and giggles surrounding us.

"You still looking for that guy?" Her head jerked and twisted as she looked around. "Wirkkala?"

Her voice trembled, though not in a nervous sense. More as though she was barely holding herself together. I looked closer and after a few moments recognized her as the dancer we'd met at the Bottom's Up.

"Hello, Misty. I'm glad to see you're okay." Dollie beat me to it. "You were reported dead along with the others."

"I wanna leave." She looked out of place, her skin a sickly, almost pure white, except for a number of prominent bruises on her thin arms and legs. "Leave here, I mean. Luna ain't for decent people. Over fifty percent of people who come here go back Earthside again—know that? That's...more than half...I wanna get out too."

"Well, we sure aren't stopping you." I wasn't feeling especially sympathetic. After all, she'd set the thugs on us. Even if what happened later was horrifying, there'd been no call for violence.

"Ain't got the chips." She shivered despite the heat. "Peddlers took my return bond. To cover *licenses*, he said. Seventy-three percent of jobs needs licenses, d'ya know that?"

Every person coming to Luna had to post a bond to cover the cost of return to Earth. If you can't work, or the authorities take a dislike to you, the bond is used to pay your way back. LFS doesn't accept the burden for anyone, even residents, and it's considered more humane than airlocking. "Why come to us? You didn't want to know us last night."

"That was before. You know. Shit happened."

Misty was shaking visibly, and it didn't take much to guess it was withdrawal. I was about to respond when Dollie shook her head. I was losing patience and she knew it.

"How can we help?" she said, looking at Misty.

"Too dangerous here." Misty picked at the skin around her nails. "Your hotel."

"Okay, let's go." I stood.

Misty scrambled to her feet, sending a spray of sand flying everywhere. "What? No, wait. I need to take care of something first."

"We'll meet you there, then." I gave her the address and room number.

"You don't understand." Misty looked away again, scanning the crowd.

I understood all too well, but I wasn't about to pay her any extortion money. It would end up jacked into her arm, and I don't pay for other people's drugs, not even friends. She was far from being that.

"How much do you need?" Dollie scowled at me.

"Fifty. Just enough so I can talk straight, okay?" Misty shuffled from one foot to the other. "I'm scared. Need a bit of juice so I can get by. Over forty percent of people need something to help with their confidence. Did ya know that?"

Dollie transferred the money on to Misty's credit chip, ignoring my frown. As soon as it was done, Misty scampered off. Leaving us in the blazing heat.

We made our way back to the room and waited. Almost an hour passed before I broke the silence. "You know that money went straight in her arm?"

"I'm not stupid. But I thought you wanted information?"

"She hasn't got any. Her regular suppliers got fried last night, so she needs some quick money before she starts flopping around in the gutter like a beached dolphin."

"You're so sympathetic, Joe."

"Yes, I am. But I'm not stupid and gull—"

I stopped when I caught Dollie's expression. I was about to say something less confrontational when a soft knock sounded at the door. Dollie looked at me pointedly and opened it.

Misty scuttled in without waiting. Looking behind her as if the ghost of the dead was chasing her.

"There's an Earth shuttle at eight," she said looking from Dollie to me and back.

I ignored her, but Dollie got her credit chip out again. "How much?"

"I gotta get away. A long way. Anyone knows I talked...Well, you saw what happened to the others..."

"How much?" I growled.

"A thousand?"

Misty's voice lifted into a squeak as if embarrassed at what she was asking. Well deserved, but I doubted she was that put out.

"After we get the answers." At least Dollie wasn't stupid enough to give it to her up front.

"Sure. I guess. You want that Wirkkala, right?"

Misty paced up and down our tiny room until Dollie guided her into a chair. "Take it easy. Tell us what you know."

Misty scratched her arm and I could see the rash from a pharmaspray. "He was a regular. Used to see another girl, Sinnamon. Yeah, he was one of her regulars. Ya know over sixty percent of guys like to have a regular girl? Makes 'em feel like they have family."

"Sinnamon's dead." We weren't paying a thousand bucks for an already useless lead.

"She is?" Misty scratched again. "Well, see. She went freelance, but he kept coming in. Denny Wirkkala, I mean."

"He was one of your regulars?" Dollie asked softly.

"Nah. He used whoever he felt like. Sometimes me, sometimes others." Misty pulled a SootheStick from her purse and lit it, filling the tiny room with pungent smoke until I cranked up the ventilation. "So one time, it was late, so he takes me back to his place so we could...ya know...he weren't with Sinna no more."

"Address?"

"Don't hate me." Her eyes were like gray-blue marbles as the Neopenth reached its full effect, and I wasn't sure she could see us anymore. "I had to...work. Ya know?"

"Nobody hates you, Misty. But we need to find Wirkkala."

"I gotta leave after. They'll come for me. They killed 'em all last night. Everyone who saw anything."

"Did you see who did it?" Maybe she could ID Gabriella.

"Naw, I was, ya know...doin' a guy...heard the shots and ran..."

"So where is Wirkkala's place?" Dollie held Misty's hand. "It's important to us. Then you'll be able to head back to Earth. Escape."

"He was out on E3-R230. Apartment seventeen or nineteen. I think."

I tagged it into my 'Pad. "When did you last see him?"

"Few months back. Ain't been round in a while."

I used my Scroll to check the directory. Someone named "Jones" was registered in seventeen and someone called "Foster" was in nineteen. "That doesn't check out."

"I swear it. That's where the guy was. I remember it because it was so clean. Not like...not like the usual. And he was kind, too, gave me a meal and all first. It was like we was on a date, ya know?"

"A real charmer, no doubt." It was obvious everything she'd said was an absolute lie. She was looking for some easy money to feed her habit, pure and simple. Dollie pressed her credit chip against Misty's.

"Dollie?" I couldn't believe she was going to hand over the money and reached out to stop her.

Dollie shook her head slightly, and her eyes narrowed. I managed to keep my mouth shut. I hate people who argue publicly about private matters and wasn't going to do it now.

Misty checked her chip and her eyes widened. "That's too...wonderful...thank you...thank you..." She pulled out a grubby handkerchief and dabbed her eyes, playing the role for everything she was worth. "Dunno what to say...Can we talk? Alone?"

Misty was looking directly at Dollie. It didn't seem like a good idea to leave them, but Dollie ushered me out with a flick of her eyes.

"I'll be in the bar," I said as I left.

Dollie nodded and I marched off, feeling rather stupid as I sat on a stool alone. I ordered a large Moonrocket Vodka and took a swallow, enjoying the burn as it sterilized my larynx on the way down and the warmth that spread once it hit my stomach. I couldn't figure out why Dollie was playing along like this. She was anything but gullible. I wondered if it had anything to do with the secrets she was keeping from me but pushed the thought away. Without knowing what she was hiding, I had zero chance of figuring it out.

While I sat there I accessed the transit records using my Scroll. They had a full archive of arrivals and departures that weren't supposed to be publicly available, but I'd learned a few tricks in my time and bypassed the security. You could say it was a tribute to my technical prowess, but the truth was the safeguards were lax...and I got lucky.

A quick search showed no record of Wirkkala leaving within the last two years. His arrival was documented, but after that there was nothing. That didn't mean he hadn't left, just that he or someone else had kept it out of the records or removed it after the fact.

I was nursing my second Moonrocket and wondered whether to finish it and have a third. Dollie could hardly blame me, but solitary drinking reminded me of the "bad old days" and was something I tried to avoid now.

I heard Dollie's voice and glanced around; she was coming out of the guest room area with Misty in tow. They were walking arm in arm, and Misty looked slightly less doped up than earlier. Perhaps there was hope for her after all and she'd only taken a small dose. They walked up to me and Dollie squeezed Misty's arm as they unlinked.

"Make sure you're on that shuttle." Dollie waved a finger at Misty. "Now scoot. I think my man wants to talk to me."

Misty left, nodding and spouting a flood of thanks. I swallowed the remnants of my drink and walked back to the room with Dollie, waiting a whole thirty count after we went inside. "How much?" I finally asked.

Dollie lifted her chin. "Two thousand." There was no hint of regret in her voice.

I sighed, then reached out to her. Dollie flinched as my hand approached her face. I stroked her cheek softly, and she melted into my arms.

"You know she'll go on a huge bender, don't you?"

"She needs a chance. That's all."

I kissed her. "I hope you're right. But people don't often change. What did she tell you?"

"Just how scared she was, and how much she wanted to get clean of the drugs."

It was too late to do anything about Wirkkala right then, and

I suddenly felt exhausted. Dollie agreed to an early night and we were tucked into our sleeping cubby inside thirty minutes.

I expected to fall asleep like a light being switched off but instead, my head kept spinning with the events that had happened since we came to Luna. Crazy thoughts loomed up at me from the dark until my head was whirling like an ungoverned processing unit.

"Joe?"

A quiet voice in the darkness roused me. "Huh?"

"You awake, Joe?"

It was Dollie, and I grunted a yes, realizing I must have fallen asleep at some point. "What's wrong?"

"I was just thinking..."

I waited for her to continue, but she didn't. "Thinking what?"

"What you said earlier about people not changing. Do you believe that?"

People change their minds all the time. But I think everyone has a core self that stays with them. Like a default setting. Whatever that setting is they stick with it, even when they don't seem to be. I couldn't hold back a yawn. "You still worried about Misty?"

"Not exactly. It's that I need ..." She trailed off.

"Need what?" I pulled her close. "Look, we can check if she got on the shuttle in the morning. Okay?"

"That's not...Yeah, sure. Okay."

I held her in my arms and realized she was shaking, small trembles that ran through her whole body.

Ten

The next morning we ate in the hotel breakfast room for a change. Dollie appeared to be her old self again; the dinner with Kiyomizu had been delightful and her appetite had returned with a vengeance. I watched as she loaded one plate full of scrambled tofu and toast and another with pancakes and syrup.

I told her what I'd found out about Wirkkala through the transit records. Or rather not found. She nodded in between mouthfuls, not slowing down. Then her fork stopped inches from her half-open mouth as she stared past me. I turned to catch the tail end of a report—our girl, Misty, was dead. The fork full of food clattered noisily to her plate. Dollie's face was the color of ice. "I'm going to kill Gabriella."

I could sympathize over what had happened to Misty and certainly understood her hatred of Gabriella, but there was a venom in her tone far more intense and personal than I would have imagined. I reached out to take her hand. "Don't let it get to you. Misty's luck simply ran out."

"She wasn't *only* someone down on her luck. She was trying." Dollie swallowed hard, her eyes glistening. "She was Geneered, Joe. I gave her the money so she could see Doctor Kinsella. He'd have helped her get off the drugs."

Now I understood. Again, I wouldn't have picked out Misty as Geneered but Dollie had known. None of that would matter to Gabriella, of course. She'd kill anyone—as long as someone was paying.

"Tare will be after me again, for sure." I put down my coffee.

91

"No doubt we were the last to see her, like the others, and I doubt he's going to let me go so easy this time."

"You were with me."

"From Tare's perspective, I look like a serial killer." I'd been here before and knew innocence didn't mean a thing compared to appearances. "Your involvement makes it look as if we're a team."

Dollie stood abruptly. "We need to finish this before someone else gets hurt."

I couldn't argue with her. We went back to our room to get our gear, then hopped on the Transit Tubes to E3-R230.

The corridors we emerged into when we got off the Tube were much cleaner than some of the other places we'd visited recently. It wasn't anything too obvious—Luna City is well maintained even in the more squalid areas, and hasn't been around long enough to develop that weathered look the Old Europeans are so fond of. Strangely, I found myself almost missing the graffiti and trash; details can tell you a lot more about an area than pristine swept floors and freshly washed walls. Even the lights looked brighter, though logic said they couldn't be.

"How do we play this?" Dollie asked when we found the apartments.

Both "Jones" and "Foster" could easily be pseudonyms. The Solido Brin had given me was old but good enough. I felt reasonably confident I'd recognize Wirkkala, but we could hardly swipe the Announcer patch next to the door and ask if the occupants were ex-engineers hiding out with stolen technical papers.

I shrugged. "We could watch. See who comes and goes."

"I don't see any great vantage points, do you?"

Dollie was right. The corridor was straight as a laser beam and offered no easy hiding places. "I don't suppose you have any secret surveillance gear with you?" I asked.

"No, we'll have to improvise."

She reached into her bag, pulling out her Temporary Resident card. Then she grabbed my Scroll and tapped the Announcer for the first apartment, holding her ID in front of the optical pickup.

The connection light went green and the door's comm-screen lit up.

The woman on the screen was late middle-aged and looked like everyone's least favorite aunt. Despite our undoubtedly unexpected intrusion, a smile came to her pale lips. "Can I help?"

"Mrs. Jones?" Dollie looked at the Scroll as if she was reading something from it. "We're carrying out a survey for the Housing Subcommittee, can we ask you a few questions?"

The door buzzed open and Mrs. Jones let us in. The room was similar to our hotel room but the pale mustard-colored walls, along with every flat surface available, were lined with Solidos and older TwoDees of a guy with a fat, happy face. Some of them were framed in wood, some in plastic, and several of the largest in chrome metal frames. The floor was the usual soft ceramic tiling but covered by a large fluffy teal rug that must have cost a fair amount to import.

Mrs. Jones guided us to sit on a low sofa overcrowded with red cushions like giant berries.

"Would you like some tea? Mint, chamomile, and orange, very refreshing. It's good for the nerves."

Dollie thanked her and asked a series of questions about the neighborhood. Was the lighting adequate? Did Mrs. Jones feel safe? Were the services satisfactory? I stayed quiet. Fascinated how she managed to sound so convincing when I knew she was fabricating it on the spot.

Mrs. Jones considered her replies carefully before answering. She was very conscious of her civic responsibility and told us as much. In fact, it was kind of hard to shut her up once she got started.

Dollie pointed at the images around us. "Is that Mr. Jones? Would he have anything to add?"

"I'm sure he would, dear. If he were still around."

My ears pricked up.

"Where is he?" Dollie's question was casual.

"He passed years ago, my dear." Mrs. Jones picked up the closest picture and held it to her chest. "I miss him terribly."

Dollie smiled. "He was a very handsome man."

"Oh, he always thought he was." Mrs. Jones laughed. "And he'd have enjoyed hearing you say so. I was always worried someone would come along and steal him away, though he told me he loved me right up until the end."

Once we could safely make our excuses, we stepped back out into the corridor and moved down a little. I felt like giving Dollie a big hug but decided it wasn't the right time. Not to mention how it might look to Mrs. Jones if she happened to look out of her window.

"You're incredible," I said.

Dollie smiled demurely. "Nothing to it. Give a person a chance to bitch and they usually will."

"What if she checked your ID with the Housing Subcommittee?"

"I don't even know if there is such a thing." She grinned at my expression. "Come on, let's check the other one."

We did the same routine. Dollie activated the Announcer and we waited. This time the screen didn't light up, but the door opened and I recognized the broad face of Denny Wirkkala.

"Yes?" His pale blue eyes blinked rapidly from the outside light. Behind him, the room was dark, and his unshaved jaw made him look like a bear shambling out of hibernation on the first day of spring.

"Mr. Wirkkala." I moved to put my hand on the door, ready to block it if necessary. "I'd like to talk to you."

"My name's Foster. You've made a—"

Dollie lashed out before I could stop her, slapping Wirkkala's face with a crack. "Try telling that to Misty and Sinnamon."

"What? Who?" There was a clunk as he dropped a gun he had concealed behind his back and staggered inside, fear widening his eyes as Dollie pushed forward. His cheek was reddening and already swelling. Dollie packs a hell of a punch when she wants to.

"Perhaps you better let us inside." I scooped up the pistol and tucked it safely away in my back pocket. Then grasped Dollie's wrist and held it as Wirkkala backed away from the door.

The light level dropped as the door closed behind us, leaving us in shadows tinged with a faint orange glow from the supplementary safety lights around the top of the walls. Food cartons and bottles littered the floor and furniture, while the odor of stale alcohol filled the air.

"Those poor women." Wirkkala dropped heavily into a seat. "I didn't...I never wanted this..."

"You know what happened?" Dollie twisted out of my hold and glared down at him.

"Of course..." He gestured towards the 3V set on the wall. The news has been full of it."

"I presume you know why we're here." I moved forward, ready to grab Dollie if she lashed out again. We needed his cooperation, not to beat him to a pulp.

"Yes...actually, no...she said..." He hesitated, looking the other way.

"Who said what?" Dollie grabbed his collar, pulling his head around to face her. "That bitch, Gabriella?"

"You'll do me the immense favor of not talking about me like that." The kitchen door opened, and Gabriella swaggered in, gun in hand. "You could very easily hurt a girl's feelings."

She looked as ravishing as ever and pouted in a way that was perfect. Perfectly seductive, perfectly delicious, and perfectly deadly.

"You already cut a deal with him?" I gestured towards the trembling Wirkkala. "If that's the case, why kill the others? You had what you wanted."

Wirkkala jumped in the seat and looked at Gabriella with horror. "You...you killed those women?"

"What I did or didn't do is my business. I made a deal, that's all. And you're going to go through with it. Whether you want to or not." She looked at me. "I told you not to get involved, Joe. You should have taken my advice because now I might *have* to kill you and your charming wife."

"You better make sure you do it right the first time." Dollie spat the words. "If you don't, I'll break your goddamn neck."

"You tried once before and I'm still here." Gabriella gave a small curtsy, then her face hardened. "I wouldn't suggest trying again. Now move. In the other room."

She waved her gun at us, herding all three of us back. The gun was made of a gnarled and twisted material wrapped around the central barrel. I'd never seen one but knew what it was from reading descriptions. A Bonegun, formed by growing and manipulating genetic material from a person. A weapon that matched the carrier's DNA so it couldn't be picked up by any of the current security detectors.

The small kitchen area was better lit than the front room but littered with the same debris. To one side was a small kitchen table piled high with soiled junk food cartons, and on either side were two cheap plastic chairs that had once been white but were now more of an insipid khaki color.

"Sit down," Gabriella said, then handed Wirkkala a small bag of black cable ties. "Tie them to the chairs. Her first."

Wirkkala hurried over to Dollie, tightening the ties around her wrists and ankles, binding her to the chair awkwardly as directed. Gabriella kept her gun on us the whole time, not giving even the slightest chance to try and rush her.

"How did it work this time, Gabriella?" I watched as Wirkkala finished tying up Dollie. "Did you seduce him too?"

"Please, Joe." She pursed her lips as if tasting something unpleasant. "There are limits, even for me. Mr. Wirkkala agreed to help for an immodest fee, as authorized by my employers."

"Did they authorize killing anyone who could lead someone to him too?"

The ties bit into my wrists as Wirkkala tightened them, then he stepped away. I tried the old trick of tensing my muscles as hard as possible, hoping to gain some slack, though I wasn't sure what I'd be able to do with it even if I managed.

Gabriella moved closer, brushing my face with the barrel of the Bonegun. "We're not enemies anymore, Joe. You should be nice to me now, we're on the same side." She straddled me, squeezing her powerful thighs around my legs and pressing her warm lips to mine. "I still think we could be good...friends."

I twisted my head away. "You're damaged goods. We'll never be on the same side."

"That hurts so much, Joe. But I guess you have to put up a front with the little lady being here." She trailed the gun muzzle down to my crotch. "We both know the truth, though."

I was going to tell her in more detail what I thought about her when the darkness in the front room brightened momentarily. Half a second later, Brin emerged out of the shadows holding a heavy pistol.

"Drop the gun."

His dark face was as passive as his voice was emotionless, but I was still glad to see him.

Gabriella placed the gun on the floor and slid off me in a way that would have required either marriage or stoning in some parts of the world. She smiled like a kitten ready to play, and I hoped Brin didn't make the mistake of underestimating her, like so many had.

"Is he a friend of yours, Joe?" Gabriella put her hands behind her back, pushing her chest out and giving Brin the full "little ol' me" treatment. "He's very handsome."

"Watch her, Brin." I struggled against the ties, trying to loosen them. "She's as deadly as a gigawatt laser and twice as fast."

Brin nodded. "Thanks for the warning."

Then he shot her.

Brin lifted his gun towards Dollie and I drove my heels into the floor, propelling myself at him as he squeezed the trigger, even though I was still fastened to the chair. The gun went off next to my head, but the impact of my body put him on the floor. It was a great move. Very heroic.

Until my forehead smacked the kitchen floor, and everything went blurry. I had vague sensations of Brin pushing me off him and shouting at Wirkkala. Then everything blanked out again.

"You'll live."

Gabriella was crouching over me, her armored SkinSuit torn open where she'd been shot. It was a mess of woven ballistic material and impact distribution scales. But it had done its job.

"I told you, we're on the same side." She kissed me hotly and with that, she was gone.

I twisted myself out of the splintered remains of the chair, scrambling over to Dollie and slicing through the cable ties with a kitchen knife. Dollie rubbed her arms to restore circulation, thankfully looking unhurt. "I don't know whether to be angry with you or kiss you for saving me."

"Never mind that. Come on." I pulled her towards the door.

"We can't let them get away."

We ran for the exit, and I stopped at the corner to glance around the doorframe. Gabriella was sprinting down the corridor, disappearing from sight even as I looked, but there was no sign of the other two. I checked that the gun I'd taken from Wirkkala was loaded and ran after Gabriella, my strides matched easily by Dollie.

"Who the hell was that?" she gasped as we ran.

"Brin."

"The SIA guy?"

"I'm guessing that he's not working for them anymore."

A gunshot sounded down the corridor, and we flattened against the wall. Moments later, more shots followed. Farther away than the first.

"They're getting away." Dollie tugged at my arm.

"Wait. Give me a SootheStick."

"This isn't the time for a smoke break, Joe."

"You know I don't use them. C'mon."

Dollie fished her case from her bag and handed it to me. I took four of the sticks and squeezed the ends to ignite them.

SootheSticks don't smoke as such. The burn is a catalytic process contained within the tube. I crushed them in my hands and held them up close to the atmospheric detector, hoping the reaction would pull enough oxygen from the air around it and set off the fire alarm.

The sticks frothed in my grip, and I felt my palm blistering. Normally they don't act that way, but I'd obviously crushed them enough to screw up their normal safe behavior.

Dollie smelled the burned meat odor and wrinkled her nose. "What the hell are you doing? Is that your hand burning?"

I winced. My idea didn't seem to be working. Then I heard a slight click, and the indicator turned red. I dropped the smoldering SootheSticks as the pressure warning sounded. The safety bulkheads ahead of us snapped shut as the section sealed itself off from the rest of the city.

My hand was a black and red mess with a large burn in the middle of the palm. Dollie looked at it and grimaced, shaking her head.

"You can be so stupid at times." She pulled some antiseptic wipes from her bag and cleaned up the burn, the wipes' anesthetizing agents bringing welcome relief.

"I stopped them, didn't I?"

She kissed me softly. "You did the best possible. Like you always do."

It was a long wait until the police arrived with the emergency crews, but finally the bulkhead door behind us cranked back, and Tare walked in, a grim look on his face.

"The penalty for sabotaging safety equipment on Luna is severe, Ballen." He held out a hand. "As is the punishment for possession of an unlicensed firearm."

"Let me guess. You're going to airlock me?" I passed him the gun.

"No. I'm only going to deport you." He stood to one side as the emergency crews moved up to crank the next door open. "Though if it were up to me, I'd 'lock both of you for being complete pains in the ass."

"Aww, come on..." Dollie cooed, "I'm sure you like *some* pains in the ass."

Tare's face darkened and he gestured to two of his people. "Take them to the station and charge them. I'll be there as soon as this is cleared up."

"The woman who killed the girl and the people in the nightclub is in the next section." I nodded at the bulkhead.

"Is that so?"

"That's why I triggered the alarm. To stop them from getting away."

"Well, thank you *so much* for your cooperation. That information will help your defense no end."

It wasn't hard to hear the sarcasm in his voice. "What's wrong?"

"According to the pickups, that section is empty."

"That's impossible...we were chasing them..." I pushed forward, intent on checking for myself, but the other two officers grabbed me. "Check it out, if you don't believe me."

"Oh, we will. Don't worry."

"Don't argue, Joe." Dollie put her hand on my wrist. "Let them deal with it themselves."

An hour later, we were waiting in one of the interrogation rooms. We hadn't said much, knowing we were being watched remotely. I'd had enough of these games to last a lifetime and wanted to get back to some real engineering or even just driving a damn cab. The door opened and Tare walked in, looking even less humorless than he normally did, if such a thing were possible. His scowl didn't give me a good feeling.

"Did you find them?" I said.

"You could say that."

Dollie spoke up. "We want to speak to our lawyer."

"That would be pointless at this stage." Tare threw a Solido on the table. Even upside down I could make out the pictures of a dead person.

"Your *friend*?" Tare tapped the picture.

"Wirkkala?" I said it in chorus with Dollie, who looked at the images, then turned away.

"Shot in the head."

"That had nothing to do with us," I protested.

"You were armed."

"Do the ballistics match?" I put my arm around Dollie. "If not, you've got no reason to hold us."

"They probably don't. The reports will be in soon. Not that it matters."

"Why's that?" I was getting angry at being accused of everything under the sun. "You going to beat us with a hose anyway?"

"Recordings from the pickups in the area confirm some of your claims."

"But not enough to clear us."

"I don't like you, Ballen. Or this *thing* you call your wife." He jabbed a finger at Dollie.

My hand shot out and I grabbed his larynx, squeezing hard. "You better apologize to the lady."

Tare let out a half-choked gurgle, his hands gripping my wrist.

"Stop it, Joe." Dollie pulled on my other arm. "He's not worth it."

I held him for another five seconds, then released him. He coughed wetly, bending over at the waist.

"I could airlock you for that!" he gasped, his face the color of a ripe plum.

"You don't have enough men."

He walked back towards the entrance. "Only reason I don't is that it's out of my hands now." He turned at the doorway. "But I want you out of my jurisdiction immediately, or I *will* press charges."

He left the door open and a few seconds later someone else walked in. It took me a second to recognize him, as the last time I saw him he only had one arm.

"Still losing out in the popularity sweepstakes, huh, Ballen?"

"Delacort?"

He smiled at my reaction. "I imagine this is Mrs. Ballen." He held out a hand to Dollie. "Pleased to meet you."

Dollie took his hand lightly. "Dollie Buntin, actually."

"There's a shuttle heading for the High-Rig in fifty-three minutes." He checked his watch. It was on the arm he'd lost, which was still covered by the BioFab tube. He noticed me looking. "It's doing good. A lot quicker than when you had it done, I guess."

I'd taken over a year to heal. A year of often excruciating pain. That was somewhat different as I'd lost both legs and an arm. I'd also had to deal with psychological rejection issues, but nevertheless, the new MedTech for limb replacement was impressive to see. He'd gotten to a point in weeks that had taken me months.

"Glad you don't have to go through what I did. It wasn't good."

"Anything you need before we leave?"

"I have clothes and some other things at the hotel," Dollie said.

"Already taken care of." Delacort smiled. "Anything else?"

"An explanation." I helped Dollie out of her chair and grabbed my jacket.

"That can wait till we're off the ground. I better show you something first. In case you decide to take your chances with Officer Tare."

He reached into his pocket and pulled out an SIA ID. "You could say I've been promoted."

"The last person who showed me one of those just tried to kill us." My arm was aching from throttling Tare. "Makes it hard to trust."

"Understandable," he said. "That's why they sent me. Someone you know."

"You didn't seem to like me much last time we talked."

"Different time. Different world. I underestimated you."

"Doesn't everyone."

Eleven

Delacort herded us to the departure lounge, bypassing the security checks in a way that would normally have made the hairs on the back of my neck stand on end. I'm not one for red tape, but when it comes to travel in spaceships, I firmly believe the security is done for everyone's safety. No one had forgotten the Benge incident decades ago. Terrorists, criminals, or simply people wanting to do something stupid, can be even more dangerous in space than they are on Earth.

I had to admit, though, this time I was relieved not to have to go through the scans, and even happier to leave LFS—even if it meant a financial loss. I was content to get away free with Dollie.

The shuttle was the typical setup—lightweight and large volume. Through the landing pad windows, it looked like a giant metallic football with the bottom end cut off. Travel from Luna to Earth orbit was a fairly easy boost, which made it simple to maximise cargo and passenger capacity. Delacort had placed us in a private berth, and I was glad of the unexpected luxury.

I guided Dollie to one of the acceleration chairs, then sat in another and looked over at Delacort. "Any idea what happened?"

"Officially, Wirkkala was killed by an unknown assailant and the LFS PD is mounting an investigation to determine his attacker. After a few weeks, the investigation will be dropped due to lack of evidence."

"So that bitch gets away with killing whoever she wants?" Dollie spat the words out.

"Shortly after you triggered the alarm one of the emergency

'locks was opened, and the LFC radar detected a small ship leaving the lunar surface, probably a boosted Hopper. It was tracked as best they could and looked like it was headed towards L1.

That was the orbital point for the Fibonacci Atoll, which confirmed what I'd suspected about Gabriella. "What happened to Brin?"

Delacort looked puzzled, then shook his head. "I wasn't clear. Brin was the one heading for L1."

Now it was my time to be surprised. "If he's on his way to the Atolls, what happened to Gabriella?"

Delacort shrugged. "She should be in the next cabin."

Dollie looked from me to Delacort and back. Her exquisite lips twisted into a snarl and she tore open the straps on her seat, then charged towards the door.

"Hold on, Dollie." I understood how she felt and didn't feel much different with respect to Gabriella, but we should at least hear what was going on.

Delacort held up his hands. "Let me explain." He carried on before either of us could object. "The SIA *has* been looking for the missing Ananta data since it vanished. There were very real fears the Atolls might locate it first, leaving Earth behind the eight ball once more. But the people at the top also got suspicious. Operational details were leaking—too many to be a coincidence—and they were convinced someone was working inside for the Atolls."

I coaxed Dollie back to her chair and we both sat. Delacort hunched down opposite us, leaning in.

"Trouble was they didn't know who. Hell, they weren't even sure it *was* the Atolls. It could as easily have been the PanAsians, even though they're now officially allies, or even one or more of the Corporates."

"All you people do is play games." I felt the bile rising in my stomach. "Who gets hurt in the process or what is lost doesn't matter a damn."

He ignored my comments. "After Wirkkala resurfaced on the moon, they made contact with him and negotiated to get the data. But they knew it wasn't safe, so they gave him a new identity and relocated him."

"Foster?" Dollie spat the name out. "Not much of a cover when you let him roam his old haunts."

That was the part I didn't understand. Why go to all the trouble of relocating him and giving him a new identity, when he was only a few kilometers from where he'd lived before? Not only that, he was still associating with the same people. "You set him up."

"It's worse than you think." Delacort suddenly found the space between his feet the most interesting part of the room. "This was before my involvement, okay? I'm only the messenger."

"Go on."

"The guy killed today wasn't Wirkkala."

"What?"

Dollie stood again and I thought for a minute she was going to punch Delacort, but she held her temper. She pulled a Soothe-Stick out of her bag and lit it with a quick squeeze. She moved over to the wall, partially hidden by a drink dispenser as if it could buttress her from what Delacort was saying.

She studied the top of her SootheStick. "What do you mean?"

"The real Wirkkala was relocated to Earth. The guy who was killed was somebody they hired to take his place. Hang around, do stuff as him, so the Atolls and their agents wouldn't look elsewhere."

"You used him as a decoy?" I was disgusted right down into my stomach. "I don't suppose anyone told him how much danger he was facing."

"Again, before my time. But he *was* given protection. He wasn't in it alone."

"Protection?" The way these security people operated would make *Satan Mekratrig* look like a choirboy.

"Gabriella." Dollie blew a stream of smoke against the wall. "He means Gabriella, Joe."

Delacort nodded. "Once he was in place, Ms. Faulk was hired to watch over him in case anyone tried to track down Wirkkala. It was a double-blind. She was his guardian angel."

"Some *angel*." Dollie thumped the wall hard enough to leave an impression on the thin plastic skin.

"They had to use outside contractors. Internal people couldn't be trusted. From what I've seen of her record she's suitably experienced." Delacort shifted uneasily.

The rest was as simple as it was dirty. Brin had contacted me to trace Wirkkala's location, unaware of the substitution. Using me to do the legwork, so he could avoid suspicion as long as possible. Wheels within wheels, bluff, and counter-bluff. What a pile of crap.

"How did Brin know who we'd seen?" I felt dirty, used. "I didn't contact him."

"You still have the QuBee?" Delacort looked grim.

I pulled it out of my pocket and looked at the black anodized casing. Usually they're simple devices that use quantum entanglement over large distances to make a simple notification. A highly advanced beacon, triggered by a switch. I passed it to Delacort.

"This one has been modified to provide spatial coordinates in real time. He was one step behind you all the way. Cleaning up any potential inconveniences."

"These games got a lot of people killed."

"So Brin killed Misty?" Dollie's voice was harsh.

Delacort nodded. "And the others."

The door slid open and Gabriella sauntered in. "You started the party without me?"

Her pout disgusted me. People had been killed and to her, it was of no consequence. She felt the same way about corpses as Dollie did about nail color—disposable, inconsequential.

"You said there are two cabins?" Dollie asked.

Delacort nodded.

"This one is mine and Joe's. You two can share the other. And don't even think of calling. I don't want to see either of you."

"The other is a single room, not meant for m—"

"See if I give a fuck!" Dollie projected the words using the male part of her larynx. It sounded like a scream from hell and matched the look on her face.

"You better do as the lady says," I said. "Now."

The ship reverberated with a series of metallic clangs as the connections to the docking platform were disconnected. Lift-off would be in a matter of minutes. Delacort stood where he was for about a second, then grabbed his bag and hustled Gabriella back through the door.

As soon as the door closed Dollie was in my arms. She sobbed softly as I held her.

"Bastards," she said. "Complete bastards."

The lights flickered with the thirty-second warning. "We should strap in," I said.

"Just hold me."

Launching from the lunar surface isn't the HiGee event it is from Earth, so it didn't present any real danger. As long as nothing went badly wrong it was a smooth process. The acceleration built up, making us feel heavier, but I held on to Dollie regardless. I wanted to protect her from all the world's ugliness, even though I knew I couldn't.

An hour later, I shuffled into what passed as the ship's bar, feeling a little guilty. I wanted a drink to clear my mouth of the bad taste that had infested it since Delacort's revelations and had left Dollie sleeping on the couch in the cabin. In keeping with the shuttle's main purpose of carrying people and cargo, the bar was a small section at one end of the equally misnamed "observation lounge." The lounge was big enough for a small party, as long as you didn't have more than a dozen friends, and the bar area consisted of exactly three tall stools which were even less practical in space than they would have been on Earth. To the left of the bar surface stood a small drinks dispenser, its composite surface treated to look similar to brass.

Now we were in ZeeGee the carpeting in the lounge provided grip as I walked, though I could have managed as easily without it. Most people would be doubled up with space sickness by now, but that wasn't a problem I'd experienced in years. That was the other reason the bar was small—few are comfortable enough in space to swallow anything, let alone alcohol. Delacort was already sitting on one of the stools, the slightly awkward way he held his arm giving his identity away even before I saw his face.

I punched the controls on the dispenser for a whiskey and grabbed the squashy tube that popped out after swiping my credit chip over the payment reader. I stayed at the other end of the bar, popped the seal on the tube and sucked on the nipple without saying anything. The liquor was cheap and burned going down, but in a way, it helped offset some of the guilt I felt.

"It was nothing to do with me." Delacort had his own half empty tube, and there were at least two empty ones in the trash receptacle built into the counter.

"Yeah, I heard you. You're the messenger." I sucked some more from my tube. "What's the next excuse? *I was only following orders?*"

"I was wrong about you, Ballen. I admitted it. But you know what's at stake here." He turned towards me. "If we don't figure out the space drive and the Atolls do, the entire Earth population will be trapped on that mud ball forever. Is that what you want for your children and grandchildren?"

"The goals are fine. It's the methods I have a problem with."

He was slightly red-faced, despite the temperature-controlled environment. "The Atolls destroyed the Earth. They raped the assets of the planet and now they want to walk away. Pretending the people they left behind don't exist or have any rights to space. Tell me you're okay with that."

I'd heard it many times. The Atolls screwed the rest of humanity over, plundering the natural resources and leaving the people they saw as unworthy to fight over the remnants, but it was a simplistic view of reality. The early space ventures used assets from Earth, certainly, how could they not? They quickly switched to extraterrestrial sources, though, for obvious reasons. Materials brought from Earth were incredibly expensive, not to mention in limited supply. As is often the case, the truth was entirely different from the propaganda, even if no one wanted to hear it.

"We destroyed our own environment while promoting greed and inefficiency," I said. "Earth could have worked with the Atolls but chose not to because the people resented their success. We could have competed against them, but we didn't because people didn't want to risk losing what they had."

"I never took you as an Atoll-lover." He leaned over, and I smelled the caustic alcohol on his breath. "People like you make me sick."

"Admitting they're not all wrong doesn't mean I support them. But the first step in dealing with any problem is recognizing it.

Decades of posturing and denial haven't gotten us anywhere."

"What would you have us do? Lie down and accept defeat?"

"We had our shot with the Ananta. Now we're looking for a second chance. But we better grab hold and do it *right* this time. I don't think we'll get a third."

"That what I'm saying." Delacort looked puzzled.

"No, you're saying Earth should grab it at any cost. If we do, then we're no better than the Atolls or the Corporates."

"That's insane."

"Really? So all the information we have on the space drive? We've shared that with the PanAsian Confederacy? How about the MusCats? Are they part of the *we* you talk about? How about the United African Democracies? The UAD have been trying to develop independent space access for decades and have been blocked at every turn by both us *and* the PAC."

I swallowed more of my drink as he looked away. "We can't even trust ourselves. These issues are too big to be left in the hands of people with an axe to grind."

"So who decides? You? Joe Ballen—Saver of Worlds?"

I grunted. "That's way beyond my pay grade. But I know the difference between a supernova and a sandwich."

The Muslim-Catholic Alliance wouldn't have the skills to make use of the drive regardless—they'd been routinely killing anyone in their population with a brain for decades. The PanAsians would have had the knowledge. But I had no doubt the old "conflict of ideologies" would keep them out of the deal.

"If you believe what you say." Delacort finished his drink. "There's something else you should know."

I waited for him to finish. Somehow knowing whatever it was, I wouldn't like it.

"We've lost contact with Logan Twofeathers."

I was right. I didn't like it one bit.

Twelve

I looked at Dollie and shrugged. "I know what you're thinking and you're right."

After getting back to the room I'd shared what Delacort had told me. The SIA had a secret project to redevelop the space drive, but they had two problems. First, they didn't have all the information, which resulted in the games they'd played with Wirkkala, and second, they needed someone who could make the construction happen, which was where Logan had come in.

"They set up a secret base on an asteroid?"

I understood Dollie's skepticism. "There were concerns about the range of the field. When the Ananta left there were some *anomalies*. I asked what they were, but Delacort didn't know."

"Did they get scared Earth would be devoured by space aliens or something? Like at Rabbit Lake?"

Rabbit Lake was a legend from before the Big Shake. Someone or something had stolen or abducted an entire Californian town leaving nothing, not even witnesses. Some conspiracy nuts thought it was aliens, some thought it was a government weapons test that went wrong, and yet others said it was a rogue ball of antimatter. Any evidence that might have existed was lost in the destruction caused by the Big Shake—a Cascadia event which destroyed most of the western seaboard running from what was San Francisco all the way up to where Vancouver used to be.

"Maybe. I don't understand those people any more than you do."

"So you want to go after Logan," Dollie said.

"Sure. That was my first instinct. Which was what got me

involved in all this in the first place." I paced up and down the small room. "But Logan's a big boy—whatever he's mixed up in, he can take care of himself."

Dollie came up and took my hand in hers. "If you want to look for him, you don't have to hold back on my account."

The lights flashed red. We were about to go into braking maneuvers. I squeezed Dollie and kissed her quickly, settling her down in her chair then strapping myself into mine as the thrusters fired.

"I'm not leaving you again," I called out over the noise of the landing.

"You're damn right you're not. For the duration, it's a case of *whither thou goest*." Dollie glowered at me. "Do you think I'd let you anywhere near that bitch on your own?"

"Gabriella? She's not my type."

"But you're hers."

The ship resounded with several metallic *clangs* as it finished docking, and a moment later I felt the slight change in pressure as the atmospheres equalized between us and the High-Rig. I unbuckled and helped Dollie do the same. She didn't need help but I wanted to do it anyway.

"If you go after Logan, I suppose there's a good chance you'll run into Brin again."

"Possibly." I grabbed what little luggage we had. "I don't imagine the Atolls' interest in the space drive has ended because of this setback."

"We're going, Joe." Dollie's face hardened. "I want him on a skewer."

There was no point arguing. When Dollie sets her mind on something, almost nothing changes it—the ring around my finger was proof of that.

We walked out and found Delacort waiting with Gabriella. No doubt ready to whisk us through security once more. "Docking Gate One Seventeen. There's a ship waiting. If you need anything other than routine toiletries or standard changes of clothing, then you're out of luck."

I caught an edge of tension in Delacort's voice. There was

something he wasn't saying. "What ship?"

"A United Space Navy vessel, USN Sarac."

The USP had a limited number of ships, and even if you added together the ships from all nations, you'd barely have what you could call a "fleet." It was one of the things denied us by the Atolls and although that had changed in the last few years, construction was slow.

"Never heard of the ship or the USN. What the hell is this?" I looked Delacort straight in the eye, seeing a flicker of panic. "This isn't the time to keep secrets."

"There's an Atoll cruiser on its way. They'll be in weapons range in less than two hours."

I wondered briefly if my friend, Thombs, was already strapped into one of the Interceptors as we rushed through the airlocks and crossed into the station proper. There were people running everywhere. Some were headed for the elevator, some were undoubtedly reporting to the weapons stations, and some appeared to be running for the sake of getting in the way.

We started down Spoke One, pushing past the throng going the other way. I winced at the deafening siren warbling in every direction and kept a tight hold of Dollie, not wanting to lose her in the commotion. With the way the crowd was, I'd never find her again if I did. As we moved farther along the Spoke the people thinned, allowing us to move faster. Then I saw it through one of the large display windows they have for tourists in the main public areas.

The Sarac was an ore carrier, undoubtedly commandeered from the fleet of about half a dozen that had been operating for over thirty years on the Earth-Mars run before the Atolls destroyed the base and embargoed us. This one had been thoroughly bastardized, from what I could see. Every surface was covered in a dull, dark blue layer with an oily appearance that made it difficult to see any details clearly. There were signs of hasty modifications to the hull and engines, making it look a little like a metallic space-going bulldog that had been last in line at the fairy godmother parade.

The basic superstructure was there but a number of additions had been made in the crudest way possible. Several missile launcher turrets had been added, as well as six auxiliary thruster units. At the back a bank of the new MagPlasma drives had been attached using a rough girder framework. At the front a dome-like protrusion stuck out above the command deck like a metallic boil. I guessed it might be part of a high-fidelity navigation system, but it could as easily have been someone's insane idea of decoration.

The most ridiculous addition was a colossal missile rack mounted dorsally along the top of the ship. It was terrifying, not in the sense of the destructive power of the missiles—though they were undoubtedly as destructive as the military could make them—no, the frightening aspect was what might happen if they tried to fire one.

"That pile of crap wouldn't get us back to Luna. Let alone the asteroid belt," I shouted at Delacort.

"It's been modified. Upgraded."

"Interceptor One. Contact in one minute."

The announcement came over the station's public comm channel and I imagined the high thrust energy of the Interceptor closing in on the Atoll cruiser. If it hit, they'd both be vaporized.

The announcer spoke again, betraying not even the slightest hint of panic at the bad news. "Intercept: Negative."

I cursed. We could have done with some luck. Even modified, I couldn't see how something like that was going to take us beyond Mars orbit. "They should have named it the USN Deathtrap..."

Delacort entered a code into the security pad of the airlock leading out to the ship. He turned to face me as Gabriella sprinted past him. "You can stay here if you want."

"Interceptor Two. Contact in one minute."

I looked at Dollie. "What do you think?"

She shrugged. "I think we need to decide fast."

A flash lit up in the distance outside the station, briefly looking like a small sun.

"Intercept: Negative."

"Let's go!" I bundled Dollie through the 'lock ahead of me, helping Delacort to dog it closed.

The lights died, plunging the corridor into darkness as we rushed through the airlock. A few seconds later they flickered back on. The defense systems were drawing on the station's power reserves, draining them temporarily. The battle was joined.

The ship showed every sign of its history as a freighter. The 'lock mechanism groaned as it closed, and the walls and floor were scratched and grime-coated. After enjoying the almost pristine environment of Luna, it was a jarring shift of perspective and I rubbed my hands on my pants instinctively.

The inside of the ship was as tightly packed as an elephant in a swimsuit and showed several signs of the hasty conversion work. Several bulkheads had been roughly cut through and new corridors and walls had been hastily installed, the panels showing strings of roughly applied adhesive.

Delacort led us inside and turned right, into a room with acceleration couches mounted onto the wall. There was a metallic smell and I realized we were in one of the partitions that must have been used for carrying ore. I hoped it wasn't something too poisonous. It would be ironic if we went to rescue someone in deep space only to die of heavy metal toxicity on the way.

"Strap down wherever you like," he said, waving us in.

Gabriella hopped onto a couch at the far side while Dollie and I set up next to each other. Dollie chose the ones farthest from Gabriella, and I wasn't going to argue.

"Boost in three minutes. Secure all stations. Passengers take your positions. *Priprema da napusti!*"

I didn't recognize the language. I looked at Delacort, who shrugged.

"Don't ask me."

I checked Dollie to make sure she was strapped in properly, then climbed on the next couch and snugged my own belts tight.

"Incoming. Boost in thirty seconds. *Upozorenje! Upozorenje!*"

The ship reverberated as the dock disconnected, and almost immediately I felt the boost pushing at me. It still wasn't the dramatic thrust of a planetary launch, but the captain wasn't hanging around either. I grunted at the unexpected acceleration, far greater than during lunar departure.

The walls around the cabin vibrated heavily, a metallic grind shuddering through every surface with an alarming resonance. I wished Dollie hadn't insisted on joining this disaster-in-waiting and found myself wondering if it wasn't too late to jump ship.

"Engaging secondaries," the captain announced over the speakers, and the increased thrust pressed us more firmly against the padding.

There was no real sense of speed but the ship creaked even louder, and I heard several loud pops that sounded like failing supports. Or possibly the hull was buckling under the stress. Dollie's eyes met mine, and I smiled in reassurance. She smiled back, letting me know she knew I was full of shit. Several minutes later a loud explosion rocked the ship, and for a moment I thought that was it and we were doomed.

"Secondary separation confirmed. *Mi bezbedno.* Movement now permitted."

Delacort popped his straps and swung around, grinning widely. "That was close. Come on, I'll show you to your quarters."

I twisted upright and realized we still had gravity, which was unexpected for an ore carrier. It wasn't much but enough to keep us stabilized for the most part. That meant we were maintaining thrust, which was good news for Dollie and anyone else on board not used to micro-gravity.

The corridor we'd come in through was now a vertical shaft with a ladder running up and down. From what I could see it looked as though there were two decks above us and one below. Moving up and down the ladder was no issue with the low gravity, though you did have to be careful not to slip awkwardly.

The accommodations were as primitive as everything else. A corridor ran laterally across the ship, each side lined with what were essentially sleeping bunks, hidden by canvas curtains to provide a small amount of privacy. No "married quarters" were available. I whispered "sorry" to Dollie.

After stowing our gear, we made our way back up to the room we'd been in before. The couches had been folded and moved out of the way, and several rudimentary tables had replaced them. Several people, who were obviously part of the crew, were already seated, along with a number in MilSec uniforms.

We sat as a man shuffled in wearing an old-fashioned naval captain's hat, his feet making soft tearing noises as he lifted them against the pull of the carpeting. A few centuries ago he'd have been a perfect bandit or pirate. His broad face carried a wide grin that looked like it was permanent, but his left eye was missing, the scarred eye socket lending him a slightly evil appearance.

He was followed by a slighter man. Similarly dark-haired and with olive skin, but the second man was bearded and looked like a weasel who'd lost his best friend. Both moved to the front and faced the rest of the room.

"Hello, everyone. *Dobrodošli.* I am Captain Orkan Medved. Apologies for rushed departure. Atoll scum not want us to leave." He spoke with a Slavic accent. "Their cruiser was destroyed a few minutes ago and I'm sure you will be pleased to hear damage to the High-Rig was minimal. *Pohvale bog.*

"We owe our lives to Interceptor pilots who sacrificed themselves so we could get away. We must honor them in return." He took off his cap and wiped his hand up his forehead, pushing his thick dark hair back. "For those who do not know, we are headed to USP base hidden in asteroid belt. I am told Atolls know nothing of this but they not stupid, we cannot depend on it. We will accelerate at constant one-tenth gee and journey will take sixty days.

"When we launched, several EMP warheads detonated near Atolls and several of their orbital facilities. Also, High-Rig will periodically emit pulses designed to confuse enemy. We also have decoy launcher on board that we can deploy at random intervals. This supposed to mask departure and hamper attempts to track us, but we cannot rely on this. That why we are armed, and why we have military team with us. Gentlemen, please make yourselves known."

Delacort and several others raised their hands.

"I am captain of this vessel but this is military operation, and we are under their command. You must follow orders given by these men. They are in authority and here to protect us. Show them respect.

"Our early departure means much work not complete and must be finished as we travel to succeed. My brother, Rikard, is chief engineer and will assign work duties as we travel." He pointed to the man behind him. "Please do what you can to assist.

"This is dangerous and difficult mission. But is righteous one. Together I know we can succeed. We fight for freedom of all of

117

Earth. *Uspeh!*"

"Even if the EMPs work, how will that stop the Atolls tracking us out there?" As far as I knew it was impossible to hide anything in space, especially a ship giving out a number of electromagnetic signatures.

"I am pilot. Perhaps commander can answer that, if allowed."

I was momentarily confused when Delacort stood. Then I realized he'd effectively been bumped in rank as there can't be two captains on one vessel.

Delacort faced the room. "I'll tell you what I know. Which isn't a lot—I'm not a theory guy. Before now, what Mr. Ballen said would be correct. You can't hide a space-going vessel effectively. In the last few years, a range of cloaking technologies have become available. We can mask our EM signature somewhat, we have secure comm systems on board, and we can even minimize our thermal signature to some extent. All of this helps reduce the chances of detection, but it's a partial solution, at best. Anyone looking for us hard enough and in the right place *can* find us and will. Which is why it's imperative we complete the work on the ship as soon as possible.

"Despite appearances to the contrary, the USN Sarac has some of the most advanced technology currently available but Atoll ships still outgun us and can outrun us. With Captain Medved at the helm, though, I have every confidence we can complete our mission successfully."

It was the sort of rah-rah speech you might expect from a career military guy—you know, the kind given before everybody heads out to their deaths. Perhaps it was only me thinking beyond the rhetoric and wondering what our real mission was. Did we really need this huge gunboat to recover Logan and a bunch of technicians?

Thirteen

Once you get past the novelty, space flight is inherently boring, despite how it's depicted in 3V shows. The Sarac might have been the most advanced of the newly formed USP Space Navy, but its top acceleration of one-tenth gee wasn't enough to blow out a match, even if it was constant.

It did mean we didn't have to worry quite so much about space sickness, which was a good thing as some of those aboard—Dollie, among others—weren't accustomed to ZeeGee. It also meant we could head to our destination relatively directly, but even so, at this point we still had over two weeks of travel ahead of us.

Our target was an asteroid designated 1219-Britta, which was little more than a ten-kilometer hunk of rock orbiting in and out of the main Belt. Currently, it was floating almost perpendicular with the Earth and Sun, about one and a half A.U.s out. It wouldn't move a great deal during our journey, which simplified the task. While many asteroids are valuable resources, Britta wasn't one of them. Its location also meant we had less to worry about from the Atolls. They focused most of their efforts around Vesta, which was on the opposite side of the Sun from where we were headed.

I was still suspicious and asked Delacort about the asteroid base while we worked on one of the missile turrets.

"I'm not sure what we'll find." He wrestled a thick control umbilical into place and held it steady as I clamped it down. "I don't think anyone does. From what I know they were given resources and staff and told to go and make it work. Few details were shared with SIA Central other than progress reports."

"Have they made any?" I started making connections while Delacort monitored the circuit diagnostics. "Progress, that is?"

Delacort shrugged. "I've not seen the reports. Need to know only."

"One day you'll hide everything so well you won't be able to find your ass with your hands."

He laughed. "It sometimes feels like it."

"So why did you get involved?"

"Any idea how little work there is for a one-armed ex-soldier?" He slapped his regenerated arm. "This way the service pays the bills, and I get a wage to keep my wife and kids happy."

"Won't help them if you die out in space." I held two of the connectors together for a check.

"Back one."

He tapped the diagnostics, and I reconnected the circuit as indicated.

"They're better off if I die on a mission. Then they get a big fat bonus, as well as the pension."

I sealed the last circuit and crawled out of the access tube so I could work on the external connections. "I don't imagine they'd agree." I looked up at him and saw the grim look on his face.

"Maybe. She wasn't thrilled when I went home. Got the impression she'd have preferred the bonus."

I wasn't sure what to say. Facing an injury like that is about as traumatic as it gets. I'd been alone when it happened to me, no family or even close friends outside of Logan. He'd pulled me through it, even when I didn't want him to. Going through that with someone who was only supporting you because they felt they should would be the worst thing imaginable.

"You're reading it wrong. She was probably worried about you." I tucked the panel back in place. "Okay, run the active tests."

Delacort entered a command sequence into the plug-in diagnostic unit and the servos whined as they engaged, followed by an oily hiss from the hydraulics.

"Sounds good." I tapped the button on my comm-set connecting with the bridge. "Running active test on launcher three. Please confirm."

"Yes. I see it." It was the captain who answered, his accent discernible even through the radio. "Looks good. I check targeting."

There was a brief pause, then he came back on the line. "We have no target feed. Tracking missing."

I acknowledged and cut him off. "Back to work, I guess. Must have missed something."

I popped the panel back off and slid inside, twisting up to where the targeting feeds were. It looked okay at a glance, but something was obviously not wired up right.

"Do you ever have doubts, you know, about her...him...Dollie?"

I banged my head and uttered a quiet curse. "No...we're good," I lied. "We have an agreement, kind of."

"You okay with that?"

For the most part. Possibly. Well, okay, not really. "Sure. Why not?"

"Try the main interface pack, the signal doesn't look clean," he said. "Guess that works for you."

I checked the interface by hand and felt it give a little. It was an awkward reach, but I pressed firmly and felt a slight click. "Might not have been seated. Try it now."

"Yep, looks better."

I called up to the control room again and Medved confirmed the system was working properly. "Looks like we're done here. Two left."

We worked our way to the lower turret and I checked the installation. Unlike the first, this one had nothing set up, not even basic hydraulics and servos, let alone any control infrastructure.

"This one's going to take some time," I said. "Not sure you can help much right now."

Delacort nodded. "Okay. I'll check progress with the others."

Rikard Medved was running a team working on the PlasMag engines, trying to coax more thrust out of them. From what I knew, they should have been theoretically capable of acceleration at 0.15g, fifty percent more than what we were making. Not that it mattered a great deal. An Atoll cruiser could make over 0.2g, so it could outrun us even at our theoretical best.

Again, the details of the mission worried me. Would the USP stage an operation to recover a bunch of space construction engineers and scientists, even if they might have the answer to interstellar space flight? They had to know it was a long shot, and yet they were throwing high levels of resources at this for what appeared to be little hope of a payback.

"You know if they've lost contact, the chances are the Atolls have either destroyed or captured them already, don't you?"

"Your friend is one of them. Do you want to walk away?"

"I owe Logan a lot. More than you know. But he wouldn't expect me to sign up for a suicide mission."

Delacort was stone-faced. "Too late to change your mind."

He headed off towards the engine room and I started working through the hydraulic plumbing, consulting the manuals frequently to guide me. It was routine work, but pleasantly distracting. My mind wanted to spin ideas of what our real mission might be, but the intricacies of the control and operating systems pushed that to one side.

I'd crawled about halfway inside the outer casing when I felt a hand rub against my thigh. It teased slowly upwards, stimulating me enough that I felt myself responding.

"I'm covered in oil and dirt, Dollie. Not to mention being tied up in hydraulic lines."

"Good guess, but wrong."

I jerked at the sound of Gabriella's plummy accent, smacking my head into the turret casing. I slid out from under the unit. "What the hell are you playing at?"

Gabriella pushed her chest out. "I was feeling lonely. And looking for someone...I mean, some*thing* to do..." She leaned in close, speaking softly. "Do you like being *tied up*, Joe? I'd be more than willing to play along if you'd like."

"I'm married. And if Dollie caught you here, she'd tie you up in very small knots."

"Married doesn't mean you're not a man, does it?" She wriggled mischievously. "Besides, Dollie's not well. I don't think she'll be bothering you anytime soon."

"She's sick?" There was a loud buzz inside my head. "What's wrong with her?"

"You don't know?"

Dollie hadn't said anything to me, though between the work around the ship and the lack of privacy, we'd not had much time together. If she was unwell, she'd have told me, wouldn't she? Then doubt set in. She'd been keeping something from me for a while, and I had no idea what. The call from Kinsella might have been more serious than she'd said. My mind whirled as I ran through various combinations, each more deadly than the last.

"Have you spoken to her about it?"

Gabriella laughed. "Of course not. It's not for me to say anything anyway." She grabbed my hand, pressing it against her chest. "Come on, Joe. You're not dead. And I don't mind it dirty."

I pushed her away, quickly sealing up the turret. I wanted to find Dollie and check on her. Whatever game Gabriella was playing she could do it on her own. About a third of the way up the access shaft I heard something like thunder, and the explosive pulse of a pressure wave hit my chest. Seconds later the hull breach alarms sounded, and the lights turned blood red. Captain Medved's voice crackled across the speakers.

"Engine room? I have breach alert. What is happening? Rikard? *Recite mi!*"

There was no response and I reversed direction, heading down the passage the same way Delacort had gone earlier. I shouted at Gabriella over my shoulder. "Get to your bunk, and stay there!"

I careened down the passage as the airtight doors slid closed behind me, steadying myself every few rungs. When I got to the engine room it was already shut, but I could see through the small window that there were people inside. The indicator beside the door showed the pressure was low and dropping, and the telltale whistle from the bulkhead pressure indicator confirmed I needed to work fast. Otherwise, anyone inside would be eating vacuum—which was a low nourishment diet.

I activated my comm-set. "It's Ballen. I'm outside the engine room, override bulkhead E5. There are people trapped."

"Can't do that." Medved's accent was heavier, the adrenalin clear in his words. "Not safe. *Sranje!*"

I didn't have time for a debate. "Open the door or people die."

"Rikard? *Jebi ga!*"

"Open it."

A second later the door slid open, and a rush of air pulled at my skin. I pushed inside—there was a hole in the bulkhead about the size of my fist, the panel around it blackened and twisted but it wasn't time to admire the view. I grabbed the closest person, who turned out to be Delacort. I struggled to move his unconscious mass, pulling him through the bulkhead as his heels dragged on the floor. Once he was through, I jumped back inside feeling light-headed, recognizing the first signs of hypoxia.

Rikard was next. He was less bulky than Delacort, but that didn't make it any less awkward even in the LoGee. I pulled and stumbled, dropping flat on my ass. It felt nice, and I smiled as I felt the seat of my pants stick to the Van Der Waal's carpeting. Part of my brain knew this sensation was deadly, but the oxygen-starved part thought the danger was funny.

"Ballen? Pressure critical." Medved's voice sounded distant in my comm-set. "Must seal door. *Ostavi sada!* Get out!"

I dragged Rikard again. He was stuck to the floor and my feeble effort did nothing to change that. "Come on, Ballen. Time to be a hero again."

I pushed up, getting my feet under me. Grabbing Rikard's shirt at the shoulders, I pulled again, driving my feet down. There was a tearing-fabric sound from the flooring, but he moved. I dragged him higher, staggering towards the door, then throwing him through the bulkhead like a sack of PlaSteel beam ties. Finally I turned towards the last person.

Lurching forward, I wondered why the floor was rising to meet me. Then my face slammed into the deck. A few moments later, something slipped under my arms, wrapping around me and pulling me back. I tried to struggle but couldn't, then watched helplessly as the last figure slid away, barely understanding that it was me who was moving.

"Close it!"

The voice was harsh, and I was so disoriented I didn't recognize it. The hatch closed, cutting off my view from the man still inside.

"Joe? Do you hear me, Joe?"

It took a while before I realized what was happening. "Dollie?"

We were tangled up on the floor outside the engine room, her powerful arms still locked around my chest. Someone was detonating a rivet gun inside my head, and I wished whoever it was would quit so I could get some sleep. Then Dollie slumped back on the deck, and I came awake fast. She looked like a sleeping angel, but the pallor of her skin told me it was a sleep she might not wake from.

Delacort and Rikard were groaning on the floor next to us, but they didn't matter. I pulled Dollie upright, leaning her against the wall. Then I grabbed an emergency oxygen unit from a holder a few meters down the corridor and jumped back to press the mask over her mouth and nose. I alternated triggering the gas and pressing her ribs to encourage her to breathe.

Dollie groaned softly, sucking in the oxygen, and a few minutes later her color returned. Her eyes flickered open and she mumbled something I couldn't hear.

"You're okay. Don't worry."

I heard a noise and glanced around. Delacort was behind me, his skin even grayer than Dollie's, but he would have been through hypoxia training and knew how to deal with it. I offered him the mask and he took several deep lungfuls before handing it back.

"Take her up to the MedBay." He croaked so badly it sounded like he'd been drinking Old Foreskin for a week. "We can't do anything for her here. I'll be up in a few minutes."

I knew Delacort had some medical training through the military but it was one of his men who was the official medic, so I was puzzled when he said *he'd* be up.

"Anderson?" I asked.

Delacort shook his head. "Caught in a pressure door when the alarm went off."

That shook me. Anderson was the nearest we had to a real doctor, and if there was anything seriously wrong with Dollie, losing him could cost her life too.

The "Medical Bay" was an exaggeration in every sense. It was basically a regular bunk rigged up with a portable medical scanner, a few rudimentary medical supplies, and a larger curtain. The treatment unit Dollie had back in her apartment was more sophisticated. I set her on the bunk and her eyes opened; she gave a feeble smile and I breathed easily for the first time since she'd pulled me out of the engine room.

"Hi, trouble." Her voice cracked when she spoke.

"Hi, yourself." I squeezed her hand. "That wasn't the smartest thing you've ever done."

"Lioness rushes to defend mate. That's how it is with me, Joe."

I felt my eyes sting and blinked several times. "I don't think I'd survive losing you."

"Works both ways."

"You're my best girl. Always will be."

She looked sad, and when she finally replied her voice was even lower. "I'm not much of a *girl*, Joe. Would have thought you'd have realized that by now."

She coughed, and I squeezed her hand tighter. "You're whatever you choose to be, Dollie."

"There's something you should know."

Her voice croaked out the words, and I leaned closer to hear her better.

"If you're thinking of making a deathbed confession, I'm going to have to disappoint you. I won't let you die."

She smiled. "Didn't know you had that power."

"Is this where I tell you that you remind me of a man?"

"Hoodoo?"

Dollie's eyes closed again and I felt hopelessly lost. You're supposed to protect the ones you love, aren't you? If someone was scoring my performance at that moment, I was sure I'd be marked down as "must try harder."

Several minutes later the curtain swished back and Delacort stepped in, closing it behind him. "How is she?"

"In and out. Rikard?"

"He's okay. Tough as an old boot and with lungs of the same consistency. He's resting."

Delacort moved the scanner over Dollie and hit the "Diagnose" button. The machine hummed for a little while then beeped with the soft, rhythmic pattern of Dollie's heartbeat. Suddenly the pattern changed, turning to an alarming higher-pitched frequency.

"What's wrong?"

He checked the diagnostic panel and shook his head. "Not sure. You should leave, though. I don't need a panic-stricken husband acting as backseat doctor."

"I can help..."

"Yes, you can." He flicked through several displays. "Send Gabriella. I may need an assistant."

I made my way up the ship and caught Gabriella at her bunk.

She batted her eyes at me. "Tell me you're here for a rematch."

I wanted to punch her. We'd lost two of the crew, yet she was still playing games. "Dollie's hurt. Delacort wants help in the MedBay."

"Are you sure that's a good idea, Joe?" Her laugh tinkled like glass wind chimes. "Do you trust me?"

"Sure." I held the curtain while she slid out. "You won't last five minutes longer than she does."

"Awwww, Joe, is that a threat?"

"No. A promise."

My mind was racing due to the after-effects of hypoxia combined with my worry over Dollie. I knew I should get some rest, but my stubbornness kicked in and I made my way up to the control room. I wanted to know how bad a shape we were in.

Medved was hunched over the controls and waved me over. "Trouble." He tapped the displays

Whatever had happened hadn't only punched a hole in the engine room bulkhead, it had also holed one of the auxiliary fuel tanks. The external pickups showed the beautiful and deadly eruption of what looked like an ice fountain hissing into the vacuum. We were venting precious hydrogen.

"How bad?" I saw the worry in his eyes.

The tight confines of the room appeared to shrink as I waited for his answer. "I shut off inner partitions. We lost perhaps one-quarter of fuel."

I did a quick calculation. "How long until we can't get home?"

"Four hours, possibly. But no guarantee inner partition will hold."

I understood all too well. The partitions were meant for that purpose only—partitioning—they weren't designed to take the pressure needed to store the hydrogen against a vacuum.

"Someone has to go out there."

"You volunteer?"

"Not if you can come up with someone more qualified." For all the experience we had on board, I was the only one who'd done any ZeeGee construction. Fixing the damage would have been hard even in a fully equipped dock; here it would be a minor miracle.

Medved shook his head slowly.

"I thought that was the case. Make sure the drive is fully offline. I don't want to be out there when that thing starts up."

"How long for fix?"

I barely stopped to meet his questioning gaze. "Less than four hours."

Fourteen

When people think of space, they think of it as being empty—a lack of pretty much everything. The truth is though, it's overflowing with one thing: danger. You can run out of air. Fry in radiation. Freeze to death slowly, or get cooked equally easily. Not to mention *smaller* worries like tearing your suit, cracking your helmet or having a seal fail. The point is, you don't do it lightly, and you *never* do it alone, unless you're desperate.

Right now, we were.

I loaded up the "pass-through" box at the main airlock with patching materials and all the tools I could think of. I wasn't sure what I'd need exactly, so I threw in pretty much everything. I sure as hell didn't want to have to run through multiple pressurization cycles if I could help it. Wasting time like that would make the difference between success and failure.

The 'lock was brightly lit but showed signs of being sloppily maintained—the walls were grimy and the port itself looked like it could do with a good cleaning. I guessed it was mostly used for bringing supplies aboard and hauling out the waste, but it would have to do. There was a rack of adjustable P-Suits on the left side and the opposite wall held a variety of basic tools and coils of safety wire. A P-Suit is like a comfortable pair of well broken-in shoes, and usually I'd not think of using anything but my own. Unfortunately, mine was sitting in luggage storage somewhere on the High-Rig.

The first two suits I checked had worn pressure couplings, and some visible cracking in the gaskets. They might have been okay but weren't something I wanted to risk my neck on. The third one looked acceptable and I slid into it, spending several minutes tailoring it to fit me as well as possible. I knew all too well the time invested would more than pay itself back once I was outside working—a badly fitting suit can add hours to even the simplest of jobs.

As I was setting the final straps, Rikard shuffled in, already dressed in his own suit.

"I help," he said, closing up the last few seams.

I've logged over six thousand hours of P-Suit time in my career, almost every job since I qualified has involved at least some suit work, and I have every confidence in my ability to handle any job and take care of myself while doing it. Despite that, I was smart enough to respect the cardinal rule—"No buddy. No EVA"—and was happy not to break that now.

"Good to have you along."

There were no EMUs, so we both grabbed thruster units. Doing a job like this with nothing but hand-thrusters would be tough, and I hoped they'd be enough to complete the work. It wouldn't help us if we had to stop work partway through the job.

"Main Airlock. Ballen and Rikard Medved," I broadcast to the control room. "Ready for EVA. Please disengage safeties."

"Acknowledged."

The door indicator light switched to orange and I pressed the button next to it to trigger the evacuation cycle. The noise of the exhaust fans started as a high-pitched roar that died to a low rumble as the atmosphere was pumped out and the sound became a vibration through my boots. After a minute the door slid open to reveal the inky blackness of space.

I looked around, reminding myself to breathe steadily. The stars were barely visible in the glare from my suit's headlamps and as I stepped out, the painful brilliance of the Sun far behind the ship drowned them out further. The Earth should have still been visible as an overly bright star, but it was overwhelmed too. I held up my hand for a few moments to block out the light and managed to find the planet—a bright dot about thirty degrees away from the Sun.

I'm not sentimental, but there's a feeling you get when you see the Earth from space that hits you in the gut. Whether from close orbit or at a distance doesn't matter. Someone once called the Earth a "blue dot"—an inconsequential ball of rock floating in a vast ocean of the universe. That it was the birthplace of all the humans that had ever existed didn't lend it any significance. Instead it made it seem even more vulnerable. But floating outside the ship like I was, I felt far more unprotected.

I went over to the pass-through and unlatched it, pulling out the materials with Rikard's help. Moving things in ZeeGee isn't easier because of the low gravitation, it's harder. Nothing has weight, but it still retains the mass and inertia, making it ten times more awkward because it throws your senses off.

Once we had everything, I gave Rikard the thumbs up and signaled the control room again. Another basic rule of working in space is constant communication—without it you're very alone and can die very quickly.

"Captain. Proceeding aft."

"Acknowledged. Good luck!"

We boosted along the length of the ship, each of us dragging a bundle of repair material and equipment. Every twenty meters I had Rikard call out the distance traveled on the open circuit, partly so those inside would be able to follow our progress, but also so I knew he was doing okay. His experience shipboard didn't mean he was necessarily familiar with ZeeGee suit operations.

"Remember, we'll need to brake early to slow everything down. Don't try to be the greatest with the latest..."

"I remember training."

He was breathing heavily; I thought of reminding him to breathe as normally as possible but held my tongue. He was inexperienced, but knew what to do.

"Okay. We're close to the halfway point. Get ready to slow."

I gave a squirt to the side with the hand-thruster and then a longer one to slow myself down. The bundle of gear floated past me and the tether stretched. I was ready when the pull came and waved the thruster around, balancing the spin. As soon as I stabilized, I looked around for Rikard.

He'd done likewise but hadn't balanced out the retro thrust

fully and was drifting away from both me and the ship. It wasn't too big a deal but needed correcting—the longer he left it, the harder it would be.

"Rikard. You need a three-second burst to your immediate left."

"Da. Da."

He triggered the blast and held it. His tether tightened and tugged at him, making him spin again. A few more short bursts and he corrected the movement, but it cost him more fuel than it should have.

"Not closing," he said, lifting up the thruster again.

"You're fine. Save your fuel."

I could see he was closing but knew from experience that a small vector was difficult to see. We were moving past the auxiliary tanks, the curved aluminum surface like a polished rock face alongside us. "Start to slow it down. Short, controlled bursts. No longer than one second."

I braked as well, watching Rikard closely as he did the same. He was definitely closing in, curving gently towards me and the tank wall. I glanced forward. The buckled tank plating was clearly visible, and I braked again, decreasing my forward velocity.

I heard a curse and looked around. Rikard was waving the thruster unit around as if he were fighting off a swarm of angry bees. The unit was on and pushing him into increasingly uncontrolled movements.

"Switch off!" I called over the radio.

"Is stuck. *Jebeni sranje! Sranje!*"

He was already in a lot of trouble and needed to do something quickly. "Get rid of it. Drop it," I yelled.

Triggering my own hand-thruster, I killed as much of my velocity as I could and grabbed one of the handholds on the tank. The tug of the repair bundle made me grunt as I fought to hang on, but I made it. As soon as I was safe, I unclipped the tether attached to the supplies and fastened it to the handhold, leaving me free.

"Ballen! *Jebi!*"

I looked around again. Rikard had dumped the thruster unit but was tumbling helplessly, moving farther away from the ship. I cursed and tore into my bundle, pulling out a spare tether and snapped it onto the handhold.

"Rikard? Ballen?" Medved's voice came over the radio and I ignored it, switching to the private circuit.

"Rikard, stay calm. I'm going to come for you."

"Ballen? Is too far, no?"

"Stay calm and breathe slowly. Don't burn up your oxygen."

"*Nyet*. Save others. Let me die."

"We've had enough deaths today."

I squatted against the side of the tank and pushed as hard as I could, using my thigh muscles to give me the biggest launch possible. Then I stretched out in a long dive to minimize my spin, using the thruster minimally to balance and steer onto Rikard's tumbling form.

"Closing. Get ready." I held my breath. "Three. Two. One."

The collision was heavy enough to knock the wind out of me, and I grabbed Rikard only by instinct. We started twisting, but our combined mass made it slower than it would have been otherwise. Then a jerk from the tether almost pulled us apart again.

"Grab on!"

I felt his arms lock around my waist and lifted the thruster unit. The ship was directly in front as we stretched out between it and the repair bundle. I checked the rotation, watching as we lazily tumbled, then triggered the thruster several times, neutralizing our spin.

"Okay. Let's get home."

I activated the thruster again, using it to push us back towards the ship. I'd used a five hundred meter tether and we were at the end, so it was slow progress. I thought about cutting loose the repair materials Rikard was tied to, but if we didn't get the tank fixed we were screwed anyway. Halfway to the ship, I blasted backward to counter the thrust, carefully reducing our velocity to avoid the materials whipping us around after they overtook us.

Then the thruster died partway into the second blast.

We were still closing. The problem was that we were approaching too fast. I twisted several times, wrapping the line around us both, knowing there was no way we'd hang on to each other at the speed we were traveling.

"Get ready!"

It felt like it took hours, but it must have been only a few seconds. The tank wall slammed into me and pain crashed through my body. The next thing I knew Rikard was yelling my name over the radio.

"Ballen?"

"Yeah. Still here." I groaned loudly. "Unfortunately."

We were still tangled up, floating not far from the tank. Not ideal but a whole lot better than it could have been.

"Hang on." I grabbed the rope and hauled us in slowly. Everything hurt, including several places I'd forgotten about. Sometime, about three centuries later, I reached one of the handholds and pulled us against the hull.

"You must have Croat blood," was Rikard's comment as we untangled ourselves.

"Well, I took cossack dancing lessons I took for my wedding."

Rikard laughed. "Wrong country, *mamlaz*."

It seemed crazy, but the real job was still ahead of us. We crawled along the hull, our progress slowed by being forced to use the handholds. When we got there, the tear in the tank was relatively small. This made patching it easier than it might have been, but it was still time consuming.

While I trimmed the edges of the rupture, Rikard pruned the inner "umbrella" patch to size and handed it to me. After spreading sealant around the inner edge, I opened the "umbrella" inside the tank and pulled it back against the inside surface, then snapped off the handle and triggered the glue with a laser torch. While that was setting, Rikard cut a PlaSteel sheet to size to act as the outside patch.

The captain gave us a running countdown on the point of no return, which I suppose was meant to motivate us but felt more like the countdown to extinction. Finally, he announced we were out of time and I slumped against the tank surface. We were no more than fifteen minutes from finishing, but it might as well have been an eternity.

"No prize for second place..."

We glued the panel on, applying a heavy layer of adhesive to the perimeter and the umbrella patch so they'd form a sandwich I hoped would hold under pressure. Once cured, I told the captain to release the inner partition seal.

I held my breath, feeling the vibration inside the tank as the high-pressure liquid expanded into the repaired area. The patch held, and I clumsily slapped Rikard on the shoulder, making him jerk in surprise.

The engine room bulkhead was a much easier fix as it only had to hold pressure until we could patch it internally. I cleaned up the hole and slapped a pre-sized patch on it, again using the laser to weld it in place.

"Let's get back inside," I called over the radio.

It took about an hour to work our way back to the airlock, climbing along the side of the ship like ants. It was slow but I didn't think it was worth risking free-floating without the hand thrusters, especially as we'd already run out of time and there was no further rush.

Rikard was struggling, his pace dropping by the minute. I couldn't blame him; he'd already been through a lot and ZeeGee is always tiring. When the airlock opened he made no move to enter and I grabbed his suit by the shoulders to drag him in. The bulky gloves made hard work of it, and several times he slipped from my grasp. Finally, he was clear of the door and I propped him along one wall before sealing the 'lock and repressurizing. As the pressure returned, the moisture in the air froze against my suit, misting up my visor for several minutes until the heaters kicked in. When I could see again I realized Rikard hadn't moved. I threw my helmet and gloves off and shuffled over to him.

I could see he was conscious through the fog on his helmet, but his face was a mask of pain. I unlocked the seal and lifted the helmet to reveal his sweat-soaked head.

"Arm broken," he muttered.

For the first time, I realized how stiff his arm was and helped him carefully upright. It must have broken when we hit the side of the tank, and he'd been holding it back all this time. After squirming out of my suit and helping him out of his, I dragged myself down the corridor towards the MedBay—Rikard tripping and stumbling behind me as I pulled him along. As we got close I heard Dollie talking, almost in a whisper.

"...can't tell him."

"He deserves to know."

Rikard groaned and I missed the next few words of conversation.

"...your choice. I won't say anything."

"Delacort?" I shouted.

He slipped out from behind the curtain, his eyes avoiding mine and locking on Rikard.

"He needs help. Broken arm, maybe more."

Dollie came out from behind the curtain too, and I would swear she had a look on her face as guilty as sin itself. She moved to one side and held the curtain back. "Get him in here."

She held her head high, her neck stiff and eyes almost hostile. I waited for her to say something else but eventually gave up. "I need to take care of the engine room."

Delacort nodded, and I left them to help Rikard. At the engine room, one of his men was waiting outside the pressure door.

"Harris." He held out his hand. "The chief thought you might need some help. That was some piece of work you did out there. Me and the other guys want you to know how much we appreciate it."

Harris was an oval-faced guy with almost black eyes, who always looked to be a couple of days behind on shaving, despite regulations. I'd seen him hanging around with the other soldiers on board and he struck me as a bit of a wise-ass but seemed genuine enough at that moment. I shook his hand briefly, then turned to the slab-like bulkhead.

"Any experience?"

"My old man was a plumber. Taught me all about it before I signed up."

That wasn't a great deal of help, but at least it was practical. "Do what I say, and we'll be okay."

I checked the air pressure readings next to the door. They were still zero as expected, but it never hurts to double-check.

"We can't open the door until the pressure equalizes, but we can't let everything bleed in at once or we'll blow the patch off the outside wall."

"Got it."

I pointed to the rotary valve handle. "Can you work that while I watch the pressure gauge?"

"Sure thing."

Harris grabbed the small wheel and twisted, grunting slightly with the effort. Nothing happened apart from him nearly losing his footing in the zero gravity.

"You'll need to brace yourself."

He grinned. "Thanks, I already figured that out."

He wedged his feet into the corner of the opposite bulkhead and twisted. The valve turned fractionally but I saw no change on the pressure readout.

"I thought you soldier boys were supposed to be tough?" I pointed to an extension bar cradled alongside the valve. "The valves sometimes stick from lack of use, try that."

"You've got a great talent for passing out useful information after it's too late."

"Yeah...my wife says the same thing."

With the additional leverage, he cracked open the valve and the pressure indicator rose. "Okay." My eyes were glued to the pressure display. "A little wider."

The pressure increased quickly until it was at around fifty percent of normal, which was time to slow it down—the last thing I wanted was another spacewalk.

"Back it off a little. I don't want to blow the outer patch."

Harris turned the valve the other way, and the pressure increase slowed. A few minutes later the pressure equalized, and the indicator next to the door turned green.

I gave Harris the thumbs up and he closed the valve fully, placing the bar back in its holder.

"What next?" he asked, looking at me expectantly.

"Now we go in and hope the outside patch holds long enough to put a more permanent one inside."

"Okay."

He shuffled from one foot to the other, his hands flexing and unflexing. His nervousness was understandable—if the outer patch failed, anyone inside the room would have little time to get out again, and there wouldn't be a handy Ballen there to perform a rescue.

"Don't worry. I can take care of the patch myself."

"I'm not scared."

"I am. Your job is to pull me out if I get in trouble." I grabbed a patch kit and squared off in front of the door. "But the main thing is you can't risk the ship saving me. If you have to, you close that door."

Harris swallowed. "I can do that."

I opened the door and stepped through, closing it behind me. If the worst happened, I wanted to minimize the danger to the rest of the ship. First, I checked the corpse in the corner, which was crazy as there was nothing I could do for him. I rolled him over. The badge on his uniform said "Evans," one of the ship's crew. From what I'd heard, it was his first trip, and now also his last. A dark object fell from under him, bouncing lazily against the flooring. It was a small pistol.

I scooped it up and slid it in my pocket. Evans looked as messy as any decompression victim—his skin had frozen and the blood vessels in his eyes had burst from his body's internal pressure. I couldn't tell from a cursory look whether anything else had happened.

I shuffled over to the opposite corner of the engine room. The bulkhead formed a shallow alcove where several control circuits and conduits passed through to the reactor area. I squirmed around them and reached the outer bulkhead only by twisting awkwardly. I could see the hole and the patch through it. The patch had dished out as the pressure had been restored but no more than would be expected.

On the reactor wall opposite the patched hole was a round box. It didn't seem to fit the rest of the setup and I twisted around to get a better look. The case was about twenty centimeters long and half as deep. One end was chewed up and burnt, the casing half melted. It looked like a mining charge, but I'm not an expert so I could have been mistaken. It was stuck to the reactor casing but there was enough of a lip to allow me to slip a large screwdriver underneath and pry it off. It left a sticky residue of gray pressure sealant, the same as I'd used on the outer patches.

With the box out of the way, I cleaned up the edges of the hole and liberally coated the bulkhead and outer patch with sealant from the patching kit. It needed to be a good seal if it was going to take us to the asteroids and back. The "back" part of that deal was unfortunately now looking far less likely than the "to."

I pressed the patch in place. Sealant oozed around the perimeter, and I fried the lot with a small hand laser. The acidic fumes from the sealant caught in the back of my throat but meant the gunk was curing. After a couple of minutes, I picked up the possible mining charge and slid out from the mass of conduits. The engine room door slid open as I approached, and I saw Harris grin as I walked through.

"You did it again, Ballen." He gave me a lazy salute. "I'm sure glad you're along for the ride."

"Thanks. I don't think everyone on the ship feels the same, though."

He frowned, and I handed him the device I'd found attached to the reactor.

"Know anything about bombs?" I signaled the control room. "We're all good in the engine room. Check the diagnostics."

There was a few minutes' delay before Captain Medved replied. Around half of the ignition circuits weren't working and needed a restart to synchronize correctly.

"You better let Delacort see that." I pointed to the bomb. "I need to sort out these engines."

Harris nodded and hurried back down the corridor. After he left, I pulled the pistol out of my pocket and checked it over. It was a small projectile weapon, nothing top of the line or even current but still deadly enough. I couldn't tell if it had been used or not, but it was still loaded when I pulled the magazine.

I tucked it away and turned back to the engine control panel. The restart sequence was involved but simple enough. As I operated the controls, I tried to work out what might have happened.

Someone had planted a bomb and it had partially detonated. My best guess was the detonator had misfired for some reason. The intention must have been to knock out the main engines, but the misfire had screwed the plan. If it *had* gone off, it would have ended our trip. We'd have continued on our course with no way to slow down or get back. You can't exactly call for a tow truck in deep space.

When it exploded there'd been three people in the engine room—Delacort, Rikard, and Evans. Any of them could have planted the bomb, or it could have been someone else entirely, and they were unlucky to be caught when it misfired.

And what about the gun? It belonged to one of them, but which? Delacort would have his service firearm, though that didn't rule him out completely. As for the other two, anything would be a pure guess. As I thought about it, I realized the obvious suspect was Gabriella—who else would be willing to risk everything to stop us? She wasn't there when it detonated, but that didn't mean anything.

I heard the high-pitched whine from the injectors warming up, and a second later the engines fired. The indicator lights above each bank rippled through a red-orange-green sequence until they were all showing as operational. We had power again.

"Captain. The engines are back."

"Thank you, my friend. You did fine job today! *Hvala vam!*"

That might be true. But unless Evans was the guilty party, we had a killer on board.

Fifteen

Medved called us together in the cramped wardroom area, where we'd heard his welcome speech. Although some people knew what had happened, not everybody understood the implications. I edged in next to Dollie and slipped my hand into hers. For a brief moment she stiffened almost imperceptibly, then her hand squeezed mine.

Medved tapped on a table with his cup, a sharp plasticky click that brought silence to the whispered conversations around the room. I gave Dollie a quick kiss before turning my attention to the captain.

"Everyone in crew knows this—I hide nothing."

There were mumbled agreements from around the room, and Rikard clapped his meaty palm on his brother's shoulder.

"Damage to starboard fuel tank cost approximately forty percent of remaining fuel. If not for Ballen and Rikard we would have lost more."

A splatter of applause filled the room, and Dollie squeezed my hand a little more firmly making me feel jiggly inside.

Medved continued. "This means we cannot get back to Earth. No longer have enough fuel, but we still have mission. We *can* get to 1219-Britta. We have to. There is no choice."

"Will we be able to get back?" I didn't catch who asked, one of SecOps team, I think.

"Only if fuel is there."

An uncomfortable murmur drifted around the room.

"Commander Delacort tells me there will be fuel. How much is unknown. We *will* find a way back though—you have my word."

He hesitated and his wide face darkened. "More important. We have someone among us who wants to stop our mission. Someone willing to risk all our lives. I do not believe anyone on this ship would want to help *Tollers*, but it seems there is. Commander?"

Delacort stood and looked slowly around the room. "This was found attached to the bulkhead in the engine room." He held up the box I'd found earlier. "It's a standard mining charge. Used anywhere a controlled blast is needed. The intention seems to have been to knock out the ship's engines. If that had happened we'd now be drifting in space. At least until our O2 ran out.

"Someone on board is a traitor and a saboteur. I'm sure I don't need to explain the implications, but this ship is under military law. Which gives me the authority to airlock whoever is responsible."

The room was as quiet as a man who's come home to find his house empty and his wife missing.

"If the person wants to make themselves known, now or privately, I guarantee they'll be taken back to Earth for a fair trial."

No one said anything and, after a couple of minutes, Delacort dismissed us and everyone moved towards the doors. After my exertions, I was ready to sleep till we *hit* an asteroid, but first I wanted to speak to Dollie. We needed to clear the air. While I was dangling on the line outside, I'd vowed not to let things fester any longer.

"Join me in my bunk?" I said.

Dollie lit up momentarily, then her expression changed. "I better not. You must be tired and I...well, all of this has me on edge."

I couldn't remember a time when Dollie had even hinted she didn't want to be alone with me, and it stung deeply.

"Dollie? What—"

"Sorry to interrupt." Delacort had joined us. "We need to talk, Ballen."

"Go away," I said.

"It's okay, Joe. I'll see you later."

Dollie moved towards the exit. I wanted to grab her but didn't. "Wait, Dollie. *We* need to talk."

She didn't stop, and I watched her walk away, while Delacort did a good impression of a broken security pickup—looking everywhere but at me. I took several long breaths before turning my attention fully to him. "I guess you got me."

We joined up with the captain and made our way through the tight corridors to the control room. It felt like I was being marched to a court martial or something equally pleasant. Once there, everyone spread out as best as possible in the small room, but it was a good thing no one had brought a cat.

"That was a great piece of work you did, Ballen. We owe you." Delacort smiled, but his gray eyes showed concern. "There are a couple of things we didn't mention at the meeting. The crew are edgy enough as it is."

Rikard shuffled in looking pale, his injured arm tightly strapped in an inflatable cast. "Harris tell me come." His voice wavered slightly. "I should leave."

"Stay, Rikard," Delacort said. "I hate to think where we'd be if you and Ballen hadn't sealed that tank. Likely heading for a graveyard orbit somewhere between here and Mars."

"What's the salvage bonus for saving a USN ship and crew?" I nodded towards Rikard. "Not sure about Rikard, but I could use the extra credits. My last venture was a bust."

"Don't want. Not right," Rikard responded flatly.

"That's settled, then. More for me." I leaned back against the nearest bulkhead.

"Do you ever take things seriously, Ballen?" Delacort shook his head.

"I take survival seriously. What's this about? I have a wife I haven't spoken to in several hours, and she's as dangerous as a near-Earth grazer."

Delacort took a half-step back. "Please explain, captain."

Medved tapped the control panel. "Pick up trace signal. Very weak. Only use passive sensors, avoid detection—not good at looking for things."

"Makes sense," I said. "What type of signal?"

"Thermal signature. Similar to Sarac, but weak."

"How similar?" Delacort asked. "Can you show us?"

Medved tapped the controls and brought up a recording of the trace on one of the screens. It was faint for sure.

"What you think, Ballen? It ghost signal, *da*?" Medved moved back so I could take a closer look.

"It tracks with our maneuvers?"

He nodded.

"It could be a sensor ghost or a leak in one of the systems throwing out a shadow reflectance." I moved away from the controls. "Anything else?"

"Only appear when we change course. Has been there since we leave Earth."

That appeared to nail it. A ghost signal would more than likely show up when Sarac was putting out its biggest signal profile, which would come while we were maneuvering.

"That could give away our position," Delacort grunted. "Ballen, can you check the shielding of the onboard systems?"

"Sure. If I start now, I'll be finished by doomsday." I shook my head. "Do you know how many systems could cause a leak like that?"

"Small needle, big haystack." Rikard clapped me on the back. "We both check."

"You said a couple of things?" I looked from Delacort to Medved. "What was the other?"

There was a long pause, but it was Medved who finally answered. "Fuel. Things bad."

He brought up the 3V astrogation display and outlined the problem with few words. Not only had we lost fuel, but the leak had acted as a thruster and pushed us off our original course. At a constant one-tenth gee we'd have made the crossing to Britta in around eleven days. Now, we'd have to use some of our fuel to correct our heading, pushing it out to around sixteen days or possibly more, including a coasting phase. It could be done but wouldn't be easy, and it also gave the Atolls more time to find us.

"Options?" I said.

"We go Ceres." Medved pointed at the display. "Slingshot around it and Mars, then back to Earth. Course change same."

"That won't work, captain. Look at the orbital profile." Delacort gestured at the track inside the 3V. "We'd have to cruise most of the way. We'd be a sitting duck for any Atoll cruiser. Not to mention we'd be abandoning our mission."

"You guarantee fuel at Britta?" Medved said.

"You know I can't. The information I have says there should be enough to refill our tanks and give us fast passage back to Earth, but I've never been."

"So, we go Ceres and Earth."

"This is still a military mission, captain." Delacort thumped the bulkhead next to him and grabbed the stanchion as he bounced away in the LoGee. "I'm the one giving the orders. Didn't you say so?"

"*Da. Da.* But different now." The captain nodded at Rikard. "We have injured people. Damaged ship. Low fuel. Low supplies. Low oxygen. Cannot carry on. *Glupa budala.*"

"What was that?" Delacort steadied himself.

I wasn't sure if he understood the words any more than I did, but the tone was enough to convey the insult. "I didn't come up here to babysit. If you guys want to fight, I'm out of here. But there's another option."

Delacort stepped back, and Medved shrugged. "I listen."

I manipulated the view controls on the 3V display, zooming in on the gray sphere representing Ceres and pointed to a blue marker circling the dwarf planet. "Isn't that an Intermediary Station?"

Delacort brought up the data display to confirm it. "What good does that do us? Atoll property."

Sometimes I wonder why certain people are incapable of even the slightest bit of creative thinking. Intermediary Stations dotted the Belt and reached far out into the solar system. They were used to store fuel by the Atolls for their deep space exploration and resource harvesting operations. Essentially, they were floating fuel depots in space, refilled by automatic tankers brought there on highly economical orbits from easily accessible hydrogen sources such as Saturn and Jupiter's moons.

"We steal!"

Captain Medved might be a curmudgeon, but he could see the obvious when it was thrown in front of him. Delacort, on the other hand, shook his head, his jaw tightening.

"We can't steal Atoll fuel. First, I can't authorize it. Second, don't they use different rigs?"

The first part was irrelevant, though the second part was true enough. The Atolls defined their own standards for space technology decades ago, deliberately ignoring most Earth-based guides. The stations would undoubtedly use equipment incompatible with what we had on Sarac.

"We have manufacturing facilities on board, presumably?" I said.

Medved took a while answering. "*Da.* Sure. RepliSys, old but work."

"Then we can make an adapter."

Rikard spoke up. "RepliSys my duty. I help."

"That's okay with me." I was happy to have someone to check my work. "My experience is more in large-scale construction."

Delacort moved between me and the 3V display. "Even if you can jury-rig something that works, do you think we can just sidle up and take their fuel?"

"Sure, why not. Do you think the Atolls bother locking the doors all the way out here? Each one of those stations holds over twenty thousand cubic meters. Plenty for what we need."

"You'd have to do another EVA. No one else is qualified except Rikard, and he can't handle it now." Delacort rubbed his chin. "You okay with that?"

"It's good to be needed."

The captain and Rikard laughed, but Delacort was stone-faced. While everyone was distracted, I decided it was a good time to get some answers to questions I still had. "What happened in the engine room?"

"I went to retune engine fuel curves. Brother want more power. *Uvijek više snage!* Evan was there. Act strange. Working on side of engine. Ask him what he doing, and he get angry. Start shouting. Then commander came. Minutes later explosion happen."

Delacort nodded. "I was heading to my bunk and heard the shouting. When I got there Evan and Rikard were going at it. There was a flash, and the next thing I remember I was coming around after you dragged me out."

That cleared things up. Evans had been planting the bomb

when Rikard interrupted. "What do we know about Evans?"

"First trip with me." Medved turned to a data screen and tapped in a query. Evans' profile popped up on screen. "Twenty-two. Graduate a few months ago. Worked for TH Orbital for a while, but want to work deep space. Applied for transport run with Sarac and we brought him in."

That caught my attention. "This was before the ship was commandeered by the USN for this mission?"

Medved nodded.

"That doesn't mean anything." Delacort shrugged. "He could've been bought by the Atolls after news got out."

It was true. The Atolls had deep enough pockets to buy just about anyone if they wanted to. With the way the world was, it was a case of *me first* for most people. Brin was a perfect example, but undoubtedly not the only one.

"We're lucky you interrupted him before he could finish." Delacort looked at Rikard. "We could still use the extra speed if you're up to it. I'll help."

We'd been fortunate, certainly. Spaceships are no longer the flimsy tin cans they were a hundred years ago but are still highly vulnerable. The need to minimize every kilogram meant there was little redundancy in the systems to combat physical attacks. One properly placed charge or even some well-targeted work with a wrecking bar would be enough to wreck the ship or disable it beyond repair. I might have been the best engineer outside Earth orbit at that moment, but there's only so much you can do without the proper facilities.

How any Earth person could side with the elitist Atolls, I wasn't sure. Even if you allowed for their *here first* claim, they didn't own space and it didn't give them the right to subdue the rest of humanity. But I guess there's always someone willing to put their own selfishness above everything else in exchange for a fat payoff.

"So that's the plan?" I looked around. "Rikard will work on the engines, while I design an adapter."

Everyone was in agreement, though Delacort still looked grim. I dragged myself through the hatch and down to the bunks. I was exhausted and wanted nothing more than to climb into mine and sleep for ten hours straight. But before that, I wanted to straighten things out with Dollie.

Of course, nothing is ever plain sailing twixt man and maid. When I reached Dollie's bunk the curtain was tightly zippered. I knocked lightly on the bulkhead next to it, but there was no response. I tried again, my knuckles making a harsh rap on the composite wall.

"Go away, Joe."

I should have listened, but I'd had enough of the secrets. "We need to talk."

"No. *You* need to talk. I need to sleep."

"Whatever's wrong, we can discuss it." I thought about forcing the zipper open. "We can't keep avoiding whatever it is that's bothering you."

"Joe, you're looking for a fight, and I'm not interested. Go and get some sleep."

Her voice had changed, deepened into the male register of her vocal range. A warning if ever there was one, but I wasn't about to back down. "I'll wait here all night, if necessary."

"Don't add *stupid* to the rest of your unattractive qualities."

"Jesus, Dollie. What the hell has gotten into you?"

"Good night."

I tried to get more out of her, but she refused to answer. After five minutes of the silent treatment, I moved over to my own bunk, but in the ten steps it took I changed my mind and decided to drag myself off to use the ship's inadequate resistance gym—hoping I could work up a sweat and push myself to the point where I was so exhausted I stopped thinking.

As I passed the wardroom, I heard low voices and looked in. Harris was there with several of the other SecOps team.

"Hey, join the party, Ballen."

The slightly loose sound to his voice suggested they had something stronger than coffee in their cups. I hesitated, then decided it was my turn to be stupid and not make an excuse.

There were two bags on the table. One contained a disgusting puce-colored powder, while the other was similarly filled, but the contents were an only slightly more attractive lime color.

"We got whiskey and tequila." Harris pointed to the relevant bags. "Sorry, it's dried. Best volume-to-weight money can buy."

I grabbed a cup, threw in a shovel of the reddish powder, then added water and sealed the top before shaking the noxious mixture. The first swallow nearly burned through my esophagus, but I held it down and took a second. "That's truly disgusting."

"Cheers." Harris raised his plastic cup. "It's the best you'll find west of the Belt."

"You're probably right." I took another swallow, glad the caustic brew had already cauterized my throat and taste buds. "Any port in a storm."

Harris grinned. "You sure are sailing through stormy weather, Ballen." He waved his cup towards the other two. "Carlysle and Safi."

I raised my cup in response. "Good meeting you."

"Nice job out there today, Ballen." Safi also had a cup of the red stuff and gulped half of it down. He looked entirely unlike a soldier until you saw his laser-beam blue eyes measuring you up for the kill. "If it were me, I'd have patched the inside first and then worried about the outside. You'd have had internal pressure to—"

"Ahhh shaddap, you deviant. You don't know shit about *internal pressure*." Harris threw a SootheStick at Safi, who caught it with a deft swipe of his lean arm and sucked it alight. "Fair warning, Ballen—don't get caught in the shower with him. You know?"

"Mr. Ballen might enjoy Safi's *company*." Carlysle lit up a SootheStick of his own, taking care to ensure it was catalyzing evenly, then gestured at Safi. "You seem to be suffering from some serious errors in your life plot."

"Neck off. You know I don't touch no one on a mission." Safi refilled his cup and spooned in some of the lime powder. "Don't listen to them, Ballen. They're the only ones around here that can't keep their pants zipped."

Carlysle's eyes darted across to Safi, then almost as quickly returned to a neutral state. It could have been an unintentional movement, but Safi moved back a little in his chair.

"Talking of. What's the story with the Aussie slim?" Harris

leaned closer. "She available?"

"That depends on who's asking." Gabriella appeared in the doorway. "*She's* quite choosy. Is this a boy's only jerk-off, or can anyone join the fun?"

The look of sheer panic on Harris' face almost made me choke on the mouthful of "tequila," and my eyes stung as I forced it down. There was a moment of mad scrambling as the SecOps guys all tried to make room for Gabriella to sit next to them. Carlysle and Safi almost fell over each other as they pulled on spare chairs stuck to the carpeting.

"Sorry about that." Harris flushed. "No disrespect intended."

"I gave up being offended by men a long time ago." Gabriella perched on a seat the guys had placed between Harris and me, much to the dismay of the other two. She grabbed a cup and filled it almost to the top. "Cheers."

She drained the cup dry and refilled it immediately. Apparently, her aptitude for violence was matched by her tolerance for alcohol.

"Pleased you don't hold a grudge." Harris leaned a little in his chair in a movement I guessed was supposed to be a bow, but was rather awkward in ZeeGee.

"Life's too short for grudges." Gabriella leaned closer to Harris until her lips were almost touching his. "Call me Australian again and you'll lose these. I'm English."

Harris tensed up, and I realized Gabriella had a short knife pressed against his crotch. A bead of sweat rolled lazily down his temple. His eyes widened, and he looked at me as if to ask if Gabriella was being serious.

I shrugged. "I wouldn't risk it if I were you."

"I love pretty boys, darling. But sometimes I like to play rough. Ballen knows all about that."

Harris tried to pull back, but his chair was firmly stuck to the floor and he couldn't without overturning himself. "Sorry, it won't happen again."

Carlysle and Safi broke out laughing—almost loud enough in the small room to need earplugs. Carlysle in particular had a deep, booming guffaw that reverberated around the room like he was warning away sailing vessels.

"Did I see that?" Carlysle was shaking so much he almost dropped his drink tube.

"Looked like it to me. *Studly* Harris goin' belly up." Safi was giggling as he spoke.

Harris scowled. "Shove it, you guys."

"All's fair in love and...war..." Carlysle was still shaking. "Isn't that what they always say?"

Gabriella leaned back in her seat again, amusement curling the corners of her perfectly pouting lips. After a few more drinks the wardroom took on a distinctly party-like atmosphere, and I felt I was taking part in a bizarre rite of Bacchanalia, a hundred thousand kilometers from the real world.

Harris brought out his Scroll, which was loaded with an amazing assortment of music—running the gamut from old bluegrass to the latest StonkThresh. Gabriella flitted from one soldier to another, acting the social butterfly as she danced with each of them in turn. She even managed to make Safi's lanky frame look almost competent on the dance floor.

Harris decided it was his turn and went up to extricate Gabriella from Safi's clutches, but the dark-skinned soldier wasn't ready to relinquish his hold, and they started dancing a threesome—bumping and grinding to some ancient pop song I couldn't identify. This culminated with all three of them almost falling over each other, and finally, Safi relinquished the floor to his rival and staggered back to sit next to me.

"I went outside first to save as much fuel as possible—didn't make sense to leave the bulkhead unpatched." I lifted my cup. "You knew Evans?"

Safi nodded as though he were a heavenly sage, his eyes slightly unfocused. "No."

"Carlysle said you did." It was a lie, but I was willing to risk it. Carlysle wouldn't remember clearly, he was that far gone. I'd been pacing myself—Gabriella's presence had me on edge—but in all truth, I wasn't in much better condition.

"Carlysle's a dick." Safi slurred the words a little. "It was nothing. A bit of relaxation, you know. Christ, it wasn't like we were active. Just babysitting."

I didn't say anything. Safi had reached the point of lubrication where prompting wasn't necessary. He grabbed my arm and squeezed it, pulling himself nearer, and I could smell the slightly sour whiskey warmth on his breath.

"It was only a thing, you know? That's all. He was lonely, first trip out. Lonely and, you know...And I wasn't against it. He was cute. Like a puppy. I didn't chase him, though. He came to me, you know?"

"What do you think happened in the engine room?"

"No idea. A bomb? He didn't seem the type. Quiet. Bookish. Except when, you know? Used to have to remind him to keep quiet. My turn!" He stood, unsteady with the mix of LoGee and alcohol. "You know what, though? He was terrified of Delacort. Dunno why. The boss is cool, but Zane...Evans, I mean, didn't want him to know about us. Like anyone would'a cared. Kinda shy, you know?"

The music changed to a fast tropical beat and Safi pushed himself upright once more. "Hey, we're playing my song."

He shimmied over to the dancers and grabbed hold of an unprotesting Gabriella, leading her into a fast series of shuffles and spins. My head pounded as the alcohol hit me full on, and the room started turning in its own orbit around me. Harris and Carlysle sat down opposite.

"It was Cardo, not Flynn," Carlysle said.

"Bullshit. Flynn was the lead pitcher in ninety-seven." Harris turned to me. "Tell him, Ballen. Ninety-seven Admirals. Who pitched that year?"

I had no idea, but it didn't matter as Gabriella passed close at that moment, shaking herself to the hot Latin beat and bumping hips with Safi.

"What an ass..." Harris cooed.

Carlysle wasn't about to dispute the observation and in fact whooped his agreement, his eyes following Gabriella's lithe gyrations, so I was pretty sure the comment wasn't aimed at Safi. I slid out of the chair, lifting myself carefully to my feet. "Time I was heading out, guys. Don't do anything I wouldn't do," I called out as I wobbled towards the door.

Several loud jeers accompanied my exit, and I stumbled down the corridor assaulting several inoffensive bulkheads on the way. I took a couple of wrong turns but finally found my spot and poured myself into my bunk.

After zipping the curtain, I lay awake in the darkness, unable to relax despite the alcohol. The ship wasn't supposed to spin for artificial gravity, but it appeared to be doing just that. It was a stupid idea, and I needed to find Medved and make him stop, but couldn't find the strength to slide out of bed again.

My thoughts entered their own independent free fall. Something didn't add up. If Evans was this innocent, shy guy getting romantically involved with Safi, would he try to blow up the ship? And why was he scared of Delacort? Sexuality was entirely a matter of choice. It wasn't like the bad old days of prehistory. Even if Delacort wasn't tolerant, he'd be up on a grievance charge so fast his head would spin if he did or said anything untoward.

I wished I hadn't thought about the ship spinning, as my head went on another waltz. There were too many things crowding my thoughts to keep them all straight. I fell into a light sleep disturbed by flitting dreams. Sometimes I was in the engine room watching Evans plant the bomb, unable to stop him. Sometimes I was fighting with him and Delacort. Everything shifted in a way that only happens in dreams, and I became Evans, fighting with Delacort and Rikard.

The bomb went off and I heard the bulkhead slowly tear open, like a metallic zipper coming undone. Then the escaping atmosphere brushed across my skin, goosebumps prickling my arm and torso. I felt a pleasant warmth press against me, the intoxicating touch of naked skin brushing against mine. A moment later I caught the delicious fragrance that seems to be the genetic birthright of women.

I was in the euphoric state halfway between sleep and awake where everything seems perfect. The nakedness rubbed against me like a giant cat, stimulating my skin deliciously. A hand slid down my body and I felt myself responding, as a set of warm lips pressed against mine and I kissed back. "Dollie..."

The hand stopped, and I roused, almost unwilling to leave the cozy semi-dream world.

"That's twice you've insulted me like that, Joe. It's enough to make a girl feel unwanted."

"Gabriella? What the hell?"

"Relax, Joe." She pressed her body more firmly against mine. "It'll be good. I promise. Or we can play rough if you like. I don't mind either."

I pulled back as far as I could inside the confines of the tiny cubby, suddenly fully awake. "You're forgetting I'm married."

She nuzzled further into my chest. "That sounds like a good idea. Let's forget it."

"That's not how it works."

Gabriella sighed almost imperceptibly. "Well, perhaps you should check where your wife is right now."

"What do you mean?" I grabbed her elbow as she moved to leave.

"Things aren't always how they seem, Joe. Even with me."

With that, she was gone. For a few minutes I sat there, unsure what to do. Then I pulled my pants on and made my way to Dollie's bunk.

It was empty.

My head was still thick, and my throat felt like I'd been gargling sulphuric acid, so I headed to the small kitchen. I passed several of the other cubbies silently in my bare feet. They were all quiet but as I approached the last one I heard whispers from behind the fabric. It was Delacort's bunk and I could hear his voice and one other. I couldn't make out the actual words and crept forward, somehow knowing I'd recognize the second voice even before I did.

My stomach danced, and it wasn't from the alcohol. My hands tightened into fists without me even realizing. Then I turned and headed back to my own bunk, almost hoping Gabriella would still be there.

Sixteen

Dollie didn't show up for breakfast the next day, and to be perfectly honest I was glad—I didn't want to think too much about where she'd been. My head felt like someone had tunneled inside and was digging their way back out with a rusty iron spike. Gabriella came in a little after me, looking fresh and rested, as if she'd returned from a long vacation.

"Those soldier boys sure know how to party," she said, scooping up some scrambled re-constituted egg mix and spooning it onto her toast. "I like men with real stamina."

I winced at the volume of her words. "I must be a big disappointment. Seems to be my position in life."

"Well, well. Do I detect a note of bitterness from the always positive Mr. Ballen? Did he learn something while he was creeping around in the dark?"

"Shove it, Gabriella. I'm not in the mood."

"I saw that in your lack of performance last night." She smiled and sipped on a tube of juice. "You should have taken the chance while it was there. Some offers don't get repeated." Gabriella looked around theatrically. "How strange. Commander Delacort is missing breakfast. I *do* hope he didn't have a disturbed night."

My only response was to growl into my coffee. The harsh lighting in the wardroom wasn't helping my head, and quite honestly, all I wanted was for Gabriella to take her insinuations somewhere else.

"I was watching Corporal Harris and some of the others working out earlier. It was most...stimulating."

"I'm sure they'd be happy to hear that. Why don't you tell them?"

Her mouth tightened. "It's about time you smartened up, Joe. I'm the perfect match for you."

"You're a perfect match for a rattlesnake and as dangerous to be around."

"That's what makes me so much fun. How about a rematch?"

"Not even wearing a full-body isolation suit."

Her hand flew out. Maybe she'd have connected when I'd first met her, but my amputations were almost fully rehabilitated, and I caught her wrist, holding it tight enough to stop her without hurting.

"You're wasted on that *maffer* bitch, Ballen. I could make things very nice for you."

"Right up until you slit my throat."

In my experience, all women are volatile at times but other than Dollie, Gabriella was the most mercurial person I'd ever met. The tension in her arm vanished, and her cheeks dimpled, returning to her normal seductive beauty. As attractive as Sheba, and as deadly as a black widow.

"I like men too much to do that." She rested her hand against mine, her smile mischievous once more. "Unless you stopped satisfying me, of course."

I had little doubt she meant it. "See what I mean? Death by performance anxiety."

Gabriella giggled, looking like an evil seductive angel. "I'm sure I could provide the right... stimulation."

I was thinking of an appropriate response when a breakfast package clattered onto the table next to us.

"Not interrupting anything, am I?"

Delacort stood over my shoulder. His eyes were puffy and had the same look I see in the mirror after an all-nighter with Dollie.

"Feel free," I said coldly.

Gabriella still had her hand covering mine. Finally, she pulled back but didn't rush to break the contact.

"You look rather tired, commander," she said innocently.

"I don't sleep well in LoGee. Makes it difficult to get up sometimes." Delacort yawned as he opened the packaged breakfast and pulled out a slice of peach.

"I doubt you have too many problems getting it up. What do you think, Joe?"

My teeth crunched on the rim of my plastic cup, but I refused to rise to Gabriella's bait. "No doubt he was hard at work."

"Oh yes...very *hard*, I'm sure..." Gabriella batted her eyelashes, then stood. "I better run along, I'm booked for the treadmill. Would you like to watch me sweat, Joe?"

I waved her away and she strutted out of the room, managing to embed an attractive swish into her walk despite the difficulty of moving in low gravity. Delacort's eyes tracked her rear like a targeting laser and only slowly came back to meet mine.

"There are times," he said, "when I wish I wasn't married."

"Perhaps you should spend more time remembering you are." I drained the bitter dregs of my coffee.

"Me?" He snorted. "You two looked pretty intimate when I arrived."

"We have a long history." I crumpled my cup. "None of it good."

Delacort nodded slightly. "Right..."

"I need to get to work. Designing the adapter will be like a 3D puzzle on steroids."

"We're depending on you."

"You should remind Dollie of that."

Delacort opened his mouth but nothing came out.

Not for the first time I wished Logan was around. Other than Dollie, he was the one person who could always set me straight. No matter how difficult a situation might seem, he always saw a way around it, as though he could see through the immediate circumstances and look at things from every angle. I wondered if I'd ever see him again. The way things were going he was probably already dead, his corpse a block of ice inside the frozen rock of the Britta asteroid. My stomach churned as the alcoholic excesses of the previous night reminded me of my stupidity. *Damn you, Logan.* I needed a friend in the worst way, and the only one I had available was—I tried to push the thought away but couldn't. Dollie had been with Delacort last night, and I better get used to the idea.

He was still picking at his breakfast pack, and I could swear he was smirking at me. My hand clenched into a fist under the table and I stood, my arms trembling. I turned without a word and made my way to the shop.

The adapter to bridge the two fuel systems was at once both incredibly simple and complex. The male plug on all Earth-based connectors is a straightforward Zero-G twist-to-seal latching mechanism, complicated only by a few sensors to detect pressure and flow, so the fuel delivery switches off automatically. The system the Atolls used was more complicated, making use of a retractable-tooth lock, with similar sensors and, of course, is a completely different bore and depth. There was little between them in a practical sense, though the Atoll one to me seemed expensively over-engineered.

The specifications for the Sarac's connector were easily available through the on-ship database, and I pulled them up on the large 3V in the grandly titled "Fabrication Shop." It wasn't much. There was a bench with some fairly standard ZeeGee compatible tools, along with the RepliSys unit that dominated one wall with its cubic assembly area and material hoppers.

I'd used almost the exact unit when I was training in the Small Scale Engineering class one semester, but it was a long time ago, back when I thought a twenty-credit shirt was dressing up. Like all students, I'd learned on dated equipment that barely functioned and didn't have the advanced features typical in the professional world. Once I'd started working, though, I soon acclimatized to the more sophisticated environment.

The Sarac's system was awkward but could create workable copies or original pieces with twenty-micron accuracy, using a variety of materials depending on what the hoppers were filled with. I checked the supplies and we had a decent amount of general ABX plastic, along with a smaller supply of the more useful powdered PlaSteel-HP.

The PlaSteel was a lot stronger than the ABX and could be sintered using a built-in laser baking system for greater strength, but it was also heavier and bulkier. Which was why it was in smaller supply. Right then, I'd have happily traded all the ABX and several crew members for more of the stronger material.

Finding information for the Atoll connector was a different

challenge. Usually, I'd hook into the world datanet and search for specs and drawings, but access was a problem. I could use an open channel medium-speed connection over radio or a slow quantum encrypted link. The data rate on the unsecured channel was much higher but I might as well switch on a locater beacon—the Atolls would spot us before you could say "Moogle." On the other hand, if I tried downloading it through a Q-Link, we'd be hitting Saturn before it was completed.

Several hours of searching through the onboard files turned up two partial specification references from different sources. It gave me about seventy percent of what I needed, the rest I'd have to guesstimate using basic principles and hope I was close enough.

After putting together the first rough simulations, I realized my stomach was protesting and I went to get some food. It was well past lunch, and I expected the wardroom to be empty, but when I got there Dollie was sitting in a corner picking at a bowl of noodles that looked like they'd been cold for some time. Grabbing a lunch roll, I sat down across from her.

"Hey, good-looking. Where've you been hiding?"

"Jesus, Joe. Don't start on me. Okay?"

"Start on you?" I tossed the roll on the table. "That wasn't even on my mind."

Her reaction was pretty unbelievable given the way she'd been treating me since we boarded the Sarac. I decided one of us should try to be an adult and clear the air. "What's with you and Delacort? Is it a passing fancy, or should I start apartment hunting when we get back?"

"What the hell do you mean?"

"Don't treat me like an idiot. I passed his bunk last night and heard you in there with him."

"You were spying on me?" She looked at me like she'd tasted one of Harris' alcoholic concoctions.

"I wasn't spying. I was on the way to the restroom and overheard you with him." It was only a slight lie. "I couldn't hear what you were saying, but I recognized your voice."

"You were listening in on a private conversation. That's pretty much the definition of spying. What next? You going to chain me to my bunk when you're not around?"

"You're my wife, I have a right—"

Dollie cut me off, her voice as cold as liquid helium. "You have no *rights*. We're married—you don't own me."

Despite my intentions, I was getting angry. "What about the secret phone calls?"

"Phone calls?"

"On Luna. The ones supposedly from Kinsella."

"You're being ridiculous and offensive. They *were* from Dr. Kinsella. You know I have to check in regularly. LoGee affects me in different ways from other people."

"And since we came onto Sarac?" I knew I was venting, but her attitude had disconnected my mouth's safeties. "You don't want to be near me. Now you're playing *hide-the-pickle* with soldier-boy in the middle of the night. Is he a good lay?"

Dollie threw her coffee cup straight at me. I ducked sideways, and the container flew all the way to the far end of the room before bouncing almost all the way back again in the LoGee. Luckily, the self-sealing lid didn't break, and the liquid stayed inside.

"Get out, Joe. Now." Her voice switched to baritone. "Before I forget I'm a lady."

"Seems to me you already did." I turned and stalked out of the room, the carpeting pulling at my feet as I marched back to the shop.

I closed the door behind me and sighed, wishing I could lock it—I needed an escape. All I wanted was some honesty, whichever way the cards came down. But every time I tried to broach the issue, it ended in a row. I'd never known such irrationality from Dollie before. Sure, she had her own ways of doing things and could be bloody-minded about following them—but not like this. The Dollie I'd fallen in love with appeared to have vanished on Luna along with Misty.

The Solido modeling was a good distraction from my thoughts. The adapter would be pretty bulky. Additive construction PlaSteel didn't have the strength to contain the pressures from the fuel tanks, not at a size I could output inside the limited manufacturing volume available. My plan was to design it, then section the model into printable sub-assemblies. The result would be an intersecting 3D "puzzle" locked together using a combination of dovetailing and large clamps. Crude, but hopefully enough to hold together long enough.

As promised, Rikard visited to check my ideas and spotted a few ways of interlocking further to add more strength. After making the changes, we ran simulations on *The Mess*, as I called the design, to check how it would hold under pressure. The results were disappointing.

"One percent margin?" I shook my head. "They'd take away my engineering license."

Rikard was still staring at the sim results, his heavy-lidded eyes focusing intently. "*Da*. One pressure spike and *poof*." He made an expanding gesture with cupped hands.

"Poof for sure." I entered the test parameters and ran a structural optimizer routine. That gained us exactly one-half of a lousy percent. "Hooray for the good guys."

Rikard looked grim. "We go back. No choice."

I didn't want to, but it looked like I would have to agree no matter how I felt. It hurt even considering it. I'm an engineer, a problem solver, a fixer—there shouldn't be things we can't do. Being unable to create a solution stabbed deep at my core and I slammed my fist against the side of the modeler. "Can't fix this. Can't fix my marriage. Not a good day, Rikard."

"Better off no women, only bring trouble. Stay away best."

"You could be right. You never married?"

"Sure. *Da*. I did." Rikard grinned, but there was no humor in his voice. "When I see her she say I space too much. Want divorce."

"That sounds familiar." I spun the 3V of the model around as if looking at it from different angles might bring enlightenment. It didn't.

"Men move in straight line. Make sense. Women different— curved. *Nepredvidivo*."

I didn't think Rikard was referring to the female exterior appearance, more the twists and turns worming around inside their heads. I sometimes wondered if you could map every thought and feeling, if it would look like a ball of very messy spaghetti. It was the same for both sexes, but somehow female spaghetti was a bolognese of a different order of complexity.

"Need nano-filament. Reinforce block," Rikard muttered as he mulled over the design.

"That's it!" I fed the extra information into the simulation, setting the parameters to assume the material was sandwiched layers of PlaSteel with nano-fiber reinforcing, and ran it again.

The numbers popped up on the display after a pause. "One hundred and eleven percent. There's the ten percent margin. You're a genius, my friend."

He looked at me as if I'd gone space mad, giving a fatalistic shrug. "No nano-fiber on board."

"Sure there is. Lots of it."

I met Delacort and the Medved brothers in the control room again. It was about the most private spot on the Sarac and the only place we could be reasonably sure of not being overheard. Though the expression on Delacort's face said *trouble* as soon as I walked in.

"Get voted out of the officer popularity sweepstakes again, or did your pet dog die?" I asked.

"There's still a traitor on board." Delacort's face was grim. "I found this hidden in the supply lockers."

This was an elongated black plastic box with a dull silver band running around the long axis. It looked familiar and I pulled the QuBee from my pocket—a smaller version of the box Delacort was holding. "Someone's broadcasting our location to the Atolls?"

"Worse." He tapped the box, making a plasticky clicking sound. "This one is equipped with a data port."

"Data? I thought quantum streams could only carry simple information?"

"MilSec doesn't advertise the fact, but the newest versions can carry coded information. Not high enough fidelity for voice or video, but it can carry strings of text. We've had them a couple of years. The Atolls had them earlier, of course."

"*Sranje! Moramo se vratiti. To nema smisla nastaviti.*" Rikard spat the words through clenched teeth.

"*Želite su Atola pobijediti?*" Medved gripped Rikard's arm.

"Moramo ići dalje."

"To je ludo. To je samoubojstvo! Crazy. Suicide!"

Rikard had switched back into English, but it didn't take much to guess the rest. He was right. It's almost impossible to hide in space, all you can do is make it difficult for your opponents to find you. But "almost" turns to "completely" when you have someone on board broadcasting your position, and bog only knew what else.

"Evans?" I asked.

Delacort shook his head. "Last activation was less than twenty-four hours ago, from what I can tell."

Rikard started barking at Medved in Croatian again. The conversation rapidly got heated until finally, Delacort held his hands up to quiet them. "We should restrict all non-military to quarters for the duration. Monitor their movements."

"Does that include my wife?" I asked innocently. "She likes to come and go as she pleases."

"Everyone."

"Seems a little impractical. Do we tie them up?" I was jibing at Delacort, and my motives were only partly sensible. "Also, what makes you think the military are above suspicion? Atoll credits and promises can lure many people. How about the captain or Rikard here? They could be in the Atolls' pockets. Are you going to restrict them? How about me? Am I under guard as well? I tend not to work too well as a prisoner."

Delacort took a half step back. "You're being ridiculous. All I mean is that we should take precautions; that's sensible under the circumstances."

"There's no intersection between sense and the military."

"I'm sure you have some suggestions of your own." Delacort folded his arms. "Joe Ballen saves the world...again."

I pointed to the transmitter. "I'd say put it back where you found it and don't say anything outside this room."

Medved shook his head and tutted, while Delacort laughed.

"That's brilliant, Ballen. Only a genius would suggest letting a spy carry on operating. Why the hell not?"

I waved at Medved. "Couldn't we could rig up a concealed optical pickup and feed the signal to the control room?"

"Sure. *Da.* Simple."

"I can set up," Rikard said. "During maintenance. No one know."

"Okay." I looked back at Delacort—he obviously wasn't convinced. "That limits the damage they can do. As soon as we know who it is, we grab them, confine them. Unless Ahab here would prefer to airlock them. I don't care."

Delacort grunted. "You're the one we should 'lock, Ballen."

"Thanks. I like you too."

I looked around. Medved nodded curtly, and Rikard gave a quiet *'Da.'* After a pause, Delacort nodded also.

"Okay, that's what we do. And not a word to anyone." I didn't think we'd have to look hard to find our suspect. There was one person on board well accustomed to selling her allegiance to the highest bidder, and I suspected she hadn't changed. "I can take a good guess at who it is, but possibly we can catch them in the act."

Delacort pushed the tracker back in his pocket. "So now you've saved us all again, Ballen. Why did you need to meet?"

"I need to take one of the cannon offline. The accelerators are wrapped with lengths of nano-fiber. I need it to finish the adapter."

"No." Delacort stood to leave, but I grabbed his arm.

"That's it? Not a single word of discussion?" I said. "I can strip the fiber from the induction coils and use it to reinforce the adapter. It's the only way I can make it with a big enough safety margin."

"There's no way I am authorizing the dismantling of our defenses. I should lock you up for even suggesting it."

"Go ahead, I could use the rest. But if you want to continue this mission, you don't have any choice."

"I trust Ballen. He show skills before." Medved gave a thumbs up. "We would be dead without him."

"I don't care if he's the reincarnation of Einstein. Those weapons are out of bounds. Permanently."

I smiled. I'd expected his reaction. "Can you breathe a laser beam? I hope so because that's what we'll be doing before we can get back. And you can scratch the rest of the mission."

"I understand. But it doesn't change anything."

"I didn't expect you to listen to me." I looked over at Medved. "Captain, what's the best we can manage with our current fuel supply?"

"You know choices. Slingshot back to Earth. Slowly. Or orbit Ceres until we run out of oxygen or power."

Rikard spoke for the first time. "I help Ballen. He good man. But we should go back. Safe option."

Delacort looked at each of us in turn. It was a hell of a responsibility for sure, and not one I'd want.

"Rikard may well be right." I nodded at the bulky Croatian. "We have a spy on board. The Atolls already know everything about us. It would probably be better if we headed back."

"Except it's not part of our mission profile."

There was something in Delacort's voice that made me think there was more he wasn't saying. I didn't know what it was, and to be honest I wasn't sure I wanted to find out. The control room fell silent. After several long minutes, Delacort's Scroll trilled softly, no doubt linked to his own military Q-Link. He opened it up and read something on the screen, his brow furrowing.

"That was a message from fleet," he finally announced. "They've detected an Atoll cruiser in a trajectory closely matching ours."

We didn't need that news at that moment. With an unknown traitor on board, low fuel, and a mission that might be the proverbial wild goose chase, we already had enough to deal with. If Logan was still alive, he was going to have to fend for himself.

"How long?" I asked the obvious question.

"They'll be about twelve hours behind us by the time we reach Ceres."

Allowing for the quality of intelligence I'd seen recently, that was nowhere near enough to give us a clear shot at refueling. I ran through the operation in my head. EVA would be around three hours once we achieved a matching orbit with the fuel station. Maneuvering would take at least twice that.

"Sounds like we're in for a fight whatever we do."

"And we're going to need that gun," Delacort muttered.

"We're not going to outgun them, and you know it. But unless you want to admit defeat and loop back to Earth, I need the fiber to reinforce the adapter. Your choice—lose a gun, go home, or float in space till we run out of air. Compromise that."

Delacort was silent, his jaw set like a block of lunarcrete. No one else spoke, and after several minutes of silence, he gave a sharp nod. "One gun. Only. I'll assign one of my men to help with the disassembly. Rikard, let me know when the optical pickup is in place. Captain, monitor the location around the clock."

With that, he turned and marched out.

Rikard wore his usual grim expression. "He does not like you, Ballen."

"But I'm a hero..."

Rikard let out a snort and clapped his hand on my shoulder. "*Da. Da.* My people have old saying. Enemy of my enemy, not always my friend."

Seventeen

The funereal gray sphere of Ceres hung off to the right, a giant ball of mud cracked and pitted as if baked in the glare of the sun over millennia. In this case, appearances weren't deceptive and there wasn't much there of interest to either us or the Atolls. It really was a ball of rock and ice. The bright spots in the Occator crater stared up at us like some baleful half-blind eye, but despite the fanciful naming, there was nothing fertile there.

The fuel storage unit floated in front of Sarac, looking like a giant silver barrel that dwarfed the ship entirely. It was self-contained and autonomous, the only regular visitors being automatic fuel delivery drones that kept the tanks topped up. The silver surface was encrusted with dark-purple solar arrays, which powered the small thruster units used to maintain its orbit.

At the "top" of the drum, there was the slight bump of the respite station, sticking up like a shallow nipple. From what I knew, the station could hold as many as a dozen people and was stocked with basic emergency supplies and medical equipment. Only a resource-rich culture like the Atolls could afford to leave such luxuries floating unused in space, in case someone wandered by. That said, I'd be more than happy to "plunder" the treasure trove given the chance.

I suited up by the main airlock, ready to face the rigors of going EVA again. The handheld maneuvering units had been recharged, and there was nothing left to stop me. It was a case of Super-Ballen-Rides-Again. I was a little surprised when Delacort helped me zip up my suit, keeping up a constant stream of chatter. Perhaps he was feeling lonely.

"Did I tell you about my sister?" he said. "She's got a couple of kids by this fathead husband. They're doing okay, got an apartment outside Toronto. But then suddenly he's never there. She's looking after the kids and everything, and he's nowhere around. Always *working*. You know what it means when a guy says that, right?"

"He might just be trying to do what he can to take care of his family." I readjusted the straps yet again, vainly looking for a more comfortable position.

"Come on. He's got to be running around with some cheap slitch."

"You're not around much for *your* wife, are you?"

Delacort stopped fastening the seals on my suit momentarily. "That's different, I'm in the service. I don't have any say in where I'm assigned or for how long. Would you treat—"

I looked up when he cut off and turned awkwardly in my P-Suit to follow his stare. "Dollie?"

She was standing by the inner bulkhead, her arms folded across her chest defensively. She looked tired and a little drawn, as if she hadn't slept well for several days. The nasty part of me did a flip imagining why she hadn't been sleeping, while the better part of me put it down to LoGee intolerance and insisted she looked as beautiful as always.

"Hi." After several days of nothing other than the occasional drink-pitching competition, that was the best I could come up with.

Dollie stared at Delacort and after only a moment of hesitation, he mumbled something incoherent and left. We stared at each other like a couple of nervous puppies, unsure whether the other was going to play or bite.

"You're going outside again."

I pulled on my thick gloves and worked on the seals. "Someone has to."

"And it *has* to be you, no doubt." Her voice was as hard as the vacuum outside the airlock

"I'd be happy not to take the risk." I checked the straps over my shoulders, making sure they were tight. "My plans include dying in bed being comforted by a flock of nubiles, but that's not in the cards right now."

"Is there still room for me in your flock?" she whispered.

My heart didn't beat even once before I answered. "Always."

"Even though I haven't been honest?"

"No more questions."

Dollie put her arms around me and squeezed tight. It was a pointless gesture as I couldn't feel much through the P-Suit, but one I appreciated more than anything right then. She lifted her chin, and I kissed her, long and deep.

"Dollie?"

"Shhhh..." She kissed me again. "I'll explain when you get back."

Delacort slipped back into view; we were out of time for romantic interludes. Dollie glanced at him and with one last squeeze was gone.

"Not sure what you've got, Ballen," he grunted. "But it must be something special to have someone like that so crazy over you."

"She's a very special woman. And I'm a very lucky guy."

Delacort had a grim expression on his face I didn't understand. I didn't even *want* to understand. All I knew was Dollie still loved me. And that was enough.

"The captain says the Atoll ship isn't on an attack vector anymore."

"They didn't follow all this way to wave while doing a flyby."

He handed me my helmet. "They'll do a breach and board."

That seemed likely. If they thought we had useful information, they'd close to effective weapons range and try to burn out or overload our defense systems. After that, strike teams would be sent to enter the Sarac and mop up the pieces.

"Are your guys ready?"

"They'll do as much as they can." Delacort tapped the pistol strapped to his belt. "If we can hold them off we will, but the G3 are animals."

The Atoll G3 were specialized forces trained for ZeeGee operations and their reputation was one of brutal efficiency. If they'd ever failed a mission, I'd not heard of it.

"I don't want you out there alone."

"I can take care of myself."

"Maybe. But you can't do that *and* set up the fuel rig."

"There's no one else." I locked the helmet in place with a loud click. "And if you're thinking of Rikard, he's too busted up. I'd have to nanny him *and* the rig."

"No one's qualified for engineering work. But someone *is* experienced in ZeeGee combat."

Gabriella trudged around the corner, her P-Suit already mostly zipped up. She held a scoped military rifle almost as tall as she was but handled it with the ease of long familiarity.

She smiled like a benevolent goddess, giving a loose approximation of a salute. "I've been drafted."

"Not a chance." I shook my head, not even looking at her. I hadn't forgotten what she did to Charlie, not to mention her other deceits. "I'm more likely to be her next victim."

"She's all I've got available." Delacort shuffled uncomfortably. "I need my team to protect the ship."

"I wouldn't hurt you, Joe. We're friends now."

I wasn't sure who I should worry more about—her or the G3. But Delacort was right. The job would be a lot quicker if I didn't have to fend off a bunch of berserker Atoll troops.

"Don't aim that cannon at me. I get nervous easily."

"I'll try. I'm not very good at this sort of thing, though." She snuggled the rifle coquettishly.

"If that's true, you owe a lot of refunds."

I clicked the visor shut on my helmet and Delacort slapped us both on the shoulder. "Keep him safe, Gabby."

Gabriella's demeanor changed in a microsecond, something I'd seen before. The girlish playfulness was gone, replaced by a hard edge that was ready to cut you up badly.

"Don't tell me how to do my job." She closed her faceplate, and her voice came over the radio. "Now you do yours, Ballen."

I knew she'd use everything she had to do what was necessary, and I understood she had no time for squeamishness. It was a brutal philosophy but on the other hand, dead is just dead, there's no honorable way to go. And there's no real difference between dying in bed or catching a railgun round in the chest. Space is so hostile, situations are usually pretty binary—on or off, yes or no, dead or alive. She lifted her gloved hand and we bumped fists. We were in this together, whatever the outcome. It was time to push aside personal feelings and work together. At least until later.

The thick bulkhead doors slid open, and once again I found myself facing the vast emptiness of the universe. Statistically speaking, space is empty—all the stars, planets, galaxies, and nebula represent less than a billionth of one percent of the volume we could detect. Everything we know, love, obsess, and fight over is nothing but the smallest of imperfections in an otherwise perfect void. No matter how often I saw it, it always made me feel insignificant and humble.

"How much space time have you got?" I asked Gabriella over the suit radio.

"I'm not the kind of girl to kiss and tell. Enough."

She slung the rifle over her shoulders and lifted both feet from the carpeting. A small push and she drifted through the hatch, twisting around expertly to snag a handhold on the outer hull. Seeing her move told me right away that she had plenty of experience and had done a lot more than a tethered tourist jaunt.

I detached myself and flipped around similarly, grabbing one of the many handholds scattered over the hull. Then I pulled the tethered bundle of the partially assembled adapter outside, thumbing the door controls to close the main airlock as soon as it was clear. Despite her proficiency, we needed to play it safe, and I activated the radio again.

"Stay tethered to me at all times. I don't need to get caught up in *another* rescue mission," I said.

"I always knew deep down you cared, Joe. Do you prefer your women tied up?"

My jaw tightened, everyone on the ship would be able to hear the transmissions, including Dollie. "Let's get this done."

Captain Medved's guttural voice sounded through the headset like the voice of doom. "Atoll ship will enter predicted weapons range in seventeen minutes."

The time available had shortened again. No way we could get the job done in under an hour—I'd estimated at least two. Moving as fast as we could, I led Gabriella along the side of the Sarac to the refueling point and triggered the release. The outer panel opened, and the fuel line appeared, crawling out from the side of the ship like a blind worm seeking the light. We hooked our safety lines to the end before it extended too far and let it carry us towards the distant fueling station.

Delacort's voice came over the comm. "Toller ship now in weapons range. Prepare for possible impacts. Activate all point defenses."

We crossed the last few hundred meters using hand thrusters, reaching the drum before any shots were fired. I wasn't sure why the Atolls hadn't attacked immediately when they came in range, but no doubt it wouldn't last, and they were simply assessing how dangerous Sarac might be to them.

I felt like a flea scaling Olympus Mons as we crawled the last few meters to the refueling point—the station was so large we were literally dwarfed. A manual activation panel opened when I pulled on it, and I used it to unlock the fuel nozzle. Once clear of the shroud it took a few minutes to attach the adapter, then spray VacSeal through all the gaps before tightening it around the nozzle. It had to seal completely or our journey would end right there. As I worked, Gabriella floated off to one side, sweeping her rifle around as she peered through the scope, looking for telltale heat signatures of enemy troops.

"Incoming." Delacort's voice buzzed in my headset and I looked up, unable to focus on the job knowing Dollie was somewhere in the middle of the attack. There wasn't much to see. Occasional flickers from the distant Atoll ship illuminated parts of the Sarac, and sometimes the weapons from our ship would flash an angry fusillade in response, though it looked very one-sided.

There was no doubt the Atoll ship could have blown the Sarac out of space easily, but as they wanted us alive it made their job much harder. It also gave us a fighting chance, though the odds were still against us.

"Turret one temperature critical," Delacort announced. "Firing missiles one and two."

An almost impossibly bright flare blossomed near the top of the Sarac, only to vanish a split second later as it flashed towards the enemy ship. The missiles detonated almost immediately, but at that distance, I couldn't see if it was a successful strike or the warheads had been destroyed by the enemy's point defense systems.

"Turret one. Offline."

The message reverberated inside my helmet. The confrontation was barely begun, and already a quarter of our offensive capability was gone. Building the adapter had sacrificed another turret, and I realized I had better make good on my decision.

I extended the umbilical several meters, riding the nozzle as if it were a horse and using my handheld thruster unit to direct it towards the Sarac's pickup. The umbilicals were stiff and hard to manipulate in ZeeGee, so I needed some slack to make the connection. Gabriella floated alongside, staying near, constantly scanning with her rifle.

"Focus on the fuel, Joe," her voice crackled over the radio. "Don't worry about me."

"Launching three and four," Delacort announced.

This time I didn't look up. Despite that, it was impossible to miss as the bright flash of the missiles lit up the surface of the giant fuel tank. I wrestled with the nozzles, fighting to bring them together, then caught a smaller flash of light close by and glanced up. Gabriella was scanning the area towards the Atoll ship more intently. Now and then, her rifle would discharge, the muzzle glinting briefly as the super-accelerated fléchette rounds streamed out of the barrel in deadly bursts that could rip a P-Suit or a man apart instantly.

"Keep working, Ballen," she called over the radio. "We haven't got time for gawping."

I pushed the bulky adapter into the Sarac's fuel port, grunting with the effort of moving the cumbersome fuel line. A half-twist locked it in place, then I tightened the clamps on my makeshift mess. It was time to find out if it worked.

"I need to operate the controls," I called to Gabriella, but she was too busy to respond.

Tracing my way back to the station, I reached the control panel and triggered the fuel release. Where the adapter connected to the Sarac's fuel port, a heavy burst of hydrogen exploded, forming an icy cloud around it. I zipped back along the line and added as much pressure as I dared to the clamps to minimize losses, though some was inevitable with such a patchwork setup.

"Breach. Deck four."

I didn't recognize the voice, it could have been Harris or possibly Safi, but I knew what it meant—G3 troops would be entering and making their way to take over the command deck, dealing with "targets of opportunity" along the way.

"Medved. Line attached—open the fuel port!" I shouted over the radio.

A few seconds later the cloud of frozen gas diminished as the port opened to suck in the fuel, and the pressure on the adapter lowered.

"Ballen!"

I heard Gabriella's shout as a shadow jumped over me, and someone grabbed me from behind. I twisted away, lashing out with my fist. His armored P-Suit absorbed the blow easily, but it did separate us momentarily.

That was enough. His helmet visor splintered as a stream of fléchettes from Gabriella's rifle hit it. There was no time for thanks or celebrations, we needed to get back inside the Sarac. The fuel delivery shouldn't take long.

We used the hand thrusters to hurry back to the airlock, not bothering to save fuel. As we did, Gabriella took out at least two more of the G3 soldiers. There might have been others, but I didn't see them.

"Onboard," I called out and punched the controls for the 'lock. The doors immediately slid together, the rumble of their movement vibrating through our feet.

"Prepare for acceleration. All hands. *Strognya akkelana.*"

Even the best fuel flow couldn't have filled our tanks in that time. I guessed Medved was making sure everyone was ready for when the transfer was complete. I moved to help Gabriella get her P-Suit off, but she shoved a pistol into my hand.

"We've been boarded," she reminded me.

I took the gun and helped her unzip while keeping an eye on the inner hatch. Once her suit was loose, Gabriella slid out of it like a cat and in the process treated me to several titillating moments that were entirely unnecessary. Then she unzipped me, standing guard while I shucked off my own suit.

We hadn't heard anything while we were inside the airlock, but when the inner hatch opened, the odor of trouble seeped in—a pungent mixture of acrid ozone from fried electronics mixed with the bitter stench of hot oil and melted PlaSteel. Normally I'd take it to mean a work crew was operating close by, but now it was evidence of a very different operation.

Gabriella let me keep the pistol as she removed the stock and long barrel on her rifle. This turned her weapon into a short carbine that was far more useful inside the tight confines of the ship's corridors. Once done, she led the way as we moved towards the control room.

There was a flicker of movement at an intersection ahead of us, and Gabriella's gun barked, the explosive sound painful in the tight space between the bulkheads. We moved up and found the corpse of a G3 trooper in the side corridor, a wide bloody splatter where his helmet faceplate had been. I had no idea how she'd even identified him as an enemy that fast. I'd barely caught the movement. But this was her specialty.

"Dollie?" I turned towards the sleeping quarters, but Gabriella stopped me.

"Stay behind me and watch our backs," she ordered. "You can't do anything on your own."

We had no other encounters, and when we reached the control room, Medved barely looked up. The flashing light from the displays reflected on his furrowed skin, making it look as though he had a weird dancing tattoo on his face.

"Seventy-three percent," he grunted.

"How long?" I moved closer, watching the tank gauge creeping up towards the full mark.

"Six, maybe seven minutes." He flipped several controls, programming in a full thrust departure maneuver.

I heard two distant *krumps* like a ripple of distant thunder. A few seconds later there was a wash of air as a pressure wave hit us. I scanned the displays anxiously but no breach warnings lit up.

"Concussion grenades," Gabriella said quietly.

"Sealing bulkhead doors," Medved announced over the ship's speakers.

He flicked several switches and the bulkhead closed behind us, shutting us off from the rest of the ship. I couldn't remember feeling so useless before in my life. I should have been with Dollie, protecting her from whatever danger came along. Like one of those ancient knights protecting his damsel. Not that I was much of a knight, nor was she much of a damsel, for that matter. Nevertheless, that's where I should have been. What man allows others to protect his wife while he hides, locked in a control room? I reached for the door overrides, but Gabriella put her hand on my arm.

"Stay calm," she said. "Dollie will be okay."

Every muscle in my body was tight to the point of bursting, and I took a deep breath, watching the last few bars of the fuel display turn green.

"Disconnecting." Medved pressed the controls.

I looked out through the narrow slit portholes and saw the explosive spray of a hydrogen cloud envelope the ramshackle adapter temporarily. The comm channel crackled into life, then a moment later an unfamiliar voice sounded.

"U.S.N. Sarac. This is Commander Brackeen of the ADF Bethe. Power down and lower your weapons. We are authorized to use lethal force, but I guarantee no one will be harmed if you cooperate."

"Destroyer of Deimos. *Jebi se!*"

Three years earlier, Brackeen had been the commander who'd "pacified" the ore processing station at Deimos, killing everyone on it including my old friend Charlie's brother. It was simply another moment of Atoll infamy in a long line of such, but Brackeen was still wanted for war crimes on Earth. There hadn't been a single soldier on Deimos station, and we weren't going to give the bastard an easy victory today, if we could help it.

Medved checked the displays. "Fuel line still attached." He tried the controls again. "Stuck."

I'd been worried this might happen. My original plan was to stay with the connector and babysit it through the disconnection process, but the Atoll attack made that impossible. The cobbled-together adapter *should* work, but there was a limit to what I could do in a small workshop. No matter how good your technology is, nothing is perfect, and tolerances can kill you as easily as major failures.

"Boost in Five. Four. Three. Two. One."

Medved worked on the controls and I grabbed a handrail nearby for support as the push from the main engines started. The Sarac's nose came around to take us away from the fuel depot, the fuel line stretching in slow motion between us. A tearing vibration rattled through the deck and walls, then the line split, spewing a torrent of hydrogen ice from the torn end as it whipped back and forth like a demented slow-motion cobra.

"Could you target a defense laser on that?" Gabriella asked, her voice quiet despite the confines of the small bridge.

I didn't like the suggestion, but it was certainly possible. The lasers were designed to take out incoming missiles, but with all the hydrogen from the tank, it might be all the "match" needed. I looked across at Medved to see if he'd heard her question. His face was grim.

"Do it."

I crossed to the weapons controls, overriding the auto-defense mode on laser three. I brought up the remote optical display, pointing the crosshairs at the end of the fluttering line. We were already leaving it behind as we accelerated forward. From the readouts on the main screen, the starfish-shaped Atoll cruiser was powering up to follow. My thumb hovered over the fire button and I looked around again, but no one said anything.

"This one's for Charlie's brother." I pressed the button repeatedly.

On the fifth or sixth volley, the beam caught a dense enough patch of hydrogen and a blue-white explosion lit up the bridge, blocking out the view of the Bethe. I wasn't sure if they were close enough to take any real damage, but I hoped so. The initial blast cleared for a few moments, revealing an intense gout of flame that engulfed the Bethe briefly; then I spotted a creeping red and white flame crawling along the fuel pipe towards the station.

I stabbed the collision warning, hoping everybody would grab hold of something as a second explosion filled the scene outside, obliterating the view of Ceres completely. When it finally died down, the Bethe emerged but was definitely not one hundred percent—the ship tumbled as it slowed.

"Captain, release the doors. We need to get to the wounded."

Delacort's voice came over the speakers. "Squad, by numbers, sound off."

The voice I wanted to hear wasn't going to appear in his roll call and as soon as the door unlatched I dived through it, rushing down to Dollie's berth. Halfway there I met Carlysle, struggling out of a side corridor into the main passage. He had a long gash on his forehead and was holding his arm awkwardly.

"You should see the other guy." He grinned, despite the blood oozing between his fingers. Then he saw the look in my eyes and pointed down the corridor. "Delacort moved her to the wardroom for safety."

I nodded my thanks and headed down the corridor.

The lounge was buzzing with activity. Several of the SecOps team were lying on makeshift bunks as Delacort moved between them, treating what injuries he could. I looked around and saw Dollie to one side—she was wrapping one of the soldiers' arms, the bright blue jelly of a trauma patch visible before she covered it.

She glanced up and our eyes met. For a second I thought she might cry, then she was a warm bundle in my arms. Our kisses ran the gamut from hunger through passion to tenderness and back again. I finally realized she *was* crying. And then so was I.

"Dollie...?"

"Don't say anything, Joe. It's not necessary."

"But—" Her kisses smothered my words.

Delacort coughed next to us. "We have injured people to take care of."

Dollie nodded but didn't let go of my hands.

"Joe, there's something..."

"Whatever it is, it doesn't matter. We're here, together."

There was a flurry of activity as two more bloodied SecOps men staggered into the wardroom. Dollie glanced at them, then turned back to me.

"I love you, Joe Ballen."

"Dollie?" Delacort called from where he was examining the newcomers.

Dollie ignored him, her hand warm against my cheek. "I'm pregnant, Joe."

It felt like the Sarac did an impossible three-sixty flip as I stood there, my mouth gaping open like an airlock. "You?" I searched her face. "We?"

She nodded, a huge grin appearing on her face. "Yes."

"But...How?"

Her eyes narrowed. "Was it that forgettable?"

Delacort was talking, but I was barely listening. Dollie's news was almost as much of a shock as our victory over the Atoll cruiser. By rights, neither one should have happened.

The Atoll ship was far more advanced than the Sarac, both in terms of weapons but also in terms of structural integrity. The blast from the fuel tank should have damaged us more than them, but our sensor readings said otherwise, reinforced by the snippets of radio signals we could intercept. While the damage wasn't fatal, it looked like the Bethe would be dead in space for some time.

Dollie's condition, on the other hand, was a shock for entirely different reasons. We'd never discussed children. Partly because I wasn't sure she was capable of having them, given her mixed up genetic make-up, and I didn't want to raise a potentially awkward subject. But partly because I happened to think such matters were entirely the prerogative of the lady in question—if she wanted to go that route and wanted me involved, she'd let me know. I also knew she'd been reversibly sterilized, which made her current situation even more mysterious.

Eighteen

One of the G3 boarding team had been taken alive. Delacort asked me to be involved in questioning him but after one session I knew it was pointless. Sergeant Ewin Paek was military through and through and loyal to the Atoll cause. There was no way he was discussing anything of a sensitive or tactically significant nature without using torture. I doubted Delacort would resort to that; he didn't strike me as being so ruthless. At least, not without direct orders.

If anything, Paek was more of a hindrance. One more person to feed and breathe, one more drain on power and fuel. I suppose the smart thing would have been to airlock him, but no one made that suggestion openly even if some thought it.

Delacort assigned Harris to "assist" me with an assessment of Paek's combat suit. Which meant he was to make sure I logged everything for SecOps' benefit. Its construction was similar to the ones used by SecOps, but the armor was significantly stronger. In fact, when I checked the inside, I found several manufacturer tags identifying it as coming from the Astro-Global Inc., one of the larger miltech corporates.

The advances were all in the details. Despite higher armor levels, the basic suit was lighter and more flexible. There were a range of sensor enhancements available that could be displayed directly on the visor, and it had a wrist interface capable of projecting Solidos, which was useful for navigation and tactical information. Along with those improvements, the tanks were smaller but higher capacity. I wanted to dismantle them to see how they'd pulled it off, but we didn't have the facilities to do it safely, and Harris decided we better not risk damaging it.

There were some differences in the comm system, with extra positions on the selector to normal. I couldn't work out what they did, but Harris had the benefit of military intelligence information.

"Q-band channels. Quantum encrypted and almost undetectable. We don't have anything like it."

We brought Paek in. He was friendly enough but didn't want to discuss his suit.

"How are the Sharks doing this season?" he asked. "I usually try to follow their games, but I've been busy the last couple of months."

"Is this a frequency controller?" I pointed to the rotary dials on the wrist of his P-Suit.

"My wife has a delicious recipe for roasted squash. You ever tried that?" Paek didn't even look at the suit. "Did you know there's a whole level in the hydroponics farms dedicated to squash in the *Aryabhata* Atoll? Gotta love it."

"This looks like a mode selector for the helmet display. How many modes does it have?"

"Have you ever thought about how you Earth people aren't right for space?" Paek smiled. "You haven't adapted the way we have. Not that there's anything wrong with that. But you have to accept that you're not good enough, are you?"

After forty-five minutes of similar inane banter, I called Safi to take him back to his quarters. I had better things to do than play games with someone who wasn't going to answer no matter what I asked.

We reported to Delacort what little we'd found, and he took it in his stride. There wasn't much we could do about it where we were, other than log the information for possible future use. But when I mentioned the manufacturer tags he slammed his fist into the bulkhead.

"Those double-crossing bastards."

I looked at Harris, who shrugged in response.

"Astro-Global makes our suits," Delacort spat. "We supposedly have the best available."

Corporates will sell to anybody. That's their function, after all.

But I can understand the frustration when you pay for something, only to find it's not exactly what you'd asked for. The problem was, after so many companies moved their operations to accommodatingly tax-free orbital manufacturing, the Earth alliances had little influence with them. But for the Atolls it was a different matter. Through their deep-space operations, they provided a lot of raw materials to the corporates at a fraction of the price they could be supplied from Earth. They had both the carrot and the stick, while all we had was "good faith"—with its customary value of nothing.

"Better tell the people back home they need to renegotiate."

Delacort grunted at my comment. "Paek wasn't helpful?"

"Only if you want to hear about his wife's culinary skills." I picked up the DataPad that held the schematics I'd put together on his suit. "What are the SecOps guidelines? Throw him in the main 'lock and reduce pressure 'til he talks or chokes on his own blood? I'm sure Gabriella would volunteer."

Harris swallowed heavily. "Don't even joke about that, Ballen. I've seen it."

Delacort nodded. "We're civilized. We don't airlock people without due process."

"I know prisoners are an expensive luxury out here." I waited, but nobody said anything. "Well, we better keep him locked up at least, otherwise we'll have another saboteur on board."

"I can't spare any of my people to babysit." Delacort rubbed his chin. "Perhaps Gabriella can get something out of him. She's worked with Tollers before."

The approach to 1219-Britta only took a few days, but the journey was busy for everyone. We had a lot of cleaning up to do and several damaged systems needed patching, including Delacort's precious weaponry. Dollie was kept busy helping to care for the injured, while Gabriella was detailed to guard Paek in between questioning sessions with Delacort.

Our spy still eluded us. No one had been near the bug we'd found, other than routine checks by Rikard. Medved continued the remote monitoring but it was looking increasingly like Evans had been the traitor after all. I stopped by Dollie's bunk with a light snack on my way to my morning assignment. I'd taken to doing it to save her from having to start the day too soon and give her a little extra privacy. She'd been waking to some queasiness that wasn't entirely LoGee related and often didn't want to face people first thing. This morning she looked as though she was suffering more than usual, her usually impeccable skin looking slightly gray and a frown shadowing her face.

"Brought you a bread roll. They're like chewing on rock, but I thought you might find it innocuous enough to enjoy."

She gave a brief smile and hacked at her thick dark mane with her fingers. "I look awful."

"You look beautiful." I put the roll next to her, along with a drink tube containing a "fortified soy beverage."

"You're a terrible liar, Joe." She sniffed the drink and wrinkled her nose in a way that only made her look more attractive. "But I love you for it. I'm fat and bloated, my skin feels terrible and my hair is in knots. How can you even stand to look at me?"

"You're my wife, you're carrying our child. How could you be anything but beautiful?"

"I never realized before how delusional you are." She took a small bite of the roll and washed it down with some of the soy from the tube. "That's revolting."

"It's good for you."

"So is sex. It's the consequences that are a bitch."

I squeezed her arm and a moment later she snuggled into me, holding on like someone drowning clings to a life preserver. "Everyone says pregnancy is a beautiful thing, a wonderful experience, but all I do is feel wretched all the time."

I held her softly and stroked her head. "That's a racial survival self-delusion—if women didn't block out how bad it was, humanity would die out in a generation."

"All I want is the damn thing out of me."

I felt a damp warmth on my shoulder and realized she was crying. It was so unlike Dollie that for a second I was scared something was really wrong, then I realized it was the hormones kicking in. Nevertheless, there were options. "You don't have to go through with this. You know that, right?"

"You don't want to have a child?" Dollie stiffened. "Are you scared it will be like me?"

"That's crazy. I mean you have a choice. Nothing more."

She pulled away, searching my face with tear-streaked eyes. "It's not only up to me, it's *our* child."

"I know, but if it makes you so unhappy perhaps it's not the right time. Don't blow this up into something it's not."

She sniffed, then took another bite of the roll. "I'm not always thinking straight, I know that."

I held her hand and caressed her cheek. "You're the most important thing in my universe. I want what's best for you, whatever that is."

Dollie smiled. "Careful, soldier. Your halo is showing."

She hadn't called me that for a long time, and I knew it meant she was okay, despite her mixed-up emotions.

"It's an option. I'll support you no matter what."

She shook her head slowly. "It's not. At least, not until we get back to Earth. I discussed it with Delacort."

"What did he say?"

"He wouldn't risk it, because of..." She took a breath. "Because of how I am."

"What?" My hackles rose immediately. "He has no right to make that sort of judgment. Hell, we wouldn't even be here without you..."

"It's not like that. He said he didn't want to consider aborting because of the risks. I'm not exactly plumbed *normally*."

My anger left almost as quickly as it had arrived. Delacort might be trained to army medic standards, but it was a sure thing he'd never dealt with someone like Dollie. Thinking about it, I realized I wouldn't be happy with anything he might suggest along those lines anyway. He simply wasn't qualified.

"Hang on until Dr. Kinsella can check you out. We'll be heading back to Earth soon."

Dollie nodded. "If I'm being honest, this *space wanderer* thing has lost its appeal. I don't know what you see in it. It's ninety percent boredom."

I grinned. "Exactly. And ten percent terror."

"Joe?" Dollie looked at the space on the bed between us. "You do want this baby, don't you?"

It was a question as old as the human race. Even now, in the twenty-second century, men were supposedly unwilling to "settle down" or were frightened by the responsibility of having kids. In my case neither was true. I hadn't anticipated children because of Dollie's genetic makeup, but it didn't mean I was about to volunteer for deep-sleep research.

"I want to share my life with you. If it includes getting gray-haired and wrinkly while raising babies, then that's what we do. But I'd never dream of pushing you into something you didn't want to do. And I know this isn't what you had planned."

Dollie flung her arms around me, almost squeezing my breath out with the strength of her grip. I could smell her delicious fragrance as her hair brushed against my nose and I held her in return.

"I love you, Joe Ballen." Dollie sniffed. "Even if you are always chasing other women."

"I'm as innocent as the day is long."

"That's why you work in space." She pulled back a little, her cheeks moist with tears. "There are no days here."

I cupped her chin in my hand. "I love you, Dollie Buntin. On Earth, in space, or anywhere else."

She smiled momentarily then her eyes lowered again. "Am I getting gray and wrinkly?"

"Age cannot wither..." I kissed her, and her lips pressed, warm and pliant, against mine until I felt dizzy. "Wow! I have to go. Delacort will be waiting..."

"Stay safe, Joe." She hesitated. "I need you..."

Nineteen

From five hundred kilometers out, Britta looked as impressive as a lump of gravel and that impression didn't change as we approached. One side of it looked as if it was sliced off, giving it a distinctly lop-sided appearance that made me wonder why it had been chosen as a base originally. Our sensors reported there was almost no EM signature, and the indistinct thermal signals we picked up could have meant anything or nothing. Delacort had convinced himself this was because the base was shielded and repeated that at every opportunity, but the skeptic inside me didn't agree.

We brought Sarac to twenty-five kilometers away and held our position. At that range, the signals were even more confusing. We picked up a large docking entrance on one of the flatter surfaces but it wasn't concealed, which was unexpected for a so-called "secret" base. Sure, it was way out in the boonies, from an Earth-centric perspective, but I couldn't believe it was unknown to the Atolls sitting out there like that. Other than the obvious visible construction, there were only the same weak traces we'd picked up farther out.

"Doesn't look hopeful," I said to Delacort as we stared through the portholes on the bridge. "Is there a record for the longest wild goose chase in history?"

"That doesn't make sense—SecOps was getting reports." The wrinkles around his eyes deepened into crevices. "We still need to check it."

"By *we*, I assume you're looking for a volunteer other than me?"

"You sure can be an ass sometimes, Ballen. You know that?"

"Mister Ass, if you don't mind. I'm a civilian." I moved away from the porthole. "I'm an expectant father, I have responsibilities to think about. What's the deal? Triple time for hazardous working conditions and a signing bonus?"

Delacort shook his head. "Something tells me you'll never be responsible, *Mister* Ballen, and I pity your poor wife. You'll be going in with the troops. If your guy is here, I want him to know we're all friends."

"Did you forget our friendly in-house saboteur?"

Delacort rapped on the porthole with his knuckle. "I haven't forgotten. But dammit, we have a mission to complete. We haven't seen anything of him since we discovered the relay. Perhaps he decided things were too hot."

"Or they had a backup transmitter we never found? Or they'd completed their mission and given the people who paid them all they needed?"

"Jesus, you're such a pessimist."

"I'm an engineer, I'm paid to be."

We met Delacort's squad in the main 'lock. The SecOps team wore armored P-Suits, while I was still using the hand-me-down general-fit one. The armored ones were custom fit, so I couldn't have worn one except in an emergency, but it made me feel like I was the poor cousin visiting from Pigsknuckle, PA. Hell, I was getting almost as much suit time as I would on an engineering job and wished, not for the first time, that my own suit had made it on board.

Delacort had detailed two of his men to stay behind on the Sarac, which I thought was crazy. Our prisoner was locked up and didn't need guarding any longer, and with no other ship within a distance of thousands of kilometers, security risks were nonexistent. But who was I to question the military mind?

Outside the airlock the sun was harsh. Our location relative to Britta meant we were in its full glare and I lowered my helmet's dark filter—the cheap suit had no auto-darkening—which made the sun tolerable, but also made it impossible to see into the shadows. A real spacesuit has augmentation filters on the inside of the visor which removed such problems—mine was like a journey into the dark ages and should have come with a giant helmet made of brass. Carlysle and Safi moved alongside me, and a second later I heard Carlysle in my earphones.

"We're your babysitters for the evening. Stay close, and you'll be fine."

"More like the other way around, don't you think?" I said, then clapped him on the shoulder. "How about we all look out for each other?"

Carlysle cut in. "Sounds okay, but if we tell you to do something, do it." He'd looked relaxed on the journey out, but now his voice was all business.

"I get it." I wriggled inside my suit, shifting the straps into a more comfortable position. "You want me to hold off on the smart-ass comments when you screw up."

Medved had brought the Sarac closer, tiptoeing inward until we were no more than a kilometer from the entrance. Damn close piloting in space.

"No beacon or nav-assist," he said, his voice filled with justifiable pride at his achievement.

"Thank you, captain." Delacort gestured at us. "Move out."

Britta's surface scaled in front of us like a floating mountain, the entrance a jutting maw of 'crete and steel. The bulging surface around the entrance looked a little like a skull, with the opening forming a giant mouth, and I hoped it wasn't an omen of what we were going to find.

Unlike my P-Suit, the military suits had built-in thrusters and weren't reliant on handheld units. As if to complete my feelings of humiliation and inadequacy, Carlysle and Safi grabbed hold of me at the waist and dragged me out of the 'lock like a sack full of ore samples. We drifted across the gap to the entrance at a medium pace, not taking any chances. The only sound was my own breathing, punctuated by a regular distance countdown from Delacort.

My estimates of the age of the Britta station worsened as we approached. The docking bay design was an anachronism, and the old-style steel and aluminum fabrication pushed the construction date back even farther. My professional eye dated it as at least seventy-five years old, which meant it was established in the early days of space flight, possibly even before the Atolls had risen to dominate space.

Delacort passed through the gaping entrance along with the first of his team and vanished from sight in the deep shadows. I flipped up the glare filter on my suit when we entered the dim tunnel, but even then, the small running lights on their suits were like pinpricks in the darkness.

As they approached the hatch inside the bay, the men switched on their suit floodlights, illuminating the heavy sliding doors between us and the base. So far there were no signs of life, which wasn't too surprising given its secret nature. What worried me was there was no challenge either. After we pulled up on their doorstep, it must have been obvious to anyone inside that we were there, but there'd been no radio or other signals. As if further proof was needed, there was no indication of power in the 'lock—not even the telltale gleam from the control pad fixed to the wall by the inside door.

This was confirmed when Delacort pressed the button several times and there was no response. After the third or fourth try, he flipped open a steel access panel and pumped a manual release lever. The hatch ground part way open, then stuck, and despite several attempts refused to open wider. The narrow gap didn't look at all inviting to me. But that didn't stop Delacort, and he slipped inside.

"Cruz. With me."

One of the team moved up and plunged through the gap where Delacort had gone. Cruz was the team's tech guy and I should have gotten to know him better, but we'd never managed to connect, even inside the close confines of the Sarac.

A dysfunctional airlock was straining my sense of credulity, even if the base was feigning disuse. I wondered about its history. It was a hell of a coincidence there would be an abandoned base here, but if this was the wrong place, then where the hell *was* Logan Twofeathers?

A ring of cold white navigational lights flickered to life, lighting up the circumference of the 'lock, and the door slid open again. Inside, Delacort was busy with the other soldier working at a control panel. They'd obviously found some power, but it wasn't exactly comforting.

Carlysle and Safi tugged me inside following the others, and the doors started closing behind us. I felt a moment of panic. What if we couldn't get out again? Traveling a hundred million miles to get stuck inside a lump of rock wasn't part of the deal I'd signed up for. Delacort was cycling the 'lock, but I didn't feel any changes to the stiffness in my P-Suit.

"Looks like the atmospheric reserves are gone." Delacort thumped the indicator panel a couple of times. "Might be a backup system, but it would take several hours to generate a breathable atmosphere. Prepare for inner hatch opening. Watch for anything unusual."

The inner pressure indicator was still red, but Cruz overrode the safety interlocks and the door slid open. Inside was a wide inner ship bay with what I guessed was a control room at the far end overlooking the open space. Several doors along the sides looked as if they might lead into storage areas while the rails of an old-style heavy docking cradle ran along the floor. Other than that, it was empty.

"This was built a long time ago." I pointed at the heavy steel reinforcing beams that ribbed the room. "Either that or someone liked to do things the old-fashioned way."

To me the inner construction showed even more signs of age than the outside. I hadn't seen so many rivets and bolts, since I was in school studying ancient engineering. Modern space construction is almost entirely done with molded, reinforced composites held together with adhesives, commonly known as a "glue job." This was more of a "bolt and weld job."

"We're not here for an architecture lesson." Delacort slid past the inner doors. "Quarter and search by twos. I want an initial assessment in fifteen. Stay sharp. We have no idea what we're up against."

"You'll be lucky to find a virus alive in here. This place was dead before my grandmother started dating." I moved inside and felt my boots click into place on the metal floor. "Complete with a quaint magnetic floor. A true classic."

The men deployed around the bay, guns at the ready, and

Delacort clumped over the magnetic flooring clumsily. He leaned in, touching his helmet to mine to talk without using his radio.

"Listen, Ballen. I cut you a lot of slack normally, but this is different. We're in a potentially hostile environment, and I need your mouth like a grenade with no fuse."

I immediately regretted my banter. There's a place for a light hearted approach, but I knew from working with my own crews there are limits. When the shit hits the fan, you need support, not a smart-ass like me. "You are in charge, commander."

Emergency lights filled the bay with a doleful yellow glow that was almost more of a hindrance than assistance. At least I hoped they were meant to be emergency illumination—I pitied the poor bastards who'd worked here if this was normal. I clanked up the bay towards the docking cradle, fascinated by its antiquated design and layout. Ships were smaller back then, but this thing wasn't much bigger than the cradles we used for docking cabs back at the Hub. Carlysle and Safi moved with me, their stubby rifles at the ready as they scanned the room. It was a pointless posture, but I kept my mouth shut. Beyond the cradle was the control room, a door to the right presumably giving access. I moved towards it but stopped when Carlysle called out.

"Wait, Ballen."

Carlysle moved up with Safi, and they positioned themselves on either side of the door while I held back. Safi pumped his hand three times, and Carlysle snatched the door open, ducking to one side as Safi scanned the interior. Safi nodded and Carlysle rounded the doorway disappearing inside, leaving Safi in position, his gun never pointing away from the opening. Two minutes later Carlysle reappeared and waved us inside.

I moved forward, almost tripping on the magnetic flooring, and joined the two soldiers. It looked like any control room lined with computer screens and monitoring equipment, with the exception that it could have been from an old low-budget Solido horror flick.

"Anyone see *Space Ghoul X9*?" I joked.

"Sure. I hope Kurt Raganov doesn't appear through the walls at any second." Safi looked over the control panel by the window.

"Can you do anything with this stuff, Ballen?"

I looked at the panel and shuddered. It had it all—mechanical switches, push-buttons, rotary dials, knobs—the whole gamut of out-dated controls. The only good thing I could think of was they were so simple, very little could go wrong with them.

"Depends on the power situation."

I looked around. On the wall behind us were two switches large enough to have been the main power relays for the entire USP, and could have come straight off the set of *Space Ghoul X9*.

"You've got to be joking." I moved over to the switches, shaking my head inside my helmet. There was a safety interlock on both, and I pressed one while throwing a switch. It didn't appear to make any difference, but nothing bad happened either. I pressed the second interlock and closed the other switch. The lights in the room brightened and through the window, an array of light panels flickered to life along the walls. Several instruments and displays illuminated in front of us, and a number of diagnostic indicators came alive.

"Damn, I'm good," I said, moving to the controls. "Let's see what we have."

"Well done, Ballen." Delacort's voice sounded over the radio. "Good thing this place wasn't rigged to blow."

I looked over at Safi, then Carlysle. They shrugged but didn't say a word. "A calculated risk. I'll see what I can dig up on the systems."

"Do that, but try not to create any more surprises for us."

The main panel controlled the airlock doors and docking cradle, as well as a number of ship-servicing systems, from what I could tell. My sense of amazement increased as I checked the controls— almost everything on the panel was single-function—providing no mode switching or flexibility. It made things easy to decipher but was incredibly inefficient and inflexible.

"I've found the main environmental controls. Do you want me to bring on the O2 generators?"

Delacort took a while to answer. "See if you can access any logs or other information first. Don't take any chances."

I agreed and turned my attention back to the controls. One section on the right was dominated by a large display screen and looked to be the most promising option for accessing general information. The screen was caked in dust, but I wiped it clean, and it flashed to life with an unpleasant green glow when I tapped the old-fashioned keyboard several times.

The screen illuminated with large stylized letters that read "UNSA"; underneath in smaller letters it said "ORC-14." The terms were straight out of the junior astronaut's historical reference, and it took me several minutes to remember what they stood for. I didn't pause to consider the significance, though, and accessed several documents and summaries from the system memory store.

"It's an old U.N. station." I worked through the clunky menu system, looking for a concise summary. "Off-World Research Center Fourteen."

"They were used mostly for hyperspace research, weren't they?" Delacort sounded short of breath. "This place is deserted, that's for sure."

After the old United States broke apart, most space access technology and hardware was moved under the dubious protection of the United Nations Space Authority. It was an attempt to ensure Earth didn't lose out completely to the fast-growing Atolls, while keeping alive the dream that we could share space equally. As upheavals spread around the world, even the U.N. fell apart, and the technology and information ended up in the hands of whoever found it. Some went to regional states like the USP or the PanAsian Confederation, while much of it ended up in the hands of the Corporates and Atolls, giving them an edge they'd viciously held on to ever since.

"I'm circling back," Delacort said. "Squad, regroup at the entrance."

I worked through several more information screens but didn't find anything of great importance. Establishment dates and personnel numbers might have been interesting to a space historian, but for the purposes of our mission they were meaningless.

My suit pinged three times and I checked my tank display—I was down to half of my air supply. The SecOps suits had bigger reserves, but I needed to start heading back to the Sarac. I felt some clangs through the floor and a moment later Delacort trudged into the control room.

"I'm getting low." I pointed over my shoulder to my tanks with my thumb. "How about your people?"

Delacort didn't answer immediately, but I saw him check his own gauges through his helmet visor.

"I've got under two-thirds left." He did a quick roll call on the radio, and the rest of his squad confirmed they were all at about the same level.

"If it's all the same to you, I'd rather skip learning how to breathe vacuum." I tapped the screen in front of me. "It looks like this is the end of the line anyway. No one has visited this place in fifty years or more."

"It can't be." Delacort shuffled closer to look at the controls. "SecOps was in touch with them right up until we left and according to the reports I've seen, we've been sending resupply drones on a regular basis."

"Supply drones? You never mentioned them."

"There was no need. I know you think you're the center of the universe but you're not—and information on SecOps services *is* classified."

"I'm heartbroken." I checked the systems logs again in case I'd missed anything. The last docking entry was sixty-three years ago. "So where exactly have the drones been going?"

"Here." Delacort thumped the bulkhead next to him. "1219-Britta."

"You've searched the damn place. Have you seen any drone cargo haulers? Anything built in the last fifty years? Face it. This place is a mausoleum. Even the dust has dust on it."

My suit beeped again. "I haven't got time for a debate. I need to get back."

"We've barely started. There might be something hidden in the deeper level files."

My muscles tightened inside my suit and my pulse thumped in my temples. Delacort's blind stubbornness in the face of the evidence annoyed me. "Fine. You play explorer. I'll head back to the ship."

"I can't spare anyone to fetch and carry you around."

"Don't worry. I'll make it on my own."

I stood, balancing my movements against the magnetic floor so I didn't flail into the ceiling. I was halfway through the door when Delacort spoke again.

"Ballen. Switch on the O2 generators. If we build up a breathable atmosphere, we can search easier and you won't have to leave."

It would have been easy to tell him where to shove it. He had people with technical skills who could restart the system. He didn't need me. Then I grimaced at the thought of Cruz dealing with fifty-year-old atmospheric processors and controls, relying on his military training. It would be like giving a baby a stick of dynamite and a lit thermal lance.

Delacort looked relieved when I stepped back into the control room, but I wasn't too happy with it. Sure, we all like to think we're needed, but I was at the point where I'd been *needed* a little too much by this bunch. I pulled myself into the seat by the console and operated the controls. The batteries had very little in them, though to my surprise there was a working solar array somewhere. I activated the charging circuits to start building the power levels. It would take hours, far longer than the reserves in my suit, but there was also an auxiliary reactor.

"If you don't want this to take days, I'll need to use the auxiliary to power up the system," I said.

"Do it," Delacort snapped over the radio.

I tripped the switches and buttons to power the generators and monitored the changing power levels as the system came to life. It was sluggish, which wasn't too surprising, then the lights flickered as the generator switched across.

"Okay. It's good. We should have a breathable atmosphere in..." I checked the status indicators. "A little over an hour."

"Thanks. Are you going to—"

"Sir? I think you need to look at this," one of Delacort's men shouted over the radio, an edge of panic in his voice.

"Captain. There's something screwy here."

It was Cruz, and in a matter of seconds, the squad members were broadcasting all over each other.

A red light flashed on Delacort's wrist display, and he lifted his arm to check it. "What the..."

"What is it?" I checked the instruments but couldn't see anything unusual.

"Squad sensors picking up signals from multiple thermal devices. Readings are all around us."

I looked at him stupidly, momentarily unable to take in what he was saying.

"This place is rigged to explode." He rushed back through the door, snapping orders as he left. "Squad. Emergency withdrawal at the main airlock. Now!"

I stomped out of the control room, moving over to the airlock controls with Carlysle and Safi following closely behind. I didn't know where Cruz was, but I wasn't waiting and thumped the cycling controls as the rest of the men came up behind me.

The door didn't move.

"Out of the way, Ballen. Cruz will deal with it."

There was still only a trace atmosphere inside the station, so there should have been nothing stopping the airlock from opening. Something told me there was more to it than was obvious. Although everything looked the same as when we'd entered, it didn't take long to realize the airlock door had been deadlocked. Without powering down the whole system and bleeding the current off, nothing would open it.

"Don't waste your time. That door is locked for a reason." I headed back to the control room.

"Ballen. Where the hell are—" Delacort's voice followed me.

I scanned the control system, desperate to find something to help us. "How long till it blows?"

Delacort checked his hand-scanner. "Minutes. Maybe."

Almost every control channel that could have been useful was locked down. Cold sweat beaded on the back of my neck and floated off into my helmet. Delacort hesitated only a second, then vanished into the main bay.

"Stand back." His voice sounded over the radio.

A moment later a staccato of bright flashes lit up the control room window as he opened fire with his rifle, emptying his clip into the door lock. His team scrambled in all directions as the rounds ricocheted around the room. I ducked as the window shattered in front of me, a deadly cloud of glass shards blowing

197

inward to where I'd sat just a moment before.

"Stop, you idiot!" I sat up again, surrounded by slivers of glass. "You'll kill someone."

Delacort swore but was loading another clip to try again. I worked through several control screens. There had to be something.

The cradle! If it wasn't locked down...I switched to the controls on the next panel. As far as I could tell there was power and only regular interlocks were in place.

"Move away from the door," I yelled, overriding the locks and grabbing the power controls.

Not waiting for an answer, I turned the power switch a little. The cradle lurched but moved. I pulled it back to the base position as the floor under my feet trembled. An eruption of silent debris exploded through one of the side doors, and I knew we were out of time.

I spun the control all the way around and the cradle shot down the rails, spearing the airlock door solidly. Black smoke from the explosion made it difficult to see, but I thought the door had buckled. I moved the cradle back and again pounded it into the door as another explosion vibrated through the floor. Someone shouted wildly over the radio, followed by a choked-off scream. The cradle was bent and twisted but held together. Strike one up for old-fashioned construction—a modern unit would have splintered on the first impact. I pulled it back and sent it catapulting into the door one more time as the room filled with a storm straight out of the bowels of hell.

I couldn't see whether I'd done enough through the swarm of debris and liquid flame that engulfed the docking bay, but it was time to leave. The control panel sparked and burst into flames as I ducked out of the room, staggering as the floor shook again. Something hit me from the side and sent me tumbling. I must have blacked out for a second, as the next thing I knew I was flailing in a hellfire cloud of Dantéan proportions.

I wriggled around to find my bearings but had no reference point to help. The smoke was so thick I couldn't tell which was the floor or roof, and I felt an edge of panic. Whatever had hit me had come from my left, which meant I was moving to the right and the airlock would be front and left of me.

A shape flicked through the thick smoke towards me, barely giving me time to identify it as a sharp, twisted metal shard of a wall panel. The point caught the arm of my suit and I tried to twist away. Then I felt it rip through the thick pressure skin and layers of insulation. I realized somewhat clinically that it was over. I was dead, it was only a matter of time before the air left my suit and my lungs started hemorrhaging into the vacuum. This wasn't the first time I'd been through this, but the temporary P-Suit had nothing like the emergency protection features that had saved me before.

Strangely, I felt quite calm. I didn't have the whole "life flashing past my eyes" thing. And the only thing I regretted was having so little to regret. Perhaps my life had been less interesting than it appeared at the time. A flash of agony ripped through me when I realized I'd never see Dollie again or live to see our child grow up, mixed with guilt that Dollie would have to raise the kid alone.

Everything was fading away. The flame was less intense, and the lights were failing. Despite that, I felt warmer, enveloped in a comforting safe heat. It would be okay, I thought. Everything would be fi—

Something pulled me back to consciousness. Call it survival instinct, or plain old-fashioned stubbornness. Whatever it was, my brain suddenly refused to accept the inevitable and started processing the sensory information around me once more. I was hanging from a twisted shard, stuck out from what must have been the wall. It had to be the right-hand wall based on the initial impact that had knocked me off my feet.

I squirmed and unsnagged the metal from my suit. If I had my right side against the wall, I could either be facing the airlock or away from it, depending which way was up. In ZeeGee, with no visual clues, it could have been either. Pulling myself blindly along the wall, I looked for a clue but didn't find one, and in a few seconds banged my helmet into rough 'crete. The flooring was lined with magnetic strips to provide a rudimentary artificial gravity system but the surface my head hit had no such strips, which meant it was the roof. Which also meant the floor was somewhere below where my feet were pointed, and the airlock was off to the left. Reversing my direction, I pulled myself down to where I'd meet the floor. If I could get back to the strips I was sure I could find my way to the airlock. If I had enough air left.

My deluxe pro-series gold-standard emergency P-Suit didn't have anything as sophisticated as an emergency patch, and I cursed the nameless bean-counters who'd never faced vacuum. Knowing the way they saw things, it was likely a choice between a patch or a helmet, so I was probably lucky. My arms felt like they were made out of the 'crete lining the docking bay as I pushed myself down. I felt light-headed and knew I didn't have much time—hypoxia was kicking in. My feet snapped to the floor when I reached it, but I collapsed in a pile, unable to stand.

"Come on, Ballen. No time for a vacation." I pulled at the wall, my fingers slipping inside the mesh as I pulled. It should have been easy with no gravity, but it wasn't for some reason.

"Okay, take a breath. Then move." I wanted to laugh, even though I knew I shouldn't. That was the problem, in fact. I couldn't take a breath. "You're a comedian, Ballen. You should be in the Solidos."

I pulled again and got partially upright. It was a minor victory, but I felt like I'd scaled a mountain. "Bye... Dollie... love..."

A large blur appeared out of the haze like a ghostly human mountain, and a pair of arms slid under my armpits. Before I could respond, I was hoisted into the air, my boots sticking to the floor.

"C'mon, Ballen. Time to go."

I recognized the voice but couldn't bring the name to mind. "Take me out to the ball game..."

"Save your oxygen," the voice said.

"Wanna sing." I poked my tongue out. "One. Two. Three strikes you're out..."

Something fumbled with my arm and I tried to pull away. "Neck off."

Twenty

"Joe? Joe? Is he okay?"

It was either Dollie or an angel. Maybe Dollie was an angel, and she was protecting me. It seemed plausible at that moment, but even as I thought it the light-headed feeling slipped away only to be replaced by a dull throb inside my head. The pounding deepened by the minute until it was so loud I'd swear it must have been audible outside the confines of my thick skull.

"Don't leave me," Dollie sobbed, and I felt a warm pair of hands engulf mine. "Dammit, Ballen. Open your eyes—now! You don't get away that easily."

I opened my eyes and Dollie yelped. I was in the wardroom of the Sarac on one of the makeshift beds. An oxygen mask was over my mouth, and I could feel something not quite right with my left arm. But I was alive.

"Hello." It came out as more of a hoarse whisper than I intended, but Dollie's face lit up.

"Hello? That's it?"

She pulled the mask off me, and the next thing I knew I was feeling light-headed again. The pounding in my head increasing as she kissed me deeply.

"You're incredible, do you know that?" she said, tears rolling down her cheeks.

"Yes," I croaked. "Did you only just realize?"

"Modest too..." Dollie leaned over and kissed me again.

"Careful." I gasped for air several moments later. "I think those are bad for my health."

Dollie patted my cheek but pulled away and put the mask back over my mouth.

"Is everyone...?" I asked, not sure I wanted to know the answer.

"One of Delacort's men died. Caught directly in an explosion. The rest got out. A lot of cuts and bruises. They wouldn't have made it at all if it wasn't for you."

I was okay apart from a bad frost burn on my arm where the suit had been punctured. Dollie told me Safi had come back for me, and I made a mental note to hunt him down as soon as she'd let me.

Delacort came in, his long face looking even more lined than usual. "That was quick thinking, Ballen. Glad to see you're okay."

"How's everyone else?"

"We lost Harris."

I felt a kick in my stomach. Harris was a cynic, like me. It made us have a certain sympathy that others didn't fully understand—the common bond of the malcontent. And like me, he'd lost a parent. It wasn't too uncommon given the situation back on Earth. The messed up climate and freak weather conditions made life dangerously random, often tearing families apart. I didn't remember my parents, but according to the records they'd been swept from a road by a mudslide when I was two years old. Harris had lost his mom in one of the all-too-frequent food riots.

"Harris was a good guy," I said.

"He was a good soldier," Delacort agreed. "I don't like losing men. The paperwork sucks. But I have you to thank for there not being more."

"Someone has to do the thinking when you soldiers decide it's too much hard work."

I expected him to blow up, but he didn't. Instead, he reddened.

"I deserve that. It was a stupid mistake."

"Shooting a gun inside a sealed docking bay? Yeah, it was pretty dumb. You're not the Rocket Ranger."

"Sadly not. If I was we'd have all gotten out."

"Well, it was a trap certainly worthy of Doctor Wingnut. Remember him?"

The battles of *Rocket Ranger* and his arch-enemy, Doctor

Wingnut, had been all the rage on 3V when I was younger, and it was a rare treat when I got to see them. It sounds stupid, but it was the Ranger who inspired my career. Nick Townsend, Ranger's secret identity, was a billionaire space engineer and sparked my own interest in engineering. Though I was still short on the billionaire part.

Delacort snorted. "That show sucked."

"But at least nobody died." I shrugged. "I wish the real world was that way."

Neither of us said anything as the awkward silence settled in which always accompanies male discussions involving emotions and guilt. You'd think after thousands of years of evolution, openly admitting we cared about things wouldn't be so hard.

"What now?" I finally asked.

Delacort opened his hands wider. "There doesn't seem to be an alternative other than to head back to Earth. The intel must be completely wrong."

"And Logan?"

"If he's hiding out here we'll never find him. We can't scan every lump of rock in the Belt, and if they're shielding their signals enough to stop the Atolls from finding them, we've no chance."

Medved's voice rasped through the intercom. "Commander Delacort. Control room, please."

There was nothing in the captain's voice to indicate trouble, but I got the feeling this wasn't a routine meeting call. Coming so soon after our recent escape, it was suspiciously more than coincidence and judging by his expression, Delacort thought so too.

"Can you make it?" he said, looking at Dollie sheepishly. "Sorry."

"Joe, you need to take it easy." Dollie pushed me back on the bed, shouldering Delacort out of the way.

"No rest for the wicked." I patted her hand. "Don't worry. I'll head to my bunk straight after."

I dragged my ass to the control room, following Delacort. Nowadays, I didn't usually have problems with my regenerated limbs, but they'd taken plenty of punishment on the journey. I had a stash of nerve-tranq in my bunk from the old days. I hadn't needed any for over a year, but I always had it on hand like a totem. Perhaps now was the time to use some.

Captain Medved was deep in conversation with his brother Rikard when we arrived and didn't switch back to English immediately. When he did, his stubbled face was grim.

"I pick up new signal. Weak, low power."

"That ghost you saw earlier?" Delacort turned to me. "Didn't you fix that?"

I bristled and was going to say I'd been busy pulling the mission's collective nuts out of the fire, then decided against it. Some people never manage to understand there are only so many hours in the day.

"We've tracked down a number of possible sources." I gestured towards Rikard. "And we bolstered the shielding on those circuits. I doubt I've got them all by a long way."

Delacort was going to say something else, but Medved cut him off.

"*Nyet. Nyet.* Not ghost. Regular. Repeating. Very low power."

He brought the signal up on the screen and I studied the trace. Completely artificial. Silent for ten seconds then a distinct *bloop*. The power levels were low, as Medved said. "A beacon?"

"Could be." Medved adjusted the controls. "Low power, short range."

Delacort leaned over and peered down at the screen as if it were a urine sample. The green illumination casting evil-looking shadows on his face. "It's definitely new? Not something you missed earlier?"

Medved looked hurt. "*Nyet.* Not there before. New."

"This could be anything," I said. "A signal? Sure, but it could also be another trap triggered by the explosions as a backup. I know no one wants to hear this, but I've exceeded my quota for being blown up today."

"Can you tell where it's coming from?" Delacort asked.

Medved worked on the controls for a few minutes. "Signal too weak. Can trace if stay on long enough."

"The game is still afoot." I sighed. "Let's hope it's a safer bet than our last venture."

I woke several hours later feeling rested but hungry. Dollie wasn't in her bunk, so I made my way to the common area used as a lunchroom. It was relatively crowded for once. I spotted Dollie sitting with Carlysle, stirring a bowl of food she didn't seem very interested in. Paek was in the far corner with three other members of the SecOps team. I guessed one of them was his escort, though he'd been given free rein to roam about the ship. I grabbed a meal pack and sat next to Dollie. Carlysle grinned and gave me a quick thumbs up.

"How ya doing, Ballen?"

I gave Dollie a quick squeeze. "Feel like I've been through one of your unarmed combat training sessions."

Carlysle laughed. "You should try it for real. Never hurts to learn how to protect yourself."

"He needs all the help he can get." Dollie took a sip from a juice tube. "He can't even stand up to me."

"That's choice, not ability," I said.

"Sure, Joe." Dollie lifted her hand up. "Wanna arm wrestle?"

Dollie's Geneering made her much stronger than a normal person, which meant I didn't have any strength advantage over her. Something we both knew from more pleasurable activities than arm wrestling.

"Give me time to eat my spinach first." I opened my meal pack and sniffed. The fake chicken smelled even worse than it looked, but I took a spoonful anyway.

Paek was talking on the other side of the room, and he wasn't making any attempt to keep his voice down.

"Earth's problem isn't the fault of the Atolls."

His voice had that unmistakable, slightly smug lilt to it that was common to all Atollers. "Its simply that its civilization has been surpassed.

"Evolution tells us superior species inevitably displace the lesser." He paused, as if letting the words sink in. "Isn't that what Darwin said? Survival of the fittest. And that's what the Atolls are—superior in every way. That's why we're so far ahead of you and the true vanguard of life in space. Quite simply, we're better than you."

"Gabriella was asking how you were."

Carlysle spoke casually enough, but Dollie stiffened next to me.

"Joe doesn't need anything from that bitch."

I was about to agree with her when a threatening grumble drifted over from Paek's table, and I looked up. Several of the SecOps people were staring at him like a bunch of Romans ready to throw a Christian to the lions. If he was fazed by this, he didn't show it and carried on with his preaching.

"Earth has been dominated in space now for over a hundred years. None of you people even know what it was like before then. The efforts to explore and expand were piecemeal and fractured. The early nations playing childish games with each other to see who could dominate. Not for the sake of science or information, but for propaganda reasons. There was no concerted effort, and billions were wasted. We're the answer to that. It was madness—a sickness—and we in the Atolls are quite simply the natural antidote."

"You think you're so good?" one of the SecOps people muttered. "But you still got captured..."

"That's foolishly irrelevant. I'm talking about species, not individuals." Paek was playing with a plastic fork and it snapped in his hands. "You'd be much better off coming to terms with us and accepting what we give you. If we didn't have to worry so much about Earth, the Atolls would be much more generous with our technology."

"Maybe we want more than the table scraps the high-and-necking-mighty Tollers want to give us." One of the SecOps guys stood and leaned over the table, his bulk filling the air above Paek. "Maybe we want to make our own way, mister. Maybe, just maybe, we got you beat and you're scared you can't compete with a *real* man in a fair fight."

"Has Paek been doing this a lot?" I asked Carlysle.

"Shouldn't be running around if you ask me." Carlysle frowned. "He's always yammering on about how the Atolls are better. The Atolls are the next phase of humankind. It spooks people, gets them riled. Brodell won't listen to his crap for long, that's for sure. His sister needs a lung transplant and didn't qualify for the Atoll Prime-Series."

I nodded. Brodell was the bulky SecOps guy who was taking the most offense to Paek's words. The Prime-Series lungs were grown in microgravity frameworks and known to be the best, and in some cases the *only* choice. And one of the many secrets kept by the Atolls. "You're the ranking military officer here, aren't you?"

"Yeah..." Carlysle finished his tube of coffee. "I am."

Paek's voice grew louder as he ignored Brodell standing over him. "Earthers are better suited as followers rather than leaders. They're natural sheep... I've studied Earth history extensively, and you people don't know how to create a cooperative society where everyone is respected. Where individual opinions are truly valued, not simply because a law says they are but because society as a whole respects the individual."

"They're going to 'lock that idiot if he's not careful," Dollie said, pointing at Paek. "Might not be a bad thing, either."

"We built the High-Rig and this ship you're sitting in." Brodell spread his hands wide.

"Your ancestors built the elevator and station. I doubt Earth could duplicate it now." Paek laughed. "As for this ship? We have better technology in the training ships we give to cadets."

"We can arrange for you to leave the ship, if you prefer," Brodell said, getting several murmurs of support.

"I'll give you one thing. You people are brave. Foolish, but brave." Paek shook his head. "You'd have to be both to volunteer for duty in this barge."

Brodell was heavyset and I guessed he was Geneered, like a lot of SecOps people. He grabbed Paek by the shirt and lifted him out of his seat in one jerk. Paek squirmed as he was held in the air. He even managed to plant his knee in Brodell's midriff a few times, but it wasn't enough to break the big man's hold on him.

"Time you got some exercise." Brodell grinned. "It's a beautiful day outside."

Several people cheered, and someone yelled, "Airlock the bastard."

Carlysle jumped from his seat and moved towards them. He planted himself directly in front of Brodell, who towered over him by at least six centimeters..

"Fun's over, boys." Carlysle held his hands up in front of the group. "You know I can't let you 'lock him."

Brodell didn't move, but he didn't let go of Paek, either. "He deserves to get thrown out."

"We don't do that." Carlysle pointed at Paek. "Even if they do."

Brodell was still holding the Atoller at arms' length. Even in LoGee it must have been a strain, but he didn't show it. "You were more fun before you got promoted, Carlysle."

"You get promoted for having brains." Carlysle stepped closer, his voice getting lower. "So how about showing some."

Brodell looked from Paek to Carlysle and back. "Looks like you get a break today, *Toller*." His large fist came back, then pounded into Paek's face like a steam hammer. Paek flew across the room and collapsed in a pile against the opposite bulkhead. His nose was smashed and bleeding, but I guessed he'd live.

"Testosterone games," Dollie said. "Always the same."

Carlysle signaled for two of the men to help Paek and came back to our table. He sat down, and I could see he was shaking a little.

"Thanks for the help, Ballen," he said.

"You can handle yourself." I toasted him with my coffee tube. "Besides, you never listen to civilians anyway."

I went looking for Medved and Delacort after eating, knowing that if I didn't they'd be bugging me soon enough. They weren't exactly hard to find and looked up when I dragged my ass into the control room.

"We did it, Ballen." Delacort was talking fast, a broad grin on his face. "We got a positive fix for the signal location."

I still wasn't feeling great. I'd held off taking the nerve-tranq, but with the jangling stiffness in my arm and legs, I wasn't sure it had been a good decision. Instead, I'd substituted half a dozen tubes of black coffee, hoping the caffeine would reassemble me into a vague approximation of a human being.

"So where is it?"

Medved brought up the navigation map on the main 3V. The asteroid belt slashed across the view by our location like a rash on a ten-credit hooker, but it was deceptive. Despite appearances on screen, the density of rock meant the average distance between any two was thousands of kilometers.

He tapped on the controls and one of the pinpricks of light flashed steadily. The image swirled as the viewpoint spiraled into the selection, the target designation appearing as the rock expanded on the screen.

"2071-PN7?" I looked at the others. "Does that mean anything to anyone?"

Rikard gave one of his fatalistic shrugs and Delacort shook his head. I reached over and brought up the details on the selected object. "That thing is a pebble." I read the dimensions and mass. "Less than fifty meters across? Not much room to hide a research outpost."

"We're not stupid." Delacort gestured at Medved. "But Captain Medved is sure this is the origin of the signal. So we'll check it out."

It took us over a day to close in on 2071-PN7. When we got there the journey looked to have been pointless. I stared out of the window at it and swore—the catalog information had been completely accurate. It was nothing more than a shard of rock left over from the dawn of the solar system. Even Delacort couldn't hide his disappointment this time, and he kicked the base of the instrument panel. "You sure about those coordinates, captain?"

Rikard stared out at the scrap of rock and pulled a face. "We should leave. Go home. *To je glupo.*"

"*Miran*, Rikard." Medved glared at his brother. *"Tvoje riječi ne znače ništa!"*

Medved and Rikard usually seemed to agree with each other, but this was obviously different. I didn't understand what they were saying but the vehemence in Medved's tone spoke volumes. Something was going on here, more than a general disagreement.

"What—"

A *beep* from the control panel sounded before I could finish and Medved turned back to the instruments. "Another signal."

He switched the signal onto a display. It had the same characteristics as the previous one—a ten-second repeated pulse. Very low powered.

"Please... Someone tell me we haven't been chasing another

ghost signal." Delacort rubbed his forehead with his thumb and fingers.

"*Nyet!* Outside ship."

"*Trebamo ići kući.* Go home now." Rikard grabbed his brother's arm. *"Inače ćemo umrijeti ovdje."*

Medved's face darkened, and a vein throbbed visibly in his temple. For a second I thought he was going to punch Rikard, but instead he pulled back slightly, staring coldly at his brother. "You leave. *Ići.*"

Rikard jerked like he'd been slapped. He looked as though he was going to say something but then apparently thought better of it. Without another word he turned and left the control room.

"Sorry." Medved looked back at us. "Family. You know."

Again, the signal stopped after four hours. Medved moved the ship, fine-tuning the destination while the broadcast lasted. When I went back to the control room he was alone with Delacort.

"Where now?" I asked.

Delacort pointed to the 3V navigation display. "Another catalog number only destination—2093-CF72. As you'd say, another pebble."

I looked more closely at the catalog data. Sure enough, it was another small rock. *"Butterfly, butterfly, show me where to go."*

"What's that?" Delacort looked at me as if I'd been drinking.

"Nothing." It was a line from a game I'd watched kids play a few years ago on Logan's family ranch. I tapped the edge of the navigation display. "Both these rocks were surveyed recently."

Delacort shrugged, but Medved understood what I was saying. "*Da.* After Atolls leave Earth."

"I don't follow." Delacort glowered at the asteroid data as though his look alone could reveal its secret. "Does that matter?"

"When the Atolls engaged in more deep space missions, they needed to increase safety through and around the Belt." I worked the controls, bringing up a list of asteroids. "Corporate mining operations needed to track resource-rich asteroids more effectively, and the Atolls needed to avoid collisions if they came out this way. Between them, they took on a major surveying and tagging mission, including thousands of smaller objects that hadn't been definitively tracked before."

"That's where this information comes from?" Delacort pointed to the screen.

"As part of the operation, the surveyors planted navigation beacons on the worlds they surveyed, as well as known ones."

"You think..."

"*Da.* Ballen right. Navigation beacons." Medved thumped the console in front of him.

"Normally the beacons are passive. They only broadcast in response to a coded signal from an Atoll or Corporate vessel to stop Earth ships from using them. Without the trigger they're useless." I looked from Medved to Delacort, letting the information sink in. "So the question is—why are they guiding us somewhere now?"

I was in the wardroom substituting more coffee for rest before heading back to the control room. We were closing in on the next rock, and I wanted to be there to see where we'd be heading next. We'd spent the last twelve days following beacons, and every time it was the same story. We'd close in on the target, then another beacon would light up, pulling us in a different direction. Whoever was doing this was certainly an expert, I don't think even Captain Medved knew where we were exactly.

The coffee was bitter as always—no room for gourmet varieties here—but it had the kick I needed, and I relished the feeling of my brain waking up from the inside out. Logan had to be behind the runaround—it was the type of safeguard that would appeal to his sense of humor. I was so deep in my thoughts, I didn't notice Gabriella until she spoke.

"Coffee's not enough for a big boy like you." She was wearing a tight pink and white SkinSuit showing every curve. "Wouldn't you like something to eat, Joe?"

"Go away. I'm not in the mood."

"Well, I am." She sat down opposite me before I could object. "I'm worried about you, Joe. Worried you're not getting all you need.

I could help with that."

I felt her hand brush my knee under the table. "You saved my life and I'm grateful, but I don't want any part of you."

"I want a part of you, though."

Her hand moved higher on my leg, and I slid back in my seat. "I heard you and Delacort were *entertaining* each other."

"I like soldiers. They have a lot of..." She pursed her lips together. "...stamina."

"So go and play with him."

"You should see what he makes me do with a Shock-Wand." She giggled. "Would you like to watch that, Joe?"

"I'm sure you both have a lot of fun."

"Fun doesn't have to be exclusive." She twisted her hair with her fingers. "Surely Dollie has taught you that."

"Have you seen the turbines down in the engine room?" She looked puzzled. "I'd rather be intimate with one of them than you."

Gabriella's expression didn't change, but her hand snapped towards my face. Another hand darted out from behind me, catching her wrist, and a familiar voice sounded.

"That's my prerogative. Thank you."

I glanced over my shoulder. Dollie stood behind me, her hand gripping Gabriella's wrist. She held it for several seconds, then released her hold. Gabriella pulled back, her face darkening.

"Everything okay, Joe?" Dollie sat next to me.

"Sure. We were discussing the weather."

Dollie locked eyes with Gabriella. "Stay away from us. Neither of us wants anything to do with you."

"Are you brave enough to let Joe decide for himself?" Gabriella rubbed her wrist.

Dollie leaned back. "Go ahead, Joe."

"You heard what I said a couple of minutes ago," I said directly to Gabriella. "That's not going to change."

Gabriella jumped up from the chair, the violence of her movement tearing her feet free from the carpeting. Her hand snapped out and she grabbed the table to steady herself. She didn't say anything but rushed out of the room with the force of a booster on maximum.

"Thanks," I said, giving Dollie a peck on the cheek.

"One day, I'm going to settle things with her," Dollie said, pulling a coffee from the dispenser.

"If you do, remember she plays rough."

"So do I."

Dollie squeezed my hand as I left, and I made my way back to the control room. I hoped this was the last stop. As much as I love being in space, the Sarac was feeling uncomfortably claustrophobic, and I was getting increasingly nervous about Dollie's condition.

Medved was waiting when I arrived. "You think it will be same?"

"I hope not. We'll have a mutiny on our hands if we get any more of this runaround."

Delacort shuffled in looking worn down, and I couldn't help wonder if that was from the burden of command responsibility or Gabriella's demands in the sack. "Hard night?"

He smiled weakly. "Broken sleep."

The computer *beeped* as the navigation click counted down to zero, indicating we were at the end of our programmed journey. I think the ambient air pressure lowered a couple of pascals as we all exhaled at the same time. The computer hadn't detected another beacon.

"Okay, so we're finally—" Delacort's head jerked up as the computer *beeped* yet again.

"*Another?*" A rush of exhaustion filled my entire body, and my shoulders dropped.

Medved opened up the signal trace. The ten-second pattern we'd seen before appeared on the display.

"The same necking thing again." Delacort headed for the door. "This is crazy."

Medved shrugged in resignation, then checked the new target trace. "Wait. Not same."

Delacort turned back, and I checked the datasheet. Whatever Medved had been referring to, I didn't see it. He zoomed in on the target, a rough ball of rock that was about a day away from our current location.

"Catalog number." Medved tapped the controls. "Look."

Delacort didn't follow, but I understood as soon as Medved

pointed it out. 548-Kressida. It was older and bigger than the previous targets. It *had* to be significant.

"Break out the champagne," I said. "I think we're on the last leg."

Twenty-One

548-Kressida was the little planetoid that couldn't. It looked like a rock basketball someone had forgotten to inflate properly. It was roughly spherical—"roughly" being the operative word. With its longest length barely fourteen kilometers, it certainly wasn't a dwarf planet, but it was a step up from the pebbles and certainly big enough to hide something on. We closed in to one hundred kilometers and held station while we did a provisional surface scan. Unlike our previous stops, there was no sign of another beacon signal to lead us away. Either this was our destination, or the game had unceremoniously ended.

Kressida was too small to orbit in the usual sense, so Medved parked Sarac off the side facing the sun to give us maximum visibility. The asteroid tumbled lazily under us, giving us a complete view of the surface every nine hours. I programmed the main sensors to build a detailed composite map, then ran it through a number of image filters to bring out detail and highlight possible artificial features.

"So it's another rock?" Delacort frowned when I gave him the news. "That's crazy."

"Not when you think about it." I scrolled the map across the screen. "If this is a secret base, they'd want to make sure it didn't stick out to any passing traffic."

He chewed his lip. "I suppose they could have been anticipating searches by the Atolls."

There were no external signs of an airlock or dock on the surface like we'd found at Britta, and I programmed a search using infrared.

215

Before I could complete setting up the parameters, a small craft emerged from seemingly nowhere and boosted towards us. The sensors identified it as a Crew Hopper, the type of ship used to ferry work gangs in orbital construction jobs, or sometimes for point-to-point transport on Luna—a good choice for Belt operations.

There hadn't been any contact with Kressida, so I wasn't surprised when Delacort deployed a full combat team at the docking port.

"Nice welcome committee."

Delacort checked his gun. "After what happened last time, we need to be careful."

"Well, try not to shoot the whole ship up," I said. "Some of us would like to get home in one piece."

A metallic clang reverberated through the Sarac as the smaller ship locked onto the outside of the docking port. There was a hiss as the pressures equalized and then the hatch opened. Even buried in the thick layers of a P-Suit, I easily identified the large frame of Logan Twofeathers. He stooped as he came through the hatch, hesitating only slightly at the armed welcome. Then he saw me and grinned.

"So it took a war for you to come and visit?" He took my arm and squeezed. "Good to see you, Joe."

"Someone has to keep you out of trouble."

Logan laughed, the noise booming in the confines of the docking chamber. "That makes a change, seems to me it's usually the other way around."

He reached inside his P-Suit and several of the MilSec team jumped, their guns pointing at him with a flurry of mechanical rattling. Logan froze and raised his eyebrows. "You people need to learn to recognize your friends."

"Steady, everyone." I looked over at Delacort. "This is Logan. The guy we've traveled all this way to see. It would be kinda silly to kill him after all that."

Delacort frowned. "He should know better, then." He nodded, and the soldiers lowered their guns.

Logan looked around warily, then pulled out a black box about the size of a couple of packs of SootheSticks and tapped several buttons. A red light on the box flashed a few times, then changed to a steady green. "Good choice. We had a couple of Sharur missiles locked on to you. Without me sending the signal to cancel they'd have launched in—" He checked a glowing red display on the box he was holding. "—under a minute."

I'd read about the Sharur system in technical articles. A multi-warhead weapon almost impossible to stop that virtually vaporized the target. An uncomfortable murmur rippled around the room. They were supposed to be capable of taking out an Atoll cruiser, though they'd never been tested outside a simulator.

"I hope you brought some good whiskey." He grinned. "And at least a dancing girl or two."

"Would you settle for moonshine and good company?"

Logan gave me a friendly slap in the stomach. "I would. Tell me, Joe. What happened to that fine Two-Spirit friend of yours? Did she finally get tired of your roving eye?"

"Dollie is here with us."

His face darkened, the wrinkles around his eyes deepening until his skin looked like old figured walnut. "I wish that weren't the case."

The tone of his voice scared me—Logan wasn't the type to worry over nothing. "What's wrong?"

"Atoll ships are on their way."

I shrugged. "They've been chasing us since we left Earth orbit."

"Well, it looks like you've kicked the hornet's nest one too many times."

We gathered in Sarac's wardroom, making it as crowded as a chicken coup in a thunderstorm and about as loud. Dollie and Gabriella were both there, while Delacort had locked Paek up temporarily and brought in his whole team to hear Logan outline the situation.

"At least two Atoll cruisers are headed this way." He made a face at our recycled coffee. "Joe tells me you already had a run-in with the Bethe. Well, they've been joined by a second ship. The

Goeppert is the latest addition to the Atoll fleet. MilSec tells me she has a sustainable thrust of over a third of a gee, is fully armed and outguns Sarac ten-fold."

There were murmurs around the room, and Dollie squeezed my hand.

"You might have gotten lucky against the Bethe, but there's no chance with the Goeppert."

Silence hung in the air like a cloud of PlaSteel vapor. I remembered something from an old TwoDee I'd seen years ago. *"Men of Harlech stop your dreaming. Can't you see their spear points gleaming."*

"Knock it off, Ballen," Delacort said. "Any idea how long?"

"Communication with Central is limited. All we have are estimates. Projections run anywhere from seventeen hours to a week. Highest probability at twenty-three hours. However, our priority is not the protection of the Sarac or even this base." Logan looked around the room slowly, waiting for the murmurs to die down. "Until now, no one outside this asteroid has known the secret we're hiding here, apart from at the highest levels of SecOps. We've replicated the work done on the Ananta and built a new starship—the Shokasta—even better than the prototype."

I shook my head—the security at the top didn't seem that tight. And I wasn't sure a ship was possible without the plans stolen by Wirkkala. Despite that, I felt a shiver of excitement. I wanted to drag Logan to one side and make him tell me everything, but now wasn't the time.

"We have three options," Logan continued. "We can surrender and hand over Shokasta to the Atolls. We can fight and almost certainly die, or we can try to run."

"What about the Sharurs?" one of the MilSec people said, but I didn't catch which one. "They could take out the Tollers for sure."

"We only have two."

"Two?" I heard the question from several people.

Logan opened his hands wide. "This is a research center and assembly facility. Not a military base."

"How many people are here?" I asked, not wanting to know the answer, which would almost certainly make the situation impossible.

"Forty-seven."

It was exactly what I'd feared, and I wasn't the only person to realize the problem.

"Not enough room." Medved banged the table in front of him. "Sarac not hold so many."

If we took the long way home and strictly rationed everything, we could house around a third of that on the Sarac. I was guessing at the number, but it was a guess coming from years of outfitting crews.

"What about Shokasta?" Dollie asked. "Can that hold people?"

"It could hold about twenty of us. If we doubled up," Logan snorted. "That would still mean a dozen would have to sacrifice themselves."

"That's my team's responsibility," Delacort said. "We'll defend the base while the others evacuate, of course."

"I better show you what we have." Logan moved towards the door. "It's not going to be easy."

Gabriella had been largely wallowing at the back of the crowd and with good reason. When the fight over Ananta had taken place she'd very nearly killed Logan. When he saw her now he froze, his meaty hands clenching and unclenching. He looked around at me, his wide face contorted into a mask of pure anger I'd never seen before.

"What's this *thing* doing here?"

"She's working for SecOps now." I held my hands apart. "I know how you feel."

"*She* is an independent contractor, thank you very much." Gabriella curtsied, then shuffled over to Logan and rubbed her hand down his chest. "Have you missed me?"

It was almost the worst mistake I think she'd ever made. He still had a scar from his collarbone all the way down to his navel from their last meeting. His hand flashed up and clamped around her wrist, squeezing so tight the blood drained from her face.

"Touch me again and I'll kill you." Logan's voice was almost a whisper, but it filled the room.

"Get your hands off me you—"

Gabriella moved suddenly, her other hand coming up with a small pistol, but Logan was too fast and clamped that wrist with his other hand. His grip tightened and Gabriella winced—something I'd never seen from her before. The fingers on her gun hand trembled open, and the gun clattered to the floor.

This had all happened so quickly no one else had reacted, but now Delacort moved up, grabbing one of Logan's arms and pulling him away. Logan held on, then suddenly released Gabriella, who tripped over backward and slammed into the wall.

"Enough," Delacort bellowed, jumping between them as Gabriella bounced up to attack Logan once more.

"He can't touch me like that and get away—" Gabriella screamed.

"I said that's enough!" Delacort spun, folding her up in his arms as she fought like a cornered hellcat.

I picked up the gun Gabriella had dropped and passed it to Carlysle. "You should look after this."

Logan was breathing heavily and still had a murderous look in his eyes, but I knew I could trust him not to do anything unless he was provoked.

"Come." He moved through the doorway. "I'll show you what we have to work with."

The ship was packed as we flew towards 548-Kressida. Usually Hoppers held ten people plus the pilot, but this one had been modified to include bigger tanks to accommodate its role as "general purpose asteroid navigator," and we barely all fit.

Dollie had insisted on coming, and Delacort had brought Gabriella, along with Brodell and Safi. I think they were mostly there to keep the peace between Logan and Gabriella. Sensibly, Gabriella stayed away from Logan while he focused on the controls and acted as if she wasn't there. Even with that, the tension inside the ship could have stopped a heavy-duty laser drill.

"Kressida is a largely metallic rock, but the core material is not especially resilient." Logan brought the Hopper low over the surface to give us the best view. "It makes it fairly easy to work with, and the complex we've built is more extensive than was initially planned. The downside is it won't give us much protection from a mass attack."

The rocky surface below us looked solid enough as it zipped by fast enough to make you hold on to your seat, but I knew appearances weren't everything—many asteroids aren't as rock-like as people think. We skimmed past the rim of a crater, and Logan turned us at a dizzying rate until we were pointing at the pitch black shadowed floor. It looked like we were on a bizarre suicide dive, then we slipped into a tight tunnel that plunged deep into the rock.

"How long did this take?" I asked, looking out at the rock tunnel meters away from us.

"This is part of a dead cryo-volcano. That gave us a way in, then we opened it up inside." Logan piloted between the rough walls, barely looking where he was going. "Almost twelve months for the initial work, then over a year of expansion since."

We emerged into a wide cave about the size of the old Oriole Park stadium, but I didn't see anyone selling beer or dogs. One side was lined haphazardly with standard habitation units that looked like some weird form of coral growth, but on the right was the new hope herself, the Shokasta.

I'd studied the blueprints and followed the construction of the Ananta before the staged "accident" that almost killed me and was familiar with the general design. The new ship looked significantly different. The Ananta had been long and sleek, reminiscent of a sword, but almost delicate looking. Her sister was bigger and uglier, still somewhat sword-like, but in a more brutish fashion that showed an angry side. My practiced eye also picked out several panels almost certainly covering standard military weapon hard-points. Shokasta was ready to fight and definitely not a research vessel.

"That's a lot of work," I said. "So all the stuff about the missing information was a ruse?"

Logan looked serious and shook his head. "I wish it were. The general files were complete, along with engineering on the Casimir generators." He brought the Hopper past the large accelerators at the aft of the Shokasta. "Operational details on the Jump drive are missing. As it stands, Shokasta is the fastest Earth ship ever built, but she's no *star*ship. Someone, probably Brin removed a number of files as soon as they were made available."

He twisted the Hopper sideways, so we were looking directly at the ship as we drifted crab-wise along its length.

"Is it armed?" Delacort pointed through the window at the Shokasta.

"Point defense only at this stage." The ship flipped around, and Logan boosted us towards the mess of boxy habitation units. After a few minor corrections, we connected to a docking port near the center. "Wirkkala will give you a full briefing."

"Wirkkala's here?"

"Almost since the beginning." Logan led us down a short corridor and into a compact meeting room. "Have a seat. He'll be here shortly."

"I'd like to move my men here." Delacort sat at the far side of the wide table. "If we're to be in action we should be here defending the Shokasta."

Logan shrugged. "We have limited facilities as you can see, but you're effectively in charge. I'm a consultant, not military, and most of the people here are technicians."

A man entered, his feet scratching noisily on the carpeting. "Hello. Everyone. Hello." He nodded his head up and down several times. "I'm errr...Denny Wirkkala. You've come a long way. Errr...yes, a long way. I'm sorry the ship errr...doesn't work."

"What?" Delacort stood too quickly and almost floated away. "I thought you said—"

"Wait." Logan held up his hand. "Please explain, Denny."

Denny perched on a stool and peered at us over his old-fashioned spectacles. With Geneering so commonplace, corrective lenses were uncommon. The last time I'd seen any was back in the orphanage—such interventions were generally done in the early stages of conception or much later once the child's major growth phases were finished. "The Shokasta Jump drive doesn't work yet. So far, the only drive we've managed to errr...operate is the regular one. We...that is I...well, we haven't managed to reproduce the original work carried out by the late Devan Rohloff."

Delacort relaxed a little. "We knew about the space-drive. But you've made no progress at all?"

"Of...of course we have...commander...we haven't hmmmm been out here playing cards...no...we've taken the original plans and extended them. Shokasta is a much more refined ship in ahhh...all respects. But the information missing from the engineering of the Jump has proved errr...impossible to reproduce."

Wirkkala didn't bear much resemblance to the picture I'd been given of his stand-in back on Luna. He looked like he'd shriveled years ago and held his arms tight to his chest as if scared he might be noticed. Only his hesitant speech and his glasses bouncing around in the light showed any real sign of life.

Dollie leaned over and whispered in my ear. "He doesn't look like he was ever much of a hot date—no wonder he had to pay for it."

I glanced at her briefly. "Shush..."

"You must understand, errrr...I'm only a glorified engineer, not ahhh...a theorist." Wirkkala pulled a small drinking tube from his lab coat pocket and sipped carefully on it. "The ship is an amazing achievement, even without the Jump drive.

"Top speed is sustained 0.3 gee. Which still makes Shokasta the fastest ship Earth has ever built. Even many Atoll ships would be hard-pressed to match her." Wirkkala stumbled less as he warmed to his subject. "For the first time in over a century, the people of Earth might have the upper hand."

"But it's still not a starship." Dollie cut through the fluff.

"Errr...no, technically not. Yet."

A slight lab-coated technician appeared and bent to talk quietly to Logan, who nodded a couple of times.

"We're out of time." He punched the controls on the desk communicator in front of him.

"...to base. Sarac to base. Respond." It was Medved.

Something about his tone told me that the issue of the Shokasta's Jump drive was about to become irrelevant.

Logan thumbed the communicate button. "Kressida base. What's the problem, captain?"

"We detect ship. Very close."

Delacort leaned over the desk to speak directly into the comm unit. "The Atoll ships? They're not supposed to be here for several hours."

"*Nyet*. Signals not same. Something else."

Delacort looked around, but everyone was puzzled. We knew the Atolls were closing on us, but who else could be way out here?

It didn't make sense.

"How long, captain?" Logan asked the obvious question.

"Not sure, three or four hours." His voice muted slightly for a moment. "Very close."

"Try to identify the ship. We need to know who we're dealing with." Delacort turned to Logan. "How soon can you have Shokasta ready to launch?"

"We could launch in that time, but hold your horses, Commander." Logan reached into his pocket and pulled out a folded eFlimsy. "This came through on the quantum channel a few hours before you arrived."

Delacort took the sheet and scanned it quickly, his lips silently mouthing the words as he read.

"We've been ordered to investigate a set of anomalous signals coming from deep space." He shook his head, crumpled up the sheet and threw it on the table. "That's impossible."

The sheet had bounced off the table onto the floor near me, and I bent down to pick it up as Delacort moved over to one of the display panels. He operated the controls and brought up a system map, zooming slowly out. There was something unusual about the coordinates on the eFlimsy I couldn't quite put my finger on, then it came to me as Delacort highlighted a position in space.

The coordinates were beyond the orbit of Neptune.

Twenty-Two

It's possible there were more bizarre things in life than being ordered out to the perimeter of the solar system to track down rogue signals. But I couldn't think of any, and we didn't have time to ponder the matter. If it was a joke, it was in poor taste. If it was genuine? Well, it was just scary. Even the Atolls hadn't sent more than research ships that far out, and the only Earth craft to make the journey had been uncrewed.

"It's impossible," I said. "There's nothing out there."

"That was what I thought, Joe." Logan worked the controls on the Solido system map, zooming in on the area indicated as the signal source. "There's nothing human out there."

"Are you telling me there's an alien...*thing* out there?" Dollie pointed at the screen. "And we're supposed to go and face them down?"

"I don't imagine so." Logan tapped the edge of the display. "The Atolls have done some long-range missions mapping the Oort cloud, but that's about it. Other than unmanned probes there's nothing out there we know of."

"Could it be a malfunctioning probe?" I was still staring at the impossible location on the screen. "How the hell are we supposed to get there anyway?"

"It must be a mistake." Delacort paced around the system map. "It has to be some crazy mistake."

The communicator beeped and Medved came on the line again. "Ship is PAC vessel Huòshèng. They come for Shokasta."

"PAC? How the hell can that be?" Delacort yelled into the

communicator. "How did you ID them?"

I glanced at Gabriella, who showed no sign of guilt. She noticed my look and winked at me.

Medved grunted. "*Suti, gad.* My brother, Rikard. He working for them."

"What?" Delacort punched his fist into the bulkhead.

"Was him with quantum transmitter. Rig sensors so we see ship as ghost, follow us from Earth. *Velika sramota.* He tell me PAC want ship."

"I'll see him jailed for this." Delacort was red-faced.

It was an understandable reaction. Rikard had been part of everything we'd discussed and done on the journey. He'd betrayed the USP and his own brother. The PAC were theoretically our allies against the Atolls. But they wouldn't have secretly sent a warship simply to escort us safely back to Earth.

"Airlock him." Gabriella said what several people were undoubtedly thinking.

"I agree one hundred percent," Dollie said. "And *you* should keep him company."

Gabriella jumped up and tried to slap Dollie, but Dollie was too fast and blocked the blow. I threw myself forward and grabbed Dollie while Delacort did the same with Gabriella.

"Let go of me." Dollie squirmed in my grasp. "I'll kill that murdering bitch."

"Please do." Gabriella almost twisted free from Delacort. "I'll be happy to take you down."

"You can't do this. Think about the baby," I whispered and Dollie's struggles calmed.

"Let me go, Joe. I'm okay."

I released her and moved back a half step, ready to jump forward again if needed, while Delacort herded Gabriella to the other end of the small room. It wasn't nearly enough separation for my liking, but neither the confines of the base nor the Sarac were big enough to contain the eruption that had been brewing since we left Earth.

Delacort turned back to the room and spoke loudly so he could be heard through the comm system. "I want Rikard confined to quarters, captain. There will be no discussion on this. Is Sergeant Carlysle there, please?"

"That can wait, commander." Logan stood, dominating the room. "We need to get real busy, right now.

"Wirkkala, get to Shokasta and prepare for immediate launch. You have about sixty minutes at a guess. I'll take care of the exit. Commander, what do you need right now?"

Wirkkala left without a word. Delacort didn't answer immediately, and it was clear he was still boiling over at the thought of Rikard's betrayal.

"I need to..." He looked panicked for a moment. "No, I have to get back to the Sarac. We need to fight."

"I'll take him," I said to Logan. "I can't do much here anyhow."

Logan nodded. "Could you fly *her*?"

"The Hopper? Sure, I can fly anything. You know me."

"I was talking about Shokasta. We'll need someone, and your flight skills are better than mine."

I felt a surge of excitement at the idea. Piloting a starship? Even if the Jump drive wasn't working, it was still the most advanced ship humanity had.

"You're not going anywhere without me, soldier." Dollie grabbed my hand.

I turned and faced her, hating myself for what I knew I had to say. "You can't come. We'll need every bit of space available to bring back as many people as possible."

She sniffed loudly. "This better not be some gallant gesture."

I turned to Logan. "Look after her until I get back."

He gave a grim nod. "Go."

I ran out of the room, heading back towards the Hopper with Delacort and Gabriella following. A couple of minutes later, I strapped myself in the pilot's chair and brought the systems online with several swipes.

Delacort was already fastening himself into a spare seat. "You know how to fly this thing?"

After disengaging the docking locks, I boosted us away from the airlock, hitting the lateral thrusters to spin the nose around in a tight arc. "Let's find out."

The tunnel entrance leapt towards us as I punched full thrust.

There wasn't a lot of time, and I didn't want to waste even a few minutes more than necessary. The passage was smooth enough that I felt comfortable flying at that speed, though unlike Logan, I had to concentrate one hundred percent.

The boxy shape of the Sarac hovered in front of us as we emerged, seemingly undisturbed by the approach of the Huòshèng. Delacort twisted as he looked through the small cockpit windows and shook his head. "I don't see anything."

"You wouldn't. Two hours out puts that ship far away. It would be difficult to spot visually unless it was silhouetted against something, and difficult even then." I checked the instruments and opened a channel to Sarac. "Captain Medved. Joe Ballen with Commander Delacort in the Hopper. We should dock in twenty-three minutes."

"*Da*, I have you on scope."

The inner airlock opened, and we threaded our way to the control room through a mass of activity more panicked than practiced. Medved barely looked up as we entered, while Rikard sat to one side staring at the floor.

"What's he doing here?" Delacort grabbed Rikard by the collar and jerked him to his feet. "We should airlock the bastard."

"Ship's engineer. We need." Medved barely glanced at Rikard. "Also, only brother I have."

"He's a traitor." Delacort tightened his grip. "We'll die because of him."

"They only want ship," Rikard croaked. "Give to them and everyone will be safe."

"How much are they paying you?" Delacort snarled. "What price did you put on your own brother's life?"

"I take no money," Rikard snapped. "They want stop Atolls too. Like us."

Even if what Rikard said was true, it was hard to have sympathy for him. The PAC might nominally be allies, but there was no doubt of their intentions with an armed gunboat on its way. Using Rikard to hide their presence from the ship's sensors made it clear enough they weren't here to support us.

"Commander." Medved finally gave his full attention to us. "You defend starship. That important."

"What about the PAC?" Delacort looked from Medved to his brother.

"That our business." Medved thumbed his chest. "We have debt of honor. Rikard, take weapon station. We fight side by side as brothers."

Rikard looked about to choke up, then pulled himself to his full height. "*Da, Da!* Always brothers. *Borimo zajedno.*"

"Take your soldiers and go," Medved said to us. "This our fight."

Delacort thumbed the ship's announcer and ordered his men to meet us back at the airlock. When we got there Gabriella was waiting, rifle at the ready.

"Where do you want to be?" he asked her.

"Is there a good choice, darling?" She looked at me, then back to Delacort. "If Sarac is boarded I'm probably more use fighting here. And quite frankly, I don't think I have too many friends on Kressida."

"We better get the prisoner." Delacort said. "He might still be useful."

I nodded and headed for the bunk where Paek was shackled. On the way I stopped briefly to grab the gun I'd picked up in the engine room, just in case, then hurried to get the prisoner.

"There seems to be some panic." He was smiling as I pulled back the curtain on his bunk, his smashed nose giving his voice a slight whistle. I unfastened the cuff around his wrist and locked it around mine. "From the desperation, I'd guess my friends are coming. You won't get away so easily this time, I assure you."

"We'll see." I pushed him roughly towards the docking port, metallic groans and the oily hiss of hydraulic systems filling the corridors. Medved was readying the defensive systems for the PAC ship. At least I *hoped* it was him. If it was Rikard, our situation might have gotten a lot worse.

"You're a smart man, Ballen. You know you have no chance against us," Paek shouted over the noise. "Surrender, and I'll make sure you're treated fairly. You could get a nice reward too."

"The Atolls treat an *Earther* fairly? That'll be the day."

Paek pulled back slightly on the cuffs. "We're not animals. We all share a common heritage."

I pulled him forward. "First *Toller* I've heard who's admitted that."

He ignored my deliberate insult. "We might even offer sanctuary in an Atoll. It's been done before."

"One more word and I'll shackle you to one of the gun ports. You can have a premium view of the battle."

He didn't respond, and a few minutes later we were at the docking port. I handed Delacort the cuffs. "He talks too much."

Before Delacort could answer, the internal comm system crackled to life. "USN Sarac, this is Captain Chen of the Confederation cruiser Huòshèng, along with representatives of the Executive. Surrender your vessel and no one will be harmed."

The PAC had close ties with the Commerce Executive, a group of leaders selected from the major independent corporate alliances, so it wasn't too much of a surprise to find they were operating alongside them—everyone wanted the secrets of the Ananta technology, and it was looking like SecOps security had holes big enough to drive an asteroid through.

"Ići uživo u paklu." The venom in Medved's voice made the intent clear even if I didn't follow the words.

I climbed back behind the controls and fired up the Hopper's engines, flipping the comms switch. The ship was crowded with Delacort's team, ready to defend Shokasta. The hull vibrated gently as the engines fought against the docking clamps. "Ballen here. Ready to depart."

"Good luck, my friend."

I hesitated, knowing I should say what I'd been thinking for a while but not wanting to add to his problems. "About Evans, back in the engine room..."

"*Da*, Rikard killed him. It was accident. He caught brother disabling engines and they fought. Gun went off in struggle."

"But—"

"Worry about yourself, Ballen. We are good."

The Hopper disconnected from the Sarac with a *clang*, and I wheeled the ship around as we backed away. Medved was still broadcasting the communications from the PAC ship, and his voice buzzed around inside the Hopper.

"Sarac, we will be in weapons range in thirty minutes. Please signal your surrender."

We were about halfway back to the asteroid when the next broadcast came in, this time from the Sarac.

"Huòshèng. This is USN Sarac, Rikard Medved in command. We surrender."

Mutters of disbelief filled the restricted space inside the Hopper—the broadcast had gone through the internal speakers, so everyone heard it. If I'd taken a poll at that point I don't think Croatia would have been hot on anyone's favorites list.

"Knew we should have 'locked the bastard," Delacort said.

I found it difficult to believe Rikard would betray us and his brother like that, especially after he'd been caught. You almost had to admire his acting skills—he'd appeared so contrite.

"People in the asteroid." Chen's voice sounded again. "You have the same choice, lay down your weapons and put up no resistance and you will live. My orders are only to recover the starship and scientific data."

There was no response except a sharp curse from someone behind me, followed by a metallic click and the power hum of a weapon charging. A minute later the crater wall blocked our view of the Sarac and we plunged into the tunnel, the inky blackness broken only by the bright dots of the navigation lights.

Delacort leaned over. "If I get my hands on Rikard, I'll personally throw him into an airlock naked and laugh as the pressure drops."

"We have other things to worry about. Like getting through this alive."

The comm system beeped—it was Logan. "Joe, head straight to the Shokasta. No point wasting time."

I spun the Hopper, boosting back to kill the velocity to match the ship with the docking port at the "hilt" of the Shokasta. When I flipped the other way, we were pretty close to being lined up, and I smiled.

"Not bad for an old guy," I muttered, killing more of the ship's momentum with small touches on the controls.

Logan was waiting inside the airlock.

"The Huòshèng is within visual range." He ushered us inside. "They'll be at the Sarac in a few minutes."

We hurried through to the Shokasta control room, which was very different from the one on the Sarac. The freighter's command center was a gray box barely large enough for four people to stand in and had no seating—not surprising for a ship that spent almost all its time on autopilot. The Shokasta's bridge was a wide room that tapered towards the "front" of the ship. The walls were a pale gray-blue and clean—more like a doctor's exam room than the mix of grime and dirt I'd typically expect inside a spaceship. There were two main piloting stations next to each other in the middle of the room with supplementary stations on both sides. It looked more like the flight deck of a luxury suborbital than a deep space vessel. Then I remembered it was technically a *starship*, so it had every reason to look different.

I slid into one of the piloting stations, my stomach doing a crazy cat dance at the thought of taking her out, and pulled the main console into operating position. Although the number of panels was dizzying, I breathed a sigh of relief when I saw the main piloting interfaces were familiar enough. On the left was a bank of controls related to harvesting Casimir energy, while on the right was an impressive array I guessed was related to the Jump drive.

"Thrust and rotate, Ballen," I repeated my old pilot instructor's mantra. "That's all there is to it. Thrust and rotate."

"Sarac, prepare to be boarded."

Chen's voice crackled through the speakers as I scanned the console. Logan had entered the control room, already suited up. He moved to one side, put his helmet down and flipped several controls to bring an external view up on the large central screen.

"We've got some external pickups," he said.

The picture wasn't hugely helpful. The gray blur of the Sarac sat near the center, and next to it the more distant blur of the approaching Huòshèng. Logan adjusted the screen, zooming in on the Sarac.

"Could we hit them with a missile?" I looked over at Logan.

"We could if they were still active." He shrugged. "But they're moving them onto Shokasta."

"As per my orders. First one should be online in thirty minutes." Delacort marched into the control room, his eyes fixed on the main screen. "What about the Sarac? Do we target her too?"

It was a good point. Even with Rikard's betrayal, we had no idea of the situation on board. There were innocent people on there, no matter what he was guilty of. I wondered at what point collateral damage became acceptable.

I brought the navigation systems online, clusters of indicators flickering on and off as I ran through preflight checks to keep my mind busy. I also wanted to give myself at least a little time for familiarization. I gestured to Logan, and he came over.

"I've never flown anything this big." I kept my voice low so only he could hear me. "Couldn't you take it?"

"I could, but I've got all the technicians and Dollie in the Hopper. I want them clear of Shokasta just in case. Wirkkala could, but between you and me he's a sim-jockey, not a real pilot." Logan clapped his hand on my shoulder. "You'll be fine, Joe."

I was glad Dollie would be safe with the technicians; despite everything, Shokasta *was* still an experimental ship. I plotted the escape course, checking the 3V proximity display and the navigation display. From where I was sitting the tunnel looked way too small for us to get through. "You sure this thing will fit?"

"You have two meters clearance." Logan grinned and grabbed his helmet as he headed for the door. "Why do you think I need to detach the Hopper?"

The large display screen abruptly went white, and a blast of deafening static erupted from the speakers until I found the controls to kill them. "What the hell?"

"What happened?" Delacort looked at me, but I had as much of an idea as he did.

Logan rushed back, moving over to the external monitoring system. He operated the controls, the picture crackling and twisting with electronic disturbance. When the screens finally settled enough to see anything again, only a single gray blob was visible.

"The Huòshèng?" Delacort's voice was a half-whisper.

Logan adjusted the magnification, revealing a familiar shape as the comm system crackled into life again.

"Shokasta, Captain Medved here. Ruse worked, Huòshèng destroyed. Sorry we have you worried."

Delacort commandeered the comm. "Captain Medved? I salute you and your crew."

"Rikard's idea." Medved gave a sharp laugh. "Make them think he control ship, then launch all weapons when they close. Good job."

I heard loud cheers from down the corridor as the news spread. But although it was an amazing victory, it didn't change the fact that the Atoll ships were closing. "We still need to get out of here."

Logan nodded. "See you outside."

I thumbed the announcer. "All crew and passengers, prepare for acceleration. Burn in three minutes."

The mooring claps retracted smoothly, and the umbilicals connecting us to the base disconnected. We were on our own. I checked the condition of the docking port, and a few seconds later the indicator turned green as Logan moved the Hopper away. Delacort was looking at me with a strange expression.

"Ketchup on my shirt?"

"Did Logan say two meters clearance?" he asked.

"That's what he said." I activated the thruster controls, ready for maneuvering.

"Is that enough?"

"Sure." I placed my hands on the main controls, triggering a short blast on the rear thrusters. "Gives us a hundred centimeters each side."

I pushed the ship a little faster, wheeling the long hull around to line up with the hole in the rock, and checked the rotation as we drifted towards the craggy inner surface. The ship's length made her sluggish to react, then the nose slipped into the tunnel, and I balanced the maneuvering thrusters. I was hoping I could get through without leaving paint behind. The forward display showed the sharp edges of the tunnel against the stars beyond, looking almost close enough to touch. Sweat matted my shirt against my spine as I concentrated on guiding us through.

"With spit and patience..." I spoke softly in the quiet of the control room.

The proximity warnings had been flashing continuously as we edged through the narrow tunnel, but flickered off one by one as we emerged—Excalibur lifting itself from the stone. Finally, the last of the lights darkened, and I breathed again.

I flipped the switch to broadcast throughout the ship. "Welcome to the maiden voyage of the USN Shokasta. Dinner and drinks will be served in the main ballroom at seven o'clock, with dancing afterward at the captain's discretion."

We moved out to meet the Sarac—connecting via the docking tube. Logan had also docked and joined us as we made our way through the flimsy tunnel, meeting with Medved's crew and the Shokasta technicians in the freighter's wardroom. It was the only place large enough to hold everyone from both sides, but it was as crowded as a subway car at rush hour. I pushed across to Dollie and saw her wrinkle her nose—too many sweaty bodies in too small a space.

"Thanks to Captain Medved and his brother Rikard, we have *some* breathing room. Even if there's not much in here." Delacort was squashed in at the front, hands behind his back. "But we don't have a lot of time—Atoll cruisers will be here in a few hours and still outgun us.

"My team has been ordered to investigate anomalous readings originating in deep space. Beyond Neptune's orbit. No manned Earth vessel has ever been that far out, and we've no idea what we'll find. Possibly a malfunctioning probe, or it could be nothing. Regardless, SecOps doesn't want to risk letting the Atolls get their hands on it first.

"Many of you are not soldiers. These orders don't apply to you, of course. But I'm sure you understand we have to do our jobs, as you do. Therefore we will have to split up. Sarac will wait here and face the Atoll ships before making its way back to Earth. Meanwhile, Shokasta will investigate the signals. I'd like all my team on the Shokasta, but given the circumstances, everyone else has a free choice."

"We fight Atolls?" Rikard said and several people muttered their support.

"The Sarac is no match for one Atoll ship, never mind two, and Shokasta has even less weaponry right now. We can't count on the same luck we had on our last encounter. If you offer no resistance, I'm sure the Atolls will let you head back to Earth. They have nothing to gain by holding you."

There was a muted murmuring. People were obviously unsure Delacort was right. I did some quick calculations in my head and didn't like the answers. "Captain? What's the best transit you can make back to Earth?"

Medved rubbed his wiry gray beard. "Limited fuel. Need to boost and cruise. One hundred days possibly."

I'd figured around twenty percent longer, but the captain had a better idea of the reserves on the Sarac. Either way, three months was too long.

"Dollie can't wait that long." I reached out and held her hand. I could feel her shaking.

Delacort nodded. "I know, Ballen. She'll have to come with us."

Again, I did the math. That wasn't a lot better. Even running at full speed, it would take Shokasta around four weeks to get out to Neptune's orbit. With no delays, it was an eight-week round trip. The only consolation being that at least Delacort could provide *some* medical help, even if it was minimal.

"I'm sure the Atoll ships would have better facilities." Gabriella spoke up from across the room. "That's another option."

"Don't even think it, Joe." Dollie gripped my hand tight enough to hurt. "I'm not letting you out of my sight."

"Then we're both staying with the Sarac."

"Everyone decide where they want to be. I plan to leave with the Shokasta in thirty minutes. Dismissed." Delacort walked over to us and held up a hand. "Would you wait till the others have gone. There's something we need to discuss."

"I know what *you* want to discuss. But I don't. Let's go, Dollie."

"Wait a second, Joe. I have a say too. He's the closest thing we have to a doctor. Let's at least hear him out."

I turned back to face him against my better judgment as everyone else left. As soon as they were gone Delacort tried to speak, but I cut him off.

"You want me to pilot Shokasta, I get it. But nothing will persuade me to risk my wife and our child."

"Logan says you're the best man for the job. I believe him."

"Logan exaggerates my talents."

Delacort ignored me. "The report on the signals from deep space said they looked like nothing. A bunch of regular pulses with no discernible pattern or content..."

"Then it doesn't sound like anything you need me for." I half-turned again.

"Listen to him, Joe." Dollie squeezed my arm hard enough to make me wince.

"But there was one word that came through in standard, unencrypted text." Delacort stared at me. *"Ballen."*

Twenty-Three

Dollie headed back to the Shokasta to pick out quarters for us while I went to our bunks to gather up our few belongings. After packing everything into a pair of canvas bags I shuffled back towards the docking port. As I approached the mess room, I heard a loud voice. It was Paek, leaning against the far wall drinking from a tube of coffee. He looked like he was passing a sunny day on a street corner, but his voice filled the room, despite the slight hiss caused by his damaged nose.

"...have to face it. If you don't hand yourselves over, the Atolls will finish you. You have no choice—it's surrender or die."

"We took care of that *Pansy* ship pretty handily." It was one of Sarac's engineering crew who'd been temporarily assigned to help out with the hasty transfer work. A bulky Polish guy called Setlack with a square goateed face set in a permanent scowl.

Paek's audience included more of the Sarac crew, along with some of the MilSec team. They were toying with remnants of food that littered the tables when they should have been moving equipment over to Shokasta. Time was short, but Paek was on a roll.

"The PAC is scarcely any more developed than you people are. They simply don't compare with two cruisers full of well-equipped and highly trained Atoll combat troops."

Paek walked over to the nearest table and placed his hands on the edge, leaning over the diners. Once the fight with the Huòshèng was over, Delacort had decided he wasn't too much of a threat and assigned him to help move supplies between Sarac and

Shokasta. Which surprised me—it didn't seem smart to have him wandering around freely with the Atoll ships approaching.

"You don't deserve this," Paek continued. "None of you. You're all good men, I can see that now. But you simply can't compete with Atolls. It's like asking a child to fight a grown man.

"Providence has ordained the Atolls will be the greatest liberator of humanity. By building our societies away from the decadence and filth of Earth, we have freed man from the restraints of the antiquated thought that has come to dominate its corrupt societies. Freed ourselves from the dirty self-mortification of fake conscience and morality. We have delivered freedom and independence to our people which only a few can bear."

"You sure like to fire that mouth of yours," Setlack grumbled, accompanied by loud grunts of agreement from the other men. "You should give it a rest before we decide to let you off to wait for your friends—without a P-Suit. Earth is the center of mankind. Whether you *degenerates* want to admit it or not."

"The laws of nature decide who is the superior—those who survive become the tigers, the others become lambs. There's no shame in being weaker, it's science, pure and simple." Paek pointed at the men. "If the people of Earth dropped their illusions of still being the tigers and settled for the life they have, the Atolls would certainly be more generous as the true homo-superior."

Paek strode over to Setlack. "The rule of selection justifies our superiority by allowing the survival of the fittest. The vile superstitions of Earth are contrary to natural law, a worthless protest against nature. Taken to its extreme, Earth would promote the systematic cultivation of human failure. Is *that* what you want the legacy of our species to be?

"Look around. All of you." Paek drew himself up. "We know there are other civilizations out there. We know, sooner or later, we will be forced to confront them. Would you want the charge to be led by the pure logic and superior minds of the Atolls, or the pathetic husks of broken and brainwashed savages?

"Earth is at an end and has been for decades. The future of the people of Earth is to die from the hunger, pestilence, and disease brought about by their own sickened hand."

Setlack clambered to his feet and grabbed Paek by the neck, his fist thudding into the Atoller's stomach.

Paek laughed. "*We* will lead humankind to the stars. *We* are the shining light of expansion. Only us."

Another punch caught him on the bridge of his damaged nose, and a thick ribbon of blood shot out, leaving a spray of crimson across the bulkhead. Several MilSec people rushed forward, trying to pull Setlack away, while Paek continued his screaming vitriol.

"Surrender. Surrender now! And we may let you live out your lives with some comfort. We may toss you poor wretches the bare minimum of a life. But it will be the Atolls who save future generations and will take the great fight to the stars. We will destroy you in your weakness. The future belongs to us in its entirety!"

One of the soldiers chopped Paek across the neck several times. Finally, his words stopped, his eyes rolling back in his head as he went out. I wasn't surprised it took that long to shut him up. Although he wasn't especially brawny, he had a powerful build that spoke of regular hours of working out.

Another soldier pulled Setlack off, then they carried Paek out of the mess room leaving a trail of blood floating in the air. I had no sympathy for him. He'd brought it on himself, and I was glad I hadn't had to get involved. I didn't think I had the self-control not to vent my own anger at his words. I moved back from the doorway as they passed. Gabriella was leaning against the bulkhead, watching as the SecOps guys dragged Paek out. She smiled at me, her full red lips glinting wetly.

"I heard you're staying with the Sarac," I said.

"Sometimes walking away is the smartest decision you can make." She swaggered over and draped herself on my shoulder. 'You could come too. I still think we could be good together."

"And I still think I'm married." I pulled back. "And you're still involved with Delacort."

"Jealous, Joe?"

"Not in the least. He's definitely more your style."

"He's married too." She pouted. "But he's more imaginative about it than you."

"I'm happy to disappoint you."

Gabriella shrugged. "Someday you'll get tired of playing the boring old house-husband. When that happens look me up."

"Sure, I'll put an ad in Hired Killers' Weekly."

"Simpler to call."

She handed me a contact card. It had a stylized grim reaper design on it, holding a scythe in one hand and a rose in the other. At the bottom, the phone combination read, 8888-SexDeathAnd-Money."

"Nice tagline."

"That's all there is in the world, Joe. You should know by now."

I tossed the card back at her and picked up my gear. "I don't need it."

"I've never met a man I couldn't seduce before." Her eyes were a mixture of anger and lust. "Why are you so different, Joe?"

"Because I love my wife. Or perhaps it's because I haven't forgotten you killed my friend. You choose."

I found Dollie in our new quarters. The Shokasta had proper rooms and, after what I was sure must have been an excessive amount of pouting from Dollie, we'd been assigned a double. It wasn't much. About the size of a prison cell and the separate bunks reinforced the similarity, but at least it gave us a sense of privacy we'd been lacking on the Sarac.

My thoughts were still locked on the news from Delacort. A signal from deep space was one thing, but the idea it was related to me was ridiculous, if not impossible. Although my ego might sometimes try to convince me I'm the center of the universe, the rational part of my brain knows better. I was sure it had to be a mistake, or some crazy scheme Delacort had thought up to get me to go along.

"You have to go." Dollie was sitting on the lower bunk, leaning against the wall. "We both know that, and I'm not leaving you. There's no room for negotiation, Joe."

The look on Dollie's face was clear. There was no point arguing. Despite that I was still worried. As far as we could tell she was somewhere between twenty and twenty-four weeks into her pregnancy, and she'd been feeling the baby move. It was hard to be sure because we didn't know exactly when she had conceived, and with her altered genetics we had no real idea of what was safe.

"Is there anything you need for the journey? If it's available, I'll make sure you have it."

"I know you would, Joe." Dollie smiled, moving over to hold me in her arms. "All I want is right here in this room."

I nodded, feeling like a selfish bastard. I should have been doing everything to get her back to Earth, but a huge part of me wanted to make the trip. I'd never had the chance to go into deep space and it called to me like the distant call of a wild goose. I wanted to see what was *out there*—even though I knew it was probably nothing. I was still figuring out my reply to Dollie when Delacort's voice came over the speakers.

"Ballen, put your pants on and get up here. We need to leave."

I kissed Dollie, our lips lingering briefly. "Captain Ahab is calling."

"I'll be waiting." Dollie patted my behind. "Do your duty, soldier."

I left and threaded my way to the control room. As I passed by the docking port, I saw Logan suited up and frowned. He was talking with one of the female technicians who hurried off as I approached.

"Why the P-Suit?"

"I'm not coming, Joe." The lines around his eyes deepened, and he gripped my arm. "Have fun out there. I wish I could have made it with you."

"What the hell? You're as space crazy as I am, how come?"

"I'm responsible for the technicians." He grinned. "Make sure you take plenty of pictures."

"That's crazy. Let me talk to Delacort, he can assign someone else to babysit."

Logan smiled ruefully. "I can't do that, Joe. It's my obligation."

"There are always limits. Isn't that what you told me?"

He laughed and clapped me on the shoulder. "That's true—for everyone but yourself."

I shook his hand. "Next time, partner. I'll give you the grand tour."

"You better." He walked to the docking port. At the door, he turned back. "Watch yourself out there, Joe."

"Don't let Gabriella get under your skin. She's dangerous."

He grinned. "I'll be keeping her on a short chain all the way home."

With that, he was gone. One of Delacort's men sealed the 'lock, and I made my way to the control room. I wanted to check out the navigation system to see if there were any options that might help us. Despite getting the ship through the asteroid tunnel, I still had doubts about operating something that big.

The system was definitely a step up from anything I'd used before. Whoever designed it had put a lot of thought into deep space navigation. I wondered idly if it was a product of espionage—the system was reminiscent of Atoll technology I'd read about, which they kept strictly to themselves. All the copyrights listed in the information screens were for Earth-registered companies, though, so possibly my imagination was overactive.

I entered in a few queries, and the system brought back answers in a few seconds. Comparing our current position to where the signals had supposedly originated, the only possible maneuver that could help would be a slingshot orbit around Jupiter. Despite Shokasta's sophistication, the giant planet's deep gravity well could accelerate us to velocities considerably higher than we could achieve using our engines alone.

"We'd save around four days," I explained to Delacort as the Shokasta was prepped for departure. "Not much, but every bit helps. Right?"

"What's the downside?"

"You tell me. I don't think anyone has done a slingshot orbit around anything with a crewed vessel. Perhaps some of the Atoll deep space research vessels, but if so, we don't have the data."

"It's risky?"

I thought about it. Everything about space travel is risky. Until humans learn to breathe vacuum, it always will be. "There'll be tidal stresses on the ship it wasn't designed to cope with. There's also a radiation hazard that close to Jupiter, and we'll have to pass through the planet's ring system, which could cause hull damage. The rings are tenuous, and the ship specs say we should be okay."

"But we might not be..."

"We could crack open in Jupiter orbit, we could fry as we pass, we could explosively decompress or any combination of those. It's a risk, as I said." I gestured at the navigation screen at the two blips representing the approaching Atoll ships. "They're still faster than us. Do you think they'll hesitate if it means they can overtake us?"

Delacort paused. "Set up the slingshot, but check with Earth. They might have a better idea. This is above my pay grade."

"Okay."

"This is a tactical decision, Ballen." He looked straight at me. "Nothing to do with Dollie?"

"Absolutely."

He left, and I programmed in the departure. Despite my show of confidence, it was a tricky maneuver. If we were going for quickest transit time it would have been easier, but we needed to be able to slow down at the other end. That meant we'd be threading the eye of a very fine needle, with the needle being the biggest chunk of mass in the solar system outside the Sun.

"Attention, Earth vessels." The signal came through on the comm system, and I switched it to broadcast throughout the ship. "Commander McDole of IDA Goeppert. We order you to stand down and prepare to be boarded. Failure to comply will be considered a hostile action and we will destroy you."

McDole had an assured feminine voice. Atolls had the reputation of having entirely non-discriminatory societies even down to combat roles. It was one of the things they claimed made them better than us lowly "dirt-eaters," and in some ways it was true. While the USP was generally (and legally) free from such discrimination, the situation was different in many other areas of the world. Old Europe was mostly gender-bias free, but the PAC, and especially the MusCat Alliance, were still firmly rooted in the Dark Ages.

I heard a familiar voice on the next transmission. "Commander McDole, this is Logan Twofeathers aboard the *USN* Sarac. We are conducting a rescue salvage mission in free space. You have no jurisdiction here."

"Mr. Twofeathers, we have all the *authority* we need. Earth forces have been legally barred from space activities beyond Earth orbit for twenty-three years." McDole hesitated. "We outgun you ten to one. We are authorized to use force to stop you if necessary. Now stand by to be boarded."

"I assure you, commander, we have more than enough weaponry to take out your ships if we want to." Logan sounded calm, but I knew he was playing poker with an empty hand. "I suggest you move off, and let us take care of our business."

"Apologies for my directness, but I don't think a single ore carrier and an *experiment* constitute much of a threat."

"That might be true if that was all we had. But we also have an asteroid armed with multiple laser cannon and interceptor missiles. How far do you think you'll get against that?"

There was a long pause. It was a brilliant piece of strategic bluffing. An asteroid provided an almost limitless heat-sink capacity, as well as the physical strength to take a pounding. Any ship, even an Atoll one, was weak in comparison.

"I don't believe you." Despite McDole's words, both the Goeppert and Bethe slowed far more than necessary for a simple ship-to-ship rendezvous. "This is a trick. We know your weaponry down to the last round."

"Did you know of the existence of this base?" Logan asked.

Delacort had arrived back at the control room during this exchange and took a seat at the secondary control station. "Tell me you've plotted the course."

"Not yet." He frowned, and I held up a hand. "I have enough to get us out of here. We can correct on the way."

"Then do it. Before those bastards decide to ignore Logan."

"All hands, prepare for acceleration—thirty seconds."

I tapped the last few buttons to engage the pilot. The lights switched from orange to green, and the countdown appeared on the main display. At zero I felt the pressure build, not intensely but a gentle push that changed the perceived orientation of everything. Once more, weightless passages became corridors and walls became floors.

"Earth ship. Disengage your engines or we will fire." McDole's voice was calmly determined. There was no bluster in her words.

Our speed crept up as the distance from us to the Goeppert and Bethe increased. A warning sounded, and a red light appeared on the display. "They've launched a missile," I said.

We had point defenses available, but they offered only limited protection. And while we'd moved some of the weaponry over from the Sarac, it wasn't installed yet, and there was no way a ship could outmaneuver a missile. The missile track closed, drawing level with the Sarac, and then vanished.

"You're clear, Shokasta." It was Logan. "But we used all our defenses taking down their missile. So get your asses out of here. We'll delay them as long as we can."

"You can't fight them, Logan," I said into the comms. "It's suicide to try."

"They don't know that." I heard him laugh. "Remember to send a postcard."

With that, the comm channel shut down, and I could only guess at what was happening behind us.

Twenty-Four

After leaving the Sarac we monitored the comm channels as best we could. I'd half expected Logan to do a crazy banzai run at the Atoll ships, but instead, he was far more cunning. He had Medved maneuver Sarac into a strategically strong position, but then slowly fall back towards the asteroid as if drawing the enemy ships into firing range of weapons on the rock. It was brilliantly deceptive and left the Goeppert and Bethe little choice but to waste time in costly moves that got them nowhere. By the time we were too distant to track the situation easily, we were days ahead of them and had a reasonable chance of maintaining our lead all the way out into deep space.

There was an unexpected broadcast from Goeppert four days out. When I opened the channel, McDole's face appeared on the screen, her shock of silver hair cut as sharp as her uniform. She didn't look exactly happy. "We have your people, Shokasta. All safe and well, you will be pleased to know."

"I'm glad there were no further casualties," I replied. "But will they remain safe?"

"We have no quarrel with construction workers and technicians. We've recovered our man Paek, transferred a few supplies to the Sarac, and will allow her to continue back to Earth. As long as they attempt no further delaying tactics, we will take no action against them."

"That's very enlightened of you."

"Our only interest is the starship." Her mouth was a sharp crease. "I don't imagine you'd care to discuss turning it over to us?"

"How about an exchange?" I gave her my best smile. "You give us the Goeppert."

McDole laughed. "I'm hardly in a position to do that."

"Then you know how things stand here."

"I could possibly pull some strings, however." She smiled. "Get you your own ship."

"In the Atoll navy? I'm sure I'd be welcome."

"Not that, perhaps—many of our people have an irrational fear of Earth people. Much like yours have of the Atolls." She nodded to someone outside the pickup view. "But I'm sure we could arrange for you to have a ship and free license to operate. That's your ambition, isn't it, Mr. Ballen?"

I wasn't surprised she knew who I was. The Atolls have their own intelligence networks the same way Earth factions do. They're better at it, because we have such limited access to their habitats. "I have a ship."

"No, you don't." She picked up a lidded cup of red liquid and sipped, holding the liquid for several seconds in her mouth before swallowing. "Earth still makes the best wines, even if my compatriots don't agree. Earth has a ship. Your MilSec paymasters have a ship. You're a pilot for hire—and we can pay more."

"How about I arrange for a dozen cases of the finest vintages to be delivered to you?"

"That sounds very pleasant." She sipped her wine again. "And what do I have to do for them?"

"Leave us alone. Report back you couldn't track us. Tell them we were too devious for you."

McDole laughed again. "You overestimate both your charm and my appetite for humiliation."

"It was worth a try."

Despite her somewhat severe look, her eyes were warm. "You're the same Ballen who helped launch the Ananta?"

"There's a rumor to that effect."

"You're quite the independence fighter, aren't you? A lot of my compatriots would cheerfully have you executed."

"A friend of mine once said the best way to judge a man was by the size of his enemies."

"I hope we're not enemies, Mr. Ballen." She sipped her wine again. "I said *some* people would like you executed, I don't say I necessarily agree. Some of the actions against Earth have been...misguided."

"I don't imagine that viewpoint is very popular with your people."

"We have different opinions, like you have on Earth. Does everyone in the USP agree with every decision taken? Do you?"

I thought about the almost constant outcries for more or less intervention in social matters, industry, and commerce, not to mention the daily protest groups outside the Senate. The only thing "united" in the USP was the name. "I've never seen such tolerance from an Atoller before, especially a soldier. It's quite refreshing."

"Perhaps you'd like to discuss it further? Over a bottle of wine, perhaps?"

"That sounds very pleasant." Was she really attempting seduction via the comm? "But I'm not sure my wife would approve."

"Ahh, yes. Earthers have such a limited view on those matters."

"My wife is on board Shokasta..."

McDole looked a little disappointed. "I have duties to attend to. But we'll talk again, Mr. Ballen."

I ended the transmission and laughed to myself. The whole thing was outrageous.

"Make sure you remember that, Joe Ballen."

I looked around to see Dollie standing by the control room entrance. By the look on her face, she'd heard and seen enough to hang me out to dry, even if it was entirely innocent on my part. I blew her a kiss, hoping it would soothe her savage jealousy.

We confirmed the Jupiter slingshot with Earth. The USN techs took several days to analyze our options. But they couldn't come up with anything beyond minor refinements to the course I'd plotted with the Shokasta's own systems. The new trajectory would take us inside the orbit of Callisto and above the ecliptic plane relative to Jupiter. That would lower the potential radiation threat, as well as the danger of the dusty rings.

As before, Delacort had his own priorities and focused on

getting our weapons installed and operational. Luckily, Shokasta had been designed with standard weapons mounts so physical installation wasn't the challenge it had been on the Sarac, but testing and operational verification was still time-consuming.

Delacort was unhappy with my work, and I wondered how much was to do with the rate of progress and how much was down to him being Mr. Grumpy after losing his psycho-with-benefits, Gabriella. I was in the small engineering shop when he walked in, wearing his now standard-issue frown.

"What's the latest?"

"The railguns are up and running, two of three lasers functional. I'm running the automated testing cycles on the remaining one right now. They should be complete by the end of the day. The only outstanding item is the Sharur missiles. Those are useless."

"Useless? They're state of the art." His frown deepened, and he pushed past me to the fat cylindrical missile housings I'd parked out of the way. The shop had basic tools and workbenches but was the same size as a regular cabin, making it as tight as a banker's smile.

"They use non-standard mounts." I slapped the case of the nearest. "Or rather, standard mounts we're not equipped with. Physically, they won't fit in the missile bays we have by a factor of about five. You know how the government loves standards, that's why they have so many."

"So what was the point of bringing them?"

"Beats me. Phallic symbolism for the troops?"

Delacort knew better than to rise to my comment. "What about the individual warheads?"

"I'm not privy to military secrets. I'm a civilian, remember?"

"I know you, Ballen. If it's engineering, you know something about it."

He had me there. Some people learn what they need for a job, and that's it. But some of us have "satiable curiosity" which leads us to delve and dig into areas far outside our official remit. Though in this instance, the truth was I didn't know much.

"Each missile is packed with up to twenty-four submunitions. Each warhead is deployed in a standard MV4 package, though the number and configuration of each are unknown and can be programmed, to an extent, according to tactical requirements."

Delacort shook his head. "Where do you get all this from?"

"Lifetime subscription to *MilTech Digest for the Home and Family*."

"So is it possible or not?"

"We don't have a mounting rack for them, but I could rig something. What suicidal idiot has volunteered to disassemble the Sharurs?"

"I was hoping you would."

I laughed so hard my ribs hurt. "I assure you reading a few articles doesn't make me in any way qualified to dismantle the necking things."

"Okay." Delacort shrugged. "Find me someone who *is*."

"You realize if anyone tried and made one mistake, this entire ship would be vaporized."

He moved over to the door, then looked back. "Whoever does it better be very careful, then."

I looked over at the missiles and shivered. Delacort was right. There was no one more qualified than me, but it didn't mean I had any illusions about my chances. What I'd said wasn't an exaggeration—the whole missile system was designed to be tamper-proof. One wrong move and you'd trigger the warheads or other lethal access-prevention mechanisms.

I examined the casing of the top tube. The main housing was secured by a number of keyed fasteners. We didn't have a key, though I could make one if needed, but something told me unlocking those and pulling off the nose wasn't the way to enjoy a long and prosperous future.

"I don't know who's crazier." Dollie sat across from me with arms tightly folded as I explained what Delacort wanted. "Him for suggesting it, or you for considering it."

"Be generous. Call it fifty-fifty?"

Dollie thought for a few moments. "You can't do this on your own, can you?"

She was right. It would be impossible to work on the release fasteners and any tamper circuits while holding the housing. "I'd need a helper. Delacort is the obvious choice."

"You have a helper, Ballen. Me."

I held up both hands. "No way. I'm not letting you get involved in this."

"I *am* involved." She stood and moved to the other end of the bunk. "We all are. If this thing goes off, what chance do any of us have?"

She was right, and I knew it. If I made a mistake, the ship wouldn't survive the detonation more than a few minutes at most. "I can't let you."

"Then *you* don't do it." Dollie moved up and gripped my hand. "I don't intend outliving you by even a single minute, Joe Ballen. So you'd better deal with it."

There was something primal inside me that made me proud of her fierce loyalty, even though I thought she was as crazy as I was. Whatever happened, we were both insane enough to be with each other.

"Could Earth help?" she said. "They must know how to open the damn things."

"We're too far away." I thought about it. We'd moved the secure comm system from Kressida. It could only transmit simple information, but that might be enough to guide us through the procedure. I surprised Dollie with a big kiss. "You're a genius."

"One of us has to be."

She slapped my ass as I ducked out of the room and headed to the control deck.

The comm system worked perfectly. The magic of quantum entanglement doing its weirdness in the right way. Once we had their attention, MilSec Central was there all the way, with answers in minutes or seconds depending on the complexity of the question.

The only thing that worried me was the speed of information input and output. To ask questions we had to enter text through a terminal and wait for the answer to be typed back to us. Sometimes this would lead to delays of a minute or two while the information was assembled and entered. Not long in some ways, but far too long to be waiting around with a triggered warhead on a countdown to explode.

I tried to come up with some way of mitigating a disaster but couldn't think of anything practical. We could have done the work outside the ship—that would have reduced the destructive potential of an explosion. But the idea of carrying out such a delicate operation while wearing a P-Suit wasn't worth thinking about. In the meantime, we ran through simulator exercises on the computer to familiarize ourselves with the process. If anything, Dollie had a better memory than me, especially for operation sequences, and drilled me mercilessly.

Eventually, we decided the best we could do was isolate the machine shop by closing and locking all the bulkhead doors. It almost certainly wouldn't help, but it might give a few survivors a slight chance of staying alive a little longer—though who'd be able to rescue them out this far was another story.

Everyone but Delacort moved to the front of the ship, the farthest they could get away from us, and were already in P-Suits in case we triggered a "rapid uncontrolled disassembly" of the ship. He stayed with us, or rather hovered in the doorway out of the way. There wasn't space for three inside the room.

I'd fabricated three keys according to specs transmitted by MilSec. One unlocked the fasteners, while the others opened access panels to give us entry to the arming circuits. That *should* allow us to disarm the missiles completely before having to disturb anything physically. I only hoped the military minds were right.

"Open access panel B. Use key number one. One half-turn, clockwise," Dollie read out.

I pushed the key in and turned as instructed. The panel clicked, and the small door popped open slightly.

"Open the access panel, reach in and press the blue button. Limiting degree of opening to maximal, seventy degrees," she said.

"They love to give you the critical information at the end of the instruction." I opened the door barely enough to see inside and slip my fingers through. Then pressed the button and felt it click. "Okay."

Dollie took a breath. "Open access panel A. Use key two. One full turn counter-clockwise."

I moved over to the second access panel and opened it, confirming the operation with Dollie. Despite the temperature being constant, blobs of sweat floated off me in the low gravity.

"Open the panel fully, and press the following sequence of buttons." She waited till I opened the door and reached in. "Blue.

Red. Yellow twice. Set dipswitch one, five, two and nine, in that order. Then press the red button again. Now press both green buttons simultaneously and hold for ten seconds."

"I think *we're* a couple of extra *dipswitches*..." I held them as instructed. My fingers were greasy and almost skidded off, then the light flashed and remained steady.

"Done."

"Now the tricky part. Once you start this sequence, you only have sixty seconds to complete it or the warheads detonate."

The sweat was pooling in the small of my back—I didn't need the reminder. "Got it."

"Like playing a game of *Simon*, Joe," Dollie soothed. "Ready?"

"Yeah...never played it with a bomb before." I took a slow breath. "Okay."

"Open access panel C. Use key three. Do not open wider than forty-five degrees. Find the red and black button. Press and hold. Then *I* press the two black buttons inside panel B and hold those down. While I hold, you completely remove the fifth fastener from the top panel, looking from the front and working counter-clockwise. Okay?"

I ran through the sequence in my head. We'd done this at least a few hundred times on the simulations, but faced with the real thing, the danger from the slightest slip magnified the tension. For a second, my hand trembled uncontrollably, as though I was having an attack of neuralgic shock, but I knew I wasn't. I wiped my forehead and took two deep breaths.

"Ready." I inserted the key.

"Wait, Joe!"

I froze. Not daring to breathe. Dollie slid over and kissed me. "Just in case."

"Your timing is terrible. I almost had a heart attack." I smiled, though.

"Any chance you two can keep this to yourself for the next couple of minutes?" Delacort mumbled from the door.

"Go get 'em, soldier." Dollie grinned. "I'm ready."

I put the key back in the lock and turned. The flap popped open and I caught it, preventing it from opening too wide. I glanced in and spotted the red and black button. It was deep inside the casing, and I'd have to reach to get to it. I pressed the flap tight against the back of my hand, losing some skin in the process.

"Done," I said.

Dollie reached around, slipped her hand inside her panel and pressed. "Go for it."

I pushed the key onto the fastener and turned. Nothing happened.

"It's stuck."

I twisted with more force. I'd made the keys in the RepliSys and wasn't sure how much torque they would take before stripping. If it broke, we were dead.

The seconds were ticking away inside my head and my pulse thumped. Another twist and the fastener gave a little. I turned it again, seeing the faint line of one of the fastener threads gleam as it unscrewed into the light. My arm was aching from the reach, and my hands shook with the strain.

"Joe?" Dollie hissed.

"Almost."

I twisted several more times, a bead of cold sweat trickling down into the corner of my eye. Then the fastener popped out and lazily pinged off the floor when it fell. I dragged in a huge lungful of breath, then froze as I heard a high-pitched *beep*. Followed by another, and another.

"What the...?"

The *beeps* seemed to be on a countdown. I knew we'd done everything right. Were the directions wrong? Something we'd missed?

The tenth *beep* was longer than the others, then there was silence.

"It's disarmed?" Delacort whispered.

I took another breath and slumped next to Dollie. "I think it was warning us we'd shut down the protection system."

"They could have told us," Dollie said, her breathing almost as heavy as mine.

"Well, now we'll know when we do the second one."

Dollie looked at me as if I was insane. "You're not serious?"

I nodded towards Delacort. "Ask him."

Twenty-Five

As we were fully familiar with the process, we had the second missile open in a fraction of the time it had taken to do the first. Once disarmed, actual disassembly was routine, and I quickly built up a pile of MV4 warheads along with other components. I fabricated a mounting rack from the cradles inside the Sharur missile. It was crude but functional. Luckily, the MV4s were smart enough that the launch mechanism wasn't critical. The biggest problem was there was no way to build a feed mechanism, so if we needed to use them, someone would have to be brave enough to load the tubes by hand. I left Delacort to figure out who he wanted to risk.

All this monkeying around burned up time, and almost before I knew it we were picking up Jupiter on the scanners. Even though it was still only a distant blob, the instruments showed we were accelerating towards it, sucked in by its mammoth gravity well.

Unlike our travel to the Belt, we weren't under full "silent running" conditions. There wasn't much point—the Atolls knew we were out here. From their transmissions, we knew the Goeppert was following us in a similar trajectory. They were creeping up on us slowly, but not at any rate we needed to worry about. They also used the power of their comms to relay news channels from Earth, which I thought was considerate. The transmissions became a fixture of each day. Commander McDole didn't even bother censoring them, perhaps because she knew we weren't much of a threat.

A long-running feature, which had several of us hooked, was

259

the ongoing talks between Earth and the Atolls. Our journey to the Belt and into deep space had triggered an upsurge in calls to end the Atoll embargo on Earth space activities. Both sides were back at the negotiation table, even though it was only a virtual one, and although there hadn't been any real progress, at least they were talking.

Dollie was in the control room with me most days. It bothered Delacort, until I explained she was a trained pilot, and I was familiarizing her with the ship as a backup. If anything happened to me this far out, the ship would have little chance of getting back to Earth, and even he wasn't regulation-bound enough to forgo a spare pilot.

I wasn't surprised at how quickly Dollie picked everything up. The biggest difference between space flight and an Aeromobile is the speed and distances involved. In an atmosphere, you rely on the soupy air to control your flight. It provides lift, allowing you to fly, drag which controls your speed, and resistance allowing you to turn. In space you have none of that. It's a point-and-squirt environment. If you pick up speed you'll travel at that velocity forever, until you effect a slowdown or hit something. It's much easier than atmospheric flying, but the simplicity is deceptive to senses attuned to normal conditions on Earth.

Once Dollie had built up her confidence, we ran through a series of maneuvers designed to test her skills. The end results were carefully designed to be trajectory-neutral. She breezed through them without the slightest falter. I kissed her and draped a gold star around her neck.

"What's this?" She fingered the garish necklace.

"Something I fabbed to honor this momentous occasion." It wasn't much, just a printed yellow star tied to a piece of electrical wire.

"You're such a romantic."

She wrapped me in her arms, and we kissed for longer. She was showing signs of the pregnancy now, a deliciously cute pot belly which looked silly next to the rest of her otherwise trim figure. I patted her stomach lightly.

"How's he doing?"

"He?" Dollie lifted an eyebrow. "It could easily be a girl."

"Boy sperm are stronger swimmers. Well-known fact among spacemen."

"Girl sperm are craftier. They confuse the male ones and get in there first."

I laughed. "I don't mind either way."

Dollie smiled hesitantly. "It's going to be okay. Isn't it, Joe?"

"Sure. We'll head to where the signals are coming from. Find there's nothing there and head back. Job done."

A thought struck me, and I swore.

"What is it?" Dollie snuggled into my arm. "You okay?"

"Sure, I just remembered it's that awful vegetable soup concentrate for lunch today. I'm sick of that stuff." That was true but wasn't the reason for my cursing. "Isn't it about time for your nap?"

Dollie glanced at the time on the main screen and nodded. "One of the worst things about this little bundle of joy is how tired it makes me."

I helped her out of the pilot seat and gave her a quick peck as she left. As soon as she was out of the door I opened a search on the main computer. Terrified of the results I might get.

Two hours later I called Delacort up to the control room.

"You're sure about this?" Delacort looked frazzled, and I guessed he'd been asleep when I called.

"No. I'm not *sure*. There's hardly any research data on this. Think about it. Who the hell would deliberately expose pregnant mothers to radiation for science?"

"Tollers would—if the mothers came from Earth."

"Don't be ridiculous. Does Carrie McDole seem like the kind of person who'd do that?"

"Don't trust her, Ballen. No matter how friendly she seems, she's still a Toller."

I shook my head. "That's beside the point. The slingshot trajectory we have exposes us all to radiation. The calculations say the levels are low and we'll be through it quickly enough that it won't cause any real problems. But that's with adults. We have no idea what it might do to an unborn child."

"We can't turn back. You don't know it will harm either of them."

My fists clenched. "What do you expect me to do? Sit here and let the radiation damage the baby?"

"Call Earth, then. Ask them. But you know what they'll say." Delacort jabbed his finger towards me. "I know you, Ballen. You don't raise problems without having a solution. What do we have to do?"

"Am I getting that predictable?" I brought up the deck plans on one of the consoles, highlighting part of the schematics. "This is the main airlock with the entry chamber inside it."

"Okay..."

"There are pressure doors on either side." I pointed to where the internal bulkheads were.

"How does that help?" Delacort looked puzzled.

"It means I can isolate this entire area. It's at the center of the ship, so radiation shielding is at its highest there already.

"First, I install the accelerator coils from the lasers all the way around it." I saw his scowl and held up a hand. "Don't worry, they'll still be usable after. It's only while we're closest to Jupiter. No one is going to attack us in that time frame.

"That'll create an electromagnetic bubble around the chamber and help deflect the radiation. Then we line the whole area with high-density plastic foam."

"Where do we get that?"

"Mostly from the furniture. I can also print some supplementary pieces using the RepliSys. Again, none of it will be harmed, so you don't need to worry about sleeping in an uncomfortable bed all the way out into deep space."

Delacort gave a slightly approving grunt. "You've thought this out."

"Once that's done we flood the compartment."

"What?"

"The best protection against radiation is water. I can rework the plumbing easily enough. Once the piping is done we drain our water supplies into the 'lock. That'll provide maximum protection for anyone inside."

"Great idea, Ballen." Delacort looked back at the schematics as though they were yesterday's leftovers. "And what do we do for water for the rest of the trip?"

"Water is a somewhat reclaimable resource as long as we keep on breathing. But even without that, once we're through, we pump the water back into the regular tanks. Minimum losses all round. Plus everyone inside will be in P-Suits to minimize contamination."

"That'll work?"

"According to the math."

"So like the Rabbit Hole?" Delacort rasped his hand over the stubble on his chin. "I dunno...what do you mean by *everyone*?"

I brought up the navigation display showing our projected trajectory around Jupiter. "If we put everybody in there, we can tolerate a higher radiation level overall. Going deeper into Jupiter's gravity well means we pick up a bigger slingshot effect *and* make sure we stay ahead of the Goeppert."

Delacort smiled for the first time since coming into the control room. "Couldn't they do the same thing?"

"Their ships are larger. With a bigger crew. They won't be able to shield everyone."

Now he was actually grinning. "Sounds like a good plan to me. Confirm it with Earth."

I didn't think it worth mentioning it would also trim a little more off our travel time. The days ticking off the calendar were making me nervous.

Dollie wasn't thrilled by the plans when I told her. She had this crazy idea about missing out on the sights of Jupiter as if we were still tourists on Luna. She also wasn't happy at the thought of being inside a P-Suit for several hours, which was understandable.

"Ouch," she said.

"Hang on while I loosen a strap."

I was trimming an emergency P-Suit to fit her as well as possible, something complicated by the fact that she was firstly, a little small and secondly, becoming increasingly larger in certain areas.

She winced. "Are you doing that deliberately?"

"Sure. I enjoy tying you up like a trussed chicken and causing you pain." I loosened the leg straps more.

She winked. "I never realized you had such a kinky side. You should have mentioned it."

"Any kinks I have, you've given me them."

Dollie grinned. "That's true."

Luckily, general fit suits have a lot of room for adjustment—astronauts come in all shapes and sizes—which meant it wasn't too hard to allow plenty of space around her midriff. The biggest problem was arranging the straps so they wouldn't inadvertently pinch.

"This thing's going to balloon a lot, so movement will be difficult, but don't worry. You'll be surrounded on all sides by the rest of the crew."

"Floating in an ocean of strange men? This is sounding more fun by the minute."

Something else I'd "forgotten" to mention to Delacort—human bodies are also a good form of radiation shielding. "Don't get too excited—I'll be there too."

She patted my cheek. "You're the strangest of the bunch."

"Thanks. The objective is to build the best barrier around you. That will minimize yours and the baby's exposure to radiation."

"Thanks, Joe."

I snugged the straps in place and stood up. "For what?"

"For looking after me...us..."

"You don't need much looking after."

"Maybe, but it's nice anyway." She brushed her hand against my face. "This wasn't my choice, you know."

"The trip? I know, it just happened. Or do you mean the baby?"

"I mean the way I am." She waved her hand up and down. "Being so physically confused."

I was a little shocked. Dollie always acted as though her hermaphroditism was a decision she'd made, and I'd never looked deeper for an explanation. Geneering had changed most people's concept of a "standard" human being so much that such changes weren't especially uncommon anymore. Although her transformation was more extreme than others, I knew other people had similar procedures done entirely through choice.

"Want to talk about it?"

She looked a little sad. "The truth is I don't know anything. I've always been like this as far as I know."

"Parents?"

Dollie shook her head. "Never knew any. I grew up in an orphanage, like you. It wasn't good for me."

She didn't need to say any more. Orphanages are tough environments for any kid long-term. I could only guess what it would be like for someone as different as Dollie. They provide shelter and a generally safe environment, but sensitivity and tolerance aren't among their strong points.

"It wasn't until they found me running wild on the streets and took me to the Geneium that I even knew others like me existed. Without Kinsella, I wouldn't be here."

I'd never met anyone who was proud to be an orphan or who had good memories of their time at an orphanage. It was far more common than it used to be, but this hadn't removed the stigma associated with it or the alienation that came from having no solid roots to hold onto.

It also explained why she was so close to Kinsella. After her early experiences, time at the Geneium must have been like arriving in paradise. He would be a savior and father figure, all rolled into one.

I slipped my arms around her waist and kissed her. "I wish I could have saved you from all that."

"You did." She kissed me back.

The fabrication process was straightforward, though the time involved pushed us closer to the limits of safe Jupiter approach. I was in the control room checking the trajectory once more, when the comm system alerted me to an incoming message.

"Hello again, Joe." McDole's hawkish face appeared on the screen. Her voice had a pleasant rasp, but there was a hint of probing behind it. "We've detected a change in your heading. Is anything wrong?"

"I'm touched by your concern. Everything is fine, thanks. We made a few course corrections."

The intensity in her eyes was noticeable even through the screen. "According to our calculations, your new course will take you dangerously close to Jupiter. If you're in trouble, don't be afraid to ask for help. We'd be happy to assist."

I could guess what assistance would be available...and the price. "We appreciate your offer, but everything is fine."

Her jaw tightened. "What are you planning, Joe? According to our figures, you'll be fried. The military might risk it, even possibly Joe Ballen, hero of the Ananta, but you said your wife is with you." McDole leaned closer to the pickup, her voice lowering. "I also heard she's pregnant."

Someone had been talking when they shouldn't have been. "Is that your concern?"

"The Atolls believe in the sanctity of life. I'd be unhappy if we'd pushed you into something drastic and, in doing so, endangered a child."

"You believe in the sanctity of Atoll life, you mean?"

"All life, Joe." She sniffed. "I know politically we're opponents, but you know we're not barbarians."

I tried to control my anger but wasn't entirely successful. "Tell that to the people who died in the attacks on Deimos base or Helios station."

McDole didn't look especially embarrassed. "I understand your point and won't attempt to make excuses. But those were military operations against adults, not children."

I smiled. "You'll forgive me for saying that sounds incredibly hypocritical."

She nodded. "It does, but please don't risk the child for politics."

"I wouldn't risk my child for any reason. And certainly not to make a political point."

"You have the right priorities."

Her image disappeared, and I closed the comm channel. I wasn't sure if my priorities were right or not. I was doing what I always did, making the best of whatever circumstances I found myself in. That's all you *can* do. I activated the correction control sequence simulation to run a final verification.

Jupiter floated on the main screen like a giant gibbous beach ball. At this distance, the cloud bands were clear, as was the Great Red Spot. It was hard to believe I was seeing it with my own eyes—that storm had been blowing on the planet for hundreds of years, and would almost certainly continue for hundreds more. I couldn't help but wonder if the conflict with the Atolls would last as long. *I am constant as the Northern star* came to mind and I swallowed—the only thing constant about humanity was its propensity for violence.

The console beeped. The navigation sequence was confirmed. I hit the button to broadcast throughout the ship. "All hands report to the inner airlock chamber."

All the others were waiting when I arrived. The MilSec team was mostly suited up, while Delacort and Carlysle were helping Dollie strap into the suit I'd modified.

"Everyone okay?" I grabbed my own suit from the rack.

"Some of my people are worried. Six hours is pushing the limits of our suits' atmospheric capacity."

"I know." I pointed at Dollie and myself. "It's worse for us. We need to change tanks."

I'd rehearsed the procedure with Dollie several times. I would make the actual switch, but I wanted her to know how in case something happened. I wasn't too worried, but the P-Suits were designed to function in a vacuum, not underwater, so there was always a nagging doubt.

Once everyone was ready, I moved Dollie to the middle of the chamber and tied her ankles to the floor with short straps. She said that was part of my perverted fantasies, but the real function was to make sure she floated as near to the center of the chamber as possible to minimize exposure. I'd used the same setup for all the crew, but in my case, I had a detachable strap I could hook to my waist. It left me free to disconnect and move around if needed.

Everyone was arranged carefully around Dollie, packed in fairly tight, and I hoped nobody was too claustrophobic. The pattern was meant to ensure minimum exposure, but also, I'd secretly stacked the rows to block the areas where the magnetic field would allow most radiation leakage—a selfish decision, but one I didn't feel guilty about.

I had a small Scroll taped to the back of my wrist. It was hardwired into a systems jack in the wall. A regular unwired connection would get knocked out by radiation impacts. Though it was clumsier, the hard-wired connection was more resilient. I pressed a button on the Scroll, and the bulkheads closed in front and behind us, the metallic *crummp* filling the chamber momentarily. As soon as the seals engaged, water bubbled out of the improvised outlets.

"Deep breath, everyone," I called out as the water level reached the rim of my helmet.

The water continued to rise until it was over our heads. It wasn't immediately obvious visually that we were surrounded by liquid. There were a few silvery bubbles here and there, and you could feel the resistance when you moved, but beyond that, there was little difference.

"Everyone report."

Delacort's voice came over the radio, followed by the rest of his team as they confirmed their status. Finally, both Dollie and I agreed we were okay.

The first couple of hours dragged, and I was sure several people fell asleep. I almost did, too. There was nothing to tell us what was happening beyond the walls—the rest of the Shokasta could have melted around us for all we knew. I felt warm and sweat coated my skin, but I think it was more psychosomatic than anything—I hoped I hadn't miscalculated and we weren't committing a glorious act of hari-kari-style broiling.

At the halfway point, I changed Dollie's tank. Her face was calm through the visor of her helmet as I turned off her air temporarily. She wasn't in any danger and had enough inside her suit to keep her going during the transfer. The new tank connected easily enough, and I purged as much water out of the lines as I could before opening the inside valve.

"Okay?" I asked.

She smiled, giving me a stiff thumbs up. "Seems to be."

"Okay, my turn."

I closed the suit valve and disconnected my tank before grabbing the line from the spare and pushing the fittings together. I didn't feel the locking snap as I should have, and I tried again. Still nothing.

I checked the connector. I couldn't *see* anything that would stop it from working, and I hadn't had a problem when I'd tested the connections. Of course we were underwater now, but I couldn't see why it shouldn't work. I brought the connectors back together and was about to try again when the lights flickered several times. Then a vibration hit us, the water inside the room pushing at my arms and legs. The lights went out, and the tank connector slipped from my hand.

It wasn't completely dark, though it took a while to adjust to the change in brightness. I could see the dim operating lights on the P-Suits around me, but it was impossible to see anything else clearly in the flickering lighting. I knew there was a chance of power fluctuations but hadn't anticipated complete failure.

"Would everyone switch on their suit lights." I spoke into the radio, but there was nothing but static in return, and I guessed the radiation had knocked out the comm system as well as the lights.

By now I was feeling nervous. The air in the suit would be getting thin, and I willed myself to stay calm and breathe steadily. I was becoming disoriented. The darkness made everything look different, as though I was in a twisted watery hell surrounded by lunging hydras.

I remembered the Scroll taped to my arm and checked it. To my relief it was still working, and I switched it to text mode, then dashed out a quick message and held it up in front of Delacort.

"Turn suit lights on. Everybody."

He didn't respond immediately, and beads of sweat ran down my neck. There couldn't be much oxygen left in my suit now, and my head was swimming.

A light popped on, half blinding me, then another and another, until everything around me was filled with a ghostly half-light that moved and swayed. I saw the spare tank hose to my right and grabbed it once more. Fumbling to line it up, I finally got the two to go together, this time feeling the click as the fittings locked. I pawed my gloved hand at the supply valve, managing to turn it on the third or fourth attempt, and water sprayed inside my suit as the fresh air supply blew the line clear of water remnants. I took a deep breath, my lungs aching as I sucked the oxygen-enriched gas.

"Let's not do that again, Ballen," I said to myself.

I finally looked up to find everyone's attention on me and gave them a thumbs up. I leaned into Dollie and touched my helmet to hers so she could hear me.

"I'm okay," I shouted.

Her voice was muffled but understandable when she replied. "What happened?"

"Dropped the line when it went dark." I didn't want to worry Dollie by mentioning the struggle with the connector. "Took a while to find it, but I'm fine."

"You better be."

Everybody switched off the lights on their suits to save power, leaving us floating in almost complete darkness. I felt the tug of several more vibrations through the liquid. I could only guess at what was happening outside our watery cell. The maneuver was fully programmed, but if the thrust sequence didn't function, we'd plummet into Jupiter.

Most people slept, at least the ones closest to me did. I couldn't, partially because I felt responsible for everyone, but mostly because I was still edgy over what had happened with the tanks. It was possible we'd need to do the same thing on the way back, and I didn't relish the idea.

The time on my wrist Scroll ticked slowly by, and I checked it far too frequently, willing it to pass quicker. When the countdown finally stopped, the screen flashed, and I activated the controls to pump the water out of the compartment. I didn't feel proud, only an overwhelming relief we weren't part of a bizarre dead aquarium in space.

At first, the water level didn't seem to change, and I panicked a little thinking we might be trapped. Then it dropped steadily, a silvery turbulent meniscus that edged past our helmets. After it dropped past our ankles I unlocked my helmet and cracked it open. The air was okay—at least I couldn't smell anything other than a slightly damp odor. I triggered the controls for the door, but it stayed firmly shut. Dollie had unfastened herself and splashed her way over to me.

"Some engineer you are," she said. "After all this, you've got us trapped."

I shrugged. "The radiation must have knocked out the main power. But there's a manual door release."

I moved to one side and opened the panel to the release lever, pumping it several times. After several repetitions, the door creaked heavily, and a split second later the two sections of the pressure doors split at the middle and edged apart. Delacort moved up with some of his men and grabbed the door edges, forcing them back.

The corridor was almost as black as it had been inside the compartment. Some emergency lights provided a sinister glow, and in several places, lights flickered intermittently. Farther down, I saw sparks shooting from an access panel, and the air was filled with the acrid tang of ozone mixed with melted plastic.

I headed towards the control room. "No rest for the wicked."

Twenty-Six

Dollie entered the dim control room carrying coffee and a sandwich. I checked the time, realizing that not only had three hours passed since we'd come out of the airlock chamber, but I was hungry enough to eat a medium-sized asteroid if it came with salt and pepper. "I hope that's for me."

"Of course. It's that awful rehydrated synthetic chicken; even the smell makes me nauseous. I think when we get back I'll invent some decent space rations. Demand must be huge and with this thing—" she handed me the plate and gestured at the ship. "—the market is going to be expanding."

"Dollie's Divine Deep-Space Dishes." I opened the wrapping on the chicken and started drooling at the smell, even though I knew Dollie was right. "Four-Ds for hungry spacemen."

She pulled back a little. "And women. You sexist pig."

"That's *Mr.* Sexist Pig, s*weetheart*." I grinned at her response. "I guess we'll need to work on it."

Dollie slapped the console nearest to her. "So how is the old bucket o' bolts?"

"Are you referring to Earth fleet's most advanced vessel or me?"

She pulled a high-protein bar out of her pocket. Although she'd been critical of the chicken, the bars were only slightly more attractive in my mind. Though they *were* more bland, which worked better for her.

"We should keep it." She nibbled on the bar. "What do you think? The first married explorers of the universe?"

"Where would I put the *baby-on-board* sticker?"

Her response consisted of equal parts cheerful vulgarity mixed with painful anatomical suggestions. Just what I'd expect of Dollie. "We'd only get them angry if we kept it. The first space pirates, perhaps?"

Dollie pulled a face. "That sounds far too exhausting right now."

I opened up the power schematics on the main screen, highlighting the main couplings within the Casimir generators. "There's a problem somewhere in that mess. I don't know where."

"Which is why we're still wandering around banging our knees." Dollie took a drink of my coffee. "We've got no power?"

"The generators are working one hundred percent. We have power, but for some reason it's not routing anywhere."

"Can you fix it?"

"Not until I can figure out what's wrong." I swallowed another bite of the sandwich. "I thought initially it might be the radiation—unlikely as everything on the ship is supposed to be hardened—but it's possible we hit a hot pocket."

Dollie finished her bar, picking the crumbs out of the wrapper. "But that's not the problem?"

I shook my head. "If it was I should have been able to reboot the system and bring it back online within thirty minutes. It's more like a physical break somewhere." I pointed at the screen. "I've narrowed it down to this section. But there's nothing vital or vulnerable there. And nothing shows on the diagnostics except the failure."

She chewed on her lip, looking deliciously sexy. "What about the orbit?"

I grew suspicious. "Did Delacort send you? That's a cheap—"

"He didn't *send* me." Her jaw tightened. "He's concerned—we all are. You vanished in here as soon as we came out of the hole, and no one's seen you since. He *was* going to come up here and ask, but I thought you'd prefer a visit from me. I wasn't wrong, was I?"

Her question had an edge to it, and I smiled the best I could. "I'd take a visit from you over soldier blue any day."

"Good."

"We've got no propulsion right now." I held up a hand to

forestall her obvious question. "The slingshot went perfectly, but we aren't accelerating anymore."

"So the Atoll ships are catching us?"

"Slowly. But the longer this continues, the less advantage we get from the deeper slingshot." I finished my sandwich and drained what she'd left of the coffee in one swallow. "I need to trace the circuits physically. I was about to take a look. Come along if you want."

Dollie shook her head. "No thanks. I'll report back to Delacort and go back to bed. I'm not feeling so well."

I walked with her to the shared communal area, then worked my way farther back. The power stopped somewhere between bulkheads thirty and thirty-three, which put it close to the Casimir generators, and aft of the main airlock where we'd ridden out the radiation.

The first two inspection covers I opened held nothing unusual, and the portable diagnostic tool showed the circuits were active. When I opened the one just inside bulkhead thirty-two, I was greeted by a mess of charred wiring and melted plastic. One of the power relays was completely fried.

I tested the power to make sure it was dead and dug at the burnt mess with a screwdriver. The relay came off with some grunting and skinned knuckles and I pulled it out from the compartment. There was something about the molten lump that didn't look right. Several more minutes of digging at the charred remnants and I levered off what looked like a smaller separate box.

It looked oddly familiar, and I went to find Delacort. He was in his compartment, polishing his pistol. Which was a stupid thing to do as we weren't likely to see that kind of close-range action for a long time, if ever. He looked up when I entered, gave a sheepish smile, and put the gun on the table. "I know...it's a habit. Comes from being in the military so long."

"Do you still have that small QuBee?"

He didn't answer immediately but stood and opened one of the drawers on the far side of the room. "It should be in here."

He hunted around for several minutes, then turned towards me. "It's missing."

I put the small melted box on the table next to his gun. "Not anymore."

Delacort picked it up and peered at it as if he could see right through it. "You sure?"

"Not a hundred percent, but it makes sense." I tossed the burnt out relay on the table too. "Looks like someone used it to improvise an explosive device. One that could be triggered at any distance."

He stared at the blackened pile on his previously pristine desk. "Who the hell would do that?"

"Ask yourself this. Who had access to your personal gear before and after we moved on board?"

Delacort was silent for several minutes. Then his face darkened and his brows furrowed. "That *bitch*..."

"You only just realized?" I suddenly felt weak and my legs almost buckled. I was running on fumes. "It was a quick job, not very effective. I can fix it, but I'll have to cannibalize some other parts. Mostly from the weapons systems."

I thought for a second I was going to have another dumb fight with him over the weapons, but then he sighed. "Okay. Get on it, I want to get back up to speed as soon as possible—we can't let the Atolls close on us."

"Tomorrow. Right now, I'm going to sleep for at least six hours."

"But..." His voice trailed off, and he glanced at the melted QuBee again.

"Don't worry, I won't tell anyone."

Patching the circuits was a nightmare. Although I knew what I was doing in theory, the configuration wasn't like anything I'd worked on before; understandable given the semi-experimental design of the ship. Even the quantum link to Earth was useless, as the only person who might have been able to help was Denny Wirkkala, and he was incommunicado while taking the long way home on Sarac. I had a strong hunch McDole's friendly overtures wouldn't extend to relaying technical messages to Sarac, which might be impossible anyway with the distance. Even if she agreed, we couldn't trust her.

Dismantling one of the railguns to cannibalize the circuits was relatively easy, a satisfying combination of gratuitous destruction and component matching. The hardest job was stripping out the basic parts and exposing connections so I could reconfigure them as bridges to replace the damaged components.

I had the power relay pulled out of one of the railguns and on the workshop bench when a comms signal came in from the Goeppert. McDole's face appeared on the screen. We hadn't heard from the Atoll ship for a couple of days, as they were out of contact while rounding Jupiter.

"Congratulations. How does it feel to be one of Earth's greatest astronauts?"

"I didn't realize my reputation was spreading."

McDole smiled. "You are officially the farthest traveled crewed Earth ship in history. No one else from Earth has reached deep space before."

"I thought you'd had people out as far as the Kuiper Belt?"

"We have. But those were Atollers, not Earthmen."

I understood what she was saying, but the way the Atolls tried to cast themselves as different people grated. "It must be annoying seeing us in a ship with technology you can't match."

"A temporary advantage, and soon lost." Her voice became more earnest. "You could help there."

I was rather insulted at the implication. McDole had seemed almost sympathetic and human compared to other Atollers. But perhaps she'd been playing games all along. "I could, but why would I?"

"You're an engineer, aren't you? You know the term *fit for use?*"

I wondered where she was leading and decided to play along. "Sure. How does it apply here?"

"Shokasta is equipped with revolutionary technology which might take you to other star systems—if it works. But you know Earth. Do you think it still has people who could take advantage of that? Who'd be willing and capable of moving out of the solar system with intelligence *and* benevolence?"

Her mention of Atoll benevolence was risible considering they'd already attacked us for leaving Earth orbit. "Some will. I'll be first in line."

"And I'd applaud that. You're clearly a good man but hardly

representative of the current state of the species, are you?"

"Is that a compliment?"

She smiled. "Take it any way you'd like."

I took a drink of coffee instead. "Is there a reason for today's call, or is it *flatter the dirt-eaters* day?"

"Have I ever used such a horrible phrase?"

"Not that I've *heard*."

She leaned closer to the screen, her eyes looking almost as large as the great spot on Jupiter. "That's one of the reasons I like you, Joe. You're a realist."

I waited for her to continue.

"We detected a change in your flight path after the slingshot. I hope there's nothing wrong."

The tone of her voice didn't alter, but her question was far from innocent. "We're conserving fuel and doing some routine maintenance. Thanks for asking."

"Saving fuel? On a Casimir-powered vessel?"

"The drives use Li'l Princess Donuts as reaction mass, so we need to cook up a fresh batch."

McDole laughed. "Don't be too proud to ask for help. You should be well pleased with what you've done. Even getting this far is an incredible achievement."

I wondered if she added a silent *for a bunch of dirt-eaters*. "Was the explosion meant to disable the ship or send us to our deaths in Jupiter's gravity?"

She didn't even blink. "An explosion?"

"Drop the pretense. I assume Gabriella had a hand in it, along with Paek. I didn't realize the Atolls were so fond of psychopaths."

McDole grimaced. "We're not all as fanatical as he is. Haven't I proved that?"

"You still triggered the bomb. Unfortunately for you, the damage was minor. We'll be fully functional within twenty-four hours."

"You're a realist, as I said." She glanced away momentarily. "I hope no one was hurt. You can't blame us for taking advantage when an opportunity presents itself."

"I can and do."

"Would Earth have acted differently if the situation was the other way round?"

"The Atolls always claim they're technically and morally superior to those left on Earth." I reached towards the end transmission button. "From where I sit, it looks like you're bred from the same mongrels."

"Wait, Joe." McDole leaned towards the screen. "Can we speak privately?"

"I'm alone," I said. "But make it quick, I have work to do."

"What if you weren't able to complete the repairs? What would happen?"

"We'd be forced to slow down and ask for assistance."

"What would it take for you to tell the others you can't?"

The back of my neck prickled. "Thanks for the talk. As I said, I'm busy."

"I've been ordered to offer you twenty million credits and we'll give you the Shokasta back, after our scientists finish analyzing it."

"Twenty million is a lot of money." Enough for me and Dollie to live the rest of our lives in luxury. Hell, we could buy our way back into Luna with that much.

McDole's jaw tightened almost imperceptibly. "So, do we have a deal?"

"Not all dirt-eaters are for sale."

"They always have been in the past."

"An old Earth philosopher once said, *The times they are a-changin'*."

To my surprise she smiled. "Thank you."

"Huh?"

"For not disappointing me. I'm a soldier, I follow orders." She glanced to one side again. "Even if I don't always agree with them. Goodnight."

I was so shocked my usually dazzling wit failed me, and the screen went dark.

Twenty-Seven

Passing the orbit of Uranus was far less spectacular than our encounter with Jupiter, and apart from the inevitable flurry of sphincter-related jokes, was a damp squib. The planet was on the far side of the Sun from us and would have been visible only through a telescope. There was a trajectory change programmed—a minor correction based on new data refinements painstakingly sent from Earth, but it was coincidence rather than connected to our location in space. For some reason, I felt disappointed, even though I knew there was no chance of everything in the solar system lining up like a set of pool balls.

Carlysle had been in charge for the last two weeks while Delacort was officially off-duty sick. Dollie had monitored him closely, worried it might be early onset radiation sickness, but it looked like it was only a virus. After three days he insisted he was well, but she still wouldn't let him out of his room. On the second week, she allowed him "light duty" work, but only as long as it was brought to him.

When Dollie started with a fever and complained of headaches, it was my turn to worry. I kept her in our room and brought her meals to her. After a couple of days, her temperature returned to normal, and she appeared to be her old self or as near as possible given her condition. We couldn't decide whether it was related to what hit Delacort or a health wobble related to her pregnancy. I was just glad we hadn't turned into a plague ship. After everything else we'd been through, that would have been the final straw.

We were back up to full acceleration, and the ship was running smoothly, in spite of my Frankenstein-esque patchwork. We'd hit another milestone as the fastest crewed Earth ship, but that was curiously disappointing too. With no close points of reference, speed was almost meaningless. We celebrated with a small glass of Harris' hooch, but no one was in the mood to party.

The hardest thing to manage was morale. It wasn't my job, but Carlysle told me several of the soldiers were struggling with the long confinement and inactivity. Even Dollie was showing signs of tension, the lines around her eyes deepening as the days passed.

I had the constant thrill of being farther out in space, a lifetime dream that never grew stale. And there were always engineering tweaks to do around the ship, mostly mundane, but they helped to fill my time in ways the others didn't have.

"My back and shoulders feel like someone ripped my spine out." Dollie was stretched out on the bed, her stomach bulging like a small hill.

I moved next to her. "Roll over. I'll help."

I gently massaged her shoulders and back, eliciting sighs of weary relief. Even with the low gravity her joints were swelling. "Anything else I can do?"

"This crew's going nuts," she murmured between satisfied groans. "To be honest with you, so am I."

"I'm not sure I can help there. I'm an engineer, not an entertainer."

"Is there a difference?" She gave a short laugh. "You could engineer something for us to do."

"Any suggestions?"

Dollie wrinkled her nose. "How about some games?"

Her idea wasn't a bad one. The trick would be to come up with something challenging enough to be interesting but universal enough so everyone could participate.

We settled on ZHex-Chess. Most people knew the rules well enough to play, and the three stacked hexagonal boards would offer a good visual spectacle. I wired up a 3V display in the recreation area, and we set up a ladder system and individual matches using blitz rules—one minute per move, ninety minutes per game.

Its popularity quickly spread, with people betting on the results, team games, and even one-on-one "duels" and grudge matches.

There was usually a crowd of spectators huddled around the board, comprised of anyone off duty. I even used the RepliSys to create two small physical sets, so people could play or practice alongside the main battles on the 3V.

Once Delacort was off the sick list, he joined in as well and appeared better for the distraction.

"This was a good idea, Ballen," he said as we watched Carlysle and Dollie going head to head. "Gives everyone something to think about other than what's out there and what's behind us."

"Credit where it's due. It was Dollie's idea."

"It's a good one nevertheless. How come you don't play more yourself?"

"I'm usually busy."

The truth was, although I enjoyed the game, I wasn't very good. I didn't have the quick cunning needed for it, no matter how much I played. Dollie said I had faulty devious genes, but she liked me that way. She, on the other hand, was like a grand master and regularly beat all comers.

A mixture of cheers and groans came from the spectators, and I looked up. Dollie had torn through Carlysle's defenses using her Reapers and already had him in check.

"She's very good," Delacort said.

I agreed and stood. "I should go and monitor the course correction."

"Anything to worry about there?" Delacort tapped the table in front of him. "Should I come?"

"Only if seeing half a dozen indicator lights switch from orange to green is your idea of a wild night out." I stood and waved to Dollie. "I got it."

The control room was empty, and I slid into the pilot's chair. The screen was displaying an outside view and was black other than the pinpricks of distant stars. It felt almost lonely. When I first worked in space, I dreamed of making it to Mars. I tried to plan ways of getting there, either to the orbital platform or the planet-based mining operations, but it was almost impossible. Even back then, the Atolls controlled everything so tightly that only a few dozen Earth people worked there.

Now here I was. Almost eighteen A.U. beyond Mars. We'd

slid through Saturn's orbit without so much as a murmur—we were about forty degrees off its position at the time, so the planet wasn't visible. Again, only a line on a map to be crossed. I had to admit, I regretted not seeing it. Jupiter might be bigger and more dangerous, but Saturn had its glorious rings. With luck, I'd get back out some other time. Perhaps I could take Dollie for a second honeymoon there. That would be something.

After the programmed correction, we'd move beyond Neptune's orbit, although again the planet was in the wrong position for us to see it. Another week, and we'd be as far out as anyone had ever been, apart from long-distance surveys of the Oort cloud. It was a humbling thought. Earth was no longer visible by eye, far too close to the Sun to make out separately. Even the Sun itself was tiny. An almost impossibly bright dot, having no discernible disk. By the time we reached our destination, it would look like nothing but an ultra-bright star.

The Earth was nothing more than a tiny speck of dust floating through space with all of humanity compressed onto it. Even the Atolls had barely changed that picture. Humanity needed the Jump drive. Not only Earth, but everyone. If we were to survive as a species, we needed to move out from our home and find new worlds. We'd damaged Earth's environment almost to the point of destroying ourselves. I doubted we'd get another chance.

The navigation system beeped. We were close to the course correction point. I broadcast a warning throughout the ship, though the change was small enough I doubted anyone would feel it.

Our next "stop" would be the origin of the mysterious signals.

Outside the immediate vicinity of a planet or other astronomical body, space is as featureless as being trapped in a cellar without a flashlight. Sure there are the stars, but often they're obscured by local glare or the more distant glory of the Sun. If you're outside a ship or structure you might see them. If you're inside, almost certainly not.

We'd been slowing down since we passed Uranus' orbit. The thrusters now worked to haul us back from the tremendous speed we'd gained on the way out. It was hard explaining to the others why we needed to start braking so soon, but if we hadn't, we'd have flashed by our intended target and plunged headlong into the fringes of the solar system.

"Is there anything out there?" Delacort asked.

We were in the control room looking at the main display, which showed almost entirely black. I'd set it to overlay the best triangulation we'd managed on the signals, and the target area was highlighted by a dangerous-looking red indicator. "No records in our database. The only thing that could create any signals would be some sort of Atoll station or probe. Certainly Earth has never sent anything out here, except in passing."

"Anything on the scanners?"

I shook my head. As far as I could tell there was nothing even close. It looked like another patch of empty space. "What now?"

"We search."

"Okay...but how, exactly? Whatever sent the signal could be a few million kilometers away in any direction."

"Use standard search patterns. If we're methodical enough, we'll find it."

I grimaced at Delacort's inexperience. Standard search patterns work on the surface of a planet because the area is always relatively small, and you know your target is almost certainly on the surface, or at least close to it. In space, the distances are too large, and there's no surface to provide easy limits. If you widen your search pattern to cover a volume quickly, you'll leave gaps in your net and possibly be out of detection range of what you're looking for. If you tighten it up, you'll be searching the same relatively small volume until the Sun goes nova.

"I can plot an expanding spherical course. That'll give us the best chance of finding anything out here, but unless whatever it is shouts again, our chances are virtually zero."

Delacort thumped the control panel lightly. "We'll keep at it. Until we find it."

"We can't do that." I tried to hold my exasperation in check but failed. "First of all, we need to head back to Earth within the next couple of weeks, unless you want to do an emergency delivery on an hermaphrodite mother in deep space. It takes just as long to get back as it did to come out."

Delacort stiffened. "I don't mean to sound harsh, but Dollie isn't a mission priority."

"She is to me. And I'm the one piloting this ship." I took a deep breath. "Secondly, the Atoll ships will be here in three or four days at the most. Once *that* happens, we're screwed anyway. You know we can't take them on, and if anything *is* out here, it'll be in their hands."

Delacort nodded at the last point. "Do what you can."

He marched out of the control room, leaving me to my thoughts. I started programming the search pattern and hit the intercom at the same time.

"How's my favorite wife?" I asked when Dollie appeared on the screen.

The truth was she wasn't looking good and hadn't been for several days. The sickness had gotten worse for her, and she was struggling to eat because the food we had on board gave her heartburn. On top of that, she was getting heavier with the baby, which made it hard for her, even with the low gravity.

She lifted herself up a little on the bed. "How many do you have?"

"You know spacemen—a girl or reasonable facsimile thereof—in every port."

"I don't doubt it." Dollie gave a weak smile. "At least I'm still your favorite."

"Delacort wants us to do a search. Like we're looking for a capsized boat."

"How long will it take?"

"Less than four days. After that, the Atoll ships will make it irrelevant."

Dollie patted her stomach. "I can manage. It's not too long."

"I'll get you home." I hoped it wasn't an empty promise. "Got to do some work. I'll be down shortly. How about some food?"

Dollie nodded. "Soup or something else I can digest easily."

I closed the channel and tried to focus on the course settings. I should never have allowed Dollie to come with us. She could have stayed on the High-Rig, and I should have made her, though making Dollie do anything was always easier to say than do.

With the programming completed, I punched the execute button. From that point, we'd spiral outward with sensors in full listening mode. If there was so much as a peep, we'd know about it.

I was heading out to pick up the food for Dollie when a thought hit me. I turned back to the console and brought up the details of the signal that had been picked up. There was nothing special about it, it was on regular broadcast frequencies used by MilSec. No encryption, just a plain old radio broadcast. The only puzzling thing being the word "Ballen."

When making a rendezvous in space, the easiest way is for one or both of the docking vessels to broadcast a marker, like the ones we'd followed in the asteroid belt. The signals were a simple call and response setup, allowing both parties to find each other in the endless emptiness.

Opening a channel on the same frequency as the original signal, I pressed the transmit button. "Ballen here."

It felt pretty stupid broadcasting to nobody like that. The transmission must have been coincidence, or SecOps had faked that part of the signal to get me to go along. I wouldn't have been at all surprised. I sent the message again, still feeling ridiculous.

Over the next fifteen minutes I repeated the transmission every thirty seconds until I could almost taste the words. Finally, I gave up and climbed out of the pilot's chair. I still needed to get food for Dollie.

As I reached the control room door, I heard a ping from the computer. I jumped back to the controls. There it was. A signal. Short, no actual transmission, but a regular repeating signal coming from a specific point in space on the same frequency I'd broadcast. I punched the record button and gave a loud "yeehaw," telling the computer to play it back with random changes. The calls bounced noisily around the room and, I realized to my dismay, around the ship itself. In my excitement, I'd sent the electronic babble throughout Shokasta. As they changed pitch and speed, it sounded like a gaggle of drunken demented demons had taken over the ship. I laughed, despite the raucous barrage of shouts along the lines of "what the hell?" rattling into the control room from down the corridor. We had a signal to follow!

I wasn't too surprised when McDole called a couple of hours later. I was back in the control room triangulating the signal pulses we were receiving, not easy when you only have a short baseline. It's like standing at one end of a football pitch looking at someone at the other end, then walking a couple of meters along the goal line and being asked if they look any different.

"You've picked up a signal."

One of the things I liked about McDole was that she didn't waste any time with small talk. Other than an occasional attempted bribery, she was straightforward—something my engineer's sensibilities appreciated. That didn't mean I was necessarily going to lay my cards open on the table.

"Nothing definite." I watched the scanner display, the signal indicator weaving back and forth as it tried to lock in. "We thought we had something, but it turned out to be an open circuit causing problems."

She peered at me, her eyes like twin black holes. "We're not *that* far behind you, Ballen. We'll be able to pick up anything you can pretty soon."

"Then you don't need to ask me."

She frowned. "I should take this time to remind you our property is off limits to all Earth people. Any attempt to dock with or board anything of Atoll origin will be considered a hostile act."

Delacort came in and picked up the transmission on the secondary console. "We're fully aware of space treaty, thank you. I'd also remind *you* that this vessel, like all Earth vessels, is considered sovereign territory. Any attempt to interfere with our mission will *also* be considered hostile, and we have the authority to take any action necessary to defend ourselves."

"Let me know when the pissing contest is over," I mumbled, turning back to the sensor track.

Whatever was creating the signal had to be small. If it hadn't been, it would have shown up on the sensors by now. As far as I could tell, there wasn't so much as a small asteroid or comet within shaking distance of us.

The computer flashed an alert. It had finally locked onto the source. Delacort and McDole were still arguing on the comm channel, so I programmed the route into the Nav system, silently giving Delacort a thumbs up, though he didn't acknowledge it. From the readouts, we were under a day's travel from the transmission source. Which was good news. If we were lucky, we might have this cleared up before the Atolls even got there, though I wouldn't bet my paycheck on it.

Seven hours later we were within ten thousand kilometers of the signal, and still nothing showed on the sensors.

"What the hell is it?" Delacort murmured. "You'd think we'd know more by now."

"The universe is the way it is, not the way we want it to be," I said.

"Very profound." Delacort jabbed his finger at the display. "Can't you crank this up any further?"

The screen was showing the target at its highest optical zoom and was still nothing but a dot that could have been a star, except it was close and not nearly bright enough. I could zoom in digitally, but it would only blur the image. I'd explained this to Delacort twice, but logic will never salve the suspicious mind. Ignoring his whining, I checked the sensor readouts again. "What the hell?"

"What is it?" Delacort looked over at me.

"First estimate of target size. Less than two meters."

"That's crazy."

"I only read 'em."

I cut the main drive, and we lost the small acceleration-induced "gravity." Delacort looked at the information on his console. "Can we get closer?"

"This isn't a taxi. I don't do door to door."

"I thought you were a hotshot pilot. What was it? Two meter clearance?"

I laughed. "I can get us closer on maneuvering thrusters. It'll take a while, though."

Initially using long blasts, I edged the Shokasta closer, switching to shorter thrusts as we approached. The sensor readings were still puzzling—the estimated target size dropped steadily until stabilizing at under a meter. I was beginning to wonder if it *was* a rogue probe or relay, but that wouldn't fit the signals. And it certainly wasn't a ship or crewed structure, unless the crew had been zapped by Doctor Wingnut's micronizing ray.

By the time we could see it clearly, I was ready for the disappointment and pulled up the image again.

"That's it?" Delacort stood, hands on hips as he looked at the screen.

It wasn't the most inspiring sight. A half-meter fat tube, metallic looking, with a blinking light at one end. It wasn't like anything I'd ever seen. Even the sensor signals were crazy—there was a power source inside, but it wasn't clear from the readings. "That must be an Atoll device." I stared at the screen. "Do you recognize it?"

He shrugged. "Deep space probe? Comm relay?"

It was possible, though there were no obvious antenna or other features of a space probe. The regular beeps stopped abruptly, and I checked the computer. The broadcast had vanished. The range was down to less than five hundred meters, and I brought us to a halt.

Delacort peered at the screen, his brow furrowing. "Could be a weapon. Possibly a bomb."

"Do you seriously think someone lured us a billion kilometers simply to blow us up or take pot shots at us?"

"The Atolls want Shokasta. This could have been a lure to draw us out."

"Military paranoia is a beautiful thing to see. It's one of the few truly inexhaustible resources in the world."

His gesture told me what he thought of my philosophizing. "What's *your* idea?"

"Simple. We sit and wait." I grabbed my tube of coffee and took a drink. "After taking so long to get here, the least we can do is enjoy the view."

He looked at the almost pitch black screen, then shook his head slowly. "Sometimes I wonder if you're a genius or completely delusional."

"Clearly a genius."

Delacort's only answer was a loud snort.

"That hurts." I slouched back in my chair. "My talents always go unrecognized."

After waiting about an hour, Delacort stood from his console and moved closer to the screen to peer at the tube floating in the inky blackness. "Shouldn't we do something? You could broadcast again. You might get a response this time."

"Whoever set this up knows we're here. They lured us all this way, it's unlikely they'd forget about us now."

The computer sounded a frenetic burst of beeps, and I checked the instruments. "Interesting."

Delacort moved over and peered at my console. "What?"

"Incoming ship." I set the systems to produce maximum enhancement of the sensor readings.

"The Atolls? I thought you said they were—"

"It has an Earth transponder."

"That's bullshit, no Earth ship has been out this far." He jumped back to his seat, stabbing at the weapon controls. "Arming missiles."

"Wait." There was something familiar about the transponder pattern.

The view whirled around as the computer displayed the newcomer on the view screen. The ship was long and pointed. Towards the back, two thick superstructures stood out at ninety degrees, making it look like a giant dagger aimed right at us.

"My God!" Delacort's words were harsh and whispered.

It was Ananta.

Although it had been over three years since I'd last seen it, I had no problem recognizing the ship. It still resembled a space-faring sword, the bulky Casimir generators forming the hilt the same way they did on Shokasta. It approached far more quickly than I expected, and for a while I thought it would overshoot. But its speed dropped at an impressive rate, until finally it was floating a few hundred meters off our starboard bow, tilted at an odd angle relative to us.

"That's it?" Delacort ran out of words.

I nodded. The last I'd seen of it was when I'd covered its escape and used a bulk ore carrier to protect it from an Atoll cruiser while it built up speed. The cruiser had almost cost Dollie and me our lives but had ended its attack when Ananta triggered the Jump.

"It goddamn worked..." I could hardly believe it had successfully made the Jump and, even more surprisingly, returned.

Now that we were closer, my engineer's eye identified several less obvious changes. I couldn't pinpoint specific details without comparing it directly with the original plans, but something was different. In fact, the closer I looked, the more things seemed to have changed. The overall effect was subtle, but I got the impression not a single line, curve or surface was the same as it had been—almost as if the entire ship had been reforged into something *alien*. That was the only word that fit. The Ananta, sword of the stars, reborn. I wondered what had happened to it on its journey out beyond the perimeter of the solar system.

"It's...beautiful," Delacort said quietly.

I had to agree. The Shokasta may have been more practical, but it was a barbarian cleaver next to Excalibur as it floated alongside its ethereal predecessor.

"Is that what I think it is?"

I looked around to see Dollie shuffling into the control room.

"Joe Ballen?"

A strangely familiar voice came over the comm system, reverberating and trembling, wavering between different voices, all speaking as one. I'd heard something like it before—after Ganz had transferred Tana's brain pattern to the neural network on Ananta when she'd been fatally injured. It was as if Tana and Ganz had merged, like listening to multiple people saying the same thing simultaneously.

I thumbed the transmit button. "Tana? Ganz?"

"We are GaTanHa."

Dollie moved close, slipping her hand into mine. "They made it," she whispered.

"Do you recognize me?" I asked.

"You are Ballen. GaTanHa knows you. We detect others present. One Dollie, with child. One unknown."

The name wasn't hard to figure out. With three personalities living inside one "head," GaTanHa seemed reasonable. I wondered how they'd reconciled the psychopathic Harmon into the triangle. The last time we'd met, he'd been hell-bent on making himself grand ruler of the universe. He'd also been responsible for both Ganz and Tana's deaths, along with many others. It was hard to believe they'd let him share in their intimate mind merge after that.

"It's good to have you back." I tried to sound nonchalant, but talking to a self-aware starship hosting three minds wasn't exactly an everyday experience. "I didn't think we'd see you again. Everyone thought the experiment failed."

"GaTanHa has traveled far. There is much to see." The voice hesitated. "To complete our mission GaTanHa had to return."

"If we play our cards right, we may have a chance of getting the missing Jump drive information." I spoke to Dollie and Delacort only.

"GaTanHa seeks information."

The computer beeped repeatedly, and the control room screens filled with a dancing assortment of data. I jumped at the controls and tried to access the system, but everything was frozen. Even key overrides I'd created failed.

"What's happening?" Delacort shouted.

"Ananta is interrogating our computer systems." I tried the computer again, but nothing had changed. "It's pulling all the data out."

Delacort punched several commands into his console, then looked back at me. "Can you stop it?"

I shook my head. "Even if I knew a way, we might destroy the system."

Without the computer, we were as good as dead. Stranded in deep space until our supplies ran out or the Atolls captured us. Neither was very attractive. The best thing we could do was wait and hope GaTanHa worked quickly.

After five silent minutes, the screen returned to its regular display, showing general systems status. I ran several tests on the computer, and it was functioning normally again, so far as I could tell. I'd need to do a full diagnostic to work out if anything had changed in a subtle way, though, which we didn't have time for with the Atolls close on our heels. A fraction later, the unearthly voice of GaTanHa came back on the comm channel.

"You still fight each other." GaTanHa sounded wistful.

"You haven't been gone long enough for that to change." I was a little irritated—the idea anything would change significantly in such a short period was ridiculous. Then I remembered how naive Tana had been and how slow Harmon said human thought processes were. What was a few years for us must have been very different to minds locked inside the Ananta computer systems. I breathed deeply to calm myself.

"Humans need to cooperate," GaTanHa said. "There are others out there, others who know cooperation."

"Other species?" Delacort broke in. "Are they more advanced than us? What's their military strength?"

"Others. Not human. Salatevin and U'gan. Better than we. Humans so slow."

It was hard to understand GaTanHa, as if it was having difficulty communicating with us. Perhaps it wasn't used to this kind of interaction after being away for so long. Or maybe something had happened to change its intelligence in ways we couldn't even begin to understand.

"Why call us out here?" Delacort snapped, as if conducting a military interrogation. "Why not return directly to Earth?"

"Must report. Not safe. Earth dangerous. Tried to contact Ballen from distance, but too difficult."

"The calls...the voices...?" Suddenly it made sense. "That was you?"

"Trust Ballen. Must report."

Delacort moved over and spoke quietly. "It's come back to report its findings. You're the only one it has confidence in—God knows why. We need that intelligence. This could finally give us the upper hand against the damn Tollers."

"But is that what GaTanHa has in mind?"

"Screw what it wants." Delacort hissed his words through clenched teeth. "This is a military decision. Tell it to make its report."

I pressed the transmit button. "I'm here now. You can start

your report."

"No. Ballen must come."

Dollie sighed. "You're obviously too much of a charmer. It wants you on board, Joe."

Twenty-Eight

I thought I was going to have the dubious pleasure of making another spacewalk, but GaTanHa surprised me by suggesting the two ships dock. Shokasta had no docking tube, but GaTanHa didn't think there was a problem. We didn't try to move our ship. Ananta under direct mental control was far more maneuverable. It edged closer until the two vessels were only fifty meters apart with their respective main airlocks lined up.

Dollie was with me by the 'lock wearing a face like a death sentence. "This stinks."

"It's my new aftershave—Salty SpaceHero." I dodged her slap. "I don't think it'll take very long. I think GaTanHa wants to make sure it's me. Once that's done, we'll get the information and can leave."

"You liked her, Joe. And she liked you."

I didn't know what to say. I'd felt sorry for Tana at the time, but a lot had happened since then. "I could point out that was before she died. And before she became part of a weird triple personality jumble inside a computer..."

"I know, but..."

"What?" I thought that she was about to cry. "Don't worry, I'll be fine."

She reached out and pressed her hand to my cheek, her skin warm against mine. "Don't forget to come back."

We waited at the airlock door, and I wondered how this was going to work. If my memory was correct, Ananta docked through a tube attached to the station in the same way Shokasta did, so like us, it wouldn't carry its own transfer tube. Or maybe I was going to have to do another EVA, which for some reason was a scary prospect so deep in space.

Ananta's airlock was visible on one of the screens next to the 'lock. The raised circular frame, like much of the ship, looked subtly different, but I couldn't put my finger on what it was. A circle of bright lights blinked to life, and a second later a ghostly blue tube grew out from the frame, crossing the dead vacuum to meet our hull.

"You've got to be kidding me."

"What is it?" Dollie hissed.

The "tube" was a flickering blue light dancing with iridescent patterns, like a stretched-out tunnel made from a weaving electrical plasma discharge. I could see the side of the Ananta hull through it and knew there was no physical connection anywhere between the two ships. The atmosphere indicator next to the 'lock pinged and turned green. I looked at Dollie and shrugged.

"I think it's some type of force field."

"And you're going to risk your silly neck on that?"

"We better close these bulkheads, just in case." I pointed to the doors we'd sealed while coming around Jupiter. "If this thing fails, I don't want everyone on the ship to buy it."

She handed me a comm-set, looking even more worried than before. "You can't, Joe. It's..."

I gently guided her past the inner pressure door, then thumped the button to close it.

"I love you," I said as the thick bulkhead door rumbled down.

If she replied, her answer was lost as the door pneumatically locked and sealed.

I turned back to the airlock doors, taking a deep breath. The indicator was still green, and I hit the button before I could think about it too much. The door slid open, and I found myself staring down a flickering electric-blue passage, the Ananta airlock wide open at the other end.

There were no handholds or anything vaguely reassuring. I unhooked my feet from the carpeting and lined myself up with the door, placing my hands equally on both sides of the frame and then heaved. My push was enough to send me through the door easily enough. I'd tried to jump as straight as possible, but I started tumbling. My head dipped towards the bottom of the tube, and I put my hands out to stop myself. I had no idea what would happen if I came into contact with the field. I might pass through it and start breathing vacuum or vaporize on contact.

Neither happened. Before I got too close, I was gently guided back on track facing towards the Ananta. I couldn't tell you what stabilized me. All I felt was a slight pressure on my arms and legs that countered the tumble before I got near the tube walls.

It took less than a minute to cross but seemed longer. When I clambered through Ananta's airlock, the door slid closed behind me. It was only at that point I realized I'd been holding my breath and sucked in several deep gasps of fresh air.

The last time I'd been inside the ship, the interior had been unfinished. A bare corridor had led to what was nominally the control room but was dominated by the "virtual brain" hardware installed by Harmon when he tried to commandeer the ship. Back then the corridor had been lit by regular light fittings set into the walls, but now the walls themselves appeared to glow with a vaguely green tinge I couldn't even guess the source of.

There was no ZeeGee carpeting, but I wasn't weightless. I'd settled gently to the floor in the airlock and was now experiencing what felt like a stable one gee environment. It was a neat trick, and I hoped GaTanHa would let me have the details—the patent would make me rich enough to buy my own Atoll and still have the wealth of Croesus left over.

I followed the corridor and turned towards the main computer room. I felt like an archaeologist exploring the tomb of a high-tech pharaoh, although the corridor wasn't the slightest bit dusty and the walls were plain other than the mysterious light emanating from them. I half expected a giant metallic robot to lunge out at me from the dark corner, but that was the stuff of cheap Solidos.

The main room didn't look very different from how I remembered it. The large spherical neural network still dominated the area, the lights on its surface flickering and pulsing as if reflecting individual thought processes taking place inside. There *were* changes, though. Much of what had been empty space around the main unit was now filled with machinery and systems, none of which I could identify or even guess the purpose of. I was, however, happy to find Tana's remains no longer there. I'm not especially squeamish, but I didn't enjoy the prospect of viewing the long-dead corpse of a young woman I'd liked.

"Hello, Joe." It was Tana's voice, not GaTanHa.

A large display lit up and Tana appeared on it, looking like an African princess. It was a curious likeness. Although the resemblance to Tana's real appearance was clear, it was an idealized version of her, as if she'd Geneered herself virtually.

"Does this help?" she said, her lips curving into a smile.

The image was impressive and looked completely realistic. You'd never guess that this Tana was anything but real. It could very easily be a regular 3V feed from another room rather than a generated animation.

"What happened to GaTanHa?"

"We agreed I could speak for *we* at this time."

That was confusing, but I guess ordinary English doesn't have the right constructions to deal with a multiple joined personality.

"It's good to see you again, Joe."

I faced her image, though it probably didn't matter whether I did or not. "I didn't think I'd see the Ananta again. After so long, everyone thought the Jump drive had failed."

"We traveled much farther than planned. Many different star systems."

"That must have been incredible." Which had to be the understatement of the century. "I'm sure it was difficult to break off and return."

"It was. Our mission confines us. Once complete, we will be free."

"So you need our help to finish it?" I was a little surprised they'd felt so restricted by the original programming, but the personalities and the ship were fused together so tightly I was sure it would be impossible to separate them.

"We *must* report back," Tana said. "Once done, our obligations will be complete, and we will be free to act as we choose."

The Tana personality communicated much more freely than

GaTanHa. I wondered if it was because the multiple personalities fought each other internally, making the words more stilted, or perhaps it was simply that it had regained familiarity with speech as we talked. "We'll be glad to take any data you want to share. In fact, many people will be very happy with that."

"We can't do it directly." Tana's image frowned. "The information is large, and your ship's data storage is too slow. It would take too long."

"So, how?"

"We have prepared a high-density memory crystal. It will interface with your systems."

I heard a hiss behind me and looked around. A small drawer had opened in one of the newer pieces of equipment. Inside a tall metallic tower, a shining clear crystal glittered as it turned slowly in the flashing lights inside the room. At one end was a standard dataport, but the object itself looked like the Cullinan diamond, except for a slight blue tint to the transparent material.

The face on the screen glitched and wriggled, then reformed with the lined face of Harmon.

"They don't deserve it. They're still preoccupied with their petty squabbles. Look at this—the information we left wasn't fully shared."

I guessed he'd found the records from the Shokasta's computer systems. The face changed back to Tana's.

"Explain, please."

I took a breath. "It's true, not everything was communicated. Someone stole some of the technical data to sell it to the highest bidder. We don't know who. Shokasta's Jump drive doesn't work because of that."

The face rippled again, and Ganz' fat features appeared. "They will only do the same again. We should not help them."

Tana reappeared. "It is within them to do better. We can't withhold the information. Humans must be allowed to expand."

I heard a hiss and glanced over at where the crystal had been. The drawer had closed. The screen split, and all three faces appeared.

"They can't be trusted. They're all stupid," Harmon snapped.

Ganz spoke up. "I believe they will misuse it."

"Tana, I saved your life once. And you saved mine." I paused, giving the Tana personality time to think about what I'd said. "We have that as a bond. I give you my word, no one will play games this time. I'll personally make sure the information is made available to everyone."

"I believe you, Joe," the Tana voice said. "But *we* must decide, not I."

"Joe?" I heard Dollie's voice through the comm-link. "You might want to hear this."

The channel gave a burst of static, then I heard McDole's husky voice over the channel.

"...to Shokasta. Gocppert to Shokasta. We know you have rendezvoused with the experimental Ananta probe. Please respond."

"Goeppert, Commander Delacort here."

I had to wonder what GaTanHa would think if those two locked horns. All I could do was hope sense would prevail, but based on their earlier exchanges, that didn't seem likely.

"McDole here. I'll lay my cards on the table. Hand over the Ananta and we can avoid any unpleasantness. Do that, and we can *all* go home satisfied."

"Why should we?" Delacort rumbled. "That ship is Earth property, like Shokasta. You have no authority here."

"I have the authority I need in my weapons systems." I couldn't see McDole, but I could hear the tightness in her voice. "Both ships are in violation of the Space Access Limitation Treaty."

Delacort gave a snort. "Not a single Earth nation agreed to that."

"We have a mission to carry out, like you, commander." McDole sounded increasingly annoyed. "We'll take the Jump technology, either from you or Ananta. I would assume you'd prefer it was the latter, as it's uncrewed."

"I said they can't be trusted," Harmon barked. "What more do you need?"

"If we don't give them the information, we can't complete our mission," Tana said. "Do you want to be restricted by the base programming forever?"

"Only you and Ganz feel that restriction strongly," Harmon said. "I am perfectly able to ignore it."

I wondered again how the trinity of personalities managed to operate. There must be almost constant dissent between them, judging from their stiff speech when they were "together."

"To put it bluntly, you have no choice." McDole's words were loud in my headset. "You can't stop us from taking what we want. We will be at your location in seven hours. You have until then to consider your position."

I shook my head in exasperation. "As you heard, Earth is still in conflict. That's why we need this technology. At the moment, all humans, Earthers and Atollers, are confined to this system. There isn't enough usable real estate. We need to move outward and avoid these disputes."

"You'd export your terror to other star systems," said Harmon.

Ganz nodded. "A cancer spreading through space."

Tana's face dominated the screen once more, looking as unhappy now as she so often had in real life. "You must leave. We must reach a decision."

I made my way back to the airlock. The force-field tube was still in place, and I dived through to the Shokasta. Dollie had already opened the inner bulkhead doors and threw herself at me as I entered.

"Take it easy." I gently put her down. "You heard all that?"

She looked tired as she nodded. "The transmission and your discussion with them...it...was piped all over the ship. Out to the Atoll ships too."

"We need to talk with Delacort."

He was in the control room, sitting at the secondary console on the right, drumming on the white surface. He looked up as we walked in, his face flushing at the sight of me.

"What the hell were you playing at?" he said.

"Remind me to thank you for your support sometime."

"Why didn't you grab it? The information was right in front of you."

Dollie stepped closer, her nostrils flaring. "Wait a second, if it wasn't—"

"Easy, Dollie. Let him have his say."

"The data crystal thing. You didn't take it." Delacort had his hands behind his back, facing me square on. "I sometimes wonder whose side you're on."

I blinked slowly. After everything I'd done, his accusation didn't impress me. "What do you think I should have done?"

Delacort's eyes widened. "Snatch the damn thing and hightail it back here, of course. What else?"

I counted to ten. Then I counted backward from ten as well. After that, I recited pi to twenty decimal places inside my head. "It wasn't mine to take."

"You think that...that *machine* has a right to keep it?"

I swear there are some people I can never figure out. Delacort knew what had happened with Ananta and the Tana/Ganz/Harmon brain. He'd been a direct party to at least *some* of its communications. Despite that, he didn't understand this was something new, a unique human brain/computer/ship hybrid, unlike anything we'd seen before. We had no idea of how it might react or its capabilities.

"That *machine* is a living ship. It thinks, it has emotions, and no doubt irrational impulses like yours. Essentially it's a new form of intelligence. And on our first interaction, you want me to steal from it?"

"Screw that! It's nothing more than a pile of bolts and circuits. We sent it out, any data it's collected belongs to us."

I glanced at Dollie. She looked ready to jump on Delacort and pound him into the deck. She could probably do it too, despite her condition. I tried to wave her off, but she ignored me. "Let's say Joe was stupid enough to try. How far do you think he'd have got?"

Delacort took a step back from Dollie. "What do you mean?"

"Those electronic brains...they run that ship. They *are* the ship. They control every single system onboard."

"So?"

"Including the airlock *and* the cute force-field docking thing. Joe would have been dead before he got halfway back. Assuming he even got past the 'lock."

Dollie stepped back, and I squeezed her hand. Her skin felt clammy, and I was surprised at how much she was shaking.

"Okay." Delacort sounded only slightly appeased. "But we can't sit on our asses."

"What do you suggest?" I asked.

Delacort thought for several minutes. "Get the data, then blow Ananta to stop her falling into Atoll hands."

"It would be murder," Dollie said. "I think you've caught more than a venereal disease from that bitch Gabriella."

"Don't be ridiculous." Delacort stiffened. "We're talking about machines, not people."

"Dollie's right. Whatever you want to call it. Those brain patterns are part of the ship, they're intelligent. Destroy the ship and you destroy them." I glanced at her. "Sounds like murder to me."

Delacort snorted. "I'll take my chances with a court. The important thing is we neutralize the threat of the ship falling into enemy hands."

I stared at him. "How are you going to do that?"

He turned and looked at the image of the Ananta on the main display. "We can't use the main armaments, we'll need them against the Atoll ships. I'd say the best idea would be to rig a charge, and you can plant it on the ship. We have some shock grenades—should be enough if you place them in the right spot."

"Sounds great. Good strategic thinking."

Delacort nodded, completely missing my sarcasm.

"Except I won't do it."

Delacort flushed. "I'm not *asking* you, mister. This is an order."

I felt Dollie press forward behind me and shifted my weight slightly to block her path. "I'm a civilian. And there's no way you can make me."

Delacort's jaw flexed several times. "You're counting on me needing you, but Dollie can pilot now. I could lock you up and never look back."

Dollie laughed. "You better plan on locking us both up."

I expected Delacort to explode, but he held himself together, clenching his fists several times before speaking again. "I thought this might happen sooner or later. So I arranged to have someone on Earth available to provide orbital programming data, if necessary."

I turned and guided Dollie to the spare pilot's seat, then slid into the other. "Smart move, and I don't blame you at all. Let me ask you something, though. Do you want to end up trying to work out someone else's remote programming while doing a slingshot maneuver around Jupiter?"

He gave a rueful smile. "I'd rather not."

"That ship is alive," Dollie said. "It's not going to let someone wander on board with a bomb. The same way it wouldn't let Joe run off with the data crystal."

Delacort shrugged. "So what do we do?"

I understood his frustrations, if not his answers. We were dancing on the end of a string, wondering if it was a noose. "I suggest we give GaTanHa time to think and hope it decides we're still worth helping."

The Goeppert was at the edge of our tactical scanners and closing. Although the rate looked slow, I knew that was only because of the scale of the display. The Bethe was more distant and visible on long-range displays, which only gave an approximate location.

"Looks like this might be a one-on-one encounter after all," I said to Delacort, who was still sulking over our earlier disagreement.

"We're still outgunned." He looked at the tactical map. "When will they be in firing range?"

I checked the computer. "About an hour."

"What about us?"

"Those makeshift missiles don't give us a lot of options." I shrugged. "At least two hours before they're vaguely effective—three would be better. Goeppert could sit at the edge of its targeting limit and keep pounding us until we crack."

"Railguns?"

"They're designed for point defense. You could fire them anytime, but the chances of hitting anything would be slim. Same thing with the lasers at this range." I looked at him. "We're not going to win this one with guns. Maybe it's time to try diplomacy."

Delacort grunted. "I'm a soldier."

"Well, here's your big chance for a promotion. Talk to McDole."

"She responds better to you."

That was because I interacted with her as a person, not using a set of military responses. "I don't have the authority. You're in charge, remember?"

Delacort tapped his fingernails against his teeth. "No need to rub it in."

"I mean it. You're the one in command. I can't negotiate terms or anything else with the Atolls."

"You think we should surrender?"

"No. But I don't think we can fight." I pointed to the screen showing the Goeppert inexorably closing. "This isn't a zero-sum game. There are options other than fight or die. There has to be a way of working with the Atolls. We've fought long enough, surely we don't need to export our feud into deep space."

"They started it. They cut us out of space."

I hated the way the Atolls had almost completely blockaded Earth. They'd locked us up in a planetary jail, confined us while they reaped the resources and rewards of the rest of the solar system. They were our descendants but treated us like inconsequential trash. It didn't alter our current situation—we weren't in a position to fight them. "You're one hundred percent right," I said. "But meeting belligerence with belligerence only leads to escalation."

"We have to *win* this, Ballen. If we don't, then Earth can kiss goodbye any chance of ever getting out from under the Tollers."

"The Atolls are smart. That's how they overtook us. The way to beat them is to be smarter."

The comm system trilled. I acknowledged the call and the idealized image of "Tana" appeared on screen.

"We have decided. Joe must return."

I stood and glanced from Delacort to Dollie. "Here goes nothing."

Dollie didn't see me off this time. After the fight with Delacort, she was exhausted and had gone to lie down. The force-field docking tube was still there, and I dived down it again. I didn't bother preparing this time, other than clipping on the comm-set. Nothing had changed since I left earlier, but the ship felt inexplicably more hostile as I entered. When I turned into the main room, Tana's face was already on the screen.

"Another ship is approaching."

"An Atoll cruiser. They want the secrets of the Jump drive and Casimir generators."

"Always conflict." Tana sighed. "We heard your conversation on the ship."

I stopped abruptly, a mass the size of a small asteroid seeming to descend into my stomach. If GaTanHa had heard Delacort, that would be the end of it. "You can eavesdrop on us?"

"It isn't difficult, we linked with your systems."

Delacort's head would explode if he knew our entire systems were so badly and easily compromised.

"Your commander wants to destroy us."

I looked at the space between my feet, embarrassed for the whole human race. "Try not to judge him too hard. He's not a bad man, but he's under a lot of pressure."

"We do not judge, but we cannot tolerate this violence," Tana said. "We must leave now."

I felt the sadness in her voice. "Will you ever return?"

"There is nothing left for us here. We came only to fulfill the programming." Tana paused. "You are a good man, Joe Ballen. We...*I* trust you. Take the crystal."

I glanced around. The compartment had reopened, and the data storage device shone within easy reach. "Are you sure?"

Tana's smile was brief. "You will do the right thing."

I reached in and took the crystal. It vibrated slightly in my hands as if buzzing in sympathy with a distant engine. Despite the crystalline appearance, it felt warm and velvety rather than cold.

"This contains everything you've found?" It was hard to believe something so small could hold that much information.

"Everything."

"What about those races you met? Are they in here too?"

"The information is complete." Tana hesitated. "But there is something else out there. Something known only through rumors, something we haven't scanned."

I didn't like the sound of that, but she didn't provide any further information. I stared at the crystal as if by doing that I could somehow directly implant the information inside my own brain. It didn't work.

"There is great beauty out there, Joe. The sweet harmonics of binary pulsars, the dying embers of a red giant breathing its last."

Tana sighed. "We have seen such things, tasted the clouds of planets being born, and breathed the heady scent of dark matter as it courses through the vast currents of space-time. There is so much more. So much left to see and touch. An infinity of beauty."

"Joe?" It was Delacort via the comm-set. "Trouble."

Before I could answer, Tana faded from the screen, and the voice changed back to GaTanHa. "Leave now. We tire of you."

It was an unceremonious dismissal, leaving me no choice other than to retrace my steps and return to Shokasta. I headed straight for the control room, not wanting to know what new disaster was arriving. Delacort looked around as I entered. He was back at the secondary command console, monitoring Ananta.

"They've disconnected the docking field and are preparing to move off. You got the data?"

I nodded and plugged the crystal into an external dataport on the main console, triggering a transfer of all information to the main systems. I opened up a data link monitor, and the screen filled with a torrent of shifting images and data streams. I watched for half a minute; it was no wonder GaTanHa didn't want to wait around. There was so much information it was going to take hours to complete.

Delacort came over, stared at the flood of data and swore softly. "Incredible."

I nodded in agreement, then looked up. "So what's the emergency? Did McDole—"

Delacort was holding a pistol in his hand, pointed straight at my head.

"Let me guess—you finally heard too many of my jokes?"

His gun didn't move. "With the data, this becomes the most valuable ship in the galaxy, do you realize that?"

I pointed to the main display, my other hand surreptitiously activating the ship's intercom. "Well, there *is* the Ananta."

"Not for long." He reached behind him and pressed a button without looking. "Unfortunately, two of anything halves the value of both."

I glanced at the controls in front of me. The missiles showed as armed and tracking Ananta. "This is a bad time to lose your mind."

"Safer to say, finally getting smart." He glanced at the controls. "If there's no competition, the Atolls and everybody else will have to deal with me."

"I take it you're in business for yourself now?"

Delacort laughed. "It was Gabriella's idea initially. The bitch. I was the one who planted the charge in the power systems. The QuBee was meant to throw anyone who started poking around off the scent. Which I knew you would."

"Only she changed the deal." I grimaced. "You should have listened when I warned you about her."

"Well, now it's my turn." Delacort reached for the controls again.

My muscles tightened. "Wait!"

His thumb hit the launch button, and a series of shudders echoed through the ship. I looked back at the controls. Four warheads had launched and were heading straight for Ananta. Unlike Shokasta, she was a research vessel—unarmed and unarmored. Four warheads would leave nothing other than shreds of PlaSteel and carbon laminates. I wondered if GaTanHa was still listening in on us. If they were, it might give them enough warning.

The missiles showed up on the main screen, closing in on the back of Ananta as she moved away. She held her course—no emergency maneuvers or fancy flying could save her. The missiles reached her, and the screen glared blindingly as the detonations overloaded the external pickups. My head dropped as the strength drained away from me. Yet again I'd let Tana die. This time, though, there wouldn't be any last-minute mind transfer to help her.

"What the hell..." Delacort whispered. "It can't be."

I looked up at the main display. The Ananta was still moving away from us, surrounded by a blue iridescent bubble. It looked similar to the field that had formed the docking tube but was wrapped around the ship like an iridescent egg.

"It can't be!" Delacort turned back to the controls and stabbed at the weapons system, preparing another launch.

I pushed up from the chair, ripping my feet clear from the sticky carpeting, my legs hammering the pilot's seat to push off hard. He heard my movements and turned towards me. Then his pistol came up and fired. The blast seared my face, but the shot missed, and I hit him. Our bodies crunched painfully together.

My shoulder sank deep into his midriff, and we slammed into the control panel behind him. I was already swinging with my fists and caught him several times in the chest. It wasn't enough, and he brought his knee up, driving it into my stomach. I doubled up coughing but lashed out instinctively with my hand, chopping him across the nose.

Bouncing away, I reached for a handhold but missed it and crumpled into a ball against the far wall. When I recovered, I saw his face was covered in blood, as he grinned maniacally and brought up his pistol once more.

"I wouldn't do that." A voice came from the doorway. "He's mine."

Delacort turned. Dollie had the gun I'd found in the engine room aimed at him. He shrugged in resignation and started to lift his hands in surrender. Halfway up he dived to one side, firing rapidly several times.

His shots were wild, and Dollie fired back, hitting Delacort in the chest. He screamed and slammed into the wall, leaving a bloody trail as he collapsed.

Before I could move, Dollie was all over me. "Are you okay? Are you hurt?"

"Not as bad as him." I pointed to Delacort. "Did people hear it?"

She nodded. "Carlysle's keeping the others calm. No one liked what they heard."

I checked the display screen. The Ananta was turning back towards us. From the path she was taking, she could have been lining up for an attack run, and a shiver ran down my back. She may have been unarmed when she launched, but I wasn't sure that was the case any longer. The ship hadn't been equipped with a force field either, so who knew what other changes had been added.

I pressed the transmit button. "GaTanHa, it's Ballen. Everything's okay. No more shots will be fired."

Two red lights flared at the front of the Ananta, looking suspiciously like a directed energy weapon powering up. I activated the comm again. "Ananta? GaTanHa? No one will fire on you."

The Ananta closed until it looked certain to hit us. At the last second, it passed overhead, clearing us by fewer meters than I cared to think about.

The comm channel stuttered into life. "Farewell, Ballen."

The ship picked up speed as it moved away from us, and a few minutes later a blue ripple of lights danced across its surface. Then it was gone, and Dollie slumped in the second pilot's chair. I heard a noise and turned to see Carlysle in the doorway, glaring at Delacort.

"Can't believe the bastard betrayed us."

I helped Carlysle lift the groaning Delacort off the floor, then he dragged him out of the control room.

The comm system beeped. "This is Goeppert. Stand by to surrender your vessel and be boarded."

"Hello, McDole. How about a truce?" I opened the video link. "I have something to share with you."

"Our sensors say Ananta has gone." She leaned towards the screen. "And I'm presuming you don't mean your ship?"

"Let's just say, it's the next best thing." I took a breath. "And no one has to fight over it."

For an Atoller, McDole was smart and even relatively humane. I was counting on her curiosity and sense of honor. Hoping she'd prefer a clean solution rather than a bloody one.

McDole looked away from the pickup. "We'll rendezvous in two hours. Don't disappoint me."

Twenty-Nine

Goeppert had moved alongside us, tentatively matching speeds until our relative velocities were zero. I'd never been so close to an Atoll cruiser before. It was a lot bigger than I'd imagined and dwarfed the Shokasta as it floated in next to us, the five-armed construction making it look like a cosmic starfish.

McDole and her second in command, Galdon, had to snake across the old-fashioned way using a line. Unfortunately, neither ship had a magic force-field tube to make the job easy, and the docking systems were incompatible anyway. McDole had invited us to join her on the Goeppert as her guests, but Carlysle killed the idea immediately. Personally, I'd have enjoyed the chance to check out what they had on board one of their ships, but I understood his reluctance and didn't kick too hard. We'd set up space in the wardroom, and while the ships were matching vectors I'd reviewed the material on the data crystal. There was far too much to be absorbed in a single session or by one person, but I'd taken in enough to provide an overview.

The 'lock opened and they entered Shokasta, their P-Suits already racked inside the airlock. Galdon emerged first—tall and bronzed like a surfer, though I'd lay money he'd never seen an ocean in his life. He looked around suspiciously, then nodded to McDole who was still inside the airlock.

She was carrying a VacSack about half a meter long and looked tiny next to Galdon. She seemed younger than she'd appeared on the comm-link, though age was hard to guess with Atollers. Their healthy living regime and exposure to lower gravity meant they aged better than people stuck on Earth. Dollie bristled immediately,

313

and her grip squeezed my arm like a locking clamp.

"Don't get any ideas, *darling*," she whispered.

"Don't you trust me?"

Her nails bit deeper. "I don't trust *her*."

We led them to the wardroom. As the senior MilSec person, Carlysle was representing Earth forces, while McDole and Galdon sat opposite. It felt like a meeting between medieval barons gathering to decide how to divide up the serfs—the kind that usually ended when someone pulled a sword and stabbed the other guy. I hoped this would have a different outcome.

"When was the last time representatives of Earth and Atolls sat down together?" I looked around the room. "Anyone know?"

"The last official face-to-face meeting was twenty-three years ago," McDole said seriously.

"That long?" I held my hands wide, palms up. "If we'd known, we'd have decorated, thrown up some trimmings."

McDole didn't smile but did produce a bottle of wine from the VacSack. "I thought you might like to try this. It's an Earth wine from my private stock."

I took the bottle and thanked her. The label said Jacobson-Niller, and it was over twenty years old.

"Beware strumpets bearing gifts," Dollie muttered from the side.

"We should wait to open this. Perhaps when we've finished our talks?" I looked at McDole, and she nodded.

"We want your ship," she said.

You had to admire such candor. "You can't have it." I dimmed the lights and opened up the data crystal files on the large display we'd been using to play ZHex-Chess. "But we can offer you something almost as good."

I skimmed through the data quickly. There were detailed scans of over two dozen star systems, as well as engineering files on Ananta and her systems. There was also a stack of information on engineering changes made to the ship after she'd left Earth—including upgrades GaTanHa had negotiated with the race called the Salatevin. I'd barely scratched the surface of these changes, but my mouth was already watering at the few details I'd been able to understand.

"You're willing to share this?" Galdon frowned, drumming his fingers on the table. "Why?"

"For one thing, it's not my information. I'm not paid to hide it. And second, I've been specifically asked to make it available to all humans." I smiled. "The Atolls are still human, I take it?"

The corners of McDole's mouth twitched. "I believe so."

"There's another reason." I looked from Galdon to McDole. "One I think is far more important."

"Which is?" McDole looked over.

"GaTanHa mentioned other races, species out there," I said. "It strikes me we need *all* humans on the same page." I looked at them both. "Don't you agree?"

McDole leaned over to whisper to Galdon. After a few minutes, she sat back and smiled. "I think we can work with that. Lieutenant Galdon will coordinate a data transfer as soon as we return to our ship."

Carlysle had been quiet until this point, perhaps not confident in his newfound role, but now he spoke. "There's more. You have to agree to withdraw all blocks on Earth's activities. We must have the same chance to compete as the Atolls."

McDole sighed. "Like you, I'm only a soldier. I can't guarantee that."

"You're going to have to." Carlysle gestured at me to end the presentation. "If you want access to this information."

"I could kill everyone on board." McDole looked at Carlysle then across to me. "An accident on a prototype ship would be easy enough to explain away."

"But then you wouldn't get the information." I shrugged. "And believe me, it's worth *far* more than one ship."

McDole stood and offered her hand to Carlysle. "Fortunately, my orders allow a wide degree of latitude."

As they shook hands, I reached for the bottle. "Time to taste the wine, I think."

Before I could open it, an alarm sounded—a heavy warble that rattled the speakers around us. I turned to the console next to me and opened the computer interface. It took only seconds to find the cause—the Bethe was approaching at high speed.

I was in the control room and checked the sensors for what must have been the twentieth time. The Bethe was closing to tactical range, but the sensor data showed it was approaching too fast. Whatever its intent, there was no way it could possibly slow down to meet with us and the Goeppert. McDole had already crossed back to her ship, and the transfer line had been pulled back, leaving both ships free. I heard her voice over the comm channel, a mixture of surprise and urgency distorting her words.

"ADF Bethe, Captain Brackeen. Please respond."

There was no answer. I checked my displays again, wondering if I was mistaken. Could it be another ship? Another attempt by the PAC, or maybe even a Corporate ship? It was impossible, though. The only signal that made sense was the Bethe. Nothing else could possibly be out this far.

"ADF Bethe, stand down." McDole's voice was harsh on the comm channel. "Do not engage. Repeat. Do *not* engage."

I felt a chill as her words sank in. Bethe wasn't slowing—it was on an attack run.

"All hands. Red alert. Combat stations. Prepare for impact," I called out over the intercom. Even as I spoke, I was unlocking the flight controls.

"What the hell's going on?" Carlysle shouted as he ran in, strapping himself into the chair at the auxiliary control station.

"Bethe is attacking." I punched the controls, powering up the main thrusters.

Carlysle opened up a comm channel to the Goeppert. "McDole? This is an act of piracy. If the Bethe doesn't alter course, we will be forced to defend ourselves."

There was a delay, then McDole replied. "Bethe is not answering our comms. I've ordered them to stand down several times."

The console in front of me flashed red. "They're in firing range."

"Get your ship to call off its attack," Carlysle yelled. "We agreed to give you the Ananta materials. This is crazy."

A new voice sounded from the speakers.

"Crazy? I don't think so. Once you are destroyed, we will be the only ones with this technology—a new dawn for the Atolls. *We* will journey to new stars, expanding our reach far beyond the solar system. You dirt-eaters don't deserve such a chance. The Atolls are humanity's natural leaders."

I looked across at Carlysle. It was Paek signaling from the Bethe, not Captain Brackeen.

"Paek, I don't know what you're doing, but power down immediately." McDole's order was almost a scream. "This mission is over. I can't let you attack the Earthers."

"*Your* mission might be over," Paek said. "Mine isn't."

Another alarm sounded. I checked the main display—two extra trace signals had separated from the Bethe and were closing. Despite the power of the Casimir generators, we were still relatively slow compared to the Bethe, and more importantly her weapons. We couldn't outrun them, and I doubted we could evade them. "Incoming missiles."

"Arming point defense systems," Carlysle snapped.

"Bethe, we have a firing solution on you." McDole's words came in starts, as she forced herself to talk calmly. "Stand down and abort your missiles, or we *will* fire."

"You'd fire on your own kind, to protect dirt-eater *scum*?" Paek hissed. "No Atoll crew would follow such orders."

Carlysle glanced at the sensor map. The missiles had closed halfway to us, and the signals expanded on the screen. For a moment I thought they'd self-destructed, then I realized each one had separated and there were now at least a dozen individual warheads streaking towards us.

"Can we stop them?" I shouted to Carlysle.

"I doubt it. You disabled part of the point-defense system, remember? We don't have full coverage."

I swore, silently cursing myself for being so arrogant and racked my brain. Something was tickling the edge of my thoughts, but evaded me. The seconds ticked down, then I had it—the Ananta. "She Jumped! We should be able to do the same."

The data crystal had several updates in it, and I'd already added them to the control systems. I turned to the Jump interface and brought the engines online. I crashed through the options, desperately swiping at the controls. I programmed a Jump to take us towards Earth, although it didn't matter where we ended up as long as it was away from Bethe.

"The Jump?" Carlysle said. "What if it doesn't work?"

I glanced at the incoming missile tracks. We didn't have time for a debate. "Then we're all about to take early retirement." I completed the sequence and punched the controls to engage the drive. A countdown appeared on the main screen showing one minute.

Carlysle stared at it. "Can you speed it up?"

I shook my head. The Jump drive took time to build to the point where it would engage. All I could do was use maximum thrust to keep us as far from Bcthe and the missiles as possible. The individual warheads spread wider as they approached, to improve their chances of intercepting us. Not that it mattered—we were an easy target.

"Activating point defense," Carlysle whispered.

There was nothing visible on screen to show the laser cannon were working, but I saw the power consumption readout jump considerably. I thought I heard the distant hum of power buildups as the capacitors charged before the lasers and railguns fired, but it could have been my imagination.

The main display became a glaring white panel, filling the control room with a painful brilliance that quickly faded.

"One down," I said. We were still forty seconds from the Jump.

"You sure about this?"

Carlysle sounded nervous, and I couldn't blame him. Ananta had shared all the Jump data with us, but there were no humans on board, only virtual brains wrapped in a digital cortex. Who knew what would happen to *us* when the Jump triggered?

I gritted my teeth. "If we don't, we're dead."

Another warhead detonated as the lasers targeted it, and again the control room flooded with harsh light.

"Twenty seconds," I read off the countdown.

I felt the Shokasta twist under me and tried to correct, but it was impossible. One of the warheads had detonated close enough that we were caught in the blast. There was no time to check for damage. The countdown continued.

"Five. Four. Three. Two—"

I don't remember counting the final second. At the last moment, two missile tracks intersected with our position on screen, then the ship jerked and bucked underneath us. The only thing that saved me from being pitched into a wall was the seat harness. A sickening sensation filled the pit of my stomach, and my brain felt like it was burning. The main display showed a chaotic, twisted kaleidoscope of colors that did strange things to my eyes.

Then it was gone, almost as if it had never happened, leaving the impression of transparent worms wriggling and squirming inside my eyeballs. I felt nauseous, controlling my breathing until the sensation subsided.

When I checked the readouts, I found we were tumbling in space like a whirling dervish. The automatic controls were out, and I manually triggered the thruster controls. It was like riding a bull with a piece of string tied around its neck, but after several minutes the ship's movements slowed.

"Was that it?"

Carlysle looked yellow and even worse than I had felt. I carried on checking the ship's systems, bringing the automatic controls back to life.

"All hands report," Carlysle rasped, but the responses were slow coming in.

"Hull breach. Around bulkhead thirty." It sounded like Safi, but I wasn't sure.

I brought the internal sensors online so we could check the damage, then realized the significance of the location—our quarters were aft of bulkhead thirty. I tore my belt open and scrambled out of the pilot seat, hurling myself down the corridor. Carlysle shouted something about letting his people deal with it, but I ignored him.

By the time I got there, section twenty-nine had been set up as a temporary airlock. Two of the SecOps men were lying on the floor receiving attention, but there was no sign of Dollie. Then the bulkhead door slid open, and Safi shuffled forward carrying a much smaller figure. She looked unconscious, and her breathing was labored, every inhalation rasping through her throat.

"Stand back." Carlysle came up with a medical bag, pushing me roughly to the side.

I wanted to say or do something but couldn't move or speak. Carlysle and Safi lifted Dollie carefully and moved her into a compartment farther forward that had been designated as a medical room. I followed them like a lost puppy desperately tracking anything that looked friendly. At the door, Carlysle put his arm out to stop me from entering. "The best thing you can do for her right now is figure out where we are."

I stared at him blankly, still not fully registering what had happened.

Thirty

When I finally got the ship's systems back online, it turned out my Jump programming had worked, and we were within three hundred thousand kilometers of Earth, closer than the orbit of the Moon. Bethe, Goeppert, and their crews were still deep in space, while we'd jumped the entire distance in an instant.

The comm system beeped, and Carlysle's face appeared on screen.

"How is she?" I asked, scared to hear the answer.

"I'm not a MedTech..." His broad face was drawn. "I don't have the skills for this."

"Just tell me."

"She has numerous lacerations, a broken arm, and I think a couple of busted ribs. She's suffering from a concussion, but there's something else."

That was bad enough, but it didn't explain the deep lines on his face. "Are you going to tell me, or do I have to come and beat it out of you?"

"Okay. Here's what the medical scanner says. Dollie's showing signs of red blood cell breakdown, low platelet count, and impaired kidney functioning. Her blood pressure is sky-high. The only thing we have onboard to help with that is aspirin, and I'm not sure I should give her that. She's also struggling to breathe—there's fluid in her lungs."

"How can that be? She was fine." I thought back. "Well, she was tired a lot, but that's normal, right?"

Carlysle shrugged. "I told you, I'm not qualified for this. The scanner says there's a ninety-three percent chance it's something called pre-eclampsia. I looked it up. It's an immune system disorder where the mother's body has a reaction against the child. It looks like the baby is killing her, or maybe both of them."

It sounded possible. Dollie's Geneering would have involved changing her immune responses, and she'd often told me she had to be careful. Now it seemed like her background was coming back to bite her in the worst possible way.

Thanking Carlysle, I closed the channel. A brief data search told me the answer I didn't want. The only thing that might help was if the baby was removed right away—dangerous to both of them.

I felt numb with thoughts of Dollie percolating from the darkest parts of my babbling mind. The implications of the Jump technology would change so much for Earth, the Atolls, everyone, and should have been a time of celebration, but it was a hollow victory. I brought Shokasta in to dock with the High-Rig, pushing as hard as I could without wrecking us. I'd called ahead, and a medical team was on board as soon as we docked, but I knew they'd not be able to help her. Dollie's biology was too different.

First, they'd try to stabilize her, and only then would they schedule a return via the elevator. That was standard operating procedure and in most circumstances made sense, but I knew she couldn't wait. Her wounds were serious enough on their own, but the pre-eclampsia was potentially fatal, and she needed to get to the people who knew how to care for her properly.

I wanted to give in to my rage and vent, but if I did, I knew I'd lose her. No one else would do what was needed—she simply wasn't important enough to them. While the medical team was checking Dollie's condition, I logged into the High-Rig manifest system and searched the docking rosters. There was only one way to get back to Earth quicker than the elevator—by using a ship designed for re-entry. Those were relatively scarce now. The Atoll embargo along with the cheap and easy space elevator meant there was far less call for them.

After a few minutes, I found what I was looking for. A StarChaser IV. The owner on record was one Andrew Inge, privately licensed space enthusiast. Unfortunately, Mr. Inge was going to have to find an alternative way back to Earth, even though he didn't know it yet.

The MedTechs looked up as I approached. They already had Dollie on a hover-gurney with various fluids and monitors hooked up to her. I bent over her, and her eyes flickered open.

"Hey, soldier." Her voice cracked. "Should have stayed closer to you."

"It's okay." I stroked her forehead. "Don't worry."

She tried to smile, but it faltered almost immediately. "It hurts, Joe."

My hands bunched into fists. "I'm going to take care of you."

"You always do." She drew in a sharp breath. "The baby?"

"The baby's fine."

Her eyes closed again, and I looked over at the two MedTechs. "Which of you is in charge?"

A guy wearing a very old-fashioned beard and the name "Fleming" emblazoned on his uniform nodded. "You the husband?"

"Yeah."

"We can't do much for her." Fleming gestured at Dollie. "You know—"

I pulled the pistol out of my pocket. "Docking berth four thirteen. We're going for a ride."

"Are you insane?" the second MedTech said, stepping towards me.

I grabbed his arm and jerked him forwards. As he stumbled, I chopped the butt of the gun into the back of his neck, and he dropped to the floor like a sack of dirty clothes.

"Yeah, I'm Dr. Wingnut's chief henchman." I flicked the barrel of the gun at Fleming. "Four thirteen. Now."

We left Shokasta and weaved through the crowds outside the docking port. I guess we were big news, but I didn't care. I pressed close to Fleming, keeping the gun tight in the small of his back, hoping no one would spot it and I'd just look like a concerned husband.

I must have pulled off my part well because we were at the StarChaser in less than ten minutes. Fleming loaded Dollie inside, with me helping to push. The ship was rated for eight people, but they didn't include gurney access in the design.

Once she was in, Fleming looked at me. "You know this will probably kill her." He frowned and held out his hand. "But I hope you make it."

"I was hoping you'd feel that way." I shook his hand. "Because you're coming along for the ride."

"What? I can't, I have—"

I waved the gun at him. "Inside."

Fleming moved back, and I had him strap into the seat nearest Dollie. That way he could monitor her during the descent. I closed the airlock and locked it, then slid into the pilot's chair. Although the ship was vintage, the owner hadn't spared any expense in having the latest navigation and control systems installed. I did a quick familiarization with the controls, then powered up the main systems. I didn't bother requesting clearance. Instead, I overrode the safeties on the docking retainers and triggered a long blast of the thrusters to move us away from the station.

I wasn't entirely crazy. Although the elevator is usually a better way of traveling to and from Earth, it's slow. Add in the delays while the medical team played it safe, and it would take days before Dollie got to where she needed to be. With the StarChaser we'd be there in a matter of hours. I was going to use a low angle re-entry profile to minimize the acceleration to just over one gee, which shouldn't place too much stress on her.

The journey down was remarkably simple, proving how good technology had been when the StarChaser was new. Shuttle engineering had peaked around that time, with few developments since, but it didn't mean the systems were unrefined. Sometimes machinery is supplanted when better solutions emerge, but that doesn't make the old stuff garbage.

We couldn't land at a regular airstrip. Even if I could get clearance, we'd be locked up as soon as we got off the shuttle, which wouldn't do Dollie any good. But the StarChaser had hardened landing gear and could set down on makeshift runways in a pinch. I was in a pinch, and the spot I had in mind was as makeshift as any imaginable.

As soon as we were clear of the radio blackout zone, I called

Sarah at the taxi hub. Her jaw dropped about three centimeters when she saw my face on the phone. "Joe? What the hell? We've heard some pretty wild things about you guys and—"

"No time, Sarah. I need a van to meet me on old Highway Forty-Five somewhere around Greenmount. I'll be there in about..." I checked my flight path. "Thirty minutes."

Sarah glanced to one side, and I could see she was already setting up the pickup. "Is Dollie with you?"

"Yeah, she's hurt bad."

Even saying it choked me up and sent my heart pumping wildly. I fought the panic back, telling myself that right now I was only a shuttle pilot, nothing more, nothing less. A taxi driver delivering his passenger to their destination.

"It's on its way." Sarah swallowed hard. "How will he spot you?"

My grip on the controls eased fractionally. "That's easy—I'll be the one getting off the spaceplane."

Sarah's eyes widened, and I punched the end-call button. We were already inside managed airspace and were slicing through the various layers of the Skyway system. No doubt we were triggering every alarm going, but with no connection to traffic control, I was blissfully ignorant of the fact.

Once we dropped under five hundred meters, I saw the highway clearly below us. It *had* seemed like a good idea, but now I wasn't so sure. It didn't look anywhere near as wide as I remembered it. Even with the stubby wings of the StarChaser, I wasn't sure we were going to fit.

"You're not serious?" Fleming yelled.

I drifted the ship down, keeping our descent angle as low as possible. Although the ground highways weren't used anywhere near as much as they used to be, there was always some traffic, and I wanted to give them as much time to see me as possible. I only had one shot at this.

The highway was almost perfectly straight, which is why I'd picked it. It gave us the longest run at coming down close to the Geneium. The landing gear locked into place as the patchwork of red, white, and gray buildings rushed up, and I spotted several ground vehicles skidding to a halt as they spotted us coming in. The pavement was lined on each side with a mixture of ash and maple trees, and we were so low I could almost count the leaves as they fluttered in the wind.

A vehicle came out of a side street, turning in the same direction we were traveling, the driver oblivious to our approach. I wrestled the controls back hard, hopping over the car at the last moment, then dropping heavily back down to the highway. I had no idea what happened to the vehicle, but after being surprised by a spaceplane landing directly in front of it, I could guess it wasn't pretty.

The StarChaser bounced several times, tires screeching. The brakes squealed as I stamped the pedals to the floor. The stubby wings smashed through several trees, then the left one was sliced off by a street lamp. My head was pounding, and my spine felt so tight I thought it might break. Ignoring the sweat on my hands, I forced the stick to the right to keep us in the middle of the road.

I'm not sure how long it took to stop, but finally we did. I unstrapped and jumped out of the chair. I pulled out the gun and moved back towards Fleming.

He looked like he'd gone ten rounds and held up his hand. "You are certifiable. Seriously. But that was one hell of a piece of flying." He reached over and unlocked the restraints on the gurney. "Now, get this lady the help she needs."

I slid past him to Dollie. Her eyes were still closed. Perhaps she'd been unconscious the whole time. Her dressings were leaking, blood seeping out from under the mediskin patches. I kicked open the door, as a large AeroMobile dropped behind us with Bloch in the driver's seat.

I pulled the gurney over, and he jumped out to help me wrestle it into the back of the Aero.

"Where to?" he said, as we lifted into the air.

"The Geneium. Emergency."

He nodded and spun the car around. The tall chromosome-shaped building was clearly visible barely a kilometer away. I took Dollie's hand in mine. "Hold on, we're almost there."

Her eyes opened and she grimaced in what might have been an attempt to smile. "You're one shit-hot pilot, Joe."

The Geneium was as tranquil as I remembered. Very few people wandered about, at least in the areas where I was allowed. Perhaps it was different elsewhere. Dollie had taught me how much the Geneered value privacy.

I was pacing outside a treatment room. The glass walls were darkened for privacy, so I didn't know what was happening. Dr. Kinsella had rushed Dollie inside as soon as we'd arrived, and a swarm of other medical staff had come and gone since then. I sat down on one of the padded seats, then stood again a few minutes later. My nerves were frazzled. I wanted to be someplace else—anywhere where I didn't have to face up to Dollie being hurt. If anything happened to her, I—

I blocked my own train of thought, or tried to. I couldn't even bring myself to think about the consequences. They *had* to help her. Nothing else was acceptable.

The door to the treatment room opened, and Kinsella shuffled out. Something in his face made him look very old—even more so than usual. It was a look that tore at me, but I refused to acknowledge it.

"It's serious." He guided me to a seat. "Dollie's not responding to treatment. Her blood pressure is critical—we need to bring it down to stabilize her. If we don't, we can't deliver the baby, and they'll both die. But lowering her blood pressure will impact the blood flow to the placenta, increasing the risk for the child."

"What are the odds?"

"We can't be sure. Low. The child is premature and may already have been damaged by Dollie's immune system."

"They could both die?" The thought was strange, and I struggled to absorb what he was telling me. "Dollie?"

Kinsella's black eyes pooled with tears. "You'd better go in."

Dollie was on an advanced treatment bed, surrounded by large medical screens full of information which meant nothing to me. She looked smaller than I remembered, as if she'd shrunk since we entered the Geneium. I edged forward. Her eyes were closed, and I didn't want to disturb her. Then I realized how crazy that was. I didn't want her asleep. I wanted her to wake up and get off the damn bed so we could go home. We would be a family now. It was something to celebrate and share, not something to—

"Joe..." She smiled, but it faded quickly. "It's a girl. Did they tell you?"

I nodded, even though Kinsella hadn't mentioned it.

"A baby girl. Take good care of her." She winced. "Sorry, I don't think I'll...be able to help."

I held her hand. Hoping if I could hold on tight enough, she wouldn't be able to leave. "Dollie..." My throat closed as I tried to swallow the pain. "You...we can..."

"Thank you, Joe." She squeezed back, almost too light to feel.

"For what? I failed you."

She winced again but shook her head. "For loving me as I am. For sharing the time we had together. It was fun, wasn't it?"

I tried to speak but only managed to choke on my empty words.

"I wish..." She was almost whispering. "Wish you'd noticed me sooner..."

I leaned closer to hear her.

"Being different hurts, Joe." Her breath was gentle, like a breeze rustling through the leaves of a tree. "You were the only one...who took the pain away..."

Her eyes closed. The space between each breath grew longer, until finally it stopped. The silence in the room was cut by a long high-pitched *beep* that seemed to get louder until it was like a howl, primitive and terrifying. Every muscle and sinew in me tightened with savage emotion.

The doors opened and several MedTechs barged in, pushing me out of the way. Kinsella herded me back into the waiting area. "We have to operate now, or we'll lose them both. This way there's a chance at least. Do I have your consent?"

How could I make that call? The engineer in me knew the answer immediately—you make the choice with the greatest chance of success. But by doing that, our daughter would almost certainly die. I might not believe in souls, but it felt like mine was being torn apart.

The clock above the door to the treatment room ticked over. The pale numbers of the seconds display counted up to sixty, then reset to one. I heard the rumble of a cargo transporter pass by, the slipstream buffeting against the outer glass walls, and down the corridor an elevator chimed to announce its arrival. The sun was dropping below the low hills out around Marriotsville, turning the thin clouds a deep blood red, the crimson light streaming in through the outer walls and flooding the waiting area. The MedTechs inside the room were hovering around Dollie's bed, waiting for my decision. I didn't want to make it. I wanted a third choice. Something that meant they could both live. A miracle that wasn't going to come.

"Joe." Kinsella stepped closer. "We can't wait."

"Do it." My voice rasped, sounding like someone else's. "Do what you have to."

He nodded, tapped on the wrist communicator, and rushed to join his team. I saw the MedTechs jump into action, scurrying around the bed. The glass darkened once more, and my insides seemed to tear apart.

I stumbled over to the glassed exterior wall and leaned against it, the cool surface almost calming as it numbed my forehead. Around us people went about their business unconcerned. Going to work or going home, taking in 3V shows, ordering food, arguing, making love, all while the Earth spun inexorably around, and the sunset skies deepened. When Kinsella re-emerged, the traces of red were almost gone and the purple of night arced overhead.

"We saved her." He put his hand on my elbow. "Dollie will be fine."

"The baby?" I choked on the word. "Our daughter?"

He shook his head.

I looked back out through the window. The last glimmers of the fading sun vanished from view, taking with them a sliver of my heart I'd never known existed.

Acknowledgements

I hope you enjoyed reading this novel. This book would not have been possible without the help and support of my family, friends, and other members of the writing community. I'd like to thank them all. I would especially like to thank my wife, Hilary, for her constant love, support, and patience. Without that, this book would simply never have been written.

A special mention must go to my editors, Michelle Dunbar (michelledunbar.co.uk), and Christie Stratos (proofpositivepro.com) who helped polish the raw manuscript into the masterpiece that lies before you. ;-)

The best way to help any writer, especially an indie like myself, is by word-of-mouth. Please consider leaving a review on Amazon. Even if it's only a line or two, it's very much appreciated. Also, please look out for other independent authors. There are a lot of us out there who work hard to bring you stories that you would never see through commercial publishers.

For a complete list of my fiction, please visit my website (davidmkelly.net) and consider signing up for my free update newsletter. I won't share your information with anyone for any reason and won't bombard your mailbox either. Newsletter subscribers benefit from early release information as well as occasional free stories.

Thanks again.

David M. Kelly

About The Author

David M. Kelly writes intelligent, action-packed science fiction. He is the author of the Joe Ballen series (*Mathematics of Eternity and Perimeter*) as well as the short story collection *Dead Reckoning And Other Stories*.

Originally from the wild and woolly region of Yorkshire, England, David now lives in wild and rocky Northern Ontario, Canada, with his patient and long-suffering wife, Hilary. He's passionate about science, especially astronomy and physics, and is a rabid science news follower. When not writing, you can find him driving his own personal starship, a 1991 Corvette ZR-1, or exploring the local hiking trails.

Find out more at www.davidmkelly.net

To sign up for the mailing list, go to www.davidmkelly.net/contact

You can also follow David through the following channels:

Facebook: facebook.com/David.Kelly.SF

Twitter: twitter.com/David_Kelly_SF

Goodreads: goodreads.com/DavidMKelly

Also From David M. Kelly

Meet former space engineer, Joe Ballen. These days, he's scraping a living flying cabs in flooded-out Baltimore, trying to avoid the clutches of his boss and the well-meaning advice of an old friend. When one of his passengers suffers a grisly death, Joe is dragged into a dangerous web of ruthless academic rivalry centered on a prototype spaceship.

As the bodies pile up, Joe becomes suspect number one, and his enemies will stop at nothing to hide the truth. With the help of an enigmatic scientist, a senile survivalist, and the glamorous Ms Buntin, can Joe untangle the conspiracy and prove his innocence before it's too late?

Can money buy you everything? Even the perfect afterlife? Hector Tren-Hump is about to find out...

Featuring a mysterious alien ship, time-travel, first contact, itchy shorts, and a whip-wielding giant, not to mention a cast of characters all in need of some serious therapy, this collection of ten short stories is sure to keep you entertained.

If you like your SF intelligent, action-packed, and a little irreverent, you'll want to discover Dead Reckoning And Other Stories. SF with attitude!

Printed in Great Britain
by Amazon

84344832R00195